Fletcher of the *BOUNTY*

Fletcher
of the
BOUNTY

A NOVEL

GRAEME LAY

FOURTH ESTATE

Fourth Estate
An imprint of HarperCollins*Publishers*

First published in 2017
by HarperCollins*Publishers* (New Zealand) Limited
Unit D1, 63 Apollo Drive, Rosedale, Auckland 0632, New Zealand
harpercollins.co.nz

HarperCollins*Publishers*
Level 13, 201 Elizabeth Street, Sydney NSW 2000, Australia
Unit D1, 63 Apollo Drive, Rosedale, Auckland 0632, New Zealand
A 53, Sector 57, Noida, UP, India
1 London Bridge Street, London SE1 9GF, United Kingdom
2 Bloor Street East, 20th floor, Toronto, Ontario M4W 1A8, Canada
195 Broadway, New York NY 10007, USA

A catalogue record for this book is available
from the National Library of New Zealand.

ISBN 978 1 7755 4106 6 (pbk)
ISBN 978 1 7754 9137 8 (ebook)

Cover design by Hazel Lam, HarperCollins Design Studio
Cover images: Palm trees by CSA Images/Printstock Collection/ Getty Images;
all other images by shutterstock.com
Author photo by Grahame Sydney
Maps by Map Illustrations
Typeset in 11.5/16pt Adobe Caslon by Kirby Jones
Printed and bound in Australia by McPhersons Printing Group
The papers used by HarperCollins in the manufacture of this book are a
natural, recyclable product made from wood grown in sustainable plantation
forests. The fibre source and manufacturing processes meet recognised
international environmental standards, and carry certification.

For the poets: Bernard, Kevin & Peter

Contents

With sloping masts and dipping prow,
As who pursued with yell and blow
Still treads the shadow of his foe,
And forward bends his head,
The ship drove fast, loud roared the blast,
And southward aye we fled.

from 'The Rime of the Ancient Mariner'
by Samuel Taylor Coleridge.

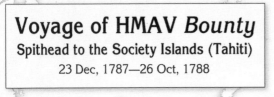

Voyage of HMAV *Bounty*
Spithead to the Society Islands (Tahiti)
23 Dec, 1787—26 Oct, 1788

Arctic Circle

ASIA

England
Spithead☐ **EUROPE**

☐ **Tenerife**
Tropic of Cancer

AFRICA

Equator

East Indies
Batavia ○   ○Timor

Indian

Tropic of Capricorn

New Holland

☐**Cape Town**   *Ocean*   Ta

Van Diemen's Land   ☐Adv
(Tasmania)

Southern   Ocean

Antarctic Circle

ANTARCTICA

Arctic
Ocean

Arctic Circle

NORTH
AMERICA

North
Pacific
Ocean

North
Atlantic
Ocean

England
Spithead

Tenerife

Sandwich Islands
(Hawaiian Islands)

Friendly
Isles
(Tonga)

Society Islands
(Tahiti)

Pitcairn Island

SOUTH
AMERICA

South
Atlantic
Ocean

New Zealand

South Pacific
Ocean

Strait of Magellan
Tierra del Fuego
Cape Horn

Antarctic Circle

20 September 1793

'I'm going now, Isabella.'

'Where?'

'To the cave.'

'Oh. Come back soon.'

'I shall.'

Baby Charles was feeding at her breast. Their elder son, Thursday October, was playing by the banyan tree outside the house. The new baby was due any day now.

Fletcher followed the path through the taypau trees, around the big plantain and the pandanus shrubs until he reached the place where several huge boulders almost blocked the trail. They were smooth and angular, as if shaped by the chisel of a giant stonemason. After making his way around the boulders, he paused to stare at the scene below him.

As on all other parts of the island, the land fell away abruptly to the sea. The slope was covered in more pandanus shrubs, with coconut and banana palms protruding through the foliage. In places the bones of the island were exposed, and where the black rocks of the land met the ocean the swells were breaking into circles of foam.

Today the ocean was unusually calm, in contrast to the turbulence Fletcher had been afflicted with for days. To rid himself of it he needed to get away from all the others, and there was only one place on the island which met this need.

Turning his back on the ocean, he began the hard climb to the escarpment. The foliage was replaced by a shelf of sloping rock, covered thinly with grit. This obliged him to climb on all fours so as not to slip back down the slope and over the precipice below. The crumbly surface always reminded him of the apple dessert topping the Christians' family cook, Betsy Coombe, used to serve them during Sunday's midday dinners.

Crawling upwards, he saw directly above of him the black cliff face. Striated horizontally, it was also pocked with caves. They resembled the eye sockets of blackened skulls. Other formations in the cliff resembled gargoyles, like the ones on the corners of the Cockermouth church he had attended as a boy.

The rays of the morning sun were shining onto the cliff, and the glare was intense. Panting in the heated air, he kept climbing.

One opening in the cliff was a great deal larger than the rest, a yawning maw in the rock. His cave, he thought of it. None of the natives — neither the men nor the women — ever came up here. They were frightened by the caves and the shapes of the cliff face; they considered the place taboo. As for the *Bounty* men, they were far too lazy to make the climb. They preferred to lie under the trees and drink their vile grog, bully the Tahitian men and fuck the Tahitian women.

But their lack of interest in this part of the island did not displease him, since he could be sure that where he was headed he was certain to be alone for as long as he wished to be.

Reaching the top of the slope and solid footing, he stood up on the rock terrace which extended along the base of the cliff. His back to the sea, he shuffled sideways for several yards until he came to the entrance to the rock hollow. Breathless, he sank down onto its gravelly floor and brushed the grit from his hands. The place stank of damp and goat shit. His shirt and hands were saturated with sweat. His hands always sweated, and not just at times like this. Whenever his emotions were aroused they began to leak, something which had embarrassed him since childhood. He took the kerchief from around his neck and mopped his hands and face.

He turned to face the ocean, spread out far below him, apparently infinite. Up here he was even above the 'hawks', the frigate birds, their wings outstretched like dark angels, riding the air waves. Terns fluttered above the coconut palms, gossiping with one another.

In spite of the heat and the strenuousness of the climb, this view was one he never tired of. The sight of the ocean and the birds, and the seclusion of the cave, brought him back here time after time. The place was balm to his wounds.

He sat staring at the ocean for a quarter of an hour, then another quarter. Today there was no sea mist, so the horizon's parabola was visible. Between it and the island there was nothing but ocean. And today it was still. No waves, no white-tops. And the colour! A blue so pure and dark it shimmered. Only where the sea met the island's rocky coastline did it break into foam.

Such vastness, such beauty.

And such distance. From his brothers, from his mother, from his other relatives and friends. From Cumbria, the region where he had grown up, and the Isle of Man, his adopted home. The knowledge that he was an outlaw, and so would never see his family or his homeland again, brought back the black fog of melancholy which beset him often now and seemed to be sinking deeper into his soul. Although this place was beyond the reach of the navy's vengeance the island had become like a prison to him. One whose walls were made not of stone but of water.

He shifted his gaze to the right, towards the bay where they had all struggled ashore nearly three years ago, and in whose water the bones of the *Bounty* now lay. They had burnt not their bridges but their ship, and with its destruction had gone their last chance of ever leaving the island. He had often wondered, had the *Bounty* not been fired, would he and those who wished to leave with him have done so?

This question continued to torment him, although leaving was now an impossibility. He and the others were in everlasting exile, from England, from Scotland, from Tahiti, from Tupuai. All of them — men, women and children — were fated to live out what remained of their lives on this island. That thought deepened the hue of the black fog. How had it come to this? In five years his life had gone from one of respectability and achievement to one of banishment and desolation.

And for that hideous descent he blamed just one man. William Bligh. The knowledge that he had sent the man to his certain death in a small boat was of little consolation to him. Bligh had wrecked his life.

On more than one occasion Fletcher had considered throwing himself from the cliff and ending it all. Lifting his head, he stared down the precipitous slope. How easy it would be to pitch himself forward and into oblivion. Only the thought of Isabella, their infant sons and their yet-to-be-born child prevented him. They were now his sole reason for living.

For almost two hours he sat at the cave entrance, wracked with regrets and loathing. Until his mind was brought back sharply to the present by an unmistakable sound coming up from below.

The crack of a musket.

He sprang to his feet and began to scramble back down the slope.

Part One

YOUNG FLETCHER

COCKERMOUTH, 15 JUNE 1778

The dark-haired lad trudged upwards, along the road to Eaglesfield. High summer, and dust from the road covered his boots. In his satchel were his schoolbooks: a times table, a nature study, his notebook and a history text, *The Story of Cumbria*. The history book had been loaned to him by Mr Rawlings, his master at Cockermouth Free Grammar School, who had pointed out to Fletcher that his family were mentioned more than once in the book.

'You are a member of one of Cumbria's oldest families, Christian,' the wigged old schoolmaster had said, his voice somewhat awed. 'And some of your father's family — over on the Isle of Man — were deemsters. Eminent judges.'

Fletcher was pleased to learn of this connection. His father had died ten years ago, when he was not yet four, so he barely remembered him. His mother said little about her late husband's family. Fletcher knew only that they had come from the Isle of Man, and that they were wealthy from their mining and farming interests. His mother, Ann Christian, always had a great deal to say about her own family, the Dixons, so much so that Fletcher grew tired of the stories about the uncles and grandparents whom he had never known. Now, at the age of fourteen, he was impatient to complete his schooling and take up a place at Cambridge, where his brother Edward was studying law. His other brother, Charles, was studying medicine in Edinburgh.

Fletcher walked on, the sweat inside his shirt causing an unpleasant itch. It was late afternoon, but still very hot. The sky was pale and streaked with feathers of cirrus. 'Such cloud formations presage fine weather,' Mr Rawlings had announced to the class while on a nature ramble earlier in the day. And after the schoolmaster's prediction had proved correct Fletcher had made a mental note to himself: cirrus means fine weather.

He left the road and walked down onto the embankment which led to the Cocker River. Its long grass, shady trees and the river itself looked invitingly cool. The elm trees were in full leaf and he went to the nearest one, threw down his satchel and lay back on the grass beneath the tree, staring up through the foliage at the blue beyond, savouring the softness and scent of the grass.

At that moment the quietness was shattered by yells coming from further along the embankment. Fletcher sat up. The yells were followed by another sound, of high-pitched crying, coming from the same direction. The crying came again, now louder. Getting to his feet, picking up his satchel, Fletcher strode through the grass towards the source of the noise.

A little further down the embankment, under another elm, were two boys. One was about Fletcher's size and age, the other much younger and smaller, only eight or nine perhaps. On the ground was an open school bag, and several sheets of paper were scattered about. The older boy's shirt was hanging loose over his breeches and his long fair hair was dishevelled. The smaller boy was wearing a brown tweed suit, the jacket front unbuttoned. The front of his jacket was being held by the older boy, who was shaking him. He shouted, 'Girly! Milksop!', then slung the smaller boy to one side, so that he lost his footing and slid to the ground. The boy cowered there, whimpering, his hands over his face. The other boy began to kick him, in the stomach, in his side, in the back of the head.

Fletcher ran to the pair. He grabbed the larger boy by his shirt collar and jerked him backwards. The boy yelped in surprise, then turned. Fletcher recognised him from school. Chudleigh, a known dimwit and bully. Fletcher flung him to the ground, then hauled him to his feet. Under his grip Chudleigh's shirt ripped and his face scrunched with fear.

The two boys were almost the same height. Bringing his face close to the other's, Fletcher snarled. 'You want to fight, Chudleigh? Then fight me.' Swinging his right hand, he brought his fist into hard contact with the side of Chudleigh's head.

Chudleigh cried out, 'No! No!'

Ignoring this, Fletcher put his left arm around Chudleigh's neck and held it there tightly. He hurled the boy to the ground, then stood back, swung his left foot and booted his backside as hard as he could. Chudleigh yelped again, and tried to scramble away on all fours.

The smaller boy was still lying on the ground, watching what was happening, his eyes popping with fright. Seeing that his tormentor was now disarmed he hesitantly got to his feet and began to do up his jacket buttons.

Chudleigh, crying now, began to crawl away in the direction of the river. Fletcher booted him in the backside again, at the same time hissing, 'Yes, crawl away, you rat. And if I see you picking on anyone smaller than yourself again, I'll give you a proper thrashing!' Finding the Chudleigh backside too inviting a target to resist, he booted it once more. Chudleigh got to his feet and began to run, this time away from the river and towards the street that led to Cockermouth's marketplace.

'Here, wipe your face.' Fletcher held his handkerchief out to the boy, who took it and began to wipe the tears from his cheeks. His hands were shaking and his mouth hung open. Fletcher gathered up the boy's papers and began to put them back into his satchel. Noticing that the papers were covered in very neat handwriting, he asked, 'Is this your homework?'

The boy shook his head. 'No. That's my writing. I like to write.'

'Oh? What do you write?'

'About things I like. Birds, trees, the sky.' Bowing his head, he said, 'That's why he was hitting me. He said that only sissies write.' He sniffed. 'And so I must be a girl, he said.'

Fletcher snorted. 'Chudleigh's a numbskull.' He handed the boy his satchel. 'Who's your teacher?'

'Mistress Debenhouse. She lets me write. She's kind.'

'So I've heard.' Straightening his collar, Fletcher picked up his own satchel. 'Well, I'd best be on my way home. You can walk with me if you like.'

The boy nodded eagerly. 'Thank you. You live at Moorland Close, don't you?'

Surprised, Fletcher replied, 'Yes. How did you know that?'

'Everyone knows your family. The Christians, and your place, Moorland Close. I've watched you in the playground too. Winning running races and doing handstands.' He gave an admiring little laugh. 'You're very good at handstands.'

Fletcher smiled. The boy was certainly observant. He had bright, intelligent eyes and a long, very straight nose. Fletcher said to him, 'If Chudleigh, or anyone else for that matter, bullies you, let me know.' He gave the boy a straight look. 'Bullies have to be stood up to. Remember that.'

The boy nodded. 'But when you're small, it's hard to.'

'Well, if it happens again, let me know, and I'll deal to him.'

They began to walk up the embankment towards the town, both with their satchels over their shoulders. There was no wind whatsoever, and the late afternoon was heavy with heat. As they walked Fletcher said, 'What's your name?'

'I'm William. William Wordsworth.'

29 May 1779

His mother was in the drawing room, sitting on the divan under the bay window. She had on a scarlet gown and her best lace bonnet, the one she had bought in Bruges a few years ago while on a tour of the Low Countries. Behind her the red velvet drapes were drawn well back, so there was a clear view of the lawn, the sun dial in its centre and the old plane tree at the foot of the slope. Under the tree was the garden seat where Fletcher liked to sit and read. Beyond the property, visible through the summer haze, were the fells and forests of the Lake District.

His mother smiled at him tightly, then gestured towards the wing-back chair beside the fireplace.

'Fletcher darling, do sit down.'

Above the fireplace was the portrait in oils of his father. Fletcher's eyes dwelt on the painting for a few moments. His father had been portrayed seated in this very room. Wearing a large wig and bearing a stern expression, Charles Christian's face was jowly, his nose prominent, the eyebrows bushy. He wore a maroon brocade waistcoat, navy blue topcoat and white breeches. An authority figure, certainly, but along with the sternness the portraitist had also captured a definite kindliness about his eyes. An attorney-at-law, Charles Christian had died aged thirty-nine, of the flux. For the umpteenth time, Fletcher wished he had known him.

Taking a seat in the chair, Fletcher returned his attention to his mother. Her expression was solemn. She was usually so animated. Her gravity made him feel a little uneasy. Had somebody in the family died? Smoothing her gown, she said, 'We need to talk about your future, Fletcher.'

He brightened. He wanted to talk about it too. In a few weeks he would leave the school he had attended for the last eight years, and would be well ready to face a new future. Away from Cockermouth.

'I'm so looking forward to going to Cambridge, Mother. This time next year—'

She heaved a sigh and her shoulders slumped. Turning away, she said quietly, 'You will not be enrolling at Cambridge, Fletcher.'

He started. 'But it was agreed—'

She held up her right hand. 'I know, I know. But circumstances have changed.'

He felt giddy. Changed? Whatever did she mean? For years it had been planned for him to attend St John's at Cambridge, like Edward, and read philosophy and law. That knowledge had driven him to succeed in his school studies, which in turn had earned him top marks in most of his subjects, especially Latin, History and English. He was more than ready for higher study. And now …

'I don't understand, Mother.' He stared at her and she seemed to shrink a little under his gaze. 'What are these circumstances?'

Placing her hands together in her lap, looking down at them, she said in the same subdued voice, 'I have become indebted.'

Her voice seemed to be coming from some foreign place. She had borrowed heavily against the Moorland Close estate, to finance Edward and Charles's educations in law and medicine. She had been struggling, secretly, for years to maintain the family's social position and finances, she said, but could no longer continue to do so. The family notary, Sir Stephen Galbraith, had advised her yesterday that her creditors were about to foreclose. Apart from Moorland Close she had virtually no assets, her debts were colossal, and as a consequence Ann Christian was insolvent.

Fletcher's hands had gone clammy. He gripped the arms of the chair. His throat tight, he asked, 'How much is the debt?'

'Six and a half thousand pounds.'

He drew breath, sharply. 'Six and a half thousand?' Then his voice failed him completely.

'Yes. On Sir Stephen's advice, I must sell Moorland Close. And you cannot go up to Cambridge. The fees—'

He found his voice. 'Sell this house?' He looked around helplessly. 'But our family has lived here for—'

She cut him off sharply. 'Do not tell me what I am already well aware of, Fletcher.' She fixed him with her beady eyes. 'It was me who brought this house to my marriage to your father. It has been in the Dixon family for generations.' She gave a dry little laugh. 'People in the town describe it as "half castle, half homestead". I'm aware of that insult.' She looked down again. 'But now I have no alternative but to sell the property to pay at least some of my creditors.'

Fletcher swallowed hard. 'Have you let my brothers know about this matter?'

She gave a wave of her left hand. It was encrusted with rings, leading Fletcher to wonder whether she had considered putting some of them on the market. 'I have written to Edward and Charles, informing them

24

of my distressing circumstances, and the reasons. Edward agrees that this house must be sold.'

'And Charles?'

'He has not yet replied.'

For some time both she and Fletcher said nothing. He felt crushed. Realising how shocked her son now was, his mother lifted her chin in a small gesture of defiance. Pursing her lips, she said, 'I did what I thought was right. The debts were incurred to guarantee my sons received the best possible education.'

Fletcher said dully, 'But it was not right, Mother. And now, unlike my brothers, I cannot go up to the university I have dreamed of attending for years.'

Closing her eyes, she began to cry. She took a handkerchief from her sleeve and held it to her face. Shoulders convulsing, she said, 'Fletcher, I am so sorry. I know how much you were looking forward to Cambridge.'

He went over to her, sat down and put his arm around her shoulders. He felt as if he had been struck about the head with a plank. His future, his family's future, dissolving. How could she have done this? His mind seething, he asked, 'Is there no way that we can keep this house?'

Eyes still shut, she shook her head. 'The debts are too great.' Head bowed, she said in a whisper, 'I am destitute. Moorland Close must be sold. For me it is either that, or the debtors' prison.'

Fletcher allowed a silence before asking, 'And after it has been sold? What will you do? What will I do?'

Lifting her head, she said in a much firmer tone, 'We will move to the Isle of Man. Edward advised me in his last letter that my English creditors have no authority there. The island has a separate jurisdiction.'

'But where will we live there? How will we live?'

Squeezing the handkerchief in her hand, she said defiantly, 'We will live at Milntown. On the estate of your father's family. They are wealthy and influential.' Her eyes narrowed. 'I brought Moorland

Close to your father, so the least his family can do is return my family's bounteousness.'

She makes it sound like a threat, Fletcher thought. Which perhaps it was.

30 SEPTEMBER 1779

Before this he had travelled no further than Cumbria, and within that region only to Carlisle and Barrow-in-Furness. During past summers they had holidayed in the two towns, alternately each year, he and his mother and his brothers, staying in terraced guest houses on the waterfront. He enjoyed those holidays, being so close to the sea, unlike Cockermouth, which was really just a river town.

During the holidays he had spent most of his days on the waterfront, staring out at the Irish Sea, watching the fishing boats returning with their catch and the merchant vessels discharging their barrels and loading timber and sacks of grain. Watching the seamen and the stevedores, Fletcher often wondered, what sort of a life was that? Living on the sea, battling the elements, visiting new ports, getting to know England's bustling coastline.

But that life was not for him. His future lay in the cloisters and quadrangles of St John's, reading history and philosophy, listening to choristers, punting on the Cam. Edward had told him so much about the place. 'It's a world in itself, Fletcher,' he had said. 'A place of unbelievable beauty, of hallowed halls, distinguished teachers and a love of learning. You will love it, brother.'

Now he and his mother were travelling by coach-and-four to Whitehaven, another busy port town on the north-west coast of England, a place of arrival and departure for the ships of Nicholson's Packet Service between the Cumbria coast and the Isle of Man, thirty-five miles away.

Fletcher and his mother had been joined in the coach by a middle-aged couple, also from Cockermouth. The woman was overweight and fussy, constantly rearranging her gown and shawl, while her husband, a small man with a face like a dried apricot, kept peering through the coach window, as if expecting a highwayman to strike.

The coach jostled along the road, shaking over the ruts and bumps. Inside, the air was stale and smelt of horse farts. Soon after they left the coaching station in Cockermouth the woman had leaned forward and said to his mother, 'I believe that Moorland Close is to be sold, madam.'

Ann Christian eyed her coldly. 'It is.'

'And you and the lad here are leaving Cockermouth.'

'We are. As must be perfectly obvious.'

Not taking the hint, the woman continued, 'I heard you'll be moving to Douglas. On the Isle of Man.'

'You heard incorrectly. My son and I will be living near Ramsey.'

'Ramsey? Never heard of it.'

'You have now.'

His mother turned away, staring out the coach's other window. With an offended expression, the woman fell back in her seat and said no more. Fletcher patted his mother's hand reassuringly. His admiration for her had grown over these past months since the news of the bankruptcy had broken. She had gone about organising her affairs crisply and without sentiment, spending most mornings seated at the table in the drawing room, quill in hand, writing letters to friends and family, and the afternoons supervising the packing up of the household belongings.

On most occasions she remained composed. But two days ago Fletcher had come across her in the drawing room, sitting in the chair by the fireplace, crying. Her hair was loose and bedraggled, which it never was, and her eyelids were puffy.

The portrait of Charles Christian had been removed earlier that day by the carriers, and taken away for storage. In the space where the painting had been hanging, a rich yellow rectangle of wallpaper stood out, contrasting with the faded lemony shade surrounding it. The yellow space was like a symbol of reproach, a metaphor for their impending loss. Upset at his mother's distress, Fletcher had done his best to comfort her, while still resentful that her reckless investments had ruined the academic future he had so long dreamed of.

Moorland Close had not yet gained a buyer, but the property was on the market, and Sir Stephen Galbraith had been instructed by Ann Christian, 'You are not to accept any offer necessarily. Instead you must insist on the best possible price you can obtain. As you well know, I need every penny I can get.'

The household furniture, carpets and paintings had been packed and placed in a warehouse in Cockermouth. The contents of the trunks strapped to the coach's roof were mainly clothes, footwear and books. The rest of the belongings would be forwarded to the Isle, once suitable accommodation had been confirmed.

The coach jolted on. Leaning back in his corner, Fletcher's mind seethed with recent memories. Farewells, so many farewells.

Mr Rawlings, the schoolmaster, shaking his hand. 'You've been a fine student, Christian. Disappointing about Cambridge, but I'm sure you'll do well, whatever vocation you eventually choose.' And he had presented Fletcher with a copy of *A Voyage towards the South Pole, and round the world. Performed in His Majesty's ships the Resolution and Adventure, in the years 1772, 1773, 1774, and 1775.* This was the account of the voyager Captain James Cook's second global circumnavigation, written by the great navigator himself. The book had been published just two years earlier. Fletcher accepted the gift gratefully, touched by the schoolmaster's consideration.

There were other farewells. The small boy whose aid he had come to a few weeks ago, Wordsworth, had approached him in the schoolyard on his last day there, and shyly presented him with a card. 'When I heard you were leaving, I wrote something for you.'

'Oh, thank you.' Opening the card Fletcher asked, 'Has Chudleigh bothered you again?'

'No, not at all. He sneers at me, but keeps away.'

'Hah! Good!'

The message read, in a small, well-formed hand:

For my friend Fletcher
Your strength and kindness go together
Close as clouds and sky, as 'twined as the weather
Wherever you go, may you stay out of danger
From peril on land or sea, or from a total stranger
Go forth, loyal friend, I will not forget you!
William

Fletcher nodded. 'It's a fine poem, Wordsworth. Thank you.' He put his hand on the boy's shoulder. 'May there be many more.'

His brother Edward came from Cambridge to farewell them. The day after he arrived, he and Fletcher walked across the property to the hill above Moorland Close. Two years older than Fletcher but a little shorter, Edward had deep-set brown eyes, a square jaw and a receding hairline.

The pair of them sat atop the hill. Tugging at a clump of grass, Edward stared into the distance, in the direction of the sea. 'I cannot begin to say how much I regret what has happened, Fletcher.'

'Your regret cannot be worse than mine.'

'All I can say is that I know you will do well, in spite of losing Cambridge.'

'How can you be sure? My prospects are so much reduced.'

'Because you're well liked and diligent. Our father's family will offer you prospects, I'm certain of it. We have uncles and cousins over on the island, and all are well connected, I believe. And their investments are considerable.'

Fletcher made no reply for some time. Then he stretched out his legs and said, 'I find it hard to forgive Mother for what has happened. It was so irresponsible.'

'Yes,' said Edward. 'But she's vulnerable now, so you must do what you can to support her until Charles and I complete our studies. When I'm qualified in the law and Charles is a practising physician, we can both help her.'

Fletcher grunted. 'But how can I help her? Now that I have been denied the chance of a higher education?' He heeled a thistle viciously. 'She has destroyed my future.'

Edward glared at him. 'Don't be so dramatic. Mother has not destroyed your future. She has merely altered it. And you never know, that alteration may be for the good. When one door shuts, another may open.'

'At the moment, all doors seem closed to me.'

'That may seem so, but something good will come your way, I'm sure of it.' He stood up. 'Come on, we must get back to the house. Mother will be expecting us.'

Fletcher met his school chums Isaac Wilkinson, Toby Hayes and Thomas Newbourn for a farewell pint at the Duck and Gun, in Cockermouth's High Street. Isaac wrote poetry; Toby and Thomas were scholars and athletes, like Fletcher. And all four young men were virgins.

The trio drank and slapped his back and toasted him good fortune. Toby said, 'I hear tell, Fletcher, that the girls on the Isle of Man are not only beautiful, they are wanton.'

Thomas grinned. 'Yes. They say the place should more properly be called the Isle of Women.'

Fletcher laughed. 'The girls there are more wanton than those in Cockermouth?'

'That's what's said,' Isaac added knowingly.

'I've heard that too,' added Toby. 'Moreover, the Isle of Man's flag, the one with three legs on it, joined at a thigh, shows three girls' legs. And the thigh is theirs.'

Warming to this topic, Isaac said, 'And it's said that the Manx girls' thighs are freely available to any good-looking young Englishman, such as yourself.'

Smiling, Fletcher said, 'Well, I shall do my best to make a scientific comparison. I shall research the subject thoroughly.'

Although the others laughed, Fletcher became pensive. His mind flashed back to another, even more poignant farewell, one which he had made last Wednesday.

'You will come back, won't you, Fletcher? Come back to me, I mean.'

'I will.'

Clarinda lay back in the grass, staring up at him. Her lightly freckled cheeks were flushed, her grey eyes wide and fixed on his. Her brown hair had been tied up in a bun on top of her head, but the comb had come loose so that her hair had fallen around her face. He found the dishevelled look irresistible.

They were lying together in the long grass, in a place well off the walking path that followed the river. She was thirteen, two years younger than him, but seemed much older. She was from a farm outside the town, and came to Cockermouth every market day to sell the eggs produced from her family's property. Since one of Fletcher's tasks was to buy the eggs for Moorland Close, he had got to know her. They had walked together regularly along the river path in the afternoons, after the market had closed. He had kissed her, often, but done nothing more. He was uncertain how to proceed after that.

He put his face close to hers, brushed her cheeks with his lips. She nibbled at his mouth. He could see, could feel, her chest rising and falling, rising and falling, and her breathing was quick, almost gasping. Coming from her was a marvellous fragrance, like nothing he had ever smelt before. Putting his face very close to hers, he drew a deep breath, absorbing her wonderful scent.

Suddenly she brought her hands up to her blouse and in one deft movement drew the blouse and the vest beneath it wide open.

Her breasts were very white, the nipples large and pink. Thinking them the most beautiful objects he had ever set his eyes upon, in an instant he was upon them, putting his lips around each in turn, feeling them swell and stiffen under his kisses. The rigidity inside his breeches tightened until it became almost painful, and he tried to adjust himself.

Clarinda giggled. 'Kiss them again,' she said, pushing her breasts up into his face.

He was only too willing to obey. At the same time he slid his right hand under her gown and between her legs.

She stiffened. 'No, Fletcher, no. Not that. Not now.'

'When, then?'

'When you come back to me. From the island. Then you can have it. Have it all.'

Inside the coach, dwelling on the memory of those wonderful breasts and the confection of her nipples, his cock hardened again. Abashed, he tried to adjust it inside his breeches with his left hand, surreptitiously, hoping his mother and the ugly old couple wouldn't notice. Managing to make himself a little more comfortable, he sank back into the corner of the coach and closed his eyes. Clarinda, Clarinda, will I ever see you again? Will that promise of your body ever be redeemed?

He managed at last to put these questions aside. But they were replaced by other, more immediate ones. What, and who, now lay ahead?

The island came into clearer focus. From the larboard mid-deck of Nicholson's two-masted packet boat *Lioness*, Fletcher could see through the mist the island's long, undulating shape. A valley was discernible, separating hills to the north-west and south-east of a small town. Visible too was a beach of pale sand and beyond it a row of dockside buildings.

The voyage across the Irish Sea from Whitehaven had taken only half a day, aided by a north-easterly wind which chopped the sea but kept the vessel moving steadily. The captain was anxious to have them inside the harbour before nightfall, the helmsman told Fletcher when he enquired about their progress.

Although the wind was dropping, at this rate they would be, Fletcher thought. He had spent most of the voyage on deck, watching the sailors going aloft and adjusting the sail-setting under the direction of the schooner's burly master, bellowing his instructions from the deck. Fletcher had watched and listened, intrigued by the business.

After they came closer to the island he went below again. His mother was accommodated in a small cabin abaft on the larboard side. Weary after yesterday's coach journey, she had taken to this berth shortly after *Lioness* cleared Whitehaven's harbour and been ill for virtually the whole crossing. Several times he had come down to check, concerned at her pallor and listlessness.

On the table beside the berth, held in place by a bracket, was the jug of water he had brought her. He poured her another tumbler full. 'More water, Mother?'

After she groaned and waved him away, he closed the cabin door and went back up on deck.

During the crossing he had felt not the slightest bit ill. Instead he found the chill of the wind and the sea's salty scent invigorating. And now there was a growing sense of anticipation. Other passengers had come up from the saloon and were standing along the starboard rail, staring at the island.

The sky was darkening now and the air had become chillier. Although the coast was in shadow, Fletcher could see that the waterfront buildings were substantial, and that ahead and a little to starboard a pair of mandible-like breakwaters enclosed the harbour entrance. Within the harbour the masts of several bare-poled ships stood up like leafless trees. Above the harbour and town was a range of forested hills.

In spite of himself, he felt a tug of emotion. This was the island where his paternal forebears had lived for many generations, where his father had grown up. Some of that land, some of those ships, may be owned by his relatives, he thought.

The master was shouting, 'Stand by to take in the flying jib! Stand by to take in the main sail!'

Men scampered up the shrouds to obey his commands. The ship's sails were reduced, she slowed and the helmsman adjusted the wheel, preparing to aim for the harbour entrance. Staring up into the yards, sails and sheets, watching the men clinging there or inching along the yardarm, working as a team, Fletcher felt a stirring of interest in their work. I could do that, he thought. It could be no harder than climbing the top boughs of the elms at Moorland Close, which he had done for years.

And if he, as a mere passenger, felt such excitement, what must it feel like to be receiving, and giving, commands to work a ship?

Driven slowly by the light airs, *Lioness* was moving closer to the harbour entrance. Turning away from the rail, Fletcher went down the companionway to let his mother know they had arrived.

Ramsey, 11 November 1779
Dear Edward,

Greetings from Ramsey! (or 'Rhumsaa', as the Manxmen call the town, in their peculiar dialect). By now you will have heard from Mother, reporting on our new life here on the Isle. She doubtless told you that for her the move has not been a very happy one. Our late father's family — including our cousin John, who is eight years older than me and unmarried — have not exactly welcomed her into the fold. I have the feeling that the family here are resentful of the fact that Father chose to live in Cumbria after he married Mother, rather than staying on the island. I have no proof of this, it is just a sense that I have. And now that Mother has been obliged to live on their charity, their umbrage is even greater. As a consequence she behaves very coolly towards the Manx Christians, making no secret of her resentment of them.

However I am warming to cousin John, and I believe the feeling is mutual. He is more like an uncle than a cousin, being much older, but does not condescend to me. Although his hair is auburn (from our Viking ancestors perhaps), in other respects he is very much like us: tall and strongly built, with deep-set hazel eyes, a heavy brow, prominent nose and cleft chin. He joked that there are so many 'John Christians' in our family tree that he should more properly be known as 'John Christian XVII'.

He has provided Mother and me with rooms at Milntown, on the ground floor of a fine building near the banks of the Auldyn River, a tributary of the Sulby, whose estuary comprises the harbour of Ramsey. The Milntown estate is very grand, the farmstead large, with battlements atop its walls, so that it resembles a castle, with a matching portico entrance. Ancient oak trees grow in the grounds of the estate, and sheep and cattle graze the fields.

Our rooms are in the east wing of the house. We have a bedroom each and share the parlour and drawing room. The latter has a well-stocked library, many family portraits adorn the walls and the windows give wide views of the gardens. Mother spends most of her time walking in the garden, writing letters and on occasion, taking the coach into Ramsey to visit the shops. Her purchases are modest, however, as money is still short for us. Her much reduced circumstances she is finding very difficult to cope with. (She was grateful to last week receive a payment from Sir Stephen, a percentage from the deposit on the impending sale of Moorland Close, although she wept when she realised that the property will soon be gone from our family forever.)

There are several horses kept on the estate, one of which John has put at my disposal. A bay gelding called Walter, he has taken me all over the estate and beyond, to an upland heath, called the 'Tops'. Between the estate and the Tops is a network of woods and narrow valleys which I have relished exploring, both on foot and on horseback. I have also ridden Walter down to the estuary of the Sulby and along the sandy beach which extends for many miles on both sides of it. Although the days are now shorter and much colder, I still find the island conducive to such excursions.

If this gives the impression that my life here is one of indolence, let me correct that notion. I spend a great deal of time cleaning out the stables, feeding and grooming the horses, and maintaining the estate — trimming the hedgerows, clearing out drains, cutting firewood and so forth. Demanding work, but I enjoy it. With winter coming soon, the livestock will have to be given additional feed, which will also be one of my responsibilities. But as I work at these duties, to earn the keep of Mother and myself, I wonder too, what else will I do with my life?

In the evenings I read a great deal. The book my teacher presented me with when I left Cockermouth School, the account of Captain Cook's second world voyage, was the first I read. It is enthralling. His ships — HMS Resolution and HMS Adventure — sailed beyond the Antarctic Circle. Surrounded by ice mountains and beset by freezing fog, the ships became separated, were reunited in New Zealand, then separated again. He almost lost his ship in Tahiti, then stayed there for a time and made friends with a chief of the island. What a voyage! Captain Cook is a truly heroic figure, an Englishman whose achievements must rank with those *of William Shakespeare and Sir Isaac Newton. As you probably know, Captain Cook is at present engaged upon yet another world voyage in Resolution. I look forward immensely to reading of that circumnavigation too, after his return.*

In the library are several volumes of Manx history. These I find most interesting. One book told me that our surname Christian is an anglicised version of the Manx name, McCrystyn, which is probably of Scots origin. Other histories say it is Scandinavian, possibly Icelandic! I never knew that. Mother must have known, but neglected to tell me. (She still shows antipathy towards father's family. John Christian's branch have a pew at the local church, St Matthew's, but Mother refuses to attend. 'I'm not a real Christian,' she says, in an attempt at humour. John's family were not amused.) Another book, one on the island's maritime history, told me about a French privateer called Captain Francois Thurot. He traded goods between Ireland and the Isle of Man, in the early years of this century. The arch-enemy of our navy, reputedly part of a planned French invasion of Britain, Thurot was defeated off the island's north-west coast in 1760. His badly damaged vessel was brought into Ramsey Bay and its timbers were used to build cottages and a bridge. The latter was named after him, Thurot Bridge. I have ridden over it!

When I raised the subject of this man with cousin John, he surprised me by saying, 'Thurot was well liked on this island. He was not seen by us as a foe.'

This brought home to me once again that Manxmen are more independent of thought than people of the English mainland. Smuggling goods from Ireland to this island is a common tradition, I've been told. The stable-hand who told me this added that the local Customs people do not make the most strenuous attempts to prevent the contraband entering the island's ports. Another indication of the Manx propensity for preferring their own laws to those of England. I see their flag — the three-legged Manx triskelion — being flown more commonly here than the English flag!

This letter will be dispatched to each of you on the Nicholson packet vessel the day after tomorrow, so you should receive it in a month or so. I trust that your studies in Cambridge and Edinburgh are progressing. I do still envy you your illustrious academic worlds, but life here is more agreeable than I anticipated. Mother and I are travelling to Douglas in a few weeks to meet some naval friends of John's.

I will write again next month,

Your loving brother,

Fletcher

PS We have a household cat with no tail, called Cassius. His lack of the usual rear feline appendage causes him no concern, as all the cats here lack tails. Strange.

He wrote a copy of the letter to Charles, then thought he would write to Clarinda as well. He would remind her of her promise to him. Then he realised this would be pointless; she could neither read nor write.

DOUGLAS, 20 JANUARY 1780

'Fletcher, meet my friend, Captain George Courtnay. Captain, my first cousin, Fletcher Christian. My late brother Charles's youngest son.'

Dressed in the uniform of a lieutenant in the Royal Navy, Courtnay was of medium height and thick at the waist, with a leathery complexion, a veined nose and pale green eyes. As he shook hands with him, Fletcher looked admiringly at his blue and white uniform, with its large cuffs and gold epaulettes. His navy tricorn was tucked under his left arm.

The trio were at a reception in the drawing room of the Douglas home of Fletcher's second cousin, Edward Taubman, and his wife Loretta. The two-storeyed red-brick Taubman house was perched upon the hill above Douglas harbour, providing wide views of the Irish Sea. On the walls of the drawing room were framed charts of the East Indies and several ornately framed seascapes. Other paintings featured coastlines with palm trees, one with a coastal fort set among tropical foliage.

'You are visiting the island on naval business, sir?' Fletcher asked Captain Courtnay.

'No. My visit is mainly social, although I'm also here to see my friend Duncan Campbell.'

John Christian explained. 'Campbell is a ship owner, with plantation interests in the West Indies. Sugar and rum. Douglas is the home port for his merchant vessels. He will be joining us shortly.' Turning the conversation back to the naval commander, he said, 'Captain Courtnay commands HMS *Eurydice*, which serves our nation in the Atlantic and Indian Oceans.'

Fletcher's eyes widened. 'The Indian Ocean? How wonderful. Have you seen much of India itself?'

'A little. The coastal ports. Bombay, Goa, Madras.'

John looked across the room. 'Ah, here's Campbell.'

The ship owner strode across the room towards the others. He was tall, with a lantern jaw and large hands, which he was holding together in front of him, as if in supplication. His expression was grave. Nodding at the others, he sighed heavily. 'I bring terrible news. Captain Cook is dead.'

Everyone stood as if turned to stone. Then Courtnay demanded, 'How?'

Campbell swallowed hard. 'Killed. In an archipelago he discovered and called the Sandwich Islands after our First Sea Lord.'

'Was he killed in battle?' John asked, his voice just above a whisper.

Campbell shook his head. 'The London news sheets just report that "He died during a fracas". On one of the islands, at some bay with an unpronounceable native name. He was beaten to death with clubs by the savages there.'

The stunned silence returned. They stared at each other with dazed expressions. Captain Cook dead? It seemed impossible. Fletcher's mind reeled. Of all Englishmen, he seemed the most destined for immortality.

'How was the news delivered?' asked Taubman.

'Overland from Russia. Following the killing, Cook's ships *Resolution* and *Discovery* sailed from the Sandwich Islands to Petropavlovsk, on the Kamchatka peninsula. Charles Clerke, Cook's second-in-command, wrote a letter to the Admiralty reporting Cook's death. It reached London ten days ago, and the news sheets last week.'

The news seeped through the room like marsh gas, bringing a pall that settled over them all. Cook the great navigator and discoverer, charterer of the Gulf of St Lawrence, Newfoundland, Tahiti, New Zealand, eastern Australia, the New Hebrides. The colossus, the titan of the Royal Navy, dead. It seemed inconceivable.

That night Fletcher lay in bed in the annex at the rear of the Taubman house, unable to sleep. He sat up, then drew aside the bedroom curtain. The moon was almost full, a shimmering disc in the eastern sky. The Irish Sea was inky, lit only by a rippling ribbon of moonlight.

But it was not the moonlight that had kept him awake, it was the knowledge that a great man had fallen, that an era of Britain's history was over. After Cook there could be no one who could compare. Yet Fletcher was also aware from his reading that there was so much of the world which was still not yet fully charted: islands, sounds, estuaries. The voyages of exploration must continue, commanders must continue to seek lands for King George. Commanders like Captain Courtnay. What places he had sailed to, what sights he must have seen on the coasts of India!

Lately Fletcher had been watching the vessels entering and leaving Ramsey and Douglas harbours. And he had come to a decision. Since Cambridge had been denied him, he would seek another future. One which offered adventure in distant lands. He would make of his life what James Cook had made of his. Drawing the curtains, he blocked out the moonlight. And before sleep came, he had decided where his future lay.

On the sea.

His mother was sitting by the fire in the parlour, knitting a scarf for Edward. The Cambridge winters were bitter, he had written to tell her, and this was her response. She had already knitted one for Charles. She looked up and smiled as Fletcher entered the room.

'Darling, welcome back. How was Douglas?'

'It was good, thank you.' He sat down on the armless chair opposite her. 'Cousin John introduced me to some very interesting people there.'

'Oh?' Clicking her needles, she asked, 'And did you hear the dreadful news? About Captain Cook?'

'Yes. People could hardly believe it. It was almost as if God himself was dead.'

'I know, I know.' She paused. 'Before you were born Charles and I once holidayed in Whitby. Such a pretty town, with small ships coming and going. The news reports said that was where Captain Cook learned navigation.'

'Yes. And where he learned to sail.' Realising that this had given him an opportunity, Fletcher looked directly at her. 'Mother, I too wish to go to sea. With the Royal Navy.'

Her fingers froze, her hands dropped, taking the wool with them. She raised her chin, frowned. 'You wish to go to sea?'

'I do. I see it as an opportunity to serve my country.' He cleared his throat. 'And see the world.'

Her frown deepened. Shaking her head, she said in a low voice, 'I forbid it, Fletcher.'

'Why?'

'You are needed here.'

He threw up his hands. 'To do what? Muck out the other Christians' stables? Feed their pigs? Chop their firewood?' He shook his head. 'That's not the life I want.'

'Fletcher, I need you. I have no one else. Edward will practise law in London, Charles is intending to serve as a surgeon in a hospital there. Should you leave this island, I will be bereft. And at the mercy of Charles's family.'

'And whose fault is that, Mother? Who lost our family fortune?'

'I did. But do not reproach me further about it. Life must go on. We are comfortably accommodated here, in spite of your father's family's resentment of me. I cannot return to Cumbria. So you and I must stay on this island. This is our future.'

'No! It may be our present, it may even be your future. But it's not mine. Can you not understand that I yearn to see the rest of the world, the one beyond this boring island?'

Her mouth became a tight line. She nodded. 'I do understand that. You are young and keen to see the world. But can you also not understand my need for your companionship? As my youngest child?' Her eyes became watery.

Fletcher looked down. He felt helpless. He hated it when she appealed to such sentiment. And yet he loved her, he did not want her left alone, did not want to heap further unhappiness upon her.

After a long silence he said, 'How would it be if I wait for a time. Say, another year and a half.' He gave her a hard look. 'Legally, Mother, I will have the right to leave then.' He attempted a smile. 'But I would rather do so with your blessing.'

Looking down, she nodded. Then after another long silence, replied with a sigh, 'Very well. When you are eighteen, you may do as you wish.'

The Isle of Man, 1781–1782

The ensuing two years seemed as long as a decade. Fletcher spent the time working on the estate, tending the sheep and cattle and the six horses in the Milntown stables, and supervising the piggery. His spare time was spent hiking or riding across the island, exploring its hills and forests.

This outdoors life suited him, and he felt fitter and stronger from the exercise, knowing that when he went to sea this conditioning would stand him in good stead.

When the weather was favourable — and this eastern side of the island was markedly drier than Cumbria — he sometimes rode up the river valley which extended inland south of Ramsey, then followed a horse trail along a gully and up to the summit of Snaefell, which at just over two thousand feet was the island's highest point.

He slipped from the saddle of his mare, Sara, and looped her reins to a bush. The broom was flaring in golden clumps across the mountaintop, between expanses of grass. While the horse grazed contentedly, Fletcher savoured the view from Snaefell's broad summit. It was a clear day in April and the visibility was good. People on the island boasted that from up here five kingdoms could be seen: the Isle of Man, Ireland, Scotland, England and the Kingdom of Heaven.

Looking east, Fletcher smiled at this notion, just another instance of the parochialism with which the island overflowed. Across the Irish Sea the mountains of Cumbria were certainly visible, and to the north he could see the coast of Scotland — Dumfries and Galloway. He turned. To the west, Ireland was hidden in a bank of cloud. As for the Kingdom of Heaven, well, that was sheer fancy. Pie in the sky, as it were. He knew too that in Cumbria there were much higher and more spectacular mountains than this one. When he was only twelve he and Charles had climbed one of them, Pillar, which was nearly three thousand feet high. And at that, only the eighth highest mountain in the Lake District. Still, the view from Snaefell was undeniably uplifting, the air fresh and invigorating.

On another occasion he rode even further, to a place called Meayll Hill, in the south of the island. On the hill was a ring of twelve burial chambers. No one could tell him who had built or inhabited these mysterious monuments, which someone described as 'prehistoric'. The word was new to him, but he knew it meant 'before history was written'. In another word, ancient.

When the weather was not conducive to riding or rambling, he spent his spare time writing to his Cumbria friends, to his brothers, or reading in the library. History was still his favourite subject. Detailed accounts of the revolutionary war in America were being published regularly now, and as cousin John subscribed to several London magazines, he read these articles avidly. Voyages of exploration were continuing, particularly in the eastern Pacific, along the western coast of the Americas, and reports of these absorbed him, too.

There was fiction in the library, as well. He read Samuel Richardson's novel *Pamela; or, Virtue Rewarded*, admired the writing, and recommended it to his mother. After reading it, she dismissed it with one word: 'dissolute'. He also read Daniel Defoe's *Robinson Crusoe*, as well as an account of the real-life inspiration for the work, the story of the Scots castaway Alexander Selkirk.

Accounts of past voyages had produced narratives of calamities and illness at sea. Reading of the voyages of the Portuguese navigator Ferdinand Magellan, and the Englishman George Anson, both of whom lost hundreds of men to the seaman's scourge, scurvy, confirmed its causes and effects. Captain Cook's chronicles made it clear that he was a visionary in the prevention of scurvy aboard his ships. His anti-scorbutic measures were so effective that he lost not a single sailor to scurvy. Accidents, other diseases, but never scurvy. Cook's record was remarkable, Fletcher realised. His physician brother had read widely of the methods used to keep scurvy at bay, and sent Fletcher copies of these scientific papers. Strictly enforced diet and shipboard hygiene, it was now generally acknowledged, were the keys to combating the vile disease. That was the secret of Cook's success during his epic voyages, Charles had concluded.

Fletcher also read the first volume of John Hawkesworth's *An account of the voyages undertaken by the order of His present Majesty for making discoveries in the Southern Hemisphere, and successively performed by Commodore Byron, Captain Wallis, Captain Carteret, and Captain Cook, in the Dolphin, the Swallow, and the Endeavour: drawn up from the journals which were kept by the several commanders, and from the papers of Joseph Banks, esq.* In 1767 the Wallis expedition had come across a beautiful uncharted high island in the mid-Pacific, which Captain Wallis named 'King George's Island' and later was known as 'Tahiti'. George Robertson had been sailing master on *Dolphin*, and had recorded in particular the trade between Wallis's sailors and the native women of King George's Island. The women first traded their carnal favours for one ten penny nail, but when they realised how hungry the sailors were for their bodies the price soon escalated to the point where the seamen were trading their hammock hooks and tearing the cleats from the *Dolphin*'s hull. When Captain Wallis found out about this commerce, Robertson wrote, 'He no longer wondered that the ship was in danger of being pulled to pieces for the nails and iron that held her together.'

Fletcher was captivated by Robertson's report. What a place was this Tahiti, where a cunny could be bought for just a nail!

Also in the library was the English translation of the book called *A Voyage round the World*, describing the expedition of the French explorer Louis Antoine de Bougainville. This included his ten-day stay, in 1768, on Tahiti. Bougainville's men too had been entranced by the island's women. Fletcher chuckled when he read the Frenchman's account of when his frigate *La Boudeuse* was standing off Tahiti:

Despite all the precautions which we took, a young girl got on board and came onto the forecastle and stood by one of the hatchways which are over the capstan. The girl let negligently fall her robe and stood for all to see, as Venus stood forth before the Phrygian shepherd; and she had the celestial shape of Venus. The sailors and soldiers rushed to get at the hatchway, and never was a capstan turned with such eagerness. We managed to restrain these bedevilled men, however, but it was no less difficult to control oneself.

After they got ashore Bougainville's men sated themselves with the island's women. He called Tahiti 'New Cythera', after the legendary Cythera, the island of Aphrodite, the Greek goddess of love.

Reading of these voyages and their perils, pleasures and triumphs, Fletcher's appetite for the world's distant places was whetted further. Yearning for his own exotic adventures, he was more conscious than ever that his time on this island was just an overture to his future career. And as far as he was concerned, that overture could not come to an end quickly enough, so that the real show could begin.

His brothers wrote to him regularly, letting him know of their progress. Charles had completed his physician's degree at Edinburgh.

He wrote: 'I am considering becoming a merchant mariner, and applying for a position as ship's surgeon on an East Indiaman. A difficult role, I imagine, but one which could take me far.'

Edward had graduated from St John's College and had been admitted to Gray's Inn, in London. He had become friends with a fellow-Cambridge man, he wrote, one William Wilberforce, a Yorkshireman and an evangelical Christian. 'I do not share his religious fervour,' Edward wrote, 'but I do whole-heartedly agree with his views on the despicable trade of slavery. Wilberforce now leads the abolitionist movement, and there is no more noble cause, I believe.'

On the Isle of Man the sea was a constant presence. Standing dockside during visits to Douglas, accompanied by the cawing of gulls and the stench of curing herrings, Fletcher observed the sloops, schooners, packet boats and privateers entering or departing from the harbour, their mooring and unmooring, the stowing and unloading of cargoes. Occasionally a storm blew in from the north, endangering the ships and their crews in Douglas harbour, and making it clear why the Tower of Refuge, the castle-like shelter built on Conister Rock in the bay, was so necessary.

He watched the merchant vessels and the Royal Navy ships being provisioned. The navy ships spent most of their time looking for smugglers' boats, which persisted in bringing contraband from Ireland or the Continent. Fletcher eavesdropped, listening to the banter, laughter and curses of the sailors, and this made him more determined than ever to become a part of their world.

As his eighteenth birthday drew closer, his anticipation of a life at sea quickened. One of Fletcher's visits to Douglas with cousin John coincided with the arrival in the harbour of the man-of-war HMS *Eurydice*, still commanded by Captain Courtnay. A 24-gunner, *Eurydice* had recently returned from duty in the Arabian Sea, and her decks were being re-caulked in the harbour.

Captain Courtnay and Fletcher and John Christian were invited to supper with the Taubmans, Edward and Loretta. In the course of the conversation Fletcher told Courtnay of his hopes for a career at sea, and

45

requested his advice regarding service with the Royal Navy. The leather-faced sea captain screwed up his eyes at the young man's question.

'A naval career? Is there a naval branch of the Christian family?' The captain's tone was interrogatory.

'None that I know of, sir,' Fletcher replied.

'And how old are you?'

'I will turn eighteen in four months.'

Courtnay grunted. 'No nautical family members. And eighteen, an advanced age for going to sea. Most mariners start at eleven or twelve years.'

Fletcher returned the captain's direct look. 'I am aware of that, sir. I'm also aware that there was no nautical tradition in Captain Cook's family. And that he first went to sea when he was nearly twenty.' He allowed a pause. 'And he didn't do so badly in the navy, did he?'

Loretta Taubman broke into peals of laughter, then picked up her napkin and placed it over her mouth. Fletcher's cousin chuckled, and even Courtnay had the grace to smile. Then, serious again, he said, 'And like Cook, you would have to start at the very bottom. On the orlop deck.'

'As an able seaman?'

'As a cabin boy.'

Taken aback, Fletcher said, 'An eighteen-year-old cabin boy?'

'Yes.' Courtnay swallowed some more red wine. 'But His Majesty's navy is noted for acknowledging talent.' He harrumphed. 'Unlike his army, which buys and sells its commissions and rewards only incompetence, it seems to me. The navy rewards merit. That is how Cook rose to the top. We gave due recognition to his obvious talents.' Turning back to Fletcher, he said, 'So I recommend that you sign on as a cabin boy, and if you prove your competence at sea you may progress to the status of midshipman.' He flicked up his eyebrows. 'And after that, who knows?'

Fletcher nodded, then hesitantly asked, 'I wonder, sir, if it would be possible for you to write a letter of introduction, for me to present to the naval authorities.'

Courtnay thought for a moment. 'That is possible. I will write to my colleague, Admiral Hood, recommending that you begin service as a cabin boy. Albeit a rather elderly one.' Becoming more genial, he added, 'Moreover, should your apprenticeship prove satisfactory, I could recommend that you are next signed on with me, on *Eurydice*, as a midshipman.'

Fletcher beamed. 'That would be wonderful, sir. Thank you.'

Two days later Fletcher met other members of the Christian clan, also friends of Edward and Loretta. John's second cousin Mary Duncan and her seventeen-year-old daughter, Isabella, were from Peel, on the west coast of the Isle of Man, where Mary's husband Roland was a shipping agent. He was currently in Belfast on business with their son, Thomas.

Isabella was studying musical composition at a school in Peel. She was tall like her mother, but there was nothing else of her mother in her features. Of slender build, with a narrow face and slightly upturned nose, she had green eyes, long auburn hair and a demure manner. She wore a pale brown gown with sleeves of lace. As she ate, Fletcher noticed her long fingers. A musician's fingers, he supposed. She said little, but he was conscious of her glancing at him from time to time. It discomfited him. What did those glances mean?

Mary Duncan was tall, with greying hair, a beaky nose and strong, somewhat masculine features. She gave Fletcher the impression of snobbery. At the supper table in the dining room she referred to his mother as 'that poor woman who was forced to sell her home', adding that 'her reduced circumstances must be so distressing for her.' Then she said to Fletcher, in a pitying tone, 'What a good thing, young man, that she has you to support her in her exile. When she has lost everything she possessed.'

Fletcher was moved to reprove her. He said forcefully, 'My mother has not lost everything, madam. She still has her family, and her health. And in time, with the help of my brothers and me, she will be restored to her former position.'

There was an uncomfortable silence. Mary Duncan pouted; Isabella looked down at her plate, her cheeks reddening.

Breaking the silence, Edward Taubman stood up and announced briskly, 'Well, John and I should retire to the library now, for a pipe and a port.' He looked at Fletcher. 'Will you join us?'

'Thank you, sir, but no. I'll take some fresh air on the terrace.'

After Loretta, Mary and Isabella said their goodnights and left the dining room, Fletcher went through the French doors and out onto the terrace at the rear of the house. There an ancient wisteria vine climbed up the wall, over the pergola above the terrace and entwined itself with the terrace's balustrade.

There was a new moon, a bright cuticle in the western sky. Stars glittered, and the air was mild. Fletcher leaned on the balustrade, still fretting over the horsey woman's comments about his mother. She was so condescending, he thought. Obviously thought herself a grande dame. But she was not so grande, and not much of a dame, either.

Continuing to brood, he saw a figure emerge from the shadows at the end of the terrace. It was Isabella, now with a cream shawl around her shoulders. She walked over to him. Tipping her head back, she stared up into his face. Although the new moon gave off little light, he was conscious of her eyes peering into his. Placing a hand on his forearm, she said earnestly, 'I must apologise for my mother's comments at supper, Fletcher. She is so crass at times. I could tell her comments offended you.'

'It is of no consequence.'

She shook her head. 'I think it is of consequence. I definitely owe you something.' She placed her hand on his.

He drew a long deep breath, and responding to her hand signal, reached out and touched her cheek. Still staring, she said quietly, 'I had heard about you, from Aunt Loretta. But you are even more handsome than she said you were.' Her fingers tightened around his wrist. His heart began to race. For a few moments neither of them moved. Then, still looking into his face, she asked quietly, 'Where is your room?'

He pointed down at the annex at the rear of the house. 'There.'

'Leave your door unlocked. I will be there shortly.'

He stared back at her, then nodded. His heart was sprinting now.

He could tell that she was far more experienced than himself, and this unnerved him. She undressed him first, removing his shirt, taking down his breeches. As he reached for her, he wondered, how had she learned to do this?

Then he ceased to think about that, and instead took her around the waist, bent and kissed her neck, her cheeks, smelling her lavender and rose water scent, marvelling at the softness of her skin. After he met her lips with his own she pulled her gown from her shoulders, then quickly removed her undergarments. He drew her towards the bed and they fell upon it together.

The first blush of sunrise was visible through the drapes when she got up, cleaned herself with the guest towel by the bed, and began to pull her gown back over her head. Sated, but transfixed still by the sight of her body, Fletcher raised himself on one elbow. 'Your mother, won't she—'

Isabella gave a little laugh. 'She sleeps like a night watchman. And snores like one too.' Putting her lips to his still-sweaty forehead, she murmured, 'Good morning, sweet cousin.'

RAMSEY, 14 MARCH 1782

Fletcher stood with his mother, dockside. His sea chest was on the wharf beside them, waiting to be taken aboard the sloop *Lady Jane*. She was tied up but readying to unmoor, bound for Liverpool. From there he would take a coach, first to Birmingham, and after several changes, eventually to Spithead. The naval authorities had informed him by letter that he would be signed on there as cabin boy on HMS *Cambridge*, an 80-gunner.

Last evening there had been a farewell dinner for him at Milntown. The mood was thoughtful rather than celebratory, and his mother's face remained overcast throughout, although when he put an arm around her shoulders and hugged her, she smiled gamely. Cousin John toasted his future, and presented him with a copy of Jonathan Swift's *Gulliver's Travels* ('To read when you're not on watch', John suggested).

At the end of the meal he made a brief speech. 'We will miss you, Fletcher,' he concluded, 'and so will the staff. You've worked well on the estate.'

'Thank you,' Fletcher replied. 'I've relished my time here. I almost feel like a Manxman now.' He paused. 'But I have to move on, to try my hand at something new.'

John nodded. 'I understand. And since you're now a Manxman, when you gain your leave, make sure you spend it here.'

'I shall.'

Two sailors took his chest and carried it up the gangplank. There was a stiff westerly wind, and men were already aloft, preparing to let go the sails. When the boatswain began his piping and the dockhands readied themselves to release the mooring ropes from the bollards, Fletcher bent and kissed his mother on the cheek. 'Bye, Mother. And good luck. I'll be back as soon as I can.'

Tears were streaming down her cheeks, a sight which filled him with guilt. How would she cope without him? In his last letter to Edward and Charles, informing them of his move, he had also urged them to visit her. Soon, he emphasised. He held her close, feeling her body convulsing, then released her gently. 'Goodbye, Mother. Goodbye.'

He turned and walked briskly up the gangplank and onto the mid-deck. Along with the exhilaration he felt was another feeling, just as strong. Relief.

The Bay of Biscay, 17 July 1782
Dearest Mother,

We have now been at sea for six weeks, and no doubt it will be another six before you will receive this, since I cannot dispatch it until we get to Plymouth next month.

Well, I am a seaman, or rather a seaboy on HMS Cambridge, the lowest of the low. Never mind, I am part of the crew, and an important part, I like to think. My tasks are menial, but demanding: cleaning, fetching, carrying, running after all others, helping keep watch. We have encountered storms in the bay, the last of which caused the mizzen mast to be sprung (cracked). Hence the need to make for Plymouth. So far we have made no contact with enemy vessels, either French or Spanish, although we have sailed as far as Cape Finisterre and some distance into the Atlantic. So my longing to visit exotic lands has not yet been realised, since the Bay of Biscay is mostly grey and unwelcoming.

Cambridge is a fine ship, and already I feel an affinity with her. Launched at Deptford in 1755, she is an 80-gunner, 3rd rate. Her guns have not yet been fired in anger on this voyage, but at practice the gunners are certainly on their mettle. The noise! No wonder most of them are deaf.

As the ship's dogsbody I was at first the target of the crew's bullies, a pair of scrofulous ABs from Bristol who threatened to beat me. I grabbed one by the shirt and lifted him clear off the floor of the mess. Then I dropped him and did the same to the other. This prompted such derision from the others that I was not bothered again by the pair. No one bullies a Christian!

I sleep in a hammock along with the able seamen, before the mast, and mess with them as well. I need to tell you about the victuals. You would be appalled at the fare we must eat, but as you know, I am never fussy about food. The navy's standard rations are: a pound of ship's biscuit daily (the others call it 'bread' but it bears no resemblance, being rock-hard), 1 lb salt pork (twice a week), 1 lb salt beef (twice a week), half a pint of pease (daily on four days), a pint of oatmeal every other day, plus two ounces of butter and four of cheese every second day. As well, we get a gallon of beer every day. So, not haute cuisine, as you would say, but I get so famished from the many exertions that I will eat anything. Our cook, Radford, is a man of great influence, the galley the most important part of our area of the ship, and the midday meal is definitely the highlight of the day. But I do miss the produce from the Christian farm, the fresh milk, eggs and bacon especially.

There is a set tradition we follow in the preparation and serving of the midday meal on board. It involves what's called 'the mess'. This means a group of men who eat their meals together. One man from each group is appointed the 'mess cook' and it's his duty to collect the day's food rations from the purser or the purser's steward.

The members of each mess take it in turn to be mess cook, and they do this for one week at a time. The mess cook also carries out some food preparation, like mixing the flour, suet and raisins for the puddings, then taking them in their bags or nets to the galley boiler. Each mess cook also prepares his men's table and puts the benches in place for them to sit on. Once the food is cooked and ready to be served, the mess cook collects it from the galley and serves it to his group. There is a tradition attached to the serving of the beef and pork, too. The mess cook carves the meat and distributes it to the others, but he must first call out 'Who shall have this?' Then another member of the mess, his back to the table, answers with his name. When all the men have been served and the meal's been eaten, the others resume their shipboard duties, while the mess cook cleans the table.

The navy is full of traditions like this, I'm learning, rituals that have been carried out for many years. I enjoy being part of them.

I only glimpse our commander, Captain Forsyth. He and his officers and the ship's sailing master lead separate lives. They meet in the Great Cabin and dine together in the officers' mess. Captain Forsyth puts in a regular appearance beside the helmsmen, though, to check our course. The ten midshipmen — all younger than me, by the look of them — also keep mostly separate from us, the lowest orders. More visible are our first officer, Lieutenant Grove, and the master, Abraham Troy. None of these take much notice of me. I am answerable mainly to the boatswain, Charlie Winscombe, and his mate, Will Anderson. Both are strict but fair, and take the time to show me the ropes when I am uncertain as to how to carry out a duty. Every day I learn something new.

When the airs are light and the ship is becalmed, we gather on the mid-deck, sing fiddle-accompanied shanties and have wrestling and boxing matches. These are keenly contested. I don't box, but I wrestle, and have won some bouts.

Another popular challenge is the leaping contest. This is to determine who can carry out a standing jump from inside one barrel and into another next *to it. The efforts cause much hilarity, with most men unable to get clear of the first barrel, let alone being able to land satisfactorily in the one next to it. But I can do it! I bunch my leg muscles, draw several breaths, clasp my hands in front of me, then spring like a frog out of the first barrel and over into the second. This dexterity must be the result of my fitness from the farm work. Whatever the reason, being able to achieve this when no one else can affords me admiration from the others. Also, my forearms are now strong enough for me to be able to hold out a musket with one hand at arm's length and keep it completely level. I do not wish to sound boastful, but this too is a feat that none of the others can manage. Physical prowess counts for a great deal aboard ship, I've learned.*

Academic competence, however, counts for nothing. Most of those on board can neither write nor read, which is why as I write this at the mess table I am receiving some strange looks from my shipmates. A quill to them is a strange instrument, far less useful than their sailors' knives, to which they are greatly attached. They even grumble at me when I read a book in my hammock by candlelight!

Every day on the ship I learn something new; every day my respect for the sea deepens. It is my vocation, I am certain of that now.

I must end now, as my watch impends. I trust that you are well and that you have had recent news from Edward and Charles. Please pass my best regards to cousin John.

Your loving son,
Fletcher

He also wrote to his brothers, and to Isabella, confessing that he would love to see her again, when he had gained enough leave to return to the Isle.

Captain Courtnay proved to be a dependable patron. After receiving a favourable report of Fletcher's conduct on HMS *Cambridge* from Captain Forsyth ('A young man of definite promise, dutiful, courageous, and educated to an unusual level'), Courtnay had written to his colleague Admiral Hood, requesting that Fletcher be added to the muster roll as a midshipman on his ship HMS *Eurydice* on her next voyage to the Far East. He had served as cabin boy on *Cambridge* for just one year.

Hood sanctioned the appointment, and Fletcher was ordered to sign on to *Eurydice*. She was to sail on 25 April 1783.

After being signed off from HMS *Cambridge* and bidding farewell to his shipmates, he travelled by coach from Spithead to Liverpool, and from there to the island, greatly looking forward to a few weeks on land and seeing again his mother and his cousins. Isabella especially.

'Mother! How are you?'

'Fletcher, darling.' Leaning back, she stared up at him. 'I'm coping. And you're even taller!'

'Ha! Must be all that salt meat and ship's biscuit.'

They sat in the garden at Milntown, under the big elm that was bursting into leaf. He told her something of his year at sea, but she showed only token interest in his new life. She said that she had heard regularly from Edward and Charles, and that they had spent Christmas with her on the island. Edward had begun practising as attorney-at-law in London, and Charles was employed as a surgeon at a hospital in Chelsea, but was still thinking of serving in the merchant marine.

His mother reported all this with more than a hint of reproach that Fletcher was the only one of her sons who was for the time being not within reasonable reach. He reminded himself to be tolerant of her attitude, knowing that she must be lonely for long periods of time. But he still found her carping tiresome.

'Your father's family have still not accepted me,' she complained. 'They keep their distance. Emotionally, I mean. And I do so much miss Cumbria.'

'I understand. I still miss it myself.' He put a hand over hers. 'But I am growing to love the sea, Mother. Even when it frightens me, I still savour its moods. And its challenges.'

She nodded, but sorrowfully, realising that this would mean his continued absence from the island for long periods. After he told her he would like to spend some time in Douglas, and see the Taubmans, he said, 'And cousin Isabella. Is there a letter here for me from her?'

'No.'

'Well, I would like to visit her, in Peel.'

His mother gave him a hooded look. 'It will not be possible to see her.'

'Why not?'

'Two months ago there was a scandal involving Isabella. John reported it to me.'

'What do you mean?'

'Isabella has eloped. To Dublin.'

For some moments Fletcher couldn't speak. Then he said, 'With whom?'

'Her music professor. He's twice her age. And has a wife and four children in Peel. The elopement scandalised the town.'

'Good grief.'

He could think of nothing else to say. But he was thinking plenty. It must have been the professor who had schooled her in the arts of love-making as well as pianoforte. And now she had gone, and he would almost certainly never see her again. Well, he wished her good fortune, but that seemed unlikely, since it was an ageing man she had run off with. But he would never forget the night they had spent together. Beautiful, wonderful, wanton Isabella.

Again he said his farewells to his family on the island and travelled to Spithead. There he was issued with his midshipman's uniform and signed on for service on Captain Courtnay's 24-gun ship, HMS *Eurydice*.

Familiar with the vessel from her visits to Douglas, Fletcher was now accommodated more comfortably mid-decks along with the other midshipmen, most of whom were five or six years younger than himself. As such, he found some of them tiresome, particularly thirteen-year-old Samuel Evans, who seemed to think Fletcher was his elder brother and never stopped following him.

The best part of his enhanced status was the midshipman's dress uniform: indigo coat with white patches on the collar and brass buttons at the cuff, cream waistcoat, white ruffled blouse, black neck cloth, ivory trousers and a belt with a scabbard for a cutlass. The crowning touch was the tall, round, black hat. Whenever he put on the uniform, he felt grand. What a change from the calico trousers, coarse shirt and fearnought jacket of his cabin-boy year.

They set sail for the Coromandel coast of eastern India on 2 May 1783, via the Cape Verde Islands and Cape Town.

Throughout May *Eurydice* made steady progress into the South Atlantic. They encountered no enemy vessels, only other British ships-of-the-line to whom they sent flag signals, but did not stop for Captain Courtnay to parley with their commanders.

For Fletcher and the other midshipmen this part of the voyage was one long lesson in seamanship. Rain, gale or sunshine, they kept strictly to their allotted duties, overseen by the officers: learning the flag signals, taking and recording soundings, marking the ship's log board, taking observations to mark her position and determine noon, running messages between the lieutenants and the captain. Each midshipman also oversaw and commanded a gun crew, ensured each member had clean clothing and that all gunnery equipment and the powder cartridges were at hand, and that the guns were ready for action at a moment's notice.

When off duty they studied the navigation manuals, trigonometry texts and the general skills of seamanship, such as the procedure for hoisting out the launches and catting the bow anchors. Every day's activities had to be recorded in their log books and handed in to the Great Cabin for reviewing by Captain Courtnay.

Unlike Fletcher's shipmates on HMS *Cambridge*, all the midshipmen were literate, although not schooled to a high level. Evans and several of the others sometimes asked him how to construct a sentence correctly or spell a word ('It's "spritsail", Evans, not "spirit-sail"', and he consistently misspelled '*Eurydice*'). And every night following supper the young men collapsed into their berths, exhausted from the demands on their day.

They reached Funchal, Madeira's capital town, off the west coast of Africa, on 10 June. The midshipmen were not permitted to go ashore there while the ship was being reprovisioned, much to Fletcher's disappointment. He had read of Captain Cook's *Endeavour*'s calling there in August 1768, during his first world voyage.

Most of the four days that *Eurydice* was anchored in the Funchal roads he spent aloft, staring at the island's forested mountains and sniffing the scent of the tropics, the smell of wet earth and foliage and wood smoke from the natives' cooking fires. He watched enviously as the ship's launches transferred onions, sugar cane, lemons, fresh beef, brandy and wine from shore to ship.

Then they weighed anchor again, prepared for the next long reach to Cape Town.

The day after the summer solstice, 23 June, *Eurydice* crossed the line. The topsails were close reefed, the course hauled up and the top gallant sails furled. The initiation rituals were observed under the direction of King Neptune, alias boatswain Robert Johnstone. Dressed in a horsehair wig and grey beard, tin crown atop his head and trident in hand, Neptune ordered every midshipman and able seaman who had not previously crossed the Equator to be liberally coated with pitch and galley filth, then tossed by the 'Trusty Shellbacks' and 'Sons of Neptune' — those crew members who had crossed the line before — into a seawater pool contained in a spare sail extended out from the starboard hull with a yard arm. The captain and officers, most of whom had paid their way out of the ducking by bribing the boatswain with a bottle of rum from their private grog supplies, watched the hilarity from the quarterdeck.

Fletcher bore the humiliation good-naturedly, and supported young Evans when he almost choked on seawater during his ducking. Fletcher had learned to swim during his boyhood, in the River Cocker, but few of the others could. Evans took his ducking gamely, but as Fletcher hoisted him clear of the water he realised that there were tears as well as seawater running down his cheeks. 'Just think, Evans,' he reassured the boy, 'you're now a Trusty Shellback yourself. So come next time, you'll be able to duck others.'

When he came back aboard, still smeared in filth, Fletcher lay on the deck and stared up through the shrouds into the blue sky and felt satisfied as well as exhausted. From now on they would be sailing in the Southern Hemisphere, where for years he had longed to be.

Cape Town, 28 July 1783
Dear Mother,

I am in Africa! Or, at least, in Cape Town, anchored in Table Bay, at the southern end of Africa. Some repairs are needed to Eurydice's rudder stock, as well as the need for fresh food and water, so we are in port for at least ten days. On two of those days I have been onshore leave, in the company of some of the other midshipmen. What a place Cape Town is! Looming above the town is a huge, flat-topped fell, aptly called Table Mountain. A river flows down from its slopes, providing fresh water for the town and any visiting ships. Cape Town's location west of the Cape of Good Hope means that nearly every ship sailing between Europe and Asia calls here for victualling, and does so too on their return voyage. The provisions are brought down to the port in vast quantities: fresh vegetables, grain, meat and wine — all produced in the town's hinterland and purchased by Eurydice's purser, George Cutler.

As it is winter here (yes, so peculiar, winter in July!), a cold wind blows down from Table Mountain, often bringing rain showers, so that we must wear our waistcoats, topcoats and hats when we are ashore. Cape Town is clustered around the waterfront, but could hardly be more different to a British port town. The buildings are very strange, tall, narrow and gabled ornately, with window boxes. Most fly the Dutch flag. The shops along the quay sell very unusual foods: smoked sausages, pickled herring served with sliced onion and gherkins, thick ham soups and spicy fried rice. I tried some of the spicy rice, it's called 'nasi goreng', a dish introduced by the Dutch from the East Indies. Delicious.

Dutch people gather on the main street and in coffee houses. The women are rather stout and plain, with black gowns and ornate, lacy bonnets. The men too are plump and well fed-looking, most with wigs, black topcoats and always smoking pipes. These Dutch people look at us curiously but do not show any sign of friendship. They do not like the English, I've been told, and it shows. Far more interesting are the African people, the 'Hottentots' as they are called. We see the men only; their women must be in the little houses at the back of the town, quite separate from their Dutch rulers. The skins of the Hottentots are very black, their hair is frizzy, their lips prominent, their noses flat. Most go barefooted in spite of the cold and their clothes are ragged. They are the beasts of burden for the Dutch and appear to be very strong, their legs muscular and sinewy. Some carry sacks of grain or flour across their shoulders, others pull handcarts piled high with produce or drive wagons pulled by oxen, all heading for the dock. Unlike the Dutch, these natives smile and greet us cheerily, calling out 'Hay-low Boss,' 'Hay-low Boss,' whenever they pass us on the street. We wave back. I feel rather sorry for them, as they are such poor creatures. I saw a Dutchman threatening a native with a stock whip and berating him with cries of, 'Lui kaffir! Lui kaffir!' I didn't know the meaning of these words, but it sounded very insulting. I didn't like it.

I will end this missive now, as the ship's noon bell has just rung, signalling that dinner will be served shortly. Pleasant as it is to be in port, I relish the prospect of setting sail again, since it means that our long haul across the Indian Ocean will soon be under way.

I shall ask one of the other midshipmen to dispatch this letter at the town's postal office when the next one goes ashore.

Your loving son,

Fletcher

By September they were in the Indian Ocean, on a due north course. Temperatures rose again and the winds were accompanied by drifting rain which saturated the decks and sails. The humidity was measured at over ninety per cent, and below decks it was sweltering. Men worked topside only in trousers, their feet bare, kerchiefs around their necks to block the sweat which streamed down their faces. The slightest exertion made it stream more. The seamen inched along the yardarms as they worked the sails, anxious not to slip.

They re-crossed the Equator on 13 October. A week later, at five degrees north, they were in the vicinity of the Maldives, a cluster of atolls scarcely above sea level. Men were posted to the top of the mainmast day and night, as the coral reefs surrounding these islands were capable of tearing open *Eurydice*'s hull. The waves breaking on the atolls' reefs were bright white, even at night, so that a man aloft could shout to the helmsmen below to warn of the approaching hazard, but the frequent squalls hid the reefs, necessitating the launch being sent ahead to check that the course was safe. From the decks and rigging they saw palms growing from the cays, and black, loin-clothed figures standing on the strand or fishing from canoes.

Once safely through the Maldives, *Eurydice* bore due east for the Gulf of Mannar and the Palk Strait separating Ceylon from India.

'Land! Land ho! Off the larboard bow!'

They rushed to the rails, and there it was, a dark mound in the mist. India. A tremor of excitement passed through the ship. Some of them had read of this legendary land, and the rest had heard other sailors' tales. India, land of strange religions and languages, of temples and turbaned rulers, of bazaars, spices, elephants and tigers. And dark-skinned, sari-clad women.

Eurydice sailed north along India's Coromandel coast, keeping well off, then into the Bay of Bengal, as far as twenty degrees north. The air was clogged with heat; the sea was the colour of mulligatawny. 'It's the water from the Ganges,' one veteran sailor told Fletcher. 'The river flowing into the bay.' And although they were out of sight of land, when they sampled the brown water it was fresh.

For two weeks they patrolled the region, tacking back and forth across the bay, seeking French vessels to attack but seeing only merchant vessels of the East India Company and native craft called parias, trading between Calcutta and Chittagong. They did not call at Calcutta, located on one of the Ganges' many mouths, and at the end of January Captain Courtnay ordered the ship to go about and follow a direct southerly course, back down the Coromandel coast.

With the apparently endless hills and plains of India usually visible off their starboard bow, they were now bound for Madras. There they would take on fresh food, water and firewood, supplies of which were running low.

Fletcher had read of Madras's history in a recently published book loaned to him by Captain Courtnay. It was entitled *The Subjugation of the French and Others by the British in East India, 1626–1780*, by Alexander Dalrymple, who had been in the employ of the British East India Company. Fletcher was aware that Dalrymple had been keen to command the Royal Navy's expedition to observe the transit of Venus in June 1769, but had been rejected because he had arrogantly insisted on also commanding the ship, something he was not entitled to do. The role was then awarded to James Cook, who proved an inspired choice.

Nevertheless, Dalrymple's history of Madras fascinated Fletcher. Its early chapters chronicled the establishment of the town, which was once just a sleepy fishing village, as far back as 1522, when the Portuguese built a trading port on the coast. In 1612 the Dutch arrived, establishing a small settlement at Pulicat, just north of Madras. Then in 1626 the British arrived, in the form of the English East India Company. The company established a factory processing the region's principal product, calico cloth, at Armagon, thirty-five miles north of Pulicat. To protect their trading interests, in 1640 the company built a small fortified settlement which they named Fort St George.

Although Madras was surrounded by territories ruled by often hostile Hindu and Moslem powers, it was Britain's old foe, France, which had captured Fort St George, in 1746. Their victory was short-lived, however, as control over the fort was regained by the British in 1749, under the Treaty of Aix-la-Chapelle. The fort was subsequently strengthened and enlarged. The British also fought the native leaders and won control of East India, known as the Kingdom of Mysore.

Fletcher appreciated the concluding statement of Dalrymple's history:

By 1780, seventeen years after the victorious conclusion of the Seven Years' War, Britain was in complete control of Madras and its surrounding region, with all her European enemies defeated and the native Hindu and Moslem authorities subjugated. Thus the conditions were ripe for the port town of Madras to become not only a vital trading and administrative centre in

eastern India, but an important base for the victorious Navy of his Majesty,
King George III. In conjunction with the other British trading towns on
the coast of the sub-continent of India, the consolidation of Madras forms
the basis for continuing British trade, prosperity and power. Greatness for
our nation lies ahead!

Eurydice was worked slowly through the mouth of the Adyar River and
into Madras Harbour. Although its entrance was only about a hundred
yards wide, once the ship was through it the river opened to the tidal
basin which comprised the harbour proper. It was crammed with ships,
mostly vessels flying the flag of the East India Company, and all at
anchor, sails furled. Much smaller native fishing vessels moved slowly
through the cluster of British ships, like small dogs among a herd of
cattle. Some were being rowed, others were under lateen sail.

Eurydice's anchors were lowered near the centre of the harbour,
alongside an East Indiaman sloop. There was little wind, and the mid-
morning sun was blistering. Fletcher and Samuel Evans leaned on the
larboard rail, near the bow, looking over towards the town, which was
built on flat land along the northern bank of the river.

A line of palm trees grew along the shore, with a few thatched huts
scattered among them. Inland, behind the town, was a series of hills,
burned brown by the sun. Smells of the land wafted across to them:
burning wood and grass, the odour of drying fish. Some distance from
the dock, to the west, was a temple, a complex structure of blocks and
towers. Directly ahead and a little way back from the river bank was a
fortress with stone walls, battlements and, above its entrance, a central
turret. The Union Jack was hanging limp from a pole atop the turret.
Dwarfing everything around it, the fort appeared impregnable.

'Fort St George,' Fletcher said.

'It's huge,' said Evans, awed. 'Are we permitted to go ashore?'

'I've not been told. I hope so. It looks an exciting town.'

'You two! Don't just stand about talking! Attend to your duties!' The
shout came from Lieutenant Drake, striding down the deck towards
them.

'Aye, sir,' replied Fletcher and Evans together. They hurried off to help release the ship's pinnace, which was being hoisted out from the foredeck.

The following day half the midshipmen, including Fletcher and Evans, were given leave to go ashore for the day. Ferried in the pinnace to one of the jetties which extended into the river, they stepped off the boat and into India.

People, people, people, everywhere. The dusty road that ran parallel to the river bank was filled with people scurrying in all directions at once, like crabs whose rock has been overturned. There were women porters in brightly coloured gowns, barefoot and bearing pottery urns on their heads, swaying gracefully as they walked. Most had gold rings through their noses. Other young women had babies strapped to their backs. Bearded men in dhotis carried baskets of goods or pulled handcarts piled high with fruit and vegetables, bound for the market across the road. There were oxen drawing carts which struggled through the hordes, their passengers turbaned, imperious men. Horned cows with bony shoulders and pale hides wandered about languorously, shitting, pissing and ignoring the human crowd. Chickens and dogs crept among the human and animal zoo. And the smells! The hot air reeked of spiced food, over-ripe fruit and vegetables, human sweat, animal and human dung.

Gagging at the stench, Fletcher and Evans fought their way through the hordes to the other side of the road. They came to a line of spice stalls, and braziers frying rice and vegetables. Behind the food stalls was a row of stone buildings, separated by alleyways. 'Black Town', they had been told this area was called. As Fletcher and Evans made their way between the stalls their female proprietors held out bowls of food and cried shrilly, 'English, English! Special food for you! Cheap, cheap!'

Feeling conspicuous amid the crowds of importuning natives, the pair struggled into the street at the rear of the market, then entered one of the alleys. On either side of it were more stalls, run by men squatting beside piles of spices and chillies heaped onto banana palm leaves. The spices were brightly coloured: saffron, red, ginger, yellow, brown.

As Fletcher and Evans made their way further into Black Town they were again assailed by shrieking vendors. 'English! English! Nice spices for you! Special! Special!'

Fletcher turned to Evans and grinned. 'We should take some back for our cook. It might improve the taste of his meat.'

Further into the alley there were no more spice stalls, just open doorways with stone steps on which men and women were sitting. The turbaned men were thin-faced and unshaven; the hollow-cheeked women wore threadbare saris and gold bangles on their wrists. All were barefooted. Some women were nursing babies which they held out to the young sailors, imploringly. 'English, English! Money, money for baby!'

Increasingly unsettled by this poverty, Evans said, 'I think we should go back to the ship. All these beggars, I don't like it.'

Fletcher shook his head. 'You can. I want to explore some more.'

As Evans turned, he said, 'Be careful.'

'I will.'

The alley grew narrower. Overhead, items of clothing dangled from bamboo poles protruding from upstairs windows or hung from balconies. Some of the washing dripped onto Fletcher and he turned up his collar. It was stifling in the alley and the mud stank, but he pressed on, excited by the exoticness he was immersed in, keen to see where the alleyway led.

A little further along, in an open doorway, stood a girl. She was quite short, not five feet in height, and wore a dark red sari. Her feet were bare and her head was uncovered, her raven-black hair hanging loose. As Fletcher approached she beamed at him. Her face was round, the skin unmarked except for a crimson dot in the centre of her forehead and a gold ring in her nose. Her most striking feature was her eyes. They were dark brown and lustrous. Still beaming, making beckoning movements with one hand, she said, 'English, English. Nice man English.'

She lifted her sari with both hands. Fletcher stared. Beneath the sari she was naked, and at the pit of her rounded belly was a mat of black hair. 'Fuck? Fuck?' she asked. Fixated, he nodded. Lifting the sari higher, she exposed her brown breasts and said, 'Money? Money?'

He nodded. They had all been allocated a small allowance by the purser for buying meals while ashore. The girl lowered her sari, stood back and ushered him into the unlit, earth-floored passage. 'Come,' she said, and he followed her. Heart pounding, he groped for the coins in his pocket. She turned, still smiling, still beckoning. 'Here, here. Fuck in here.'

From out of the darkness to his right, a figure rushed at him, one arm raised, in its hand a cosh. Fletcher just had time to see that the figure was male, skinny, and that it wore just a loincloth, before the cosh came down on his head.

It was his midshipman's hat that saved him. Although his head rang with the blow, and red lights danced behind his eyes, the hat absorbed most of the blow's force. And although he reeled from it, that gave him time to retaliate. He reached out, grabbed the cosh before the man had time to strike another blow, and hauled on it as hard as he could. His assailant came forward, stumbled, fell on his face. The cosh fell to the ground. Fletcher bent, grabbed the man's hair, hauled him upwards. He was very light. Fletcher swung his right arm and struck the man on the side of the face. He cried out, spitting blood. Fletcher hit him again, then hurled him against the opposite wall.

Before running from the building, Fletcher turned and looked for the girl. She had disappeared.

It was halfway through his second voyage to India on *Eurydice* that Fletcher received a summons from Captain Courtnay's servant, ordering him to report to him in the Great Cabin. That was still a part of the ship to which, as a mere midshipman, he was usually denied entry. The servant, Dunmorton, knocked on the door of the captain's cabin then opened it. Captain Courtnay rose.

'Christian, come in.' He waved his hand at a chair opposite him. 'Sit down.' There was a pipe on the table in front of the captain, and a small knife.

Staring at Fletcher, the commander rubbed his chin. 'You've been with *Eurydice* for almost a year, is that correct?'

'It is, sir. I signed on in April last year.'

'Yes.' He picked up his pipe and began to ream out the bowl with the knife. Fletcher watched him, puzzled. He had ordered him here just to tell him what he already knew?

The captain leaned back in his chair. 'I've been impressed with your performance, Christian, throughout the two voyages. The way you work with the younger midshipmen, and support them. Your leadership has not gone unnoticed.'

Fletcher shrugged. 'I'm older, so I help them when they need it. It's no more than my duty to do so, sir.'

'Many would not see it that way,' said Courtnay. 'The other thing that impresses me is your logbook. For a midshipman, it's the best-kept I've ever read. The care you take with the written word is impressive.'

'I had the advantage of attending a very good school, sir.'

'Evidently.' He stared at Fletcher across the table. 'As from tomorrow, I'm promoting you to Acting Lieutenant. And Watch Leader.'

Fletcher's head spun. Acting Lieutenant? Watch Leader? For some moments he couldn't speak. As Courtnay took a wad of tobacco from a pouch and filled his pipe bowl, Fletcher said at last, 'This comes as a great surprise to me, sir.'

'An agreeable one, I trust.'

'Yes. But it usually takes several years of experience to be offered a commission.'

'True. But the fact that I'm offering you one after two years at sea is testimony to your capabilities. You are strict, yet the men like you.' He grunted. 'A rare combination.'

'I am honoured, sir. Thank you.'

'Good. Tomorrow Dunmorton will issue you with your lieutenant's uniform. And from now on you will dine with us in the Officers' Mess.' He stood up and walked to the cabinet under the bookcase. 'Now, let's celebrate your promotion with a glass of brandy.'

Fletcher revelled his new status on *Eurydice*. There appeared to be little resentment among the other midshipmen over his elevation. Indeed, they seemed pleased. 'Acting Lieutenant,' said Evans proudly, as if it was himself who had been promoted. 'But you will still visit us in our quarters, won't you?'

Fletcher mimed a cuff to his ear. 'Not if you ask stupid questions like that, lad.' He grinned. 'But of course I will.'

Shortly after *Eurydice* finished her latest tour of duty and Fletcher returned to the Isle on leave, there was a startling international development. After negotiations at the highest level, a deal had been brokered and a peace agreement reached between Britain and the new nation, the United States of America. France, which had supported America, was badly in debt from the war, and could not continue fighting.

The Treaty of Paris was signed on 3 September 1783 by representatives of King George III for Britain and those from the United States, whose delegates included the redoubtable Benjamin Franklin. Negotiations had begun in April 1782, and had continued into the next year before the treaty was eventually signed. This ended the American Revolutionary War. There were separate peace treaties between Britain and the nations that had supported the American cause: France, Spain and the Dutch Republic. Peace had again descended on Europe.

But the concord brought unexpected consequences.

'A letter for you, Fletcher.' His mother turned it over. 'It looks very official. From the Admiralty.'

Ann Christian was now living in upstairs rooms in a house in Woodbourne Road, Douglas, three streets back from the Promenade. She had been financially assisted in this move by Edward, Charles and Fletcher. It was a comfortable property. The rooms all had sloping walls papered with heraldic scenes; there was a fireplace in the small drawing room; and sash windows gave views of Douglas Bay, the harbour and Onchan Head. Apple and plum trees grew in the small walled garden at the rear of the house. Fletcher was staying with his mother, sleeping in the small bedroom at the rear of the building.

'I'm grateful to you,' she told him, 'for helping me escape from Milntown.' He pressed his lips together, to avoid clicking his tongue in irritation. Escape? Why dramatise the move? Why didn't she just accept her improved position and be done with it?

They were seated on a chaise longue under one of the drawing room windows. His mother handed him the letter and he opened it eagerly. Was the Admiralty writing to offer him a permanent commission?

21 November 1784

Dear Acting Lieutenant Christian,

You have doubtless read of the cessation of hostilities between Great Britain, France and the United States of America. This is a development to be greatly welcomed, as it will save our nation considerably in lives and capital. Accordingly, the Chancellor of the Exchequer has announced that the activities of Great Britain's Army and Navy will be substantially reduced, and henceforth military personnel will be retained on half pay. The vessel on which you last served, HMS Eurydice, will be kept in dock at Deptford, and will not sail on active service again in the foreseeable future.

We know that you will rejoice in the new peace agreement as ratified by the Treaty of Paris and will look forward, as we do, to a future for Britain and Europe of peace and prosperity.

Yours faithfully,

Philip Stephens, Secretary to the Admiralty, Whitehall, London.

'What is the news?' his mother asked.

He handed her the letter. She read it, and her brow creased. 'No further service? Half pay?'

Nodding, he stared out the window. His career in the navy, shattered. No more voyages to India, no more training on the high seas, no more promotions. Half pay — a shilling a day — would scarcely support him on land. His mind clouded over. Just when his tide had begun to flow strongly, it had turned and ebbed, leaving him stranded on this dull island.

'What will you do?' asked his mother, still clutching the letter.

Quite unable to answer, he just shook his head.

Later that day he climbed Bray Hill at the back of the town and sat gazing at the sea. The sun was bright and the features of the harbour's Tower of Refuge were clearly defined. To banish the view, he looked down. In his mind a black fog had formed, and lodged there. It blotted out his future. Confined to land? He couldn't bear it. The sea had become his life: he couldn't renounce it and become a landlubber. Everything he had learned over the last two years — and that was plenty — was now gone to waste. Sod the peace treaty.

The last two years had been the best of his life. He had become accustomed to, and savoured, the endless, ever-changing sea. The exhilaration of sails and gales, the howl of the wind in the shrouds, the creaking of the strakes, the pitching and rolling of the ship. And the rambunctious camaraderie of the lower deck, then the more formal company of the officers' mess. The shores of India, the smells of its ports and their foods, the chatter of native voices, the allure of exotic women. None of that could ever be matched by a life on land.

He shook his head, but could not dislodge the blackness in there. His hands had gone clammy, and he wiped them on his breeches. Assailed by despair, he put his head in his hands. What could he do? Where could he go? He certainly couldn't stay here on this island with his difficult mother.

It was another hour before he got up and walked back down the hill and into the town. There was a glimmer of hope on the horizon, he thought. Cousin John, who knew everyone who made a living on land, could speak to Captain Courtnay, who knew everyone here who made a living on the sea.

The Douglas Club was on the Douglas waterfront, a two-level stone building covered in Virginia creeper whose bare winter vines clung to its walls like clutching fingers. The building's windows were mullioned, its porticoed entrance dignified.

The air in the social room was thick with smoke from a coal fire and the pipes of most of the members. A candelabrum hung from a ceiling rose, its multiple flames casting light over the room. On the walls were paintings of hunting scenes and sea battles. The flag of the Isle of Man hung above a servery, on which were carafes of wine, port and brandy. A Negro waiter moved through the crowd of members, holding out a silver salver upon which they placed their glasses for him to refill.

Looking around, Fletcher saw that he was the only person present who wasn't wearing a wig. Most of the members were in their forties; a few very elderly ones must have been over fifty. Their faces were universally rubicund, their bellies bulged beneath their waistcoats. The room thrummed with hail-fellow-well-met greetings, loud conversations and even louder guffawing.

Fletcher noticed someone he had met before, Duncan Campbell, standing by the servery, engaged in earnest conversation with another man of about the same age. Campbell owned ships that traded between England and the West Indies. 'Sugar Rum Campbell, we call him,' John Christian had said. Campbell also owned several prison ships — hulks moored in the Thames in which convicted felons were kept. This venture had made him even wealthier.

John beckoned the Negro waiter over and placed his own and Fletcher's glass on his tray. 'Another two brandies, there's a good fellow,' he said. Turning back to Fletcher, he made an exasperated face. 'I've just been told that Courtnay's away in Liverpool at the moment, so can't be here this evening.' He brightened. 'However, I asked Campbell to invite someone else along who may be able to help you. He's had extensive naval experience and is married to Campbell's niece, Elizabeth Betham, who's from Douglas. Campbell is influential, so that connection may be helpful to you.' He put a hand on Fletcher's shoulder. 'One way or another, young man, we'll get you back to sea again.'

'Thank you. I appreciate it.'

Looking across the room, Fletcher saw another man enter. He was short — barely five feet — but sturdy and stiff-shouldered. Wigged, he wore a dark blue frock coat, white hose and highly polished boots. He looked about thirty. Noticing John, he moved through the crowd and approached him.

John held out his hand. 'William, welcome.'

'Thank you. It's good to be in here and out of the cold.' He turned to Fletcher. 'And this is?'

'My cousin Fletcher. Ann Christian's son. Fletcher, meet Lieutenant William Bligh, late of His Majesty's navy.'

The first thing that struck Fletcher was the man's eyes. They were pale blue and as piercing as gimlets. Being short, he had to tilt his head to meet Fletcher's gaze, but the eyes kept boring into his. Fletcher noted his other features: a broad, pale forehead, pointed nose, a full, shapely mouth and a small chin.

He shook Fletcher's hand. 'Well, another Christian. Good evening.'

John said, 'Lieutenant Bligh served with Captain Cook on HMS *Resolution*.'

Fletcher gasped. 'How wonderful.' Then realising the insensitivity of his reaction, corrected himself. 'Not wonderful, perhaps, but memorable, surely.'

As they talked Fletcher was disconcerted by the man's eyes, which continued to track him until he was obliged to look away. Although he seemed a little distant, he did show interest in Fletcher's experiences on *Eurydice*. He had met Captain Courtnay on more than one occasion, Bligh told him.

'Well, I'll leave you to chat,' John said, and moved away in the direction of Campbell.

As Fletcher and Bligh talked, the older man appeared to relax. They had some things in common, most notably the fact that they had both been discharged from the navy on half pay. 'My naval career ended two years ago,' Bligh announced with obvious resentment, 'and isn't likely to be resurrected unless war breaks out. In which case both of us will be needed again.'

Fletcher nodded. He and this fellow Bligh were both in the same boat, so to speak. Or rather, not in one.

Bligh asked about Fletcher's family. When told that his father had been a lawyer in Cumbria and that his brothers had attended Cambridge and Edinburgh universities, Bligh's eyes widened. He had been born in Plymouth, he said, where his father had worked in the Customs department. He had first gone to sea at the age of fifteen, on the warship HMS *Hunter*.

Fletcher was intrigued by this, but more by the fact that this man had sailed with Cook. He pressed him for details of that voyage and Cook's violent death in the Sandwich Islands. But at mention of this, Bligh's expression dimmed. He said tersely, 'I have nothing to add to what has already been written about that voyage. Now I must go and talk to Campbell.' And he turned away.

Staring after him, Fletcher frowned. What an unusual fellow. So changeable.

Later that evening, walking back along the waterfront with John, Fletcher learned more about Bligh. Although his cousin related the story matter-of-factly, it was obvious to Fletcher that it had caused great interest in Isle of Man society.

'Bligh earned a reputation while on Cook's last voyage as a fine navigator and hydrographer. An accomplished cartographer, too. So when he was discharged and put on half pay, he took it badly.'

'I know the feeling,' Fletcher put in.

'But you're young and single. Bligh is a married man with a baby daughter. When he and Betsy moved here they were penurious, so she went to her Uncle Duncan and asked for help. He loaned them money to lease and furnish a house in Douglas. And Bligh is now in Campbell's employ.' He tapped his nose and laughed. 'On this island the saying that it's not what you know, it's who you know is very true.'

Fletcher said, 'Bligh became disgruntled when I asked him about his voyage with Cook. Why was that, do you think? I really wanted to know about it.'

'Well, Bligh feels he was done an injustice following that voyage. He was sailing master on Cook's *Resolution*. And a diligent one, by all accounts. He carried out surveys, charting coastlines all along the

72

way. Of the Kerguelen Island, Van Diemen's Land, the Sandwich Isles, North America.' He put his hand on his tricorn to hold it in place against the wind. 'Bligh's mate on *Resolution* was Henry Roberts. Now the charts from the voyage are being published, and Roberts claims the credit for them and for the engravings that were produced. Bligh is receiving no credit for his great work.'

'That's unjust, surely.'

'Indeed it is. Roberts was never a proper surveyor, and Bligh is. And he's bitter with Roberts over the way he has purloined his charts.'

'I don't blame him.'

They walked on in silence for a time. The wind had strengthened and waves were being driven against the sea wall. It was chilly, too. Fletcher wrapped his topcoat more firmly about him and tightened his scarf. A storm was brewing.

John went on. 'However, Bligh's career as a merchant mariner is blossoming. He has commanded two West Indiamen on the Caribbean route.' He chuckled. 'It's well known that Campbell is paying Bligh far more than he got in the navy. An annual salary of five hundred pounds. And now he's been given command of Campbell's merchantman, *Britannia.*'

A spark flashed in Fletcher's mind. Why should he not become a merchant mariner, as Bligh had done? Royal Navy or merchant marine, a ship was a ship, after all.

After considering the matter for some time, he composed a letter, one which required a great deal of writing and rewriting, first in pencil, then finally with quill and ink.

8 July 1785

Dear Captain Bligh,

You may recall that we met at the Douglas Club, when I was in the company of my cousin, John Christian. We had in common the distressing fact that both of us had been paid off by the navy following the signing of the Treaty of Paris. I had served for two years on HMS Eurydice as a midshipman, and was promoted to Acting Lieutenant by Captain George Courtnay.

I hold a strong desire to return to sea, as during my two years on HMS Eurydice I grew to love the life. It is now over six months since I was last at sea, and I miss it sorely. I am aware that you have been granted leave from our King's navy and have gained the command of the West Indiaman, Britannia. Allow me to congratulate you on this appointment, I am sure that this will further consolidate your already successful career as a merchant marine commander.

Since my career in the Royal Navy has been similarly truncated for the foreseeable future, I would respectfully request to apply for a position aboard your latest vessel and serve on her when she next sails for the West Indies. I believe I possess all the necessary skills to make myself an asset on a merchantman such as Britannia.

Next September I will be twenty-one years of age, and I am willing to serve in whatever capacity it may take, in order to return to the sea. Please allow me, sir, to do so.

I am, sir, your obliged and very humble servant,

Fletcher Christian

He read and reread the letter. Was it too boastful? Unduly modest? Had anything important been omitted? When he was satisfied, he completed the final draft, placed the sheet of notepaper in an envelope and delivered it to the residence in Douglas where William and Elizabeth Bligh lived. He felt confident at his prospects. How could the man possibly decline such a request?

Four days later he received a reply.

12 July 1785

Dear Fletcher Christian,

Thank you for your letter, in which you request to be added to the muster roll of my vessel, Britannia. However as the ship's complement is full, I must decline your request.

Yours faithfully,

William Bligh

Once again the black fog threatened to return. What had seemed like a chance had been dashed, in just three lines. Damn the man! His mother, who had brought the letter to him, asked to see it. Clicking her tongue, she cast it aside. 'The man is a fool, Fletcher, to refuse you.'

'He's by no means a fool, Mother. But he is a trifle strange.'

'In what way?'

'I can't say, exactly. Just somehow … strange.'

'Would it help to write to Mr Campbell? He owns the ship, after all.'

'No. It is the captain's role to appoint his crew. I should try again, I think. Make my case more forcibly.'

'I will phrase the new letter for you, darling.'

He shot her an irritated look. 'Thank you, Mother, but no. I've sailed to India. Twice. So I'm capable of writing a persuasive letter.'

She looked away, obviously offended, and Fletcher retired to his room.

15 July 1785

Dear Captain Bligh,

I regret that you were not able to include me on the muster roll of Britannia, for her forthcoming voyage to Jamaica. Perhaps, sir, I did not make my desire to return to sea clearly enough. You must be aware, since we share the experience, of how discouraging it was when we were compulsorily retired from active naval duties. For me this was like a blow to the guts, one which I did not think I would recover from, since the sea has come to run so strongly in my veins. Yours too, of that I am certain. So I would prevail upon you, sir, to reconsider, and accept me as a crewman on Britannia. Wages are no object; I only wish to learn more of the skills of professional seamanship, and if you would permit me to mess with the gentlemen, I will readily enter your ship as a foremaster, until there is a vacancy among the officers. We midshipmen are gentlemen, we never pull at a rope; I should even be glad to go one voyage in that situation, for there may be occasions when officers may be called upon to do the duties of a common man.

All I ask for, sir, is the chance to prove myself.

I remain, your obliged and most humble servant,

Fletcher Christian

A reply came two days later.

Dear Fletcher Christian,

Coincidentally, the gunner on Britannia has fallen ill and cannot sail when we weigh next month for the West Indies. I presume you are familiar with the duties of a gunner, from your time as a supervising midshipman on Eurydice. Aboard Britannia, you will work as a rating and mess as an officer.

Report to my ship in Douglas Harbour at your earliest convenience, to receive further instructions.

Yours faithfully,

William Bligh

Elated, Fletcher read and reread the letter.

When he arrived on the waterfront, crewmen were busy loading goods onto *Britannia*. She was tied up to the main wharf, and the sailors were lugging sacks and barrels up gangplanks under the direction of the boatswain. The ship's purser stood by, carefully noting the nature of the cargo and the quantities.

Also on the wharf was a hansom cab, drawn by a chestnut mare. It became obvious for whom the cab was waiting when William Bligh emerged from below decks in the company of a youngish woman. He helped her across one of the gangplanks and ushered her out onto the deck. Seeing Fletcher, he led her by the arm to him.

'My wife Elizabeth, Fletcher Christian. Betsy, this is Fletcher Christian, who is to join the crew of *Britannia*.'

Fletcher inclined his head respectfully. 'Mistress Bligh, good day.'

She was about thirty, with thick black hair which cascaded over her shoulders. Her eyes were brown, her eyebrows two perfect arcs, her face round, the nose slightly aquiline, the cheeks rouged. Her gown was pale grey with an ornate collar tied with a bow of matching silk. Her figure was petite. The overall effect was prettiness and daintiness combined.

Lifting her chin a little, she appraised Fletcher carefully. 'I know your Manx family, naturally, Mr Christian.'

They chatted briefly. She and William were leaving the island soon, she said, and were moving to Lambeth, in London. 'I must leave now.' She smiled. 'It was very nice to meet you.'

'Likewise,' replied Fletcher, bowing to her. She really was very pretty.

Britannia was one hundred and seventy feet long, weighed eleven hundred tons and carried forty cannons as a defence against piracy. Her holds were capacious and she carried a crew of eighty-six, mostly seasoned merchantmen.

It took four and a half weeks for her to cross the Atlantic from England to the West Indies. 'Crossing the pond', as the old-timers put it. Taking advantage of the easterly winds and complementary currents, they sailed south-west until they reached the Tropic of Cancer. They then approached the islands of the Greater Antilles from the north, driven by a following wind.

It was late afternoon and rain was sweeping over the ship from the north. Screams came from the masthead. It was Charlie Rogers, the man on watch. 'White water! Off the larboard bow! Bring her about! Bring her about!'

Britannia lurched, her timbers growled, then with terrible slowness and canvas slumping, she came about, missing the uncharted reef with only yards to spare.

That evening Captain Bligh rewarded Rogers with a double ration of rum.

The following day, in clear weather, they passed safely through the Windward Passage between Haiti and Hispaniola.

Fletcher stood at *Britannia*'s mid-deck rail, looking out at Port Royal, Kingston, Jamaica. It was late afternoon, and there had been rain, but the sky was now clear, though the air remained sticky. There was the smell of the sea and the smell of the land, and both were heady. Looking shoreward, he felt the same expectation he had experienced when *Eurydice* arrived in Madras. The atmosphere was similar too: the sultry air, the smoke from open fires, the earthy smells of the tropics drifting across to the ship.

Men were already aloft, furling *Britannia*'s sails in preparation for docking, and the helmsmen were working the ship carefully towards the quay. Port Royal harbour contained several other merchantmen, most at anchor, although some were docked and discharging cargo. A ship of the line, HMS *Valiant*, was the largest vessel in the harbour. Her marines could be seen drilling on deck. Negroes, naked from the waist up, pulling carts or with sacks across their shoulders, were struggling towards the quay with their loads. Scarlet-jacketed infantrymen were patrolling the waterfront with muskets shouldered.

Captain Bligh had told Fletcher something of Jamaica's history. The French, coveting the island for its sugar cane, had in 1758 sent a fleet to try to take her from the British. Admiral Rodney intercepted the French fleet in the Straits Passage of Dominica and defeated it decisively, enabling the British to retain control of the Caribbean's sugar islands.

Bligh concluded, 'Our Navigation Act makes it illegal for Jamaica to trade with the so-called United States of America. And there's a problem with the smuggling out of sugar from these islands.' He looked peeved. 'All the more reason to regret the Admiralty's decision to run the navy down. If they hadn't done so we could be apprehending smugglers in a man-of-war in these waters, the way I used to in the Irish Sea.'

A road ran parallel to the shoreline, lined with warehouses, a Customs House, goods stores and an army barracks flying the British flag. Red jackets were on sentry duty beside its entrance. An avenue, lined on both sides with coconut palms, led off to the right, shadowing the shoreline.

The governor's mansion was sited at the rear of Kingston, atop a hillock. Fletcher trained his spyglass on the building. It was two-storeyed, built of stone, with a veranda along its frontage. The British flag was hoisted above its entrance.

'A grand sight, is it not?' said Bligh.

'It is, sir.'

'Our nation's power, for all to see.' He produced his spyglass and held it to his eye. 'Campbell once told me that Kingston's streets were built on a grid system. The ones that form the town boundaries are wide, to allow easier wagon transport to the plantations and back.'

'Where are the plantations, sir?'

'To the north, on the plains at Liguanea.' He swung his spyglass in that direction. 'That's where the sugar cane is grown. Rice, too.' Smoke billowed from that area. 'The cane fields are being fired in preparation for the harvest.'

Fletcher nodded. 'When will we go ashore, sir?'

'In the morning. I shall first report to the governor, then visit Campbell's plantation.' He lowered his 'scope. 'You're welcome to accompany me. Would you like that?'

'I would, sir. Thank you.'

For the first two weeks of the voyage Captain Bligh had remained aloof, treating Fletcher like any other member of the crew. He accepted this; after all, the man was ten years his senior. But as the voyage progressed his manner began to change. Fletcher was conscious of being observed as he undertook his deck duties, particularly the care of the swivel guns. Once he was stopped and asked how he was finding the voyage. Fletcher replied candidly that conditions on this ship were not as rigorous as they had been on *Eurydice*. Here things were less regimented. He also pointed out that it was a welcome change not having armed marines on board to enforce naval discipline. He appreciated this difference. Then he smiled wryly at the captain. 'But the food is much the same.'

One day during the third week, conditions being favourable, the captain accorded Fletcher the responsibility of shooting the sun at midday and recording the ship's position. After he did so satisfactorily, from then on Fletcher was conscious of the captain taking a personal interest in his nautical education. He felt grateful for this. Already familiar with the fundamentals of seamanship — boxing the compass, splicing, knotting, reefing, furling — he was now being tutored by his commander in the more esoteric skills: keeping an estimate of a ship's progress by dead reckoning and taking observations using the sun or stars. These, he knew, were significant skills.

At the end of the third week Fletcher was invited to dine with the officers in their mess. There he appreciated the difference in the table conversations; from the crudities and grumblings of the lower deck to the more mature discussions of the captain and his officers. Here the talk was of politics, books and voyaging. Evidently Fletcher had passed some sort of unwritten test, as a few days later he was again invited to the captain's cabin. There, over coffee, Captain Bligh showed him his charts and explained in detail the course he was plotting for *Britannia*'s sailing master, Charlie Rogers.

Fletcher's knowledge of navigation was enhanced by this. Always eager to learn, he looked forward to these sessions and began to warm to the commander. This captain, he realised, was an exceptional seaman. No wonder Captain Cook had appointed him sailing master on *Resolution*. Even as a twenty-two-year-old, Bligh must have been an outstanding candidate for the role.

While on *Eurydice*, Fletcher had witnessed floggings of ordinary seamen, standard naval punishment for transgressions such as insolence to an officer or negligence while on duty. Once Captain Courtnay had ordered an able seaman to receive twenty strokes of the cat for drawing a knife on the cook and threatening to cut off his balls after he was served putrid meat. But a curious thing about Captain Bligh was that not once during *Britannia*'s voyage out did he order a man flogged.

This, Fletcher soon realised, was probably because he had an even sharper arrow in his quiver — his tongue. Never had he heard a man curse like this captain. Any seaman who contravened regulations was hauled before him on deck and treated not to physical but verbal violence. After one hapless seaman, John Gibling, was caught in the act of stealing the rum ration of the master, Rogers, he was stood before the quarterdeck in front of the crew. There the captain brought down curses upon him like a shower of molten lead.

'God damn you, Gibling, you thieving fucking swine. Blast and bugger your eyes, you're no better than a burnt-arsed whore! Steal again, you nackle-arse, and I'll have you keel-hauled to buggery.' He leaned over the railing. 'What have you got to say for yourself, you fucking arse-licker?'

Gibling shook his head. 'Nothin', Captain.'

'Well then, you thieving, arse-licking pig-fucker, get below and hand your rum ration over to Rogers!'

Gibling, head hanging, trembling with shame and humiliation, slunk down the nearest companionway. He never stole again.

Fletcher witnessed this admonishment in amazement. How could a man change so rapidly in manner from the urbane character of the Great Cabin to the foul-mouthed name-caller topside? A man would prefer strokes of the cat rather than be abused in this manner. And, he wondered, what would demure Elizabeth Bligh think if she heard such cursing?

The other odd thing was that when the captain's fulminations were over, he reverted instantly to a calm demeanour, as if not a single curse had passed his lips.

Moreover, the commander never uttered so much as a 'damn' in Fletcher's presence. His language was mild, his demeanour considerate, even avuncular. Fletcher was by now invited to dine in the officers' mess every other day.

The increasing interest that the captain was taking in his gunner's progress did not go unnoticed by the rest of the crew. *Britannia*'s first mate was Edward Lamb, a hollow-cheeked fellow with close-together eyes. One morning as he and Fletcher sat in the bow, splicing a damaged sheet, Lamb remarked, 'I hear the captain's had you to dine with him again.'

'He has. What of it?'

'You're just a gunner. Gunners don't eat with the officers.'

'They do if they're invited to. And I was.'

'The old man must be playing favourites, then.'

Hacking at the cordage with his knife, Fletcher scowled. 'Jealous are you, Lamb? That he's not invited you?'

Lamb snorted. 'Jealous be buggered. I only eat with the men. The real men.'

He said no more, causing Fletcher to wonder what on earth he meant by that remark.

The Governor of Jamaica, Sir Thomas Norcroft, provided the captain with an open, two-horse carriage and a driver, so that they could make their visit to one of Campbell's plantations. It was to the north of Kingston, occupying the whole of a river plain which the river meandered across. Each of its flood plains was covered in a forest of mature sugar cane.

Fletcher observed the scene before him with awe. A field of cane, its stalks blackened from recent firing, was being harvested by men, women and children. All Negroes. The cane stalks were tall, much taller than the workers, and the men wielded long knives, slicing the stalks off at ground level, then trimming the leaves, working their way steadily into the blackened forest. Their canvas trousers were smeared with reddish dirt and soot.

Behind them, women wearing threadbare cotton frocks and with coloured scarves around their heads collected up the cut stalks. Dozens of children in short pants were helping the women, coming along behind them, scooping up armfuls of cane and putting them onto wagons to which teams of draught horses were harnessed. All the workers were barefoot and in the midday heat their arms rose and fell, rose and fell, their muscular bodies glistening with sweat.

Overseeing the cutting and loading were two Englishmen in broad-brimmed hats, open shirts, heavy trousers and boots. Muskets slung over their shoulders, stock whips in their hands, they strode up and down behind the workers, urging them on with guttural cries. More white overseers were supervising the loading of the big sugar stalks onto the wagons, ready for conveying to the mill. One overseer had a huge-headed Staffordshire bull terrier on a lead and was patrolling up and down with the dog behind the line of workers. Fletcher noticed the children glancing at the dog with frightened eyes.

Slaves, Fletcher thought, these are all slaves. Human beings who have been bought and sold like livestock.

The windmill was further along the road, its four sails turning languidly in the breeze. More male slaves were feeding the cane stalks into the mill for crushing between steel rollers; others were carrying away the cane juice in buckets and loading them onto another wagon.

Fletcher and his captain observed the industrious scene for some time, without speaking. But as he watched, Fletcher recalled the words from one of Edward's letters, sent from Gray's Inn:

Slavery is an abominable institution, Fletcher. No civilised nation can possibly condone it. That English companies are a part of it is a stain on our nation. My friend Wilberforce is doing everything in his power to make the practice unlawful. He intends to stand for Parliament, and if elected will rally the abolitionist cause at Westminster.

Yet here, before Fletcher's very eyes, an Englishman's plantation was operating, based on slave labour. Fletcher did not know how exactly much profit Campbell was making from his plantations, but knew it must be considerable. Even after the cost of feeding the slaves and paying for the transport of the commodities back to England, the price they fetched there was so high that the man must be making a fortune. And he was doing so off the backs of these poor wretches.

Just then one of the overseers blew a whistle and called out, 'Luncheon! Luncheon!'

Other Negro women carried an urn, some loaves of bread and a bunch of bananas from an open fire over to a banyan tree beside the road. The workers put down their knives, walked over to the tree, dipped their mugs into the urn, took some of the bread and fruit and sank down under the tree. There, panting and sweating, they sipped their tea. Only then did Fletcher notice that several of the men were shackled together at the ankles.

The captain had said nothing for some time. He just stared at the slaves with an impassive expression.

Feeling the need to comment on the proceedings, Fletcher said, 'Slavery, sir, I think is immoral. Those poor people.'

The captain looked at him curiously. 'You sound like an abolitionist, Christian.'

'I believe I am, sir. My brother certainly is. He's a friend of William Wilberforce's.'

The captain harrumphed. 'A troublemaker, that fellow. Hewers of wood and drawers of water. That is the destiny of the nigger race.'

'Who said so, sir?'

'The Bible.' He stared upwards. 'Joshua, chapter 9, verse 23. "Now therefore, you are cursed, and you shall never cease being slaves, both hewers of wood and drawers of water, for the house of my God".'

Taken aback, Fletcher said, 'Slavery is condoned in the Bible?'

'It is. And since the Bible is God's word, we must accept it.' Bligh squinted. 'Moreover, if the cane wasn't harvested and processed, then we would not be employed by Campbell, would we?' He stared at Fletcher. 'Either of us.'

Fletcher made no reply. His conscience had been pricked by this remark. The captain's point was valid: in a way they owed their present position to this business, vile though it was. He stared again at the group of black people huddled under the tree, seeking shade as they ate their miserable lunch, the women feeding their children. This is not right, he thought, and the Bible is wrong. But he said nothing more.

Hearing a loud crack, then another, Fletcher saw the overseer with the dog waving his whip. He cracked it again, then shouted at the slaves. 'Right, you lot, break's over. Get up and back to work! Now!' Again his whip cracked. The people rose, slowly, the women shepherding the children towards the cane.

It was a scene Fletcher would never forget.

On the way back to the ship he sat in silence in the open carriage, filled with conflicting emotions: anger, sorrow, disbelief. And, mostly, guilt. Beside him, the captain said nothing. He just looked around approvingly at the cane fields, flourishing under the West Indian sun.

The return voyage would be tougher, the captain warned Fletcher, as *Britannia* would face mostly adverse winds. And again he was given lessons in navigation. In the Great Cabin the captain had a chart of the West Atlantic laid out on the table, weighed down with lead ingots. Yesterday they had tacked cautiously west of the low-lying Caicos Islands and were now sailing on a north-easterly course towards the Atlantic.

Holding a pair of dividers, the captain stepped them carefully across the chart. 'Our current approximate position is here, some miles east of the Bahamas. The latest coordinates are longitude 73° west, latitude 25° north.' He glanced overhead at the dangling compass. Its needle confirmed they were on a NNE course.

'We should cross the Tropic of Cancer the day after tomorrow. Then, still on this course, at about latitude 33° north, we will pick up the Gulf Stream. Thereafter we will be borne along by it.' He stared at Fletcher. 'The current was so-named by Benjamin Franklin, did you know that?' Fletcher shook his head. 'Yes, he named the Gulf Stream in 1770. Clever chap, for an American. The stream is a powerful current, driven by wind stress, as Franklin realised. It has long been used for the west to east Atlantic crossing. Cook certainly made use of it, whenever he sailed to England from Newfoundland.'

Fletcher watched closely as the captain again stepped the dividers. 'At about here, 40° north, we shall alter course and bear due east.' He closed the dividers. 'My reckoning is that we will sight the south coast of England in late November.' He leaned back. 'Any questions?'

'No sir. Thank you for the information.'

As they sailed further north, the temperatures grew cooler and the barometer dropped. Conditions topside were wet and unpleasant. Fletcher's days were filled with his menial shipboard duties: checking the cannons and shot, re-caulking leaking seams, greasing the blocks with pork fat. All under a darkened sky and a slate-grey sea.

Britannia bore these conditions well, driving into the swells and keeping on an even keel. Her belly bulged with hundreds of barrels filled with sugar, molasses and rum. The ship reeked like a distillery, and when the crew received their daily grog ration, unlike the navy's it was not diluted. As the Atlantic days grew colder, the Jamaica rum warmed the crew's guts mightily.

It was during their second-to-last night at sea, while coasting the south littoral of the Isle of Wight, that Fletcher and his captain shared a last supper in the Great Cabin, over some of Campbell's over-proof rum. The two men sat facing each other across the table, which had been cleared of its plates by the captain's servant.

Captain Bligh's face, normally marble-white, was slightly flushed and his blouse collar was undone. Fletcher sipped a little of the rum from his tankard and winced. Too strong. Without warning *Britannia* rolled heavily and both men clutched their tankards. As the ship settled again the captain took a mouthful of rum, then set his tankard down on the table. He let out a long sigh. 'Christian, there's something I want you to know before we are discharged.'

'Yes, sir?'

The captain waved his right hand. 'Enough of this "sir". Call me William from now on. In private only, of course. And in private I shall refer to you as Fletcher.'

Fletcher blinked with surprise. 'Very well … William.'

The captain leaned forward. 'And I'd like you to know this.' He stared into Fletcher's eyes. 'I have appreciated your company during this voyage.'

'Thank you. And I have appreciated yours. It's been a privilege to regularly dine with you. And to learn so much along the way. I'm grateful.'

William waved a hand dismissively. 'You learn quickly. One day you'll have your own command, I'm certain of that.' He took another mouthful of rum. 'But what I also want you to know is how much I appreciate the company of someone with your background.'

'I don't follow you, William.'

The captain sat back. 'Your family are important people. Betsy has told me how elevated they have been, in island society, for generations.

Your father's family were judges on the Isle of Man. Your mother's family too, by all accounts, were notable people. Landowners in Cumbria.' He made a face. 'Whereas my family were always just petty officials.' He looked away.

It took a few moments for Fletcher to take this in. Then he said, 'William, with respect, that is ridiculous. What counts is what you have achieved. You served with Cook, you surveyed new lands, you've circumnavigated the world, you've commanded naval ships. It's a distinguished record.'

William grunted. 'Don't think I was seeking praise. I wasn't. Those who go in search of praise seldom find it.' He belched, and Fletcher realised he was a little drunk. In vino veritas, he thought.

Bligh continued, 'I want you to know how much I respect your lineage, and your education. In this profession one must rub shoulders with many blockheads and ruffians. An uncivilised lot. Even some officers are less than couth. To keep the company of a … of a refined man, has done my spirits good.'

Fletcher looked down. 'I like to think that I get on well with all the men. It's important to do so, below decks.'

'Indeed, indeed. But you have many natural advantages. You are tall, handsome, athletic. Your barrel jumping trick, the men love that.' He held out his tankard and clinked it with Fletcher's. 'So, thank you, Fletcher, for your good fellowship.' He reached for the rum decanter. 'Now, let's have another drink.'

Embarrassed now by this effusion, Fletcher said, 'And thank you, William, for your fellowship.'

But he wondered, how could a man given to disgusting cursing be drawn to the company of those who valued sensibility?

They raised the Downs on 14 November and docked at Wapping the following day. After a team of Customs officials had done their work and the cargo had been authorised for discharge, the imposing figure of Duncan Campbell was waiting on the dock to greet them. Stouter than ever, he wore a black topcoat, a matching tricorn and shoes with outsized brass buckles, highly polished.

The ship's manifest documents in one hand, he shook William's hand with the other. 'Splendid work, Bligh. A fine cargo, safely delivered. The profits will be considerable.' Noticing Fletcher disembarking with his sea chest, he extended his hand to the young man. 'Christian. Welcome back. How was the voyage?'

'Very good, sir, thank you. I've learned a great deal.'

'And do you now return to the Isle of Man?'

'A little later, yes. After I've paid a visit to my brothers in the City. But I promised my mother I would be home for Christmas.'

'Hah, there's a dutiful son. Do pass my fondest regards to John Christian and the Taubmans.'

Fletcher farewelled William on the dock. The captain would spend Christmas in Lambeth with Elizabeth and their baby daughters, Mary and Harriet. Looking cheerier than Fletcher had ever seen him, he shook his hand. 'You've done well, Fletcher. I hope you will sail with us again.'

'Is that possible?'

Still gripping his hand, William nodded. '*Britannia* will sail again for the West Indies. In February, Campbell estimates. I shall let you know if there's a position aboard for you.'

After three days in London, Fletcher took a coach to Liverpool and the packet boat across to Douglas. There he moved back into the room at the rear of his mother's townhouse.

If he had found life in Douglas quiet before, it was now utterly silent. There were few ships in the harbour, and its water was as grey as a sheet of lead. Snow fell the day before Christmas, coming in flurries from the north and settling on the hills above the town.

He walked the lifeless streets, climbed Bray's Hill and stared seaward, then returned to sit on the waterfront, willing the time to go faster. The dark fog that had invaded his mind before began to hover once again. He found himself brooding, longing to get away. His mother irritated him more than ever, forever imagining slights from the Christians and gossiping about the family and the townsfolk. ('Mary Duncan was struck with the flux.' 'There was a brawl on the waterfront, between a press gang and some local youths.' 'Loretta fell from her horse and broke her leg.' 'Isabella Duncan has had a child by her adulterous lover.')

Of these titbits, only the last one moved him in any way. No wonder she had never replied to any of his letters. Poor Isabella. That night with her he would never forget. Whenever he was pleasuring himself — shaking the snake, as the saying had it, and such shaking was not infrequent — it was always Isabella he had in mind.

His only other solace was meeting cousin John in the Douglas Club and discussing the West Indies voyage with him. John was a good listener and showed gratifying interest in the expedition, and Jamaica. The club still had its Negro servant, Joseph. Remembering the shackled slaves in the cane fields, Fletcher went out of his way to treat him courteously. Joseph was a very decent fellow, and by returning his kindness Fletcher in a small way assuaged the guilt he still felt at his nation's sanctioning of West Indian slavery.

Adding to his frustrations, he heard nothing more from William. As the New Year came and went and there was still no word, he became increasingly despondent. The fog in his head darkened. Would he ever get to sea again?

Then in mid-January, he received a letter.

Durham Place, Lambeth
Dear Fletcher,

I trust you and your family are well on the island. Your relatives must have enjoyed hearing of your voyage to the far side of the Atlantic, as have Betsy and our two infant daughters. And what delights they have afforded me over Yuletide and the New Year. Betsy's parents, Dr Richard and Mrs Betham, have been our guests at Christmas, and greatly appreciated the pleasures of the London social scene.

I hope that 1787 will bring us both good health and good fortune.

With that in mind, I am delighted to inform you that I have been contracted again by Campbell to command Britannia on a voyage to the

West Indies, to deliver trade goods to our compatriots there, and procure and convey to London more commodities from his Jamaica plantations. Furthermore, Campbell having received such positive reports from me pertaining to your diligence during our recent voyage, he has suggested that I once again engage your services.

I will be very pleased to do so, and hereby offer you the position as second mate aboard Britannia for the duration of her next voyage. That date is set down for no earlier than the 8th of February and no later than the 20th of the same month of this year.

Should you accept this offer, it will afford Betsy and myself great pleasure if you could spend time with our household in Lambeth in the days prior to the departure of Britannia.

I am,

Yours faithfully,

William Bligh

Fletcher set the letter down. Second mate. Wonderful.

The cab stopped in front of the block of townhouses. Fletcher got out, paid the driver and looked up at the Bligh house, which was the second in from the left of the block.

The brown brick, three-storeyed house was newish-looking. A flight of steps led up to the front entrance, lined on both sides with black spear-top railings. The door was navy blue, and above it was a wide white arch set into the brick. It matched the frames of the sash windows in the walls to the right and left of the entrance.

Fletcher rapped on the front door with its brass knocker.

The maidservant showed him into the drawing room, where William, Betsy and their infant daughters were waiting. The room was small, its walls papered dark green with gold floral patterns. A coal fire was burning in the grate and above it on an oak mantelpiece was a collection of South Sea artefacts: a carved club, a jade adze, fans of woven pandanus and an elaborate headdress with a crest of red feathers. Above all this was an oil painting of a ship in full sail, flying the Royal Navy ensign.

Elizabeth greeted Fletcher affably. Her pale blue gown was fastened at the front with a cameo brooch. Her hair hung loose and there were dark crescents under her eyes. Tiredness from child-caring, Fletcher presumed. The baby was in a cane crib under the window; the other daughter was stacking blocks in front of the fire.

William, in open-necked blouse, blue waistcoat, white hose and soft shoes, explained the significance of the mantelpiece artefacts. 'The headdress is from the Sandwich Islands, from the island the natives call O-why-hee. That was where Cook was murdered. The club and fans are from Nomuka, in the Friendly Isles; the jade adze is from New Zealand. Poo-na-moo, the natives there call it.'

Fletcher glanced up at the painting. The ship's name was painted across the stern: HMS *Resolution*.

'A fine ship by all accounts, William.'

'Certainly. She was Cook's favourite vessel, he once told me. Took him around the world twice.' He corrected himself. 'One and a half times.'

After the maid brought in tea and scones, they sat round the fire chatting. Whenever William mentioned the forthcoming voyage, Fletcher noticed Elizabeth's expression darkening. After a time she fell silent.

He stayed with the Blighs for three days, sleeping in an attic room at the top of the house. At times he was kept awake at night by the persistent crying of the baby, from the floor below his. By day he walked with William along the Thames path, or crossed the river to Westminster and took coffee at Wallbrooke's, in the Haymarket. At the house he spent time playing with the little girl, Mary, whom he found delightful. Just starting to speak, she found his name hard to pronounce. 'Lecture', she called him, climbing on his back and pretending to ride him to Banbury Cross. Fletcher envied William these domestic delights, and the companionship of a wife and children. One day, he hoped, he would have such a loving family.

It was on his final day in the Bligh house, when William had gone off for a meeting with Campbell, that Elizabeth poured her heart out to him. Over morning tea in the parlour, they had been talking about the imminent voyage, and estimating how long it would take William away from England. Elizabeth said: 'It's hard being the wife of a sea captain, Fletcher. The long absences, the uncertainties. Being left with the babies, and with little Harriet being such a sickly child, it wears me down.' Her eyes began to water.

Fletcher nodded. He could imagine how hard it was, and he felt for her. But would the benefits not compensate? The generous salary that Campbell paid her husband, the security of a career in the merchant marine. However, he did not venture to say this, and Elizabeth seemed to want to continue confiding in him.

'After he returned with *Resolution*, after being away for over four years, William wrote to Elizabeth Cook, Captain Cook's widow, expressing his condolences over her husband's murder.' She plucked a handkerchief from her gown sleeve and dabbed at her eyes. 'And do you know what Mistress Cook did?' Fletcher shook his head. 'Although she replied to William, she also wrote a note to me, inviting me to meet her. At her house in Clapham.'

'Did you go?'

'I did. It was an honour to be invited. What a brave woman she was, not knowing where her husband was for all those years, then never seeing him again. And before that, the deaths of three of her young children.' She took a deep breath, almost faltered. 'Mistress Cook told me that people used to say that her husband only came ashore to father children. A cruel remark, but not without some truth.' She sighed heavily and stared at Fletcher with her tired eyes. 'I am with child again myself, you see.'

The second voyage to the West Indies afforded Fletcher further valuable experience. As second mate he was accorded the privilege of dining with the ship's officers regularly. Throughout the voyage William was his usual efficient self, both at sea and on land, negotiating contracts in Kingston, then bringing Campbell another valuable cargo of sugar-derived products home to London. And although Fletcher still disapproved of the human exploitation that was the foundation of this profiting, the pleasure of once more being at sea, then in an exotic port, had the effect of overriding this concern. The authority that accompanied the role of second mate he relished, too. On navigational matters William took him into his confidence, so that at times Fletcher felt that the commander was becoming almost a father figure to him, replacing the natural one he had never known. His respect for the man grew. Yet in a way he still didn't really know William. He was such a contradictory man.

Shortly after their return to England, while he was again the Blighs' guest at Durham Place, William divulged to Fletcher a unique opportunity which had just arisen. The autumn nights were drawing in and they were seated in front of the fire, drinking port wine. William said in a low, almost conspiratorial voice, 'You know of Sir Joseph Banks?'

'Of course. Our greatest natural philosopher.'

'Indeed. And a great thinker.' He set his glass down on the fireside table. 'While in Wapping yesterday, meeting with Campbell, I heard of a scheme which Banks has devised.'

'What sort of scheme?'

'*Artocarpus altilis*. Do you know what that is?'

'Breadfruit.'

William's face fell. 'How did you know that?'

'I've read Sir Joseph's journal, the account of his time on Tahiti with Cook. Breadfruit is a staple of the Tahitian diet. A remarkable fruit, he says.'

'Yes. Dampier first described its qualities, observed during his circumnavigation, way back in 1688.' William sipped his port. '*Artocarpus altilis* grows prolifically in some parts of the tropics. When the fruit is baked and the crust removed, on the inside its flesh is white and tender. As delicious and nourishing as a penny loaf, Dampier said. So, literally, food growing on trees. Banks also observed that even Cook's common seamen loved breadfruit, and we know how conservative they are in their eating habits. I too saw how palatable the men found baked breadfruit when I was in the Society Islands with Cook in '77.'

'What exactly is Banks' scheme?'

William explained. Since Britain lost the War of Independence, food could no longer be imported to the West Indies from North America. But supplies were needed there to sustain the plantation slaves. Campbell complained that the cost of feeding the slaves on his plantations with food imported from Britain was eating into his profits. Something had to be done.

After Campbell discussed this dilemma with Banks, the naturalist had come up with a plan. Since the climate of the West Indies — alternating wet and dry seasons, and hot all year round — was very similar to that of Tahiti, Banks suggested that young breadfruit plants be taken from that island and transported to the West Indies. There the plants would grow, mature and provide a cheap food source for the slaves. Campbell had enthusiastically endorsed this novel idea.

At this point Fletcher interrupted. 'But William, is it feasible to take young tropical tree plants around the world? Carry them on a ship for weeks from Tahiti? Wouldn't they die of the cold in the high latitudes? While being taken round the Horn, for instance?'

'I had the same doubts. But Banks being Banks, he has a solution to that problem.' A botanist would accompany the expedition to oversee the collecting of the young plants. These would be accommodated in special conditions, aboard a specially fitted-out part of the ship, kept warm by a cabin stove, kept watered by an irrigation system. In that way the breadfruit could be successfully transported across the world.

William concluded: 'The scheme has the support of King George and the Admiralty, and the expedition will be underwritten by the Royal Navy.'

Fletcher nodded thoughtfully. 'It's certainly original. Banks is very enterprising. But it's also challenging. Does he suggest who might lead such an expedition?'

'He does.' William patted his chest. 'And it's me. He has nominated me to lead it.'

94

He went to the escritoire and handed Fletcher an as-yet unposted letter he had written to Banks. It was his reply to the invitation to lead the breadfruit transporting expedition. William smiled and said, 'Do tell me if my phrasing is unsuitable in any way.'

Durham Place, Lambeth, 6 August 1787
Sir, I arrived yesterday from Jamaica and should have instantly paid my respects to you, had Mr Campbell not told me you were not to return from the country until Thursday. I have heard the flattering news of your great goodness to me, intending to honour me with the command of the vessel you propose should go to the South Sea, for which, after offering you my most grateful thanks I can only assure you I shall endeavour, and I hope succeed, in deserving such a trust.

I await your commands, and am with the sincerest respect, Sir, your obliged and very Humble Servant.
Wm Bligh.

'Well?' William demanded.

Fletcher frowned. 'Don't you think its tone is a trifle ...' He searched for the right word. 'Obsequious?'

William half-closed his eyes. 'What does that mean, exactly?'

'Fawning.'

'Fawning? Not at all. Sir Joseph is a baronet, the President of the Royal Society, and I'm expressing my gratitude to him. To a man of a much higher station than myself, for his unique offer.'

'Well, the tone is certainly one of gratitude.'

Fletcher was being evasive. He did think the letter excessive. Grovelling, even. But he had his own future to think of. If William Bligh was to command an expedition to Tahiti, he wanted to be part of it. Desperately.

Part Two

A VOYAGE TO TAHITI

Deptford, London, 16 August 1787

They stood dockside at the Naval Yard. Moored beside them was a solitary ship, a merchantman, unflagged and with her three masts bare. A team of carpenters were busy about her decks, measuring, sawing, hammering. It was apparent from the network of ropes and pulleys dangling from the masts that they had been shortened. It was a fine London afternoon and the workmen were shirtless in the heat.

William stared at the vessel and recited: 'Built in Hull three years ago, served as a coastal trader. Coal, mainly. Two hundred and thirty tons, ninety-one feet long, just under twenty-five feet in breadth. Chosen by Sir Joseph, purchased last month by the Navy Board, for less than two thousand pounds.'

'Her name?' asked Fletcher.

'*Bethia*. But that will be changed.' He peered over the edge of the dock and at the hull. 'She's been sheathed with copper to keep out the *teredo navalis*.'

'What boats will she carry?'

'Two cutters, one of eighteen feet, the other sixteen, and a launch. The launch is not yet finished. I insisted that it be a decent size, twenty-three feet. The naval contractors will deliver the three boats after the rigging's completed.'

Although Fletcher nodded, looking down at *Bethia*'s decks he wondered how a launch of such size could be accommodated there, as well as two cutters.

They walked along to the bow. Her figurehead was of a woman in a riding habit. Staring along the vessel's larboard flank, Fletcher observed, 'She seems small, for what she will be expected to achieve.'

'Yes. But there will be more modifications. Before I ordered them topped, the masts were far too tall. They would have carried too much top weight for wild weather. And the ballast was excessive; I've ordered it reduced from forty-five to nineteen tons.' He clicked his tongue impatiently. 'There will be much more to do if we're to get her to sea by September.'

Just then there was the shrill call of a ship's whistle, and seconds later another vessel appeared at the stern of *Bethia*. It was a launch, coming downriver. The four naval oarsmen shipped their oars and the launch glided into the dock alongside the ship. Seated on a central thwart were two middle-aged men, dressed formally.

William's jaw dropped. 'Good God, I believe that's Sir Joseph.'

The launch was tied up and two men climbed the steps to the dock, Banks leading. He was well-built and fleshy-faced; the man with him was thin and long-necked. As both removed their tricorns, William came forward. 'Sir Joseph.' He dipped his head and held out his hand. 'William Bligh of His Majesty's Navy.' He turned to Fletcher. 'And this is Fletcher Christian, late of the company of the merchantman *Britannia*, which I commanded.'

Banks nodded. 'Ah, yes, Bligh, it's good to meet you at last.' He stood back. 'Now, meet my good friend Lord Sydney, one of King George's Secretaries of State. Sydney and I have planned your forthcoming voyage.'

Fletcher felt awed to be in the presence of the famous naturalist, the man who had underwritten Cook's first world voyage, and who had sailed with him to Tahiti to observe the 1769 transit of Venus. He recalled Banks' colourful account of the voyage and knew of his great reputation as a botanical collector.

Banks and Sydney observed *Bethia* with discerning expressions, then Banks said, 'So this is our Tahiti breadfruit transporter. She looks sturdy.'

'If a trifle small, sir,' Fletcher felt obliged to point out.

Lord Sydney gave him a sharp look. 'She is to carry breadfruit plants, Christian, not niggers or grain.'

Fletcher coloured slightly at this rebuke; William gave a small, apologetic cough. 'I am certain she will prove adequate, my lord.'

Sydney nodded. 'This will be a vital expedition, Bligh. To provide year-round sustenance for our niggers in the West Indies so that greater profits will accrue to our plantation owners. And to our government.'

'Quite so, my lord,' said William. 'And I was delighted to learn that botanist David Nelson is to be part of my company. He sailed with Cook and myself on our voyage in search of the Northwest Passage.'

Banks nodded. 'And collected many new botanical specimens from the North Pacific. Nelson is an admirable fellow. As his assistant I've appointed one William Brown, another experienced gardener.'

William turned to Lord Sydney. 'May I ask you, my lord, what number of marines will accompany the expedition?'

Sydney gave him an austere look. 'There will be no marines, Bligh. There will not be room.' He tugged at a flap of loose flesh at his throat. 'The ship will carry four short-carriage four-pound guns and ten half-pounder swivel guns. There will be muskets and other firearms, properly stowed, but no marine contingent.'

There was a stiff silence. William swallowed, then said, 'But should there be difficulties with the natives, my lord—'

Banks laughed knowingly. 'You are going to Tahiti, Bligh, not the murderous Sandwich Islands. Tahiti is Aphrodite's Island, the island of love. As I well remember from '69.' He smirked. 'The year of soixante-neuf, so to speak. The Tahitian men will welcome you with open arms; their women will welcome you with open legs.' He smiled. 'So marines will be unnecessary.'

William's cheeks turned pink; Fletcher grinned. Banks looked again at the ship. 'Well, let's go below and inspect the modifications. By the way, Lord Sydney and I have renamed her. She's to be called the *Bounty*. His Majesty's Armed Vessel *Bounty*.' He chuckled. 'Bounty being shorthand for bountiful, naturally.'

Below decks in the stern, Fletcher stared in amazement at what the carpenters had done. Where there would normally have been a great cabin, extending the width of the ship, there was now a fully fitted-out conservatory.

Banks explained, 'Originally this cabin extended eleven feet from the stern; it now reaches thirty feet for'ard, nearly as far as the aft hatchway. Nearly a trebling in size.' He nodded with satisfaction at this statistic.

Fletcher looked around, intrigued by the adaptation. Shelves lined the walls of the cabin, filled with empty earthenware pots. Several platforms in the centre of the space, separated by aisles, held planks to contain more pots. There were gratings in the ceiling and scuttles on the starboard and larboard sides to admit fresh air. On the inner wall a stove had been installed and the floor was lined with a sheet of lead.

Lord Sydney reached out and tested the firmness of one of the pot racks. He grunted with satisfaction. 'The first plan allowed for five hundred pots, but Banks and I decided she should carry more. One hundred and twenty-nine more, to be precise.' From his tone it was easy to tell what value the secretary placed on precision.

The conservatory was undeniably impressive, Fletcher thought. Inspired, even. But how, he wondered, would the captain and crew — forty-five men in all — be accommodated in the remainder of the ship?

Banks and Sydney, having seen and approved of the greenhouse, wished to see nothing more of the ship. William went topside to see the dignitaries off, while Fletcher carried on with his inspection forward of the conservatory. He crept through the ship, head bent, encountering the familiar lower-deck odours of stale food and lantern smoke, overlaid with the less unwholesome smell of freshly applied spar varnish.

It was obvious that the accommodation would be cramped in the extreme. William's cabin — already nameplated — was amidships on the lower deck, starboard side. It was, to be charitable, compact. Fletcher peered inside it, thinking, just as well he's a small man.

The master's cabin was opposite the captain's, at the foot of the rear stairway. The captain's dining room and pantry — also small — were between the stairway and the forecastle. The space for the master's mates and the midshipmen was aft of the forward stairway. Fletcher paid close attention to this area, aware that this was where he was to be accommodated.

The rest of the crew, thirty-three men, and the galley, were to be crammed into the forecastle, in a space near the bow which Fletcher estimated to be only about twenty feet wide and forty feet long. It was dark, without scuttles, and Fletcher's head cleared the ceiling by just a couple of inches. There were half-finished pens which would hold livestock — sheep, pigs and goats — alongside the crew's quarters.

He went down into the hold. William had pointed out that the quarters of the specialist crew — the boatswain, carpenter, steward, surgeon, Bligh's clerk, the gunner and the botanists — would be quartered here, on mezzanine decks added to either end of the hold. Fletcher noted that the headroom of this accommodation was higher, about seven feet.

Following the inspection, Fletcher and William took a ferry upriver to the City, and took refreshments in Garraway's coffee house. There Fletcher listened to William's litany of grumbles.

'As you pointed out, the vessel is too small. Far too small for a two-year voyage. And the company is insufficient. Forty-five men. And of that number, only twenty-two able seamen. To maintain the watches, handle the sails, do any running repairs — let alone look after the breadfruit plants.' He sipped his coffee. 'No marines to enforce my authority or guard against theft by the natives.' His blue eyes flashed. 'And I am not to be promoted to captain's rank, merely a lieutenant. As such, I am granted no officers, only three midshipmen. Were I to be a post captain, which I deserve to be, I would be entitled to one or two lieutenants to help me enforce discipline.' His lip curled. 'And not only will I command the ship, I am to be the purser as well, responsible for the issuing of rations, the welfare of the crew and their disciplining. Oh, and the purchase of the breadfruit plants.' He sniffed. 'And for all these responsibilities, I am to be paid the princely sum of four shillings a day. Seventy pounds a year.'

Fletcher started. 'Seventy pounds only?'

'You heard me. Quite a reduction, from the five hundred pounds Campbell paid me to command *Britannia*.'

Fletcher was shocked. He immediately thought of Betsy and her woes. This would only add to them. At least her husband's absences in the West Indies had been offset by his generous salary, and voyages of about a four-month duration. This expedition would be for at least two years, and on a salary decline of … He did a quick calculation: eighty-six per cent!

Attempting to offer some consolation, he said, 'I'm sure that when the breadfruit scheme is brought to fruition, other rewards will flow to you.'

William raised his eyebrows sceptically. 'Perhaps. They will need to, given the Navy Board's niggardliness and the Admiralty's failure to promote me.' Fletcher was about to comment again but William held up his hand. 'Oh yes, I know in peacetime promotions are seldom made, except at sea. But with my record on *Resolution*, my surveying, my navigating …' Again his eyes flashed. 'What more must I do, to receive a captain's rank? Furthermore, as you well know, for these past four years I've become used to working with merchants, men who believe in rewarding those who serve them well. And do so handsomely. But now I am given massive responsibilities by the navy for miserly recompense and no promotion.'

Fletcher listened to this tirade sympathetically. He well understood William's frustrations and wounded pride. Yet overriding these sympathies for his friend was his own anticipation of the forthcoming voyage and the excitements it promised. Sailing in the wake of Cook into the South Atlantic, doubling Cape Horn and into the South Sea. The delights of Bougainville's New Cythera and all that Tahitian cunny. He didn't care about the overcrowding on board: he would sleep in the maintop so long as he got to Tahiti.

This reverie was broken by William producing a sheaf of papers from his briefcase and saying, 'At least I was permitted to appoint the company myself, without interference from the petty officials in Whitehall.' He handed the sheet to Fletcher. 'All are volunteers. There will be no pressed men on board.'

Headed with the crest of the Admiralty, it was the ship's muster roll, listing names and designations. Fletcher scanned it. Apart from the gardeners Nelson and Brown, at first glance the other names meant nothing to him. Curious about the man designated Master, whose role he knew would be important, he asked, 'Who is John Fryer?'

'He's from Norfolk, thirty-four, newly married. Been seven years in the navy, was captured and imprisoned by the French for a year and a half. Most able, from his record.'

Paying more attention to the names, Fletcher said, 'Lawrence Lebogue, sailmaker.' He looked up. 'I remember him from *Britannia*. But he's old. Must be nearly forty.'

'No matter for a sailmaker. Cook had John Ravenhill on *Endeavour*, and he was over seventy. Poor sod died on the way home, though.'

Another name on the roll stood out for Fletcher. 'Peter Heywood, Acting Midshipman. I knew a Heywood family on the Isle of Man. Is he related to them?'

'He is. I know the lad. He was nominated by Betsy's parents. He's the son of close friends of theirs. His father's a deemster, like your forebears. Peter is only fifteen, but he's a cheerful boy and keen as mustard to go to sea. He'll stay with Betsy and me before we sail.' He paused. 'Another of the midshipmen, John Hallett, is also only fifteen. Betsy recommended him, he's the brother of a London friend of hers. She also recommended Thomas Hayward, whose family she knows. The other midshipman, George Stewart, I invited to join the expedition because his parents took great care of me when *Resolution* was forced to take shelter from storms off Stromness, in Orkney, back in 1780.'

Fletcher thought, how important patronage is in such matters. He recalled cousin John's words: 'It's not what you know, it's who you know.' That seemed truer than ever. The Blighs' personal connections had been responsible for several of the crew being added to the list. Handing back the roll, he said, 'The Isle of Man is well represented, William.'

William gave a rare smile. 'Indeed. So perhaps *Bethia*, or I should say *Bounty*, should fly the Manx flag instead of the ensign.'

* * *

Over the next few weeks Fletcher and William met regularly, at Garraway's and at a Shoreditch tavern, the Crab and Lobster, to discuss the expedition. Although William continued to cavil ('The carpenters have still not finished the livestock pens', 'I still await my sailing orders from the Admiralty', 'Three men on the roll have scarpered and will need to be replaced'), his sense of expectation was obvious as the departure date neared.

By early October the trade goods had been purchased and were being stowed in *Bounty*'s hold. Again William shared the details with Fletcher, reading from the bill of lading: 'Two hundred and thirty-four chisels, of various sizes. Four gross of knives, eight hundredweight of spike nails, four dozen hand saws, fourteen dozen hatchets, ten dozen gimlets, fourteen dozen looking glasses, eight pounds of glass beads — red, white and blue — and seventy-two shirts.' He handed the list to Fletcher. 'A considerable total. In value, over one hundred and twenty-five pounds.' He pouted. 'Nearly twice my meagre salary.'

Fletcher whistled softly as he looked at the list. 'All goods, William. No money will be paid?'

'I will be allowed one hundred ducats to cover expenses in ports beyond the South Sea. But in Tahiti real money has no use. The only currency the natives value is iron. Have you read Hawkesworth's account of the *Dolphin* voyage?'

'I have. *Dolphin* was nearly torn apart for its nails.'

'Yes. And when I was there with Cook, the natives demanded more and more iron items.' He took a spoonful of sugar and stirred it into his coffee. 'But it's only fair that we recompense the Tahitians for their breadfruit plants.'

Fletcher nodded. 'And what of the provisioning?'

'It continues, ordered by myself and overseen by the Victualling Board. We are provisioning for a year and a half. The balance will be obtained from the natives — mainly pork, poultry, fruits and vegetables. My time with Cook convinced me that diet is vital to a crew's health. There will be no scurvy on *Bounty*, of that I'm determined. So there will be sauerkraut, malt, juice of wort, portable soup, wheat and barley instead of oatmeal.' His expression became harsh. 'And by God the men will eat it, every day. Cook made it a flogging offence not to, and I'll do the same.'

They strolled along the path that led to the Tower of London. It was autumn now and the air was biting, the river water murky, the sky gravestone grey. A few merchantmen were working their way upriver, struggling to find favourable wind. The shouts of their crewmen carried across to the river bank.

'I must say, Fletcher, that I'm looking forward to the blue skies of the South Sea.'

'As I am. In fact I find myself thinking of those skies a great deal.'

William stopped, placed his hands behind his back and stared up at Fletcher. 'Allow me to say how much I have valued your support over these last weeks.'

Fletcher shrugged. 'It's the least I could do. I'm repaying the help you've given me. Were it not for you I would still be on the Isle of Man, lamenting my lack of prospects. Now, I'm confident that when we return from Tahiti I will be qualified to be commissioned as a lieutenant.'

'I'm sure that that will be the case.' William flexed his shoulders awkwardly. 'But I want you to know how much I value your friendship. I admire you a great deal, do you know that?'

Embarrassed, and avoiding William's gaze, Fletcher said, 'It's been a pleasure to serve with you. And the anticipation of our voyage to Tahiti is one I cannot suppress.'

William grunted his agreement, and they resumed their walk. Hands still behind his back, he said, '*Bounty* will be ready to unmoor the week after next.' He scowled. 'Yet I still have not received my official sailing orders, sod the slack swine in Whitehall. So I've decided to wait no longer. We will set sail for Spithead on the second of November and I'll collect my orders from there.'

On 3 September *Bounty* was unmoored from Deptford dock and dropped downriver. There her provisioning was carried out, under

William's strict supervision. Fletcher stayed with his brother Edward for a few days, in his rooms in Chancery Lane, then in mid-October returned briefly to Douglas to farewell his mother, cousin John and the Taubmans.

Although the aim of *Bounty*'s forthcoming voyage was officially a close secret, thanks to the Isle of Man's connection with some of its crew the ship's destination, if not its special mission, was common knowledge. The islanders expressed great pleasure that William, Fletcher and young Peter Heywood were to be a part of the expedition. The South Sea in general, and Tahiti in particular, had been popular subjects for local journal readers ever since Wallis's discovery of the island.

Fletcher's mother reported that his brother Charles, now medically qualified, had been on a voyage to Madras and Macao, as ship's surgeon on the merchantman *Middlesex*. He would return to England shortly, she had been advised in a letter forwarded by the East India Company. Fletcher immediately regretted that this meant they would not be able to meet and discuss Charles's voyage.

Once again Fletcher stood on the dock at Douglas harbour, waiting to board the packet to Liverpool. His mother, her face pale and drawn, bonneted and with a woollen shawl wrapped around her shoulders against the biting north wind, hugged him. 'Goodbye darling. Safe voyage. Do take care.'

'I shall. And the two years will go quickly. Then I shall be back here again with you. And, I hope, in the uniform of a naval lieutenant.'

'Two years!' Tears sprang into her eyes. 'Charles will probably be away again, too, so all I have now is Edward.' She heaved a sigh and closed her eyes. Tears leaked from beneath the lids.

Fletcher hugged her, then planted a kiss on her forehead. 'Goodbye, Mother. I will write from Tenerife, since we shall be calling there. And I will be back before you know I've gone.'

He hugged her once more, then walked quickly up the gangplank.

On 28 October *Bounty* was unmoored from the dock at Long Reach on the lower Thames, where her four-pounders, swivel guns and arms chests, including muskets, pistols, ammunition and cutlasses, had been taken aboard and stowed. Then, with a growing sense of inquisitiveness among the crew ('What is our exact destination?' 'What sort of a man is Captain Bligh?' 'How long will it be before we see England again?') HMAV *Bounty* made for the Channel.

Although the winds there were mainly unfavourable, the little ship handled the conditions well, and on 4 November *Bounty* was anchored securely in the Solent. William was rowed across to Portsmouth, where he had obtained lodgings for Betsy and their daughters. There they would say their farewells. Fletcher had intended to remain on the *Bounty*, in order to get to know more of the crew, but next morning he saw entering the Solent from the west a three-masted merchantman, flying the flag of the East India Company. Peering through his spyglass, he saw it was the *Middlesex*. Brother Charles's ship. He had not missed him after all.

'Charles! Welcome home!'

'Fletcher! How good it is to see you!'

After meeting on the Plymouth waterfront, the brothers quickly repaired to a nearby tavern, where over pints of ale and pork pies they caught up on all their news. Charles, at twenty-seven, was only three years senior to Fletcher but looked much older. His eyes were sunken, his cheeks gaunt and unshaven.

He explained why. 'I picked up an illness in Madras. Found it hard to keep food down.' He smiled ruefully. 'A case of "physician, heal thyself", as Saint Luke put it. Moreover, on the voyage home, there was a mutiny aboard *Middlesex*, and I was involved.'

'A mutiny? For what reason?'

'The captain, one John Rogers, proved to be a tyrant. His actions towards his crew became intolerable. One seaman, William Greace, was ordered to be flogged to death, merely for insolence. And indeed the poor sod almost bled his life away. After I treated him, he recovered, then obtained a loaded pistol and aimed it at Rogers. Our first officer, George Aitken, supported Greace, as did I. The second officer struck Rogers in anger.'

'Did you and the others take control of the ship?'

'No. Rogers persuaded some of the able seamen to overpower us. We were then locked in our cabins.'

There was a long silence as Fletcher absorbed this shocking news. Then he said, 'And now, what is your punishment?'

Charles's eyebrows knitted. 'I am censured by the company, and suspended from further service with them for two years.' He laughed. 'Something that bothers me not at all.' He shook his head. 'I am done with the sea, Fletcher. To serve on a ship under a monster like Rogers is a ghastly experience.' He took a draught from his tankard. 'As officers we had no option but to take action against his abuse of authority. It was our moral duty, we agreed. We were driven to it by the captain's behaviour.' He rubbed his tired eyes. 'Despots must be stood up to, Fletcher.'

Fletcher nodded. 'I understand. Your hand was forced. Yet, if it had happened on a Royal Navy vessel—'

Charles held up his hand. 'I know, I know. We would have been hanged from the yardarm. But because it occurred on a merchant ship, and we reported Rogers' detestable behaviour truthfully, with witnesses to support us, we will receive no further punishment. We've been paid, and Rogers has been fined by the company. Five hundred pounds.' He gave Fletcher a cautionary look. 'So, brother, choose your captain carefully.'

'There is no choice in the matter, as you well know.'

'I jest, of course.' He raised his chin. 'So, this William Bligh, is he a fair man?'

'He is. And he's a fine navigator. He's resentful at the way the Admiralty's treated him, but I find that understandable.' Fletcher drank more ale. 'And to my surprise, he confides in me. He's become a friend.'

'Good. So your voyage will doubtless be a memorable one.' Charles added reflectively, 'In my experience, men cooped up below decks for long periods are tempted to lose their tolerance for one another. The smallest of habits begin to irritate, then infuriate. And when that happens, men can act irrationally.' He got to his feet. 'Now brother, that's enough talk of irrationality. Allow me to buy you another pint.'

Bounty was still not able to leave Spithead. Although William's sailing orders from the Admiralty had at last been delivered to the ship, and the crew had been given two months' pay in advance, the elements were against them. *Bounty* was forced first into St Helen's harbour, on the east coast of the Isle of Wight, and after attempting to leave from there was driven across to Spithead by the wind and confined there for the next fortnight. After they again tried to get clear of the Channel, the winds threatened to blow the ship onto the Normandy coast. Once more the winds forced them back to Spithead. Throughout the ship, frustrations deepened. It was now December. Whenever would they get shot of the sodding Solent?

Hunched over his charts of the Atlantic, William griped to Fletcher and *Bounty*'s master, John Fryer: 'The shortest route to Tahiti is via the Horn, yet by the time we reach there the southern winter will be imminent. We may be out of season.' He ground his teeth in frustration. 'So I'm sending a note to Banks, asking that he obtain permission from the Admiralty for us to seek an alternative route, should it prove necessary to do so.'

In a reply dispatched with unusual promptness to the *Bounty*, the Admiralty granted William its discretionary consent for another route to be sought. But only if this was unavoidable.

At last the wind changed. On 23 December 1787, HMAV *Bounty* and her forty-five-man complement was able to weigh anchor and begin her long voyage to the far side of the world.

Santa Cruz, Tenerife, Canary Islands, 10 January 1788
Dearest Mother,
We arrived in this port four days ago and anchored in the roads of Santa Cruz, to the north-east of Tenerife, the largest of the seven Canary Islands. It was a relief to do so, since the beginning of the voyage was arduous in the extreme. Gales struck us two days after we left Spithead, and we spent

Christmas Eve battling enormous seas. There was some respite on Christmas Day, when the weather abated, and William (Captain Bligh) ordered beef and plum pudding for midday dinner, with an extra ration of grog. But when we reached the Atlantic, Bounty was struck by a succession of rollers. The ship was flooded, the stern windows driven in by the force of the waves and some of the precious navigational instruments damaged, including an azimuth compass. The drenched ship was bitterly cold below decks, and I have seldom seen men so chilled and miserable. William ordered rum added to their beer, which eased their discomfort somewhat. The storm also caused some spare spars to be washed overboard, the boats were damaged, and our biscuit stores saturated with sea water. Several barrels of beer, though tied to the deck, were also washed away.

Not a propitious beginning! Things can only get better, I decided.

As we sailed south and the temperatures increased, we were able to dry our sodden gear and food under the welcome sun. Lebogue the sailmaker and Purcell the carpenter were hard at work repairing the sails, rigging and boats. Now that we have plain sailing at last, I will relate to you something of our shipboard routine.

William insists that the ship be always kept meticulously clean below decks, a policy he tells me was bequeathed to him by Captain Cook. William values Cook's policies highly and implements them rigorously himself. For instance, when the weather permits it, the hatches are kept open to admit fresh air and the lower decks are fumigated with gunpowder and vinegar. William also insists that every Sunday the crew's clothing and bedding is washed, dried and aired. Naturally, I was familiar with these practices from my time with him on Britannia, so I readily accept them. The men grumbled at this policy in the beginning, but now go along with it as a normal part of shipboard routine. They have also come to accept the anti-scorbutic diet he prescribes for them, albeit reluctantly, to ward off the scurvy. At first they screwed their faces up at the sauerkraut, juice of wort and soup, but as on Cook's ships, when the men knew the officers ate it with gusto they emulated them. Anything is preferable to scurvy, even the most dullard sailor knows.

I am greatly admiring of William's consideration for his men. After the Sunday cleaning below decks he personally inspects their clothing and persons. He then calls the men together to listen to his reading of the Articles of War. This is a reminder of their obligations, and the severity of the punishments should they transgress any of the navy's rules. For example, refusal to obey an officer's command, dereliction of watch duty or, heaven forbid, mutiny. Again, I assume this is Cook's influence. After reciting the articles, William takes divine service, using the Common Book of Prayer. He takes this seriously, although few of the rest of us do. Then, and you will find this hard to imagine, he orders us to dance on deck, for up to two hours! Our jigging is accompanied by a fiddle, played by one of the able seamen, Michael Byrne, who is so short of sight as to be virtually blind. But sightless or not, he plays a fair fiddle, I have to say, and the exercise can do us no harm. Often we collapse with laughter, which is no bad thing either.

After we lowered the anchors in Santa Cruz harbour, it was my honour to be declared by William to be his and King George's representative while ashore. As a mere mate on Bounty, I was greatly surprised, and honoured, to be so designated. It was my assumption that master's mate William Elphinstone, who is my elder by fourteen years, would be asked to do this. However when offered the role, I agreed to it with alacrity. After the disappointment of being kept aboard when we called at Cape Verde in 1783, while serving on HMS Eurydice, you can imagine my delight at being taken ashore at Santa Cruz.

The island of Tenerife is ruled by Spain, so William asked me to pay his respects to the Governor, a nobleman called Marquis de Branciforte. I did so, at the Governor's residence, an elaborate building on the Santa Cruz waterfront. De Branciforte is a tall, strongly built man with a dark goatee. He wears an overly ornate uniform, complete with gold-braided epaulettes and a heavily plumed hat, so that he put me in mind of a peacock. Although the Governor greeted me affably enough, he also had a conceited manner. This was confirmed when after I introduced myself and explained that I was the Bounty's mate, the Governor's interpreter told me: 'So you are not the commander. Where is your commander?'

I told him that Captain Bligh was busy on board attending to the very important matter of overseeing the provisioning and stowage of the supplies and, as purser, balancing his books. But William had told me to convey the *message to the Governor that he would fire a salute to him with the ship's guns, provided that a matching salute was fired in return by his Excellency's cannons. There was a long reply by the Governor to this suggestion, which was translated as: 'My guns are only fired in recognition of a person of equal rank to myself.' What vanity! As a consequence, no guns were fired to salute either party. But I departed from his residence on genial enough terms, considering that the Spanish are not natural allies of ours.*

That incident excepted, I found the visit to Santa Cruz exciting. It is hot, exotic and loomed over by a volcano, Mt Teide. The mountain is over 12,000 feet high, its summit reaching to the clouds. Stupendous! Although it is mid-winter, tropical flowers still bloom on the island, and our gardener, Nelson, has gone ashore to botanise. The people of Tenerife, most of whom are Negroes, are very poor and raggedly clothed, and ruled over autocratically by the markedly wealthy Spaniards. Their women are haughty and did not even deign to reply when I greeted them in my only two words of Spanish ('Buenos dias'). The town's streets are tidy enough, and there are several Catholic churches, and a fort, and above the town, innumerable vineyards. There being no marines aboard Bounty, for safety I was accompanied by two of the ship's ABs, Thomas Burkett and John Millward. They amused me by asking, when we got ashore, 'Where are all the canaries, then, Fletch?' The poor fellows did not know that the name 'Canary' comes from the Latin word 'Canaria', meaning 'Dogs'. There were certainly plenty of them. Once again, I am grateful to my schooling in Latin from Cockermouth days! (Burkett also ventured to suggest, after I informed him of the word's meaning, that 'the Isle of Dogs', in London's dockland, should really be called 'the Isle of Canaries'. We all had a good laugh about that one.)

I was also commissioned by our purser (i.e. Captain Bligh) to purchase more provisions while ashore. I did so, in the company of John Samuel, Bounty's clerk. Regrettably, as it is not the growing season, fresh food supplies at an acceptable price were not freely available. The usual tropical fruits and vegetables — oranges, figs, sweet potatoes, pumpkins — were of poor quality, as was the island's beef. The chickens were exorbitantly priced at three shillings each! However the wine supplies were almost limitless, so we purchased over 850 gallons of vin ordinaire, along with two hogsheads of vintage Canary wine, intended for Sir Joseph Banks' cellar. Let us hope that His Eminence's hogsheads are not broached by the crew before we return with them to London! In that case an immediate suspect would be our perpetually drunk surgeon, Thomas Huggan. I never knew a man to drink so much. I hope I am never in need of his 'services'. Thank the Lord, Huggan's assistant, Thomas Ledward, is usually sober.

We also take aboard casks of fresh water, the cost five shillings per ton. All these provisions are delivered to the ship by local boatmen. It has taken four full days to stow all the provisions.

I must end now. There is an English merchantman, Penelope, alongside us in the Santa Cruz roads. As she is bound for London, I shall convey this letter to her purser, with instructions to hand it to the postal authorities in London. In this way you should receive my news by the spring. I am also writing to Charles and Edward.

William is sending reports on our progress to Sir Joseph Banks, Lord Sydney and Duncan Campbell. Since our next stop will be the South Sea, there will be no further opportunity for me to write to you until our return voyage, next year.

Until then, I am, as always,
Your loving son,
Fletcher

On 11 January 1788 they weighed and set sail westward, in the direction of the coast of South America.

On the morning of their fourth day out, boatswain Cole called for the entire ship's company to assemble mid-deck. In full dress uniform, William addressed the men: 'Good day to you all.' Placing his hands on the rail, he stared down at the assembly. 'Now that we have been at sea for three weeks, I can inform you of the expedition's destination and intent, along with other important matters.' As the men stared up at him there was almost complete silence, broken only by the slop and gurgle of the swells against the hull. William cleared his throat. 'We are bound for the island of Tahiti, in the South Sea, by the shortest possible route, via the South Atlantic, Tierra del Fuego and Cape Horn.'

There were murmurs among the assembly. Some of them exchanged knowing looks. Everyone knew of the Horn's reputation, which was fearsome, but they also knew of Tahiti's, for very different reasons.

'While in Tahiti we will take aboard many young breadfruit plants for transportation to our islands in the West Indies. *Bounty*'s gardeners, Nelson and Brown, will be in charge of this collecting. The young plants will be accommodated in the modified cabin in the stern, which doubtless many of you have been curious about. Expect that part of *Bounty* to be a floating greenhouse upon our return voyage.'

He paused to allow a ripple of amusement to subside. 'Because of the lateness of our departure — through no fault of mine, I'm bound to point out — the season is far spent. Doubling Cape Horn, probably in April, during the onset of the Southern winter, will test all our skills of seamanship. I know you will all be equal to the task.' He leaned forward. 'I have been impressed so far with your teamwork and diligence, which has brought us here, almost to the Tropic, without further mishap after the gales that beset us in the North Atlantic. Be assured, upon our return to England, all of you will receive promotion.'

A murmur of approbation passed through the men.

'And while on the subject of promotion, I wish to announce that master's mate Fletcher Christian is henceforth designated Acting Lieutenant Christian, a position which, as you will all be aware, carries additional rights and responsibilities. Mr Christian fulfilled that role while serving aboard HMS *Eurydice* in the Indian Ocean.'

Thomas Burkett, standing to Fletcher's left, nudged him and muttered, 'You will still speak to us, won't you?' To his right, *Bounty*'s master, Fryer, stared straight ahead, stony-faced. A tall, ascetic figure, he never smiled.

The announcement came as no surprise to Fletcher. Last night he had again dined with William in his cabin. After his servant, John Smith, had brought their food and wine, William raised his tankard. It was filled with Canary Islands red wine.

'Good health, Fletcher.'

'And to yours.'

They drank, then William leaned back in his chair. 'I have news for you, Fletcher.'

'Oh?'

'I'm promoting you to lieutenant. Acting Lieutenant.'

Fletcher was taken aback. 'Why so, sir?'

'For an expedition of this importance, one officer is insufficient. Since the Admiralty denied me another, I'm using my authority while at sea to appoint one. And that officer is yourself.'

'But should the promotion not go to Fryer? As master?'

William waved his hand airily. 'No. Fryer's current role is too important. No commander has ever promoted a sailing master while at sea.' He gazed directly at Fletcher. 'You are the one.'

'I must admit, William, I'm flattered.'

'It's fully deserved. You're competent. No, more than competent. You're highly capable. The men like you, and respect you. And you were promoted to Acting Lieutenant on Eurydice, were you not?'

'Yes. That too came as a surprise. An agreeable one, naturally.'

'Good, good. You have a bright naval future, Fletcher, I'm certain of that. Now, let's drink to Acting Lieutenant Fletcher Christian of HMAV Bounty.'

They clinked tankards again and locked eyes. William's were very bright.

Now William's gaze swept the assembled company. 'Additional matters. From tomorrow onwards on we will stand three watches, not two. So your duty hours will be four hours on, and off eight, instead of four hours on and four off. This will afford you all more time for relaxation. Mr Christian will be in command of the third watch.'

He moved on to the more mundane. The bread allowance was to be cut by a third, to conserve supplies. The remaining bread supply was to be kept in casks, to minimise infestation by vermin. After they crossed the line and reached the latitudes of the South Atlantic, they would all be issued with heavy weather jackets.

Every day after four o'clock the fiddle-accompanied dancing continued. Byrne's fiddling, and their dancing, was accompanied by the singing of shanties. One of the most popular of these was 'Admiral Benbow', whose lyrics were taught to them by sailmaker Lebogue, the oldest and most-travelled sailor aboard:

Come all you sailors bold – Lend an ear lend an ear
Come all you sailors bold lend an ear

It's of our Admiral's fame – Brave Benbow called by name
How he fought on the main – You shall hear

Brave Benbow he set sail – For to fight for to fight
Brave Benbow he set sail for to fight

Brave Benbow he set sail – With a fine and pleasant gale
But his captains they turned tail – In a fright

Says Kirby unto Wade – I will run, I will run
Says Kirby unto Wade I will run – I value not disgrace

Nor the losing of my place – My enemies I'll not face with a gun
'Twas the Ruby and Noah's Ark – Fought the French fought
*   the French*

'Twas the Ruby and Noah's Ark fought the French
And there was ten in all – Poor souls they fought them all

They valued them not all – Nor their stench
It was our Admiral's lot – With a chain shot with a chain shot

It was our Admiral's lot with a chain shot – Our Admiral lost his legs
And to his men he begs – Fight on my boys he says – 'Tis my lot

Following the dancing, William again recited the Articles of War. Bored now by the repetition of the dire consequences of any wrongdoing, the men shuffled restlessly. But a week out of Santa Cruz, to conclude the customary bulletin, William declared in a more cheerful tone: 'For today's midday meal, fresh meat will be served to you all. Tenerife wine will accompany the meat, along with the usual ration of grog.'

A shout went up from surgeon Huggan, leaning against the mainmast. 'Huzzah for Captain Bligh!' He was already drunk.

Although the winds continued to be favourable, the Atlantic air was sweltering, the humidity close to one hundred per cent. When the rain came, usually in the late afternoon, it was mainly in short heavy bursts, and when it did William ordered awnings spread above the deck to catch it. The rainwater refreshed the water butts, and the awning protected the men against the rays of the tropical sun when the skies cleared.

William continued to enforce his regime of cleanliness below decks, with the regular washings with vinegar and gunpowder. The humidity caused a malignant mould to form, so that it had to be constantly scrubbed from the walls and ceiling. The crew's clothing and bedding was ordered to be aired whenever the weather made this possible.

The benefits of this regime became obvious: the crew remained free of illness, and morale was buoyant. There had not been a single flogging.

They crossed the line on 14 February, accompanied by much-reduced rituals. William disapproved of ducking, he told Fletcher. So the first-timers — twenty-seven in all — were merely tarred, then shaved with a piece of iron barrel-hoop. Three bottles of rum were shared, and each man was issued with a half pint of wine. The crew became euphoric. 'We are now in the Southern Hemisphere!' they exclaimed to one another.

Fletcher relished his new role and the responsibility that came with it. The black fog which had at one time lodged in his mind was a thing of the past. Everything that lay before him was now filled with purpose, promise and expectation. He had never been so determined to fulfil those hopes and had never been better placed to do so. And for that he had one man to thank — his captain, William.

Peter Heywood was on morning watch at the main masthead when Fletcher scaled the rigging to join him. *Bounty* was in full sail with a following wind, and the sun was near its midday zenith. Even though Heywood and Fletcher were eight years apart in age, their common Manx background meant they always had much to talk about. Both were now barefoot, wearing only their crewman's calico trousers. Fletcher's torso was streaming with sweat; Peter's shoulders were pink from the sun. Below, the helmsmen were holding *Bounty* on a south-westerly course and she was making a steady four knots. There were just a few streaks of cloud high in the sky's blue dome.

Suddenly Fletcher pointed to starboard. 'Look!'

'What? Oh, yes. How wonderful.'

A school of porpoises, sleek and glistening, was swimming alongside the ship. They turned their bodies, plunging, rearing and grinning like a troupe of performing clowns. Above them, a flock of petrels dipped and soared, and much higher above them, a fork-tailed frigate bird glided, peering down at the ship. Yesterday whales had broached just a few yards from the larboard bow, their spouting spraying the decks. Master-at-arms Charles Churchill fired at them with a musket, but he may as well have been using a pea-shooter.

Fletcher and Peter chatted. Both were pleased with their allocated roles on the ship, both had ambitions to gain permanent commissions, both agreed that a life at sea was the only one to be contemplated. And both had lately been dreaming of Tahitian maidens.

'They say,' mused Peter, 'that the price of a Tahitian woman is just one nail.'

Fletcher smiled. 'I've read that too. And do you know, there are thousands of nails in the hold.'

'Blast and bugger your bloody eyes, you putrid lump of Cornish shit!'

Startled, they looked down. Matthew Quintal was standing before the mainmast, hands dangling at his sides. William was standing in front of him and Fryer was behind the captain. William turned to *Bounty*'s master. 'What was it that this broken arse said to you, Mr Fryer?'

'He said, after I told him to clean the head properly, "You can go and fuck yourself, Fryer. That's not my shit".'

William put his face closer to Quintal's. 'Is that what you said, you fucking arse-licker?'

Quintal raised his chin. 'Yeah, I said it. 'Cause it needed to be said.'

'Oh? It needed to be said, did it? Well, I'll tell you something else that needs to be said, Quintal.' He turned back to Fryer. 'This burnt-arse shit bag, this Cornish pasty, is to receive two dozen lashes for his insolence and contempt.' He stood back. 'Tell Morrison to let the cat out of the bag. And order the men to watch.'

Quintal stood at the grating, tied at the wrists and ankles. There was a wooden peg between his teeth. William read the charges, announced the sentence, then stood back for boatswain's mate Morrison, who had the cat-o'-nine-tails at the ready.

One, two, three. Quintal began to quiver. Morrison's arm rose and fell. Four, five, six. Teeth clamped on the peg, Quintal's eyes bulged. Morrison continued to lay it on. Seven, eight, nine. Quintal's back was turning red. Ten, eleven, twelve. Gobbets of flesh and blood flew. Quintal was squirming.

William snapped at Morrison. 'Right. Throw water over him. Salt water. Then give him another twelve.'

When the ropes were untied, Quintal staggered backwards and reeled. His entire back was bloodied and pulpy. Face dripping with sweat, chest heaving, he spat out the peg and eyeballed not Morrison, but his master and commander. For some seconds he stared into William's face. His expression was of such loathing that it imprinted itself indelibly on the consciousness of every witness to it. Fletcher in particular would never forget it.

By March they were sailing down the east coast of South America, out of sight of land and driven by the south-east trade wind. Temperatures fell but the seas were moderate, so much so that they were able to cover up to thirty nautical miles daily. When it rained it now came with less intensity. Men trailed lines and hooks baited with pork rind, caught plump porpoises and hauled them aboard. Their steaks made a welcome change from their otherwise monotonous diet of salt pork and beef.

'Land! Land! Off the starboard bow!'

The cry came from able seaman Alex Smith, from the masthead. It was mid-afternoon on 22 March and the autumn sky was clear, the sun low.

From the decks they saw an expanse of undulating land. Hours earlier Fletcher had shot the sun at midday and reported to William that they had reached 54° 47' South latitude.

Standing alongside him, Peter nudged Fletcher. 'What is it?'

'Tierra del Fuego. We're approaching the south of South America.' He put his spyglass to his eye. A headland and a long rocky island, streaked with snow, came into view. He and William had studied the charts of Tierra del Fuego's coast last evening, in the captain's cabin. 'That must be Cape San Diego,' Fletcher told Peter, spyglass still trained on the island. 'And to the west, Staten Island.'

'So we're nearing Cape Horn?'

'We are.'

Grinning, Peter waved his hand at the gently rolling swells. 'The infamous Cape Horn? Look at this sea — it couldn't be kinder.'

The ocean had turned into a mass of moving mountains, moving in several directions at once. They came at the ship from all quarters, rearing then collapsing onto *Bounty*'s bow and decks. Seawater streamed over the ship, poured down the companionways and into the cabins; the wind howled in the rigging like a pack of feuding wolves.

Standing by the aft companionway, mate Elphinstone screamed at the few crewmen who were not aloft, 'More men to the pumps! More! More! Ellison, Muspratt, get below and lend a hand! Look fast there! Fast!'

Another cry came from Fryer on the quarterdeck, yelling up at the top men, who were swaying crazily as the ship arced like an over-wound metronome. 'Shorten the foresail! Take in the main!'

One of the released mainmast sails, freed from its sheet, was caught by the wind and wrapped itself around the mast. The ship began to vibrate, then lurch. The men aloft hugged the yards, their feet supported by loops of rope; the men on deck stumbled about like drunkards, clutching at the rails and sheets for a handhold. With every wave that struck the ship the force knocked them down. They glissaded along the deck, slammed into the gunwales, boats or masts, cursing their hurt.

The mountains of black water kept rushing at *Bounty*. It was as if a huge dam had ruptured somewhere in the mountains of Tierra del Fuego and its lake's contents were pouring down over them. As swell after mountainous swell struck *Bounty*, she pitched with punishing force, pluckily defying her massive attackers.

At the helm, quartermasters Norton and Linkletter had lashed themselves to the wheel. William and Fletcher stood behind them, both caped, tricorns tied under their chins, staring up at the close-reefed topsails and the three nearly bare masts swaying like tree trunks in an earthquake.

Sheets of rain, driven by the gale-force westerlies, swept over the ship, so that for the crew the whole world seemed to have turned to water. Water that was black and icy and driven into their faces like grapeshot. It was impossible to know the time of day, or what if any westward progress they were making. All they knew for certain was that they and *Bounty* were fighting for their lives.

'Hold your course! Hold your course!' Legs apart, William braced himself and bellowed at the helmsmen. 'Bring her to! Keep her into the wind! Hard into the wind!'

Fletcher yelled in his ear. 'Have you ever seen a sea such as this?'

'Never! This is the worst!' He stumbled, then recovered. 'And it is all the sodding Admiralty's fault!'

'What? For the gale?'

William turned to him, his eyes wild. 'Yes! If those swine-fucking quill-pushers in Whitehall had got off their lardy arses, we would have left England two months earlier and not missed the season at the Cape!'

The ship lurched again, even more violently, and William dropped to his knees. Fletcher helped him to his feet and together they reached for the quarterdeck rail and gripped it. Then, looking up, Fletcher screamed, 'Oh, Jesus!'

To larboard, a wall of black water was rearing above them, as high as the mainmast.

The wind tore at its curling crest, then the giant comber collapsed and the ship was engulfed. There were cries from below as *Bounty* fell on her beam ends. The top men hugged the yards for dear life, miniature figures high in the sky, unable to move up or down. The ship rose, then righted herself. Sheets of water raced across the decks, then drained through the scuttles. But she had no sooner come onto an even keel when another gigantic wave reared, this time off the starboard bow, rushed towards the ship and fell upon her like a feeding beast.

Hours passed. The gale continued. There was snow, then hail, which froze their fingers and blasted their faces. William ordered all the hatches battened down, so that the only entrance to the lower deck was through the aft hatchway. But the sea was relentless, continuing to pour into the lower decks, saturating the crew's clothes and bedding.

For over three weeks they fought off the Cape Horn gales. The tiny ship was like a toy, a plaything of the gusts which abated for only a few hours, when they switched briefly to the east and the sun broke through. During these brief respites the crew attempted to dry their wet clothes and bedding, but hours later the wind resumed its assault, again from the west.

After Fryer reported that the ship was leaking, William ordered the pumps manned through all three watches, day after day. Below decks the men off duty lay in their berths, noses running, rendered speechless by the cold and wet, unable to get up, puking if they ate, joints aching with the cold and damp. The cook struggled to keep alight the galley stove, the sole source of heat, with lengths of dampened wood. William ordered the crew to have grog that was full-strength, not diluted, to help combat the cold. Hot soup and boiled wheat and sugar helped too. He also allowed some of the men whose berths were wet to have his cabin at night, in turns, so that they might get some sleep. Fletcher observed this humane gesture, and admired him for it.

There were casualties. Quartermaster Linkletter fell into the fore cockpit and was concussed; seaman Skinner was slammed into the mainmast base and bruised his spine. Both were treated by assistant surgeon Ledward, who was himself stricken with a chill. Surgeon Huggan, intoxicated from his private grog supply, ventured topside briefly, then in rapid retreat tumbled down the after ladder and dislocated his shoulder. Upon regaining consciousness Huggan croaked to Ledward: 'Never mind the shoulder, get me more grog.' Ledward shook his head and shoved the shoulder back into place.

Below decks, frustrations worsened. There was a brawl in the galley as men tried to huddle closer to the fire-box and the cook's ribs were broken. Another scuffle resulted in Churchill's hand being burned. Heywood, desperate for sleep, was late for his duty. When this was reported to William, without hesitation William told the midshipman: 'No excuses, Heywood. You are mastheaded. Now.' The lad spent five miserable hours aloft when the gale was at its most violent.

Fletcher moved constantly about the ship, below decks and topside. He helped man the pumps at night, then during the hours of dismal daylight went aloft to keep the sails reefed tight. He ordered ropes tied across the deck so the men had something to hold on to. He relieved quartermaster Norton when he was too exhausted to hold the wheel. Worn out himself, Fletcher barely slept.

On 17 April, at midday, William had to get Fletcher to tie him to the mainmast in order for him to take his sextant sights. At that point Fletcher realised they had all had enough. 'It's too much,' he told William as he untied him. *Bounty* rolled again, wildly, and they both snatched at the mainmast ladder. 'We can't go on.'

William looked at him with furious eyes. Then he nodded curtly and turned away.

An hour later, with the ship still pitching madly, William called for the men to assemble below decks. Standing before them, saturated, he declared: 'You have all put up a brave fight against the elements. I could ask no more of any crew. But the conditions these last twenty-nine days have exceeded the worst I have ever experienced at sea.' He tipped his head back and grimaced. 'It is clear that we cannot proceed westward. Accordingly, we shall go about and set a course for Cape Town.'

Some of the crew closed their eyes and gave thanks. There were ragged cheers from others. Several were close to tears. Scotsman McCoy muttered to his Cornish mate Quintal, 'Fuck Cape Horn forever, let's have the Cape of Good Hope.'

Fletcher put a consoling hand on William's shoulder. 'This isn't a defeat,' he told him. 'It's just a setback.'

'Thank you, thank you,' William replied wearily. Then he retired to his cabin to plot *Bounty*'s reversed course.

False Bay, Cape Town, 24 May 1788
Dearest Mother,

You will doubtless be surprised to receive this letter from Cape Town, after the one I sent from Tenerife earlier in the year averred that you would not hear from me again until my return to England. None of us aboard Bounty suspected that we would be in Cape Town at this time.

We are now in this Dutch colony, rather than Tahiti, because the adverse gale-force winds of Cape Horn did not permit us safe passage through to the South Sea. After several gruelling weeks of battling wind and sea, we could not pass around the Horn. William puts the blame for this on our late departure from England, and it is true that had we been even three weeks earlier at the Cape, we may well have passed through the Le Maire Strait under more favourable conditions. Our gunner, Peckover, who sailed on all three world voyages with Captain Cook, told me that he had never seen seas like the ones at the Horn, for height and length of swell. So it was with considerable relief that we turned and sailed east, reaching Cape Town five weeks later.

Now that 'flaming June' is almost upon you on the Isle of Man, you will be enjoying long summer days on the island. Perhaps Edward and Charles have paid you a visit in the past weeks. If they have not, then this missive may compensate.

You will recall that I have been in this port before, while serving on HMS Eurydice. It is good to be back and enjoying the benefits of European civilisation again, albeit briefly. Bounty took such a battering in the South Atlantic that she requires much repairing: her decks need recaulking and many of her sails and much of her rigging must be replaced. Naturally, we also need to reprovision before venturing to traverse the Indian Ocean. Fortunately the facilities in this Dutch town are well used to providing the goods and services which voyaging ships require. There are seven other ships in the harbour, all Dutch East Indiamen.

William complains at the cost of all this — as purser he must make the necessary purchases and account for every expense, an onerous task. Pilfering, or the suspicion of it, is a constant problem. When a cask of cheese was opened, the supplies of it were found to be short by several cheeses. William declared that a theft had occurred, and stopped the men's cheese rations. When aroused, he has a fiery temper and will brook no dissent (as is his right as commander). As a protest against his cheese policy, the men refused to eat their butter allowance until the cheese ration was restored, thereby cutting off their noses to spite their faces (or rather, their stomachs). Such are the petty problems that plague a ship's purser! I cannot emphasise too strongly the importance that food assumes during a long sea voyage. Meals are one of the few pleasures available to seamen, so to lose any food allowance is a loss more keenly felt than anything similar on land, where replacement commodities can be readily obtained. William is particularly sensitive about this matter, and is only too aware of the importance of keeping scurvy at bay. He insists that the men eat a breakfast of hot oatmeal, and also insists that they take their dried malt, sauerkraut and portable soup. They obey, knowing that like Cook's men they will be lashed if they do not (I have to say, though, that William spares the lash far more than Cook did, in his

127

accounts. There have been only two floggings so far on Bounty; one for insolence while at sea and the other here at Cape Town for want of duty in heaving a lead-line).

Provisions are being ferried to the ship from the shore; fresh beef and Cape wine, sheep and goats to replace those who died of the cold earlier, and bags of seeds which gardener Nelson will plant in Tahiti: apples, corn, lemons and oranges. Thus, we may be taking the Tahitians' breadfruit, but we will bequeath them our English fruits!

I will end here, as I must also write to Charles and Edward, and to cousin John. I will ensure that all my letters are dispatched on the next ship to England which sails from this port. It is William's expectation that we will be provisioned and our sails and rigging overhauled by the end of June. After which we will weigh anchor and again set sail for Tahiti, this time via Van Diemen's Land. But wherever I may be, my thoughts will also be with you.

I am,

Your loving son,

Fletcher

Fletcher and Peter wandered along the Cape Town waterfront, both wearing their hats and capes, both walking with the sailor's gait that the Cape Horn sea had bestowed upon them. After a week spent helping with the cleaning and repairing of *Bounty*, they had been given two days' leave. Winter was approaching in Southern Africa: the sky was a hard, bright blue and the profile of Table Mountain, looming above the town, was silhouetted against the blueness. The day was windless, the harbour water metallic. *Bounty* was at anchor in the bay alongside a much larger East Indiaman.

The cobbled streets were bustling with carriages, carts and wagons, men on horseback and pedestrians. Dutch women in clogs, baskets on their arms, stood about talking outside the coffee houses and shops, and there were smells in the air of freshly baked bread, smoked sausages, spices, cigar smoke and horse and oxen dung.

Barefoot Hottentot labourers staggered along the dock, laden down with sacks of flour; a few of their women, infants strapped to their backs, were sweeping the cobbles with brushwood brooms. Pairs of Dutch marines in orange uniforms strolled along, muskets with fixed bayonets shouldered. Thin cats wandered about, looking up at the passers-by hopefully. Fletcher was eating a smoked sausage he had bought from a street vendor. 'Here you go,' he said, tossing the nearest cat a piece of sausage. It was snapped up.

Staring up at Table Mountain, Peter said, 'I like it here, Fletcher. It's so different from anywhere I've been before. The mountain, the town, the people. All so different.'

Fletcher nodded. 'Very different from Douglas, certainly.'

They came to the end of the waterfront, where a canal flowed into the harbour. There were streets on both sides of the canal, and a humpbacked bridge crossed it. Barges were tied up to bollards on one side of the canal and bargemen were loading sacks of grain and barrels of wine onto them from wagons, ready to be transferred to the ships in the harbour.

They crossed the bridge. The street on the other side was lined with more gabled buildings, taverns, warehouses, sail lofts and chandleries. On the corner was a two-storeyed brick tavern with a swinging sign above its door, bearing a painting of a red-faced man with huge side-whiskers, and the name 'Ambroos'.

'Fancy an ale?' Fletcher asked Peter.

'Yes!'

They went inside. The room was large, with bare wooden floors and several high tables and stools. Mullioned windows were set into the wall facing the harbour. A few middle-aged Dutchmen sat at the tables, smoking clay pipes and playing cards. There was a wood fire stove burning in one corner, with an iron pot on its hot plate, and a servery occupied the rear wall. A staircase led up to the next floor from beside the servery. The men at the tables looked up at the two young men as they entered, muttered among themselves, then returned to their card games.

Behind the servery was a stout, balding man of about fifty, with a white beard and cheeks as red as the ones on the tavern sign. His waistcoat was unbuttoned, exposing a stained blouse. Fletcher and Peter greeted him and ordered tankards of beer. As he poured them from the barrel on the counter, the man asked, 'Which is your ship?'

They told him, and he smiled. His teeth were yellow, his beard smoke-stained. 'Ja, ja, *Bounty*. I watch her come in, the other day.' Passing the pewter tankards over, he announced, 'My name Ambroos.' They told him theirs, then took two of the stools at the servery and drank the ale. It was malty and refreshing. They chatted with the proprietor, telling him about their tribulations at the Horn and how pleased they were to be here, safely. But they made sure not to divulge the purpose of *Bounty*'s voyage.

When they were on their second beers the Dutchman leaned forward, and asked them in a low voice, 'You want a woman?'

Both were momentarily disconcerted. Then Fletcher asked, 'To hire?'

'Ja.'

Fletcher looked at Peter. 'You want one?'

Startled, Peter said, 'I don't know. Do you?'

'Yes!' He asked Ambroos, 'You have a woman for sale?'

'Ja. Very pretty.'

'Can we see her?' Fletcher asked.

By way of an answer he came out from behind the servery and walked up the stairs. A few minutes later he returned with a tall blonde woman of about thirty, in a pale beige gown. Her flaxen hair was tied back, her bearing was upright and the gown was tight-fitting, emphasising her breasts, waist and hips. The man led her to Fletcher and Peter, and said, 'This is Meike.' He said to her, 'English.'

She looked them up and down, first Fletcher, then Peter. Her face was oval-shaped, her complexion pale and unmarked, her eyes grey. Her nose was slightly upturned, her lips shapely and like her cheeks, entirely unpainted.

In a moment, Fletcher was in love. Peter too kept staring at her. Both were speechless. She was so beautiful.

Ambroos leered. 'Meike,' he said again. 'Pretty.' She gave him a sharp look, then stared at Fletcher and pointed upstairs. Her expression hardened. 'You vant?' she demanded.

Fletcher recalled Madras, and how he had been deceived and attacked. Then he dismissed the thought. This was different, this was a white woman, being sold by a white man. Breathing heavily, he said to the man, 'How much?'

'Ten guilder. For each time, ten guilder.'

Fletcher looked at Peter, uncertain. 'That is …?'

Peter frowned. 'I think five shillings.'

Fletcher winced. A small fortune. He had only a few pence, hardly enough for another sausage and one more ale. Peter shook his head. 'I've only six pence to my name,' he said. Fletcher looked again at Meike. Her expression was now expectant as she tucked a stray lock of hair behind one ear. She was so alluring. And so obtainable. For a hefty price. But he had to have her. Must have her. It had been so long since Isabella.

To the Dutchman he said, 'Tell her, I will get the money. I will come back tomorrow and pay you ten guilders.'

The man spoke to her in Dutch. Meike pouted and looked sceptical. She turned away. Eyes fixed on her, Fletcher swallowed hard then repeated, 'I will come back. Tomorrow afternoon. With the money.' He tugged at Peter's sleeve. 'Come on.'

'Where are we going?'

'Back to the ship.'

'Come!'

Following his knock, Fletcher entered William's cabin. He was bent over his desk, quill in hand, an accounts book open in front of him. Fletcher could see columns of figures. He looked up. 'Fletcher, come in. Sit down.' Pushing the book to one side, he indicated the spare chair. Fletcher took it.

'So,' William said, 'how was ashore?'

'Very good. It's an interesting town. The last we shall see for some time.'

'Indeed. Tahiti and its breadfruit await us.'

Easing himself into the chair, Fletcher said, 'While in the town I came upon an artisan's studio. It belonged to a Dutch wood carver. He makes exquisite carvings of African animals. I was very taken with his work.'

'Did you purchase any?'

'Sadly, no. They are costly and, well, I have virtually no money. In the hand, that is.' William nodded, and Fletcher pressed on. 'So I wonder, William, if you would be prepared to advance me a sum of money so I can buy some of the carvings.'

'For yourself?'

'No, no. For my cousin. John Christian. You remember John, he's something of a collector of exotic artefacts. I'd like to buy him some of the carvings.'

William's brow furrowed. 'What sum would you need, to purchase them?'

'His price in Dutch currency is twenty guilders for six carvings. In our currency, ten shillings. That is the sum I would like to borrow. It would be repayable immediately upon our return to England, naturally.'

There was a longish pause. Then William said, 'It's a considerable sum, but I will advance you the money.' He placed a hand on Fletcher's arm. 'And I do so because you are a trusted friend.'

He took a key from his waistcoat pocket, went to the cabinet beside his bed and unlocked it. He withdrew a metal box and took from it a sheaf of Dutch currency. He counted out several notes then passed them over, saying, 'Twenty guilders.' He smiled and added, 'You may like to bargain with the Dutch artist. Obtain the carvings for a lesser price.'

'I shall certainly try.' Folding the notes, Fletcher said, 'I'm very grateful to you, William. Cousin John will be, too.'

William held up his hand. 'It's a loan, remember, not a gift.'

'I understand. And it will be repaid.'

William nodded. But he also had a strange expression on his face, one that Fletcher could not fathom. Something between doubt and triumph.

But although he could not really comprehend the meaning of that look, Fletcher later recalled that it may have been from that moment onwards that William's feelings towards him shifted. It was as if he knew that Fletcher now had a moral as well as a financial obligation towards him.

She undressed carefully, removing her gown and undergarments, then folding them and placing them on the chest at the foot of the four-poster bed. Lying upon it, Fletcher watched, entranced, as she revealed her alabaster body. And by the time she came to the bed and lay down with him, he was beside himself with desire.

At last spent, they began to talk, Fletcher overflowing with gratitude for her softness, her suppleness, her capacity for giving.

Meike struggled with her English, but they managed.

She had been married to the captain of an East India merchantman, she told him. From Rotterdam. He was part-owner of this tavern. But two years ago his ship foundered in the monsoon, off the coast of Batavia. Although the ship was within sight of land, it went down with the loss of all but a few hands. Her husband had left her with many debts to repay, and she needed to meet them before she could return to Holland. They had had no children.

'Are you making enough money to repay the debts?' he asked her.

She smiled, drowsily. 'Ja. I make money. But I must share with Ambroos.'

Again he was aroused by the sight and scent of her, her porcelain skin and the depths of her grey eyes. But he had given her all his loan money. He explained. 'Meike, I'm so sorry. I have no more guilders for you.'

Still smiling, she said, 'No mind the money. I like you, Fletcher, you are a nice man. You can have this time for free.' She stroked his face. 'But doan tell Ambroos.'

That evening over supper, William asked, 'The purchase of the curios went satisfactorily, Fletcher?'

'Oh yes. They are very fine carvings.'

'Good, good.' William gave a thin smile. 'Can you show them to me?'

Fletcher swallowed, then coughed to cover his discomfort. Putting his kerchief to his mouth, he said, 'Oh excuse me.' Recovering, he replied, 'I'm afraid I've already dispatched the carvings to my cousin. From the postal bureau, this afternoon. It was important that I consign them immediately, to catch the next sailing to London.'

William gave a little grunt, and looked away. Fletcher said hastily, 'I also found an excellent coffee house, a little way back from the waterfront. Jacob's. Fine coffee, excellent sausages. Would you like to join me there for luncheon tomorrow?'

William drummed his fingers on the table then shook his head. 'No, no. I have other business to attend to.'

Van Diemen's Land, 21 August 1788

The bay was on an island in the south of Van Diemen's Land, in the extreme south of New Holland. William chose this place for replenishment because he had been here with Cook in *Resolution* eleven years earlier, and had partly surveyed the bay's coastline. Englishman Tobias Furneaux had named the bay 'Adventure' in 1773, after his ship and Cook's *Resolution* had become separated in Antarctic waters. *Adventure* had stayed in the bay for five days.

It had taken *Bounty* twenty-three days of hard sailing to get to Adventure Bay from Cape Town. After her anchors were lowered near the centre of the bay, Fletcher and William studied the land from the quarterdeck. The captain's pleasure at returning to the place he had been the very first to properly survey was obvious.

Today Adventure Bay was bathed in spring sunshine, and the land looked inviting. Ranges of hills, covered in forest, rose above the coast. A large bird — some sort of eagle — was gliding above the bay, and a few twirls of smoke arose from the forest, confirming that there were people here.

Looking to the north, they saw that the land tapered away to a low isthmus, covered in dry scrub, which was joined to another humped island. Between the isthmus and the headland at the eastern end of the bay the land looked inviting. Along the coast were stretches of golden sand, separated by shelves of rock.

Fletcher lowered his spyglass. 'The bay is well wooded. Is there water?'

'Yes. A stream flows into the sea there.' He pointed to a place halfway along the shore.

'What of the natives?'

'A strange people. Black, primitive and ugly, but not aggressive. They have no seagoing vessels, and live by hunting.' He slipped his spyglass into its holder. 'They should cause us no trouble.' He pointed to a rock shelf to their left. 'With Cook we first landed there. But we'll put in further along, closer to the stream mouth.'

The men were already busy on deck, preparing to hoist out the boats, supervised by boatswain Cole. William said to Fletcher, 'You're in charge of the wooding party. Take Purcell and four others. Peckover's in charge of the watering. I'll go with Nelson, to do some planting. Fruit trees, mainly.' He stared again at the land. 'Apples should grow well in this place.'

Fletcher, Purcell and the others did not need to go far to get the wood. Trees grew everywhere, from forest giants to scrubby ti tree. It was cool and dry within the forest, and the absence of undergrowth made it easy for the party to work their way into it. Crows perched on boughs and pairs of green and red parrots squawked at them from the trees then flew away; a long-tailed furry animal scampered away at their approach.

They reached a stand of tall ti tree. 'Right, lads,' said Fletcher. 'Let's get cutting.'

It soon became clear that Purcell resented this work. A scrawny fellow with outsize ears, he cursed as he hacked at a ti-tree trunk with an axe. Lowering it, he spat on the ground. 'Fuck this job,' he said.

Fletcher paused in his cutting. 'Why's that?' he demanded.

'I'm a carpenter, a skilled worker, not a fuckin' woodcutter.'

'We all need wood for the galley. Just get on with it.'

He stood back and his ti tree crashed to the ground. More parrots squawked and flew off. Further away, Muspratt and Thompson were doing their cutting. Purcell swung his axe at the tree trunk, still cursing.

When they dragged their wood out onto the beach, Purcell was still in a foul mood, flinging his onto a pile. Fletcher moved further along the beach to see how far Peckover's party had progressed with the filling of the water casks. As he did so William and Nelson emerged from the bushline, both with packs on their backs.

William walked up to the wood pile. Removing his pack, he glared at the carpenter. 'What's this, Purcell?'

'Wood, innit.'

'And what's it for?'

Purcell, truculently: 'The galley.'

'No it isn't. It's too long.' He bent down, picked up a long piece of ti tree and thrust it in Purcell's face. 'Can you see this fitting into the fire-box?'

'It will if it's cut down.'

'Then why didn't you do so? Look at it. It's all too big. For the galley, or stowage. You're an idiot, Purcell.'

Purcell glared back. 'And all you can do is criticise. A man can't do anything right.' He picked up his axe and tossed it at William. 'You want the right-sized wood? Chop it yourself.' He walked away.

The rest looked at each other in shock. This was insubordination of the worst kind. Much worse than Quintal's rudeness, which had incurred a severe flogging.

Fletcher, who had overheard the altercation, went up to William. 'Intolerable insolence, Captain. Shall I take him back to the ship and confine him?' As a warrant officer, Purcell could not be lashed, but some action had to be taken.

For a moment William looked confused. Then he recovered. 'No, no.' He shouted at the carpenter's back, 'Purcell! Come here!'

Purcell returned, his face flushed and his big ears pink from the sun. Standing before the captain, he looked down and awaited his judgment.

'Since you can't cut firewood properly, Purcell,' William said, 'I shall give you a very simple job. A job befitting a simpleton. Go and help unload the water casks.' He waved his hand. 'And from now on you'll be assigned labourer's duties.'

Purcell gave him a contemptuous look, then turned and trudged off towards the stream mouth. Fletcher said to William, 'Is that sufficient admonishment, Captain? For such disrespect?'

'It is.' William's face had reddened. 'And it's not your place to question my judgment. You were in charge of the wooding party — why didn't you insist that the wood was cut to proper lengths?'

Irked, Fletcher replied, 'I fully intended to after it was taken down to the beach. It was more straightforward to drag the lengths here uncut.'

William made no reply. Instead he stalked off. Staring after him, Fletcher thought, the man has a very short fuse. And a vicious tongue with which to light it. He was familiar with the verbal abuse William was so adept at from their time on *Britannia*. But then his judgments had been sound. Now he seemed indecisive and inconsistent. Why is he so reluctant to punish Purcell, when the man had shown such open contempt towards him? He ought in the very least to have been confined below decks as a punishment. He stared out at the bay where *Bounty* was riding at anchor. William as a naval commander was displaying tendencies which he had never shown during his merchant service.

Why had he changed?

Other matters concerned Fletcher. The unity the crew had displayed while they battled the Horn storms now seemed under strain. Although there had been only the two floggings so far, fissures were appearing among the *Bounty*'s company, cracks that Fletcher thought were widening under the rays of the Antipodean sun.

He thought back over the last few weeks. Leading the disaffected was the master, Fryer. Churlish to the core, he was keeping more and more to himself, not even joining the other officers for meals. Was he aggrieved that Fletcher had been promoted over him? Fletcher decided not — Fryer disliked everyone. And the feeling was reciprocated: no one liked him either.

Then there was the surgeon, Huggan. All now realised he was not merely incompetent, but because of his constant inebriation he was a liability. When James Valentine, a fit twenty-eight-year-old able seaman, became ill after Cape Town, Huggan opened Valentine's arm and let blood flow from the incision. This was standard treatment. But the wound was left uncleaned, became inflamed, and the man's general condition worsened. After Huggan applied blisters to his chest instead of his back, Valentine grew very ill.

William visited the patient in the forecastle and saw how serious his condition had become. He berated the surgeon. 'You're a drunken sot, Huggan. You're a fucking disgrace to medicine.' The surgeon stumbled away, muttering incomprehensibly.

Among all the company general unease deepened. If you couldn't rely on the surgeon for competence, who could you rely on?

And the case of Purcell was not over. Sentenced by William to carry out labouring duties, he complained that his warrant officer status prohibited his doing this work as well. Fletcher looked on as William told the carpenter that unless he obeyed his order he would be denied any provisions. He added, 'And anyone who comes to your assistance with their own provisions will also be punished.'

Realising this edict made his situation untenable, Purcell carried out the labourer's duties, but did so with undisguised bitterness.

William gloated to Fletcher, 'You see? I've put the scraggy sod in his place.' Fletcher said nothing but thought, all this rancour over lengths of unchopped firewood. He did his best to stay clear of the growing discord, but remained concerned about the widening cracks in the company, and the fact that William's behaviour was becoming so unbecoming. He did concede, though, that some of his outbursts were understandable. He shared William's dislike of the surly Fryer, and was relieved that his own health remained sound so that he had no need of Huggan's worthless treatments.

As a distraction from these conflicts, Fletcher firmed up his friendship with Peter Heywood. Since the midshipman's schooling had been disrupted by his joining the expedition, Fletcher began tutoring the lad in Latin, Greek and mathematics. He proved an able student, and was grateful for the help. Fletcher and Peter also got on well with another of the midshipmen, George Stewart, a stocky Orkney Islander. Fletcher, Peter and George found they had much in common: a curiosity about exotic cultures and a desire to learn all they could about them.

Twenty-one-year-old midshipman Ned Young was another the trio got on well with. Part-West Indian, Ned had curly, coal-black hair and rotting front teeth. He was an exuberant character who made it clear that he was on the voyage to have as good a time as possible. William disliked Young for this attitude, once remarking to Fletcher, 'He's a feckless fellow. It's his nigger blood coming through.'

During their stay at Adventure Bay the friendship between Fletcher, Heywood and Stewart, and to a lesser extent Young, intensified. This comradeship marked them apart from the other crewmen, who showed little interest in learning much about anything. Another exception to this rule was boatswain's mate James Morrison. A Scotsman, he was a well-read young man, and was known to be keeping a journal, against regulations. But Morrison kept very much to himself, which was not unfitting, given that one of his roles was to administer the lash. As such, he was obliged to keep his distance. But Fletcher found Morrison to be a literate, reflective man.

On one of their last days at the bay, Fletcher, Heywood and Stewart went for a walk along the shore. Gardener Nelson, just returned from his last planting, joined them. Wide-brimmed straw hat on his head, he enthusiastically described the work he had carried out on the eastern side of the bay: 'I've planted apple trees, grapevines, peach stones and pear seeds. Corn and cherries, too.' He looked up at the clear sky. 'In this climate, they should do well.' He smiled with satisfaction. 'So when you lads come back to this bay in years to come, you'll have fruit and wine aplenty!'

Just then five native men emerged from the bush and wandered down to the water. They were naked, slender and woolly haired, their facial features concealed under a thick layer of soot. Nelson stared at one of them, an elderly hunchback. 'Good God, that fellow. The cripple. I saw him when I was here with Cook.'

'Are you sure it's the same one?' asked Fletcher.

'Yes. That deformity, it's unmistakable.' Nelson hailed him. 'Hello! Hello!'

Looking up from his bent position, the man grinned, revealing that he had no teeth. The other Aboriginals chuckled. Nelson pointed to himself and said, 'I met you here once before. Eleven years ago. Are you keeping well?'

Not understanding a word, the hunchback went, 'Huh, huh, huh.' He was still grinning. Fletcher took his handkerchief from his pocket and gave it to the man. He examined it carefully, then put it on the top of his head. When the other Aboriginals burst out laughing, the visitors joined in.

After this all-round mirth the natives walked back into the bush, making melodic little cries as they went, which could have been song.

It was something of a relief when on 5 September, now fully provisioned, *Bounty*'s anchor was weighed and she sailed from Adventure Bay. All experienced officers knew that discipline was much more difficult to enforce onshore than aboard ship, when duties kept everyone occupied and purposeful and there were few distractions from the tasks at hand. Also, all aboard *Bounty* were impatient to reach their real destination.

William had set a south-east course which would loop them around the south of New Zealand, to take advantage of the Roaring Forties. They would then follow a north-east course, to pick up the mid-latitude trade winds. That would take them on a path to the west, and thence to the Windward Group of the Society Islands, the primary island of which was Tahiti.

140

The afternoon dancing routine resumed, with Byrne fiddling on, his poor eyes firmly shut against the sun. As the crew jigged and jumped and sang their shanties, their minds were concentrated on what lay ahead on Tahiti, although few of those thoughts related to breadfruit.

Meanwhile, two men aboard did their best to discredit the belief that discipline was more enforceable at sea than on land. They were John Fryer and Thomas Huggan.

The relationship between Fryer and his captain was becoming rancorous. Walking past William's cabin, Fletcher overheard a quarrel between the captain and the master. It was something to do with Fryer refusing to countersign the expenses book, a duty which had to be done monthly.

Fryer's voice grew louder. 'I refuse to sign it unless you also sign a statement certifying that my behaviour on the voyage so far has been exemplary.'

A snort from William. 'What's the point of that, man? The voyage is not even half over. I shall report on your conduct, but not until we return.'

Fryer stormed from the cabin, scowling at Fletcher as he passed.

Later over dinner, William discussed the conversation with Fletcher. He was mystified by Fryer's demand: 'Why does he want me to certify him now? It's almost as if he anticipates trouble on the ship and wants me to cover his arse, should there be any sort of enquiry when we get back home.'

'Did you sign a statement testifying to his behaviour?'

'I did not.'

Later that afternoon William called for all hands to assemble on the main deck. Once again he read the Articles of War, referring to the rules regarding 'Printed Instructions', specifically the mandatory joint signing of the expenses book by the master and the captain.

Fryer was standing on one side of William, Fletcher on the other. William's clerk, Samuel, held out the open expenses book and a quill to Fryer. With the entire crew looking on, William demanded, 'Now, sign it, Mr Fryer.'

Snatching the quill from Samuel, Fryer said loudly, 'I sign in obedience to your orders, but this may be cancelled thereafter.' And he scrawled his signature. The men looked on, incredulous. Ignoring Fryer, William told them, 'Return to your duties!'

Afterwards, in his cabin, William remarked to Fletcher, gleefully, 'You see? He signed. I was able to call the bugger's bluff.'

Fletcher said nothing, knowing that everyone else who had witnessed the altercation interpreted it differently. Fryer had not technically disobeyed a command. But his signing had been accompanied by a caveat, virtually a threat, and one which verged on the mutinous. But like Purcell, Fryer had not been punished for his open disdain. It was one of the most extraordinary scenes any of them had witnessed. What was the captain thinking?

A few days later Fletcher heard Fryer shout at William outside his cabin, 'I'll not dine with you again on this ship!' It was then that Fletcher realised that the rift between the master and the captain was unbridgeable. This knowledge troubled him. What could he do to bridge the divide between them?

On 9 October, James Valentine died.

After Huggan reported the death to William, he said, 'The man was a case of scurvy, Captain.' He made a rumbling noise. 'And I have found others.'

William erupted. 'Scurvy? On my ship? You lying fucking swine, Huggan, you pathetic apology for a surgeon. There's never been an instance of scurvy on my ship. My dietary regime precludes it. Valentine died from your botched bloodletting and general bungling!'

Huggan stumbled away to his private grog supply.

The next day Valentine was given a sea burial, the naval rites conducted by a sombre William. The mood throughout the ship was forlorn. Apart from the crew's sorrow at the death, any hand lost put more of a strain on the others to work the ship.

Valentine's only possessions — two shirts, one pair of trousers and a pair of boots — were given to the men who had cared for him during his dying hours.

25 OCTOBER 1788

A cry came from George Stewart, at *Bounty*'s masthead. It was late afternoon.

'Land! Land! To starboard!'

The sun was low, the sky pale, and *Bounty* was being driven by a ten-knot wind. Those on deck rushed to the starboard rails. The ones aloft clung to the rigging or leaned over the yards. As *Bounty* began to raise the island, all were reduced to silence at what was becoming clearer by the minute.

Peaks, jagged and forested, rose from the sea. They soared like spires into the sky and their slopes were creased into valleys. It was an ethereal sight, like a vision of an island.

Tahiti.

It had taken them ten months to get here. They had sailed twenty-seven thousand nautical miles, at an average of one hundred and eight miles a day. The voyage had been arduous, but now that their destination was in sight their tribulations were forgotten.

Away to the north-west, off the starboard quarter, was another mountainous island, its steep flanks illuminated by the sinking sun. It too had a saw-tooth profile.

The sun sank lower and the sky began to take on a blush. As *Bounty* came closer to the island ahead of them they saw that the mountains swept down to the coast, levelling out onto a plain covered with trees. They were mostly coconut palms, their crowns inclined towards the sea. Interspersed with them were much sturdier trees.

William joined Fletcher and Peter on the quarterdeck. Below them, Fryer stood behind the helmsman, Linkletter, and the boatswain, Cole. It was very hot, and they were all in their shirtsleeves.

'Two points to larboard,' Fryer ordered, eyes on the compass. Linkletter moved the wheel: *Bounty* swung, shuddered, then settled again.

William murmured, 'Quite a sight, is it not?'

Fletcher shook his head in wonder. 'Amazing. I've never seen anything like it.'

'Those mountains …' Peter began, then was lost for words.

William smiled. 'Cook told me that although he had approached Tahiti several times, he could never get over the sight. He was not a sentimental man, but he loved this island.'

Fletcher pointed towards the more distant island. 'What is that one?'

'Moorea,' William told him. 'The people in the north of the island are the enemies of the Tahitians. After our goats were stolen there, Cook laid waste to several villages.'

Bounty came closer to their destination and they saw a ruffle of white water directly ahead. The reef. The ocean swells were streaming towards it, then erupting in bursts of spray which hung in the air briefly, then dissolved into the blue. Inside the reef the lagoon water was still and shiny, in contrast to the choppy water surrounding them. A few hundred yards to starboard a flock of feeding terns, wings fluttering, were hovering, then diving into the sea.

Fletcher kept staring at the island, mesmerised. He had heard that Tahiti was beautiful, but this was beyond expectations. The reef and lagoon, those mountains, the valleys, the forest. This place must be like no other on Earth.

William called down to Linkletter, 'Bring her to, we'll not go in until the morning. The pass is four leagues to the north-west.' And to Cole he ordered, 'Call the crew to assemble.'

William looked at his sheet of prepared notes, then down at the men. 'The following are your instructions while ashore on this island. Any infringement of them will incur the severest of penalties.

'Firstly, there is to be no mention of the death of our great Captain Cook. The fact that he was killed by Indians could work to our fatal disadvantage. If questioned, say that Tute — that is what the Tahitians call him — is retired from the sea and living in Peretane, their name for Britain.

'Secondly, make no mention yet of the purpose of our expedition. The fact that we are here to acquire breadfruit plants is a matter which I alone will negotiate with the island's leaders. Until I do so, divulge nothing of our intentions.

'You are to treat the natives with every possible consideration. Remember, we will be guests on their island, so behave towards them as all good guests should. Do not steal or show violence of any kind. Fire upon them only if your own life is in peril.

'I warn you, however, that the Tahitians, like all natives, have a propensity to thieve. Therefore it is your responsibility, if placed in charge of valuable implements, firearms in particular, to guard those items with every possible care. Should they be stolen, their cost will be charged against you. Furthermore, it is forbidden for you to exchange any item of *Bounty*'s store for items which the natives may wish to exchange.

'I am appointing Peckover in charge of all trade with the natives. As many of you know, he sailed to these islands with Cook on all three of his voyages, and consequently speaks the natives' language well. Peckover?' The gunner held up his hand. He was a wiry man with greying hair tied back in a queue. 'I trust you to carry out that important duty with due diligence and honesty. Is that clear?'

'Aye, Captain.'

'So, the rest of you, always bear this in mind: any trade that you wish to carry out with the natives must be done only through Peckover.'

William folded his sheet of notes. 'One more instruction. Before the arrival of Europeans there were no venereals on this island. But when I came here with Cook in '77, many of the natives were poxed. We deduced that the venereals had been introduced here by Bougainville's men who came in 1768, then the Spanish, who came in '74. Like Cook, I am determined that we will not spread the venereals further among the Tahitians. To this end, no one who shows venereal symptoms will be permitted ashore. You are all required to be examined today by surgeon Huggan.' William's gaze swept the company. 'Huggan? Where's Huggan?'

When his hand did not appear, McCoy called out, 'He must be sleeping orf the grog, Captain.' The crew chortled. William called down to McCoy, 'In that case, go down and wake him. And get him to examine your cock first.'

'Maeva!' 'Maeva!' 'Maeva!'
   'Taio!' 'Taio!' 'Taio!'

The cries of 'Welcome!' and 'Friend!' came from the mouths of hundreds of Tahitians. Their canoes had put out from the shore at first light as *Bounty* was being worked through the pass and into Matavai Bay. Some canoes carried drummers whose frantic beating filled the morning air. Many of the people were chanting and a few men blew on conches, so that the bay thrummed with ecstatic sounds.

Two hundred yards from the shore, Fryer ordered *Bounty*'s bow anchors lowered. The outriggers surrounded the ship, and their occupants — women, men and children — swarmed aboard. They smiled delightedly at the crew, whose mouths were agog at the invasion. The women — most bare-breasted and in bark cloth skirts, their brown skin glistening with monoi oil — carried garlands of the native blossom, tiare, which they placed around the necks of all the sailors. The Tahitian men carried woven baskets of pork, fish and fruit which they placed at the base of the mainmast.

The sailors continued to stare, entranced. Most had experienced nothing like the warmth and spontaneity of this all-embracing reception.

William and Fletcher, both in dress uniform on the quarterdeck, stood out as the ship's leaders. Accordingly, they were garlanded more heavily than the rest. Bedecked with the blossoms, Fletcher brought a garland up to his nose. Its fragrance was sweet and heady, almost intoxicating.

The captain asked Peckover to tell the Tahitian men that he wished to speak to their leaders. The gunner, obviously enjoying this new

146

responsibility, stepped forward. Although his Tahitian was stumbling, the men understood, nodding and muttering, 'Ae, ae, ae.'

Peckover reported to William. 'Some chiefs will come aboard tomorrow.'

Already the garlanded crew were choosing women and taking them by the hand. Some were leading them down the companionways, their intention obvious. Fletcher looked at William to gauge his reaction. He appeared unconcerned, so much so that Fletcher, surprised, asked William, 'You have no objection to the women going below?'

'No.' He leaned over the rail. 'If we allow the Tahitians to establish friendships, to find special taios, to use their word, then they are more likely to cooperate, and allow us to have their breadfruit.'

'But the venereals—'

William waved a hand dismissively. 'Huggan has assured me that none of the men are infected.'

Fletcher looked away, thinking this improbable. Several of the men had told him they had symptoms of the pox. Again he wondered at William's judgment. Placing his faith in Huggan's diagnosis, when he had recently castigated the surgeon for his incompetence, was at the very least optimistic. Not that Fletcher blamed the men for their lust: under the circumstances it was entirely understandable. He longed for some cunny himself. After all, disregarding the sooty creatures of Adventure Bay, it was many months since any of them had seen a woman. And for him the Dutch woman, Meike, was now just a distant memory.

So the women stayed, and below decks there was mass, joyful copulation. The law of supply and demand greatly favoured the crew. For every seaman there were two or more women. Several times a hammock's ropes broke, sending its occupants — a heaving man and two frantic females — tumbling to the boards. After nightfall, others fucked on the decks. Fletcher looked on enviously; William pretended it wasn't happening.

Next morning *Bounty* was moved to a more secure anchorage, closer to the shore. Five chiefs were paddled out and came aboard. After gifts were exchanged — beads and mirrors for cooked pigs and plantains — Peckover was able to establish that these were only minor leaders. William was disappointed by their lack of status, but they assured him that their paramount chief, Tu, would shortly be brought out to meet him.

Through Peckover, one of the chiefs, a rotund fellow, asked, 'How is Tute?'

William replied. 'Captain Tute is very well. He is retired from the sea now, and is living with Mrs Cook and their children in their house in London.'

The man frowned. Again with Peckover translating, he said: 'Another ship from Peretane came to Tahiti, a few months ago. Its name was *Lady Penrhyn*. Some of its sailors told us that Tute had been killed, in Hawaii, years ago.'

Colouring slightly, William shook his head. 'No, no, Tute lives. And he sent me, his son, to Tahiti, to send his best wishes to the people here.'

The chiefs looked confused for a moment. Then one asked, 'You are the son of Tute?'

'Yes. I, William Bligh, am the son of Captain Cook.'

The men's faces broke into smiles. 'Ah, ah. Maeva, Parai, son of Tute. Manuia Parai!'

Observing these blatant untruths, Fletcher smiled. When it suited his purposes, the man could lie at the drop of a cocked hat.

He peered again at the land through his spyglass, impatient to get ashore. Point Venus, where Cook observed the transit of the planet nineteen years ago, was a level promontory covered in coconut palms, plantains and breadfruit trees. Fletcher saw that a stream flowed into the lagoon from the centre of the point, and that the western shore of Matavai Bay was bordered by a black-sand beach. He raised his spyglass a little. Inland the terrain rose steeply, first to forested foothills, then to the jagged peaks they had first seen two days ago. Steep-sided valleys separated the mountains; waterfalls cascaded down their sides, glittering in the morning sun. Bruise-black rainclouds were gathering about the mountaintops.

Clearly, Fletcher decided, Point Venus would be the ideal collection centre for the breadfruit plants, as well as for making repairs to the ship. There was wood and water aplenty nearby. Coconuts, too. Swinging his spyglass to the right, he could see a mile or so away a clearing in which there was a large, open-sided house, thatched with palm fronds. Smoke from an earth oven beside the house rose into the air. Could that be the paramount chief's residence?

Later that morning William held a briefing with Fletcher, Heywood, Peckover and the gardeners, Nelson and Brown. 'You will all go ashore today,' he ordered. 'Take spare sails and a tent with you, and erect them as shelters, in the centre of Point Venus. That will comprise our shore encampment and the site for a breadfruit plant nursery. Able seamen Lamb, Ellison, Tinkler and Williams will go with you, to assist.

'Acting Lieutenant Christian, you will stay ashore and be in charge of the camp. Take all your necessary belongings, including your hammock. The seamen will be issued with muskets, as a deterrent against thieving by the natives. Armourer Coleman will also go ashore too, and set up a forge on the point. The axes and knives we traded with the natives back in '77 are sorely in need of repair, I've been told.' William paused. 'We must do everything we can to earn the natives' friendship, so that the breadfruit plants will accrue to the nursery. Peckover, you will use your linguistic skills as trade supervisor for the breadfruit.'

Fletcher was delighted to be given his new role. Once ashore, he slung his hammock between the trunks of two coconut palms. Looking up into their crowns, he saw clusters of yellow nuts. Food and drink, growing at his front and back door! Stripping to the waist, he supervised the erection of the tarpaulin shelters. The ship's boats had transported the hundreds of pots to the shore, and Nelson and Brown were stacking them under the trees, ready for filling with earth and breadfruit shoots. Nelson explained to Fletcher that the breadfruit grows not from seeds, but from suckers and shoots from a mature tree's roots. Tanned and bearded, Nelson contrasted strongly with Brown, who was short, tubby and in spite of his name, very pale. But both men looked the part of dedicated horticulturalists, wearing wreaths of tiare flowers around the crowns of their straw hats.

Later that day William came ashore and inspected the camp. There had been squally rain in the morning but the sky had cleared, although the ground was still damp under the palms and the air was muggy. The improvised shelters, their corners roped firmly to palm tree trunks, had held up well in the wind and rain.

Fletcher offered William a coconut and he swigged its juice. Nodding approvingly at the pots, now laid out in serried rows, he said, 'A miniature Kew Gardens. Sir Joseph Banks would be delighted.' He tossed the nut aside. 'Fletcher, I am shortly to meet Tu, the Tahitians' high chief. When I do, I want you to be there too.'

'Why so?'

'Tu is, Peckover reports, from the highest class of Tahitians. He's the ari'i rahi, the highest chief. He's also been an arioi, another exclusive class. So it's fitting that you accompany me when I meet him.'

'I don't follow you, William.'

'You, too, are of an upper-class background.'

Fletcher found it hard not to laugh. 'William, I am from the aristocracy of Cumbria and the Isle of Man. Minor aristocracy. He is a paramount chief. All the chief and I have in common is that we are both islanders.'

William's expression became strained. 'My point is, Fletcher, that you are from a class higher than my own. And it shows in your bearing. The Tahitian people are greatly conscious of status. Cook learned that, and so did Banks. The Tahitian rulers truly respect only those of a class similar to themselves. Those men who visited us at first were lesser chiefs. Tu is the most important leader. Those of his class have contempt for the lower class, the manahune, and even more so for the very lowest class, the teu teu. Conversely, they have deep respect for the upper class.

'It's my impression that most of the women who have come aboard *Bounty* are teu teu.' He snorted. 'Fitting, since most of our crew are from England's lowest class. Our own teu teu. But as I said, there is no one else among *Bounty*'s company who is of your elevated background. I have the authority of naval command, you have the authority which stems from your lineage. So it's fitting that you are with me when I meet with the high chief. It will help our cause.' His eyes bored into Fletcher's. 'All right?'

'Very well.' But he thought, that is a very odd stance for the captain to adopt.

When Tu, his wife and their retinue were paddled into Matavai Bay in their pahi, a large double-hulled canoe, Fletcher greeted them on the beach, dressed in his officer's uniform. That too was suitable protocol, William had told him. The chief must be met by a person in authority, in keeping with his great status.

Tu certainly looked the part. He was tall, well over six feet, and powerfully built. A tangled bush of dark curly hair covered the sides of his face. He had a straggled moustache, a prominent nose and a small clump of wiry hair on his chin. Itia, his wife, was short and very fat, with long dark hair which hung loose. Both leaders were wrapped in several layers of white bark cloth.

Fletcher offered the chief and his wife his hand and greeted them the way Peckover had instructed him. 'Ia ora na. Maeva. To'u i'oa o, Lieutenant Fletcher Christian, of King George's ship, HMAV *Bounty*.'

Visibly impressed with Fletcher's uniform and demeanour, Tu inclined his head respectfully, then said, 'Maururu roa. To'u i'oa o, Tu. Ia ora na. Maeva.'

They were paddled out to the ship in the pahi. The three men and three women manahune accompanying the leaders had baskets of food in their laps. One man carried something wrapped in tapa cloth.

The canoe drew alongside *Bounty* and they all disembarked, Fletcher leading. Itia was so ungainly it took two seamen to get her up onto the deck. William greeted them at the starboard gate, removing his cocked hat and bowing. 'Welcome, Chief Tu. Welcome Mistress Itia. Welcome to this ship of the navy of King George of Peretane, HMAV *Bounty*.'

Fletcher stood back, now deferring to William. Observing the scene, he saw that it had a slightly absurd aspect. William was so

151

short, the chief so tall, the one pale, the other bronzed. William's head reached only to Tu's chest. Because of this, his authority seemed diminished. Fletcher had been told that the natives revered physical size and prowess. If that was so, William did not stack up. Yet Tu was treating him respectfully, in keeping with his status as commander of this vaka nui, this big ship.

On deck, gifts were given and received. Lengths of bark cloth, a large cooked pig and some breadfruit from the Tahitians were exchanged for adzes, axes, knives, files, a saw and mirrors from William to Tu. To Itia, William presented beads, necklaces and earrings. To Fletcher's amusement Itia showed indifference towards these geegaws, indicating that she was much more interested in the axes.

Tu then beckoned a man to come forward, the one who was carrying the parcel. He handed it to Tu, who handed it to William, who opened it.

'Good God ...'

It was a portrait of James Cook, painted in oils on canvas. His expression was stern, his features haggard.

Fletcher stared at it, amazed. 'Who did it?' he asked William.

'John Webber, our artist, when we were here in '77.' He said to Tu, 'You have been looking after this for many years?'

The chief nodded. 'Tute ari'i no Tahiti.'

Peckover translated. 'That means, he calls the picture "Cook, the high chief of Tahiti". It is a treasured object to his people, I think.'

'Yes, yes.' William handed the portrait back. 'You must keep it. Tute's son orders you to keep his portrait. Forever.'

William and Tu then exchanged names, signifying that each was now the valued taio of the other. William murmured to Fletcher, 'Being taios means we will always support each other. Including supplying plenty of breadfruit for us.'

They went below decks to the dining room, Itia included. William told Fletcher that normally Tahitian men and women dined separately, but Itia's distinguished status meant that this edict would be waived. With Peckover's language skills again being put to good use, William explained the purpose of their visit. What they needed, he told Tu, were young uru, breadfruit plants, to take back to King George of Peretane. He wished to grow them in his palace garden, in London.

Tu nodded, Parai could have all the uru he wished. He also explained that Matari'i'i'raro, the Season of Scarcity when the breadfruit was not mature, was nearly over. Matari'i'i'ni'a, the Season of Plenty, when much rain came, would shortly be upon them. The breadfruit would from then on be ripening, he said. But the young breadfruit shoots would be suitable for transplanting now.

As the chief and his entourage were farewelled, Tu told them that William, Fletcher and Peckover — who had obviously earned mana from his good spoken Tahitian — would be welcome as Tu's guests the next day, at his fare nui, his big house along the coast at Pare. He would send a servant to guide them there.

Nudging Fletcher, William said jubilantly, 'You see? My tactics worked.' Aware that Peckover had overheard him, he warned, 'Don't bother translating that.'

The trio walked inland, guided by a barefoot boy. In spite of the cloying heat, both William and Fletcher again wore their uniforms, including cocked hats; William had buckled on his sword. Peckover, though, wore a plain jacket and cap.

A well-formed trail led up through the forest, then veered right and ran parallel to the coast. Overhead were the crowns of huge trees: tamanu, toa, mape and uru, their leaves dripping from recent rain. Shrubs of flowering aute, fara and tiare grew prolifically, and clumps of plantains were everywhere. The foliage exuded an earthy smell, overlaid with the scent of wild herbs. Colourful parrots called to one another, then flew away at the men's approach. William and Fletcher swatted away insistent, buzzing insects with their hats.

After an hour's walk through the forest, trailing the boy, they were all sweating profusely and it was a relief when they reached a clearing. 'Here it is,' Peckover announced, panting. 'The fare nui of chief Tu.'

Built atop a long mound, the house occupied the centre of the clearing. A crowd of onlookers had gathered around it, and they burst into excited conversations as the servant boy and the trio of Popa'a — foreigners — emerged from the forest. Some of the women began to sing and sway their hips; others tossed tiare blossoms at the visitors.

The house was open-sided, its palm-frond roof supported by timber posts. Tu and Itia, both still wrapped in white cloth cloaks, greeted their guests by touching noses, then led them into the house. A mat of bark cloth like a hall runner was laid out along the length of the building, and seated at one end was Tu's extended family, including his father, grey-haired Teina, and Tu's young son. Behind them on a wooden platform was a display of food: two large cooked pigs, several baked tuna, sticks of sugar cane and fruits of all kinds. A large carved 'ava bowl had been placed in front of the food.

Tu went to William and wound a length of white bark cloth around his shoulders. It was large and bulky. Encased in this cloth carapace, his bare head protruding from it, William resembled an albino turtle, Fletcher thought.

Tu indicated that he and William should walk the length of the long mat and back again. As they did so Tu's voice boomed out. 'Parai, taio. Tama e Tute!' 'Good friend Bligh! Son of Tute!'

The spectators looking on echoed his acclamation, crying out 'Fa'aitoito!' 'Well said!'

Fletcher sat to one side, observing the scene and the ceremony. He was entranced. The cheering and singing crowd, the women's seductive dancing, the exoticness and exuberance — it was all captivating.

Tu and William sat down in front of the chief's family, with Fletcher and Peckover to one side. A servant filled a coconut shell cup with 'ava and handed it to Tu, who drank from it, then passed it to William. He sipped it, then passed the cup on hurriedly to Fletcher. He took a mouthful. It looked and tasted like a muddy puddle, but had an aftertaste that was refreshing. Thirst-quenching, too, although it left his lips a little numb.

As Fletcher passed the shell cup to Peckover, he noticed someone on the other side of the fare, next to one of the pillars. A young woman, sitting cross-legged on a mat by herself, wearing a cape of white bark cloth. She had a mane of long black hair and a scarlet hibiscus flower behind her right ear.

Unable to resist, and seeing that William was now eating with Tu's party, Fletcher went over to her. He indicated that he wished to sit next to her. 'Ia ora na. May I?'

She nodded, then looked at him inquisitively. Her face was oval, her nose slightly flattened, her cheekbones prominent. She looked to be in her mid-twenties. He sat down and crossed his legs, then beckoned Peckover over. 'Tell her who I am, and where I'm from.'

Peckover said to her, 'O Fletcher Christian to'u i'oa. No te mai rau Peretane.'

She nodded, then tapped her breast. 'O Mauatua to'u i'oa.' Her eyes were lustrous, almost black.

'Ah ...' said Fletcher, rolling the vowels. 'Mow-ah-too-ah.'

'Ae.'

She smiled, showing bright white teeth, then placed her hands in her lap. She stared at his uniform, then his face, assessing both. He noticed that the back of her right hand, and all her fingers, were intricately tattooed. The fingers themselves were very long and slender. Like Isabella's.

Fletcher said to Peckover. 'Tell her, tell Mauatua, that she is very beautiful.'

He did so, and she smiled. She's not unused to compliments, Fletcher thought.

He wanted to be with her, alone.

'Ask her, if she would like to walk with me.'

As Peckover did so he watched anxiously for her reaction. She blushed slightly, then posed a question. Peckover said, 'She wants to know when.'

'Now.'

Peckover asked her and she responded unhesitatingly. 'Ae.'

Then she reached out and put her hand on Fletcher's sweaty brow. She held it there for a moment, frowned, then said, 'Mahanahana.'

'She says you're very hot,' Peckover said.

Fletcher nodded, only too aware of that fact.

When she stood up, Fletcher was taken aback. She was very tall, only a little less so than he was. And slender-limbed. She glanced around. People were watching. She gestured for him to follow.

Peckover returned to his interpreting duties. When Fletcher looked across at William, he saw that he was deep in mimed conversation with Tu and Itia.

Fletcher and Mauatua passed through the crowd of spectators, she leading. The people murmured to one another and nodded approvingly at the handsome pair.

She walked tall and perfectly upright, her head held high. She didn't follow the path that he had come by, instead turning off to the right and along another, steeper trail. 'Where are we going?' he asked. She stopped, looked at him quizzically. 'Where are we going?' he repeated, pointing ahead. She nodded, understanding, then made sweeping gestures with her arms. He frowned, then said, 'Swimming?' Without replying she resumed walking, her bare feet pressing into the mud of the track. He followed, admiring her slim figure and the mane of coal-black hair.

He heard the sound of gushing water before he saw the cascade. Brushing aside some ferns, she led him into a clearing. Above it was a waterfall, pouring into a pool several yards across. The water streamed through a chasm between two boulders, then crashed into the pool. Around it were grasses with bright yellow and red flowers and a little further back, forest giants with enormous boughs, epiphytes entwined around them. The water streamed out through a channel on the lower side of the pool.

Sheltered from any breeze, the clearing was searingly hot. Overhead the sky was as blue and bright as a stained-glass window.

Mauatua pointed at the waterfall. 'Vaiharuru,' she said.

'Vay-ha-roo-roo,' he repeated, and she smiled at his clumsy inflections.

'Aita. No. Vai-ha-*ru*-ru.'

She sat on the sedge at the edge of the pool and slipped her feet into the water, indicating that Fletcher should do the same. He tugged off his muddy boots, then removed his hat and jacket. Rolling up his hose, he put his feet into the water. In spite of the sweltering air, it was icy cold, and he gasped at the contrast. Laughing, Mauatua flicked back her hair.

Fletcher rubbed his bare feet. Becoming accustomed to the cold, he sighed with pleasure at the water's freshness. Beside him, Mauatua cupped some in her hands and splashed it over her face. Noticing again the tattoos on her right hand, he took it in his. Tracing the intricate, blue-black lines, which resembled a glove of blue lace, he asked, 'Was it painful? To have this done?' He thought for a moment, then screwed up his face and flinched hard, miming pain.

Understanding, she nodded, and mimicked his pained expression. 'Ae. Tah-tau.'

'Tattoo.'

She shook her head. 'Aita. *Tah*-tau.'

They both laughed.

Then, without warning, she stood up and removed her cape and skirt. Fletcher gasped. Her skin was pale, and shone with monoi oil. He stared, spellbound.

Then she turned, took a few steps forward, raised her arms and dived neatly into the pool. She vanished for several seconds. The red hibiscus flower bobbed to the surface and floated there. She surfaced, her face towards him, her mouth wide open. She swept her hair back, then beckoned him forward. Seconds later he was beside her in the cool, translucent water.

'I am Fletcher Christian,' he said, standing on the sandy floor of the pool and touching his chest.

She shook her head. The surname was unpronounceable to her. She reached out and touched his shoulder. 'Tee-ter-ree-ah-naw.'

He was newly christened. Titereano.

He took her in his arms. They were both cool now, and dripping. He put his face to hers, his mouth seeking her lips. But she pulled away, saying 'Nei, nei,' and instead put her nose against his, and blew a breath through it. It was warm, and smelled of something sweet. Some sort of fruit, perhaps. They touched noses again, then he held her, and they went to the grass at the side of the pool.

Minutes later they came together.

And from that moment on, the lives of both of them were changed forever.

TAHITI, OCTOBER 1788–APRIL 1789

Later, he would recall those weeks as the happiest of his life. His role as commander of the shore camp, never demanding, became less so as the weeks went by. It required him only to oversee the breadfruit collecting of the gardeners and ensure that the duty seamen maintained security at the nursery. This was not difficult, as there was no thieving by the local Tahitians. In fact they seemed pleased to help, willingly transferring the cut shoots to the camp, and assisting to pot them.

Mauatua's family fare was a fifteen-minute walk east of Point Venus, on an elevated headland. From now on Fletcher stayed there, calling at the plant nursery every other day to check on the potting. When he realised his presence was largely superfluous — Nelson and Brown were preoccupied with their horticultural duties — he paid fewer visits to the point.

Consequently he saw less and less of William. So did the rest of the crew. The captain either entertained Tu, Itia and their feti'i — the extended family — aboard *Bounty*, or was a guest ashore, at the fare nui at Pare or at one of the marae along Tahiti's northern coast. It became obvious to the crew that William preferred the company of the Tahitian chiefs to them.

That suited the crew, too. Once the essential maintenance on *Bounty* had been carried out — the sails dried and repaired, the seams recaulked, the rigging checked — they idled their time away, both on the ship and ashore. They fished with lines from the decks, then brought aboard and cooked their catches. If rostered for shore leave by Fryer, they roamed the coastal plain with their taios. Many brought women back to the ship. There the vahines stayed, had sex and helped prepare meals in the galley, cooking the fish and the pork they brought aboard. *Bounty* had become a comfortable hub, lacking authority. The very antithesis of a Royal Navy ship.

Late in October William paid a visit to Point Venus when Fletcher was there. After glancing at the rows of potted plants, he told Fletcher, 'I am to be the honoured guest at another heiva today. At Papy-noo. I will be paddled along the lagoon to the marae there. I will probably stay three days.'

In the tropical heat he still wore his formal uniform. Adjusting his wig, he added, 'These people continue to treat me royally. Two days ago, at Aru-aye, I was carried across a river by four warriors, then borne onto the marae on their shoulders.' He added as an afterthought, 'Fryer remains in charge of *Bounty*.'

He strode off, clerk Samuel following with a canvas pack filled with gifts for his hosts. McCoy, one of the guards on greenhouse duty, had overheard William's little speech. He sniggered, and remarked to his friend Quintal, 'Thinks hisself the fuckin' king of Tahiti now.'

Although Fletcher ignored the comment, he had come to much the same conclusion. William's sense of his own importance was being inflated through the hospitality of the natives towards him. But this munificence, Fletcher believed, derived principally from William's gift-giving, and his ongoing dissemination of the fiction that he was the son of Captain Tute.

Fletcher's days were now filled with love-making, swimming and exploring the forest with Mauatua. They swam at the waterfall pool, Vaiharuru, and at Matavai Bay's beach. Never in his life had Fletcher felt so clean and fit and healthy. Leaving his uniform at the encampment, most days he wore just his sailor's trousers. His skin was becoming deeply tanned. He not only looked like a native, he felt like one.

And Mauatua's lithe body continued to enchant him.

Once, while kissing her bare armpit, he asked, 'Why is there no hair here?' He stroked her bare mons Veneris. 'Or here?'

She laughed. 'We take away hair. Like this.' She reached for one of his pubic hairs, and plucked it between her fingers. Wincing, he said, 'I will leave my hair there. But I shall take on the responsibility of plucking yours.'

A natural linguist, Fletcher picked up her language quickly, appreciating the vowel-rich Tahitian. The names of trees, plants, flowers and places he absorbed and memorised, while at the same time teaching her English words and phrases. The Tahitian phrase 'Aita papu' — 'I don't understand' — and its English equivalent, they used less and less.

There were other words they taught one another. 'What is your name for this?' he asked, caressing her. 'Raho,' she said, gasping. 'You call?'

'Cunny.'

She reached down and took him in hand, tenderly. 'We call this one ure.'

'Ah,' said Fletcher. 'Ure and raho. Nice names. They go well together.'

She told him of her lineage. Her family were high-born: her now-deceased father had been an important ari'i. She had been brought up mainly by her grandmother, Tetua. It was she who had rolled Mauatua's fingers between hers when she was a baby, and stretched them, every day, so that they grew long and slender. Grandmother Tetua had also pressed Mauatua's baby nose with her forefinger for a few minutes each day, so that it became slightly flattened. Long fingers and a flattened nose, Mauatua explained, signified beauty. Her mother, Maoiti, encouraged her to weave and plait and make bark cloth, activities which, unlike working the soil, would protect her fine fingers. 'Only teu teu put their hands in the earth,' her mother told her.

'Your hands are beautiful,' Fletcher said, tracing the outline of her tattoos. 'And your nose.' He brought his gently onto hers. She laughed with delight.

160

She was eager to learn about his family and how they lived. When he told her they had once owned a fare nui and fenua — a big house and land — but had lost both, she was mystified. 'How can land be lost?' she asked, waving her fingers towards the horizon to suggest infinity. 'Land is owned by a feti'i forever.'

Fletcher shook his head. 'Not in Peretane,' he said. 'My family's land has gone from us forever.'

Mauatua looked horrified: to her, such a loss was inconceivable. Then, when he told her about the Isle of Man, she asked what trees grew on Fletcher's island. Breadfruit? Coconuts? Bananas?

'No,' he replied each time, at the same time loving her for the questions.

She remembered the visits that Captain Tute had made to her island, even though she had been only a little girl during his first one. Her grandmother had been a taio of Tute's and took her to see the sacred Webber portrait at Tu's fare. Everyone had loved the great Captain Tute.

One morning she took Fletcher a little way inland and showed him a garden plot and English vegetables whose seeds had been planted by Tute's gardener during his second visit to Tahiti. Although the plot had been invaded by weeds, the plants were still growing vigorously, and seeding. Her people collected the seeds, to grow the English plants in their own gardens. He told her the names of the vegetables in the plot and she repeated them carefully: 'Pum-kin. Pee. Pean. Pars-nip. Car-rot. Ca-bage.'

Peter Heywood had also made a special taio, a cheery girl with almond eyes called Maire. Also a member of Mauatua's chiefly extended family, Maire had the habit of breaking into song whenever she felt happy, a state which she seemed constantly in when with Peter. And as she sang, her hands traced patterns in the air and she swayed her hips languidly.

Peter had moved into Maire's family's fare at Arue, where he was made very welcome. He too was learning Tahitian, under Maire's tutelage. 'Her name means Fern of the Gods,' he told Fletcher.

'Tahitian's an uncomplicated language. There are no genders, no declensions, no conjugations. Although the vowels are pronounced more like they are in Spanish, there are just five of them, as in English.' He showed Fletcher a notebook. 'I'm compiling a dictionary.' In it he had listed common words and phrases in Tahitian, and their English equivalents.

He recited one entry to Fletcher, speaking like a schoolmaster to his pupil: 'O vai to oe i'oa? Meaning, "What is your name?" O Peter to'u i'oa. My name is Peter.' He said challengingly, 'Get it, Fletcher?'

'Yes. Mauatua has already taught me how to say that. O Titereano to'u i 'oa.'

'Impressive. Now, can you say "I love you"?' Peter was grinning.

'Ae. Ua here vauia oe.' He smiled. 'It is a statement I have had much cause to use, recently.'

'Indeed, I have used it much myself.' Peter laughed. 'It's a most common statement to make, on this island.' He brandished the notebook. 'When we return to England I shall get this published.'

Fletcher nodded, but the words 'return to England' were chilling. Although he often thought of his family, he thought less and less of England or the Isle of Man. What he had discovered on this island, especially the love of Mauatua, was precious. When she lay in his arms on the fare mat, their love-making complete, his thoughts began to border on the subversive. Why should he return to England? For the sake of a few hundred sodding breadfruit plants? Which were destined to sustain a system he despised — slavery.

He lay on his back staring up at the underside of the palm fronds. Mauatua was asleep now beside him. The scent of their bodies, combined with that of the tipani blooms and monoi oil, clung about them both. Closing his eyes, he thought, this island could be where the rest of my life could lie.

One morning he and Mauatua walked through the forest so she could show him her people's special marae, Tarahoi. It was forbidden for her to go onto the marae because it was only for men, she told him. 'For vahine it is ra'a. Forbidden. But you can go.'

162

They emerged from the forest, hand-in-hand, and entered a large clearing. Mauatua stood well back while Fletcher walked over to the marae.

It consisted of a series of tiered stone slab platforms, rising in steps and culminating in what looked like an altar, also of stone. Surrounding the complex were coconut palms, flowering tipani trees and pandanus shrubs. To one side of the marae was a squat statue carved from pitted red stone, about six feet high and five feet wide.

Fletcher walked up to the highest tier. On it was a wooden frame, and dangling from it were strips of bark cloth and dozens of bleached human jawbones. Heaps of other bones lay beneath the frame. There were several rotting pig carcasses there too, putrid and swarming with flies.

Although the marae setting was bucolic, the sight of the bones and the stench of the rotting flesh made Fletcher blench. There was a sinister atmosphere about this place: it reeked of violent death. How many gruesome ceremonies, he wondered, had it witnessed?

Mauatua had earlier told him something of the terrible war that had occurred between her people and those who lived at Tahiti-Iti, at the other end of the island, when she was a little girl. There had been many, many deaths, she said.

Fletcher's misgivings about the marae's purpose were confirmed after he rejoined her at the edge of the forest. He asked her, 'Whose bones are those on the marae? Enemies of your people?'

She hesitated, searching for the words. 'Not enemies.' She mimed someone being struck on the back of the head. 'Men killed for atua. For gods.'

He understood. 'Sacrifice. Human sacrifice.'

'Suck-ree-fice.' She rolled the word around in her mouth.

'Who were they? The people sacrificed?'

'Teu teu man. Always teu teu man killed for atua.' They weren't killed on the marae, she explained, they were killed elsewhere, then their bodies were brought here. She explained this matter-of-factly.

'And that statue?' He pointed at the stone image.

'Tee-kee. Atua.'

'A god?'

'Ae. Teekee atua. Tapu.' She pointed towards the serrated peaks that loomed above the clearing. Bunches of dark clouds were roiling over their summits. Mauatua waved her hand in that direction. 'In mountains, many, many marae.'

On their return to Matavai, the clouds broke and rain fell in torrents. As they sheltered under a huge banyan tree, Mauatua looked out at the rain. 'Matari'i'i'ni'a. Te tau miti rahi,' she announced. 'Season of plenty, season of rain and storms, has started.'

On the last day of November Fletcher put on trousers, shirt and boots and returned to *Bounty*. He needed to collect a notebook, quill and ink from his cabin. He had decided it was time he started a journal recording his experiences on Tahiti, a decision inspired by his reading of the vivid journal Banks had kept back in 1769.

While searching for the writing materials among his belongings, Fletcher was struck by how constricted the cabin was, compared to his accommodation ashore. Being back here was like being a prisoner in a cell, or a cock in a coop. The air was fetid, still stinking of the body odours which had been washed away in Matavai Bay and at the waterfall pool. In confirmation of the cabin's cramped nature, as he stood up he cracked his head on the ceiling. Leaving the cabin, rubbing his scalp, he saw William entering his. The captain stopped, and looked surprised.

'Fletcher, good day. We have seen so little of each other of late.' He held open his cabin door. 'Come and chat.'

They sat facing each other over the table. William was wigless, and wore just his blouse and breeches. Fletcher noticed he had put on weight: the blouse now strained to cope with his bulging belly. His parsnip-pale face contrasted with the crescents of darkness under his eyes. Fame is obviously an exhausting business, Fletcher thought.

They chatted. William was affable and relaxed. Yes, Nelson and Brown were doing a grand job. They had already collected several hundred breadfruit plants. No, there had been hardly any thefts by the Tahitians. But yes, the time was dragging on. What was supposed to take eight weeks had already taken ten. But no, it was not his fault: that was caused by their delay in leaving England. And yes, the Admiralty officials were to blame for the lateness, for they had caused *Bounty*'s much-delayed departure and subsequent loss of time. If they had sailed when they were supposed to, the work would have been finished by now.

Fletcher listened without comment to this familiar litany. As always, William sounded both confident and condemnatory. If there was a fault, it always lay elsewhere.

Changing the subject, Fletcher said, 'I've been told that the storm season is imminent here.'

'Really?' William sounded unconcerned.

'Yes. So it occurred to me that *Bounty* should be moved to a more sheltered anchorage. For reasons of safety.'

'Oh? You know what the weather is going to do, do you?'

Ignoring his sarcasm, Fletcher said, 'Evidently from December onwards, wild weather often comes from the north. In which case *Bounty* could be vulnerable.'

'Today the sky is blue, the wind merely a zephyr. The ship is firmly anchored fore and aft. We cannot waste time moving her.'

Fletcher shrugged. 'The decision is yours. I merely suggested the move.'

William met his level look. For some moments he was silent, staring intently at Fletcher to the extent that it made him feel uneasy. He looked away. Feeling his hands becoming slippery, he rubbed them on his breeches.

Then, changing tack, William said, 'Two days ago I was the guest at a heiva, at Aroo-aye. It was most interesting. Along with the usual singing, dancing, drumming and all the rest of it, there were some mahoo there.' He paused. 'Do you know what mahoo are?'

'I've been told. Men who behave like women.'

'That's right. Big strong men, but they wear flowers and shell jewellery, and exhibit female mannerisms.' William rubbed at his stubbly chin. 'Curious about the mahoo's private parts, I took the chance to closely examine one. I asked, first, naturally, if he, or she, I should say, would let me look closely between its legs. The mahoo agreed, then lay down and opened its legs. And I examined it closely.' William gave a half-smile. 'The penis and testicles had been pulled right back and tied, so that they were hardly visible. They had shrivelled almost entirely away. The cock and balls being hidden helps them to act like a female. Remarkable, don't you think?'

Fletcher made no comment. But he thought, if a short, bewigged English sea captain got down and examined my cock and balls, they would certainly shrivel.

Still with an odd half-smile, William continued his report. 'I asked one of the chiefs if the mahoo indulge in carnal activities. He explained to me — by mime — that they perform fellatio. No sodomy. And only on their superiors, as a sexual service. Very interesting, don't you think?'

Fletcher just nodded. Where is this conversation headed?

William leaned back and put his hands behind his head. 'I'm told you have a woman on the shore,' he said. Fletcher gave a short nod. William tilted his head slightly. 'Is she any good?'

'What do you mean?'

'In the carnal sense.' His eyes were now tightly focused. 'I assume you are knowing her carnally. So, as I said, is she any good?'

Affronted, feeling himself colouring, Fletcher said, 'I consider that an improper question. It is no business but my own. And Mauatua's.' He met William's stare. 'Would you answer such a question if I asked it of you and Betsy?'

William made a scoffing noise. 'No. But the situations are not comparable. Betsy is my wife. You and the native woman are not married.' He gave a little laugh. 'At least I assume you and she have not gone through a form of native marriage, shall we say.'

'You assume correctly.' Fletcher stood up. 'And I have no wish to continue this conversation.'

William also got to his feet. His expression changed. Looking up into Fletcher's face, he put his right hand on his wrist and held it there. He said, falteringly, 'We are friends, are we not?'

Fletcher swallowed. 'I believe so. I'm grateful for what you've done for me.'

William nodded. 'So I do want you to know that after we leave Tahiti, should you feel ... in want of companionship, of comfort, you need look no further than this cabin.' His hand was trembling, his stare intense, his pupils dilated.

Fletcher pulled his arm away. Speechless at the implications of these words, he could only shake his head in revulsion. He turned abruptly and left the cabin. As he did so, William called, 'Don't forget, Fletcher, you owe me money!'

'Good God. Listen to that!'

Fletcher sat up. Naked beside him, Mauatua stirred. The noise came again, a massive thunderclap, seeming to be directly above the fare. Then another, and another boom, echoing from the mountains. Mauatua woke. There was a crack like musket fire, then a flash of lightning across the sky, momentarily turning the night into day. A second later the light was gone and darkness returned. With it came rain that fell in torrents, drenching the surrounding forest, the fare and everything else beneath it. Water poured from the little house's eaves and formed pools that began to rise around the building. Wind began to blow from the north-west. It quickly grew stronger. In minutes it was tearing at the foliage and blowing rain and leaves into the fare. They heard branches cracking.

Mauatua reached for her cape. 'Te tau miti rahi,' she said. 'It has come.'

Daylight came, but the rain was still so intense that visibility was limited, and the wind was gaining strength. Leaving Mauatua in the fare, Fletcher trudged barefoot through the forest to Point Venus. Once there he stopped. The Tuauru stream was in spate, gushing across the point in a brown flood, carrying palm fronds, coconuts and tree branches with it. On the other side of the stream, in front of the breadfruit nursery, Nelson and Brown were frantically digging a channel to divert the flow away from the plants. It was obvious that if a diversion was not dug, all the plants would be lost.

Fletcher waded into the swollen stream, pushing against the trunks of the palm trees to stop himself being swept into the lagoon. Half-swimming, half-wading, dodging the debris being swept along by the water, he reached the other side of the stream.

The two gardeners, drenched and wild-eyed, were working desperately at their channel. 'Get another spade!' Nelson shouted at him through the wind and rain. The wind was ripping fronds from the palms and hurling them across the point.

The three of them kept digging into the sandy soil and chopping at palm roots, at the same time watching anxiously as the rising stream waters came closer, aware that the storm was placing the entire raison d'être for the expedition in jeopardy. The sail-cloth covering the breadfruit plants sagged under the weight of the water which cascaded from its edges, forming curtains of water all around the nursery.

After an hour of frantic digging and mounding dirt and sand into a dyke around the nursery, a moat of sorts had begun to redirect the flood water. Now, instead of rising it was running into the ditch and gushing from the end that led down to the lagoon. The muddy water continued to stream across the point, but the water was coming no closer to the precious plants.

Chests heaving, Fletcher and the gardeners stayed their spades. Shouting above the storm, Nelson said, 'I think we've done it.' Fletcher nodded. They rested on the spades, soaked but relieved.

It was daylight now. Although the wind was still raging the rain had eased and they could see out into the lagoon. Staring through the palms and into the mist, Fletcher said, 'Oh Christ, the ship.'

Bounty, bare-poled, was pitching as wildly as a bucking mare and straining at her cables. Forward of the ship the reef was no longer visible: it was covered completely by huge waves being driven in from the open sea by the gale. It was as if the lagoon had been completely swallowed by the sea. Waves were striking *Bounty*'s bow and pouring over her decks. The ship was being battered like a toy ship by the elements, and it was obvious that if her cables broke she would be doomed. Fletcher could just discern through the mist a group of men on her foredeck trying to lower a second bower anchor. Others were battening down the mid-deck hatches. Not a soul was aloft.

Shouting above the wind, Nelson said, 'Should we go out and help?'

Fletcher shook his head. 'We'd never get there.' This view was confirmed when a great comber reared, then crashed down on the shore in front of them.

They watched anxiously from the shore for three hours. *Bounty*'s anchors held, and gradually the wind began to abate. After it at last died away, Fletcher and the gardeners were taken out to the ship in one of Tu's canoes, which had battled its way into the bay from Pare and picked them up.

Aboard *Bounty* Nelson and Brown, with Fletcher standing behind them, reported to William that the plants had been saved. Clearly relieved at the news, he thanked the three of them. 'Well done, well done,' he concluded. He gave not the slightest indication to Fletcher that their recent altercation had taken place. It was as if it had been completely deleted from his memory. Unlike Fletcher, who could not forget it.

Fryer joined them. 'What are we to do with the ship?' he asked William. Now that the storm season had struck, it was clear that their present anchorage was unsafe. Resisting the temptation to point out that his earlier warning had been correct, Fletcher suggested to the others that *Bounty* be moved further west, out of the path of the storm season's prevailing winds. Mauatua had told him of a cove at a place called Toaroa. 'Very peaceful there,' she said. 'No waves.'

William considered this, then said, 'I thought a bay on the island of Moorea would be a suitable place to ride out the storm season.' He pointed to the north-west, the direction in which the other island lay. 'We found a fine sheltered bay there, with Cook, on the north coast.'

Fletcher replied, 'That would not be advisable, in my opinion.'

William looked at him peevishly. 'Oh? Why not?'

'The leader of the people of Moorea, Mahine, is Tu's mortal enemy. Our chief would be mightily aggrieved if we were to seek sanctuary there. He would see it as a betrayal of our friendship. Moreover, we would have to move all the breadfruit plants across to Moorea.'

Fryer nodded. 'I agree. I think it best if we move the ship around to this place you suggested, Christian. To—, To—'

'Toaroa. Yes, I'm told it's sheltered, from almost every wind. And it's near Pare, and therefore close to Tu's bailiwick.'

William grunted, suggesting a concession. 'Very well, Fryer, order the men to—'

There was a banging on the cabin door, then it was thrust open. The flushed face of assistant surgeon Ledward appeared. 'Begging your pardon, Captain, but it's Mr Huggan. He's very poorly.'

They went to his berth. The surgeon was in his cot, unconscious. His face was grey, his eyes open but unseeing. The berth stank of piss, shit and vomit. There was puke all over Huggan's shirt front, and on the cabin floor was a port bottle, next to a slurry of vomit. William picked the bottle up. It was empty. Tossing it aside, he made a hissing sound.

Huggan was breathing, but his breath was coming in a series of rasps and rattles. Then he made a noise like a lowing bull, and gave a groan. And was silent.

Ledward went to him, took his left wrist and felt for a pulse. After feeling it for some time, he turned to the others and shook his head. 'He's finished,' he said. 'Choked on his own vomit.' He looked away, closed his eyes. However unsatisfactory Huggan was, the man had been his colleague.

William scowled. 'The drunken, inept fool. He killed Valentine, and now he's killed himself. Poetic justice.' He grimaced. 'He shamed his honourable profession.' To Ledward he said, 'You shall have his berth, and his position. But first, clean up this filth.' He glared at Huggan's corpse. 'We'll take the sod ashore and inter him there. Burying him at sea would pollute the ocean.'

Huggan was interred on Point Venus the next day, his grave aligned firmly east to west, in accordance with the rising and the setting of the sun. Tu, whose permission they had gained to allow the burial, had instructed that it be done this way. Priests from 'Rima' — Spanish missionaries from Lima — had told Tu that Popa'a people must be buried that way.

The day before Christmas the Point Venus encampment was struck and the breadfruit plants taken out to *Bounty*'s greenhouse cabin. Early on Christmas morning her anchors were weighed, the sails raised, and the ship turned several points to the west.

It soon became obvious that the move would not be straightforward. Swells still surged within the lagoon, which was stained brown with floodwaters, and *Bounty* had to be hauled across the wind. The sails were furled, the boats launched and Fryer climbed to the masthead to direct the oarsmen from above.

Getting *Bounty* under way early in the morning, when the sun was low, proved a mistake. Even from overhead Fryer could not see the coral heads clearly. An hour after the move began, *Bounty* graunched, then shuddered to a halt. She had gone aground on a shoal and the for'ard part of the ship was no longer afloat. Fryer screamed down at the men in the launch. 'Haul her off! Haul her off!' Lines were thrown, the oars were worked frantically. Had she been holed by the coral?

Fletcher stood in the bow above the remaining catted anchor, helping direct the rescue. The other anchor and its cable, lowered to stabilise the ship, had also become fouled on the coral.

It became obvious to Fletcher that a vital aspect of crewing — teamwork — was now missing. As they fought to haul the ship off and untangle the cable, the men yelled and swore at one another. Several of them tumbled into the lagoon, then surfaced, cursing even louder. Fryer, yelling in all directions, seemed unable to coordinate the haulage.

Fletcher watched William observing all this from the quarterdeck, his expression thunderous. *Why doesn't he intervene? Why is he leaving the mess for Fryer to clean up?* Aware that Tu and his people would be observing this incompetence from the shore, he could only conclude that William did not want to be associated with the disorder.

By standing apart from it, he could lay the blame for the mess at the feet of Fryer.

Slowly, laboriously, *Bounty* was hauled off the coral, then worked along the lagoon. Hours later she reached Toaroa and her anchors were lowered in a small bay. It was obvious that this location was indeed more advantageous than Matavai Bay. Toaroa was protected from the north-westerlies by prominent reefs, there was an adjacent promontory where a new shore encampment could be set up, and Tu and Itia's fare nui was close by. After Isaac Martin, a competent swimmer, submerged and groped at *Bounty*'s keel, he was able to report that it was still intact.

The ship was made secure in her new anchorage. Throughout the procedure Fryer remained livid, aware that he had been made to appear ineffectual before an audience. William has made yet another enemy, Fletcher concluded, one whom he could ill afford to make. He didn't like Fryer either, but the man's role was important to the expedition.

Because the move had taken so long, the company celebrated Christmas late, on 28 December. William allowed a double ration of grog. He also ordered that a cannon and some muskets be fired. The detonations terrified the locals, but had the effect of reminding those on the shore of the power of the Popa'a weapons. There must be no hostility from the natives, William reminded his officers over their belated Christmas dinner.

The New Year — 1789 — was imminent, and the season of storms well under way. Tu informed William that te tau miti rahi would last for 'another four moons'. For all that time the winds would be unfavourable for a return voyage via the Endeavour Straits, William announced to the others. He also told them he had discounted going to the West Indies via Cape Horn, as the winds there would also be adverse during this season. Accordingly, *Bounty* and her cherished cargo could not possibly leave Tahiti before April, when the storm season was over and the south-easterly trades would begin to blow again.

William had intended that they would be on Tahiti for twelve weeks; by the time they left it would be closer to five months. How would they spend this additional time?

Once again only a few of the ship's company had work which occupied them constructively. The crew went back to their taios, Nelson and Brown resumed their potting, and William spent most of his time hosting Tahiti's notables aboard or being feted ashore by various chiefs. When Tu, Itia and their entourage came aboard they always brought pork, fish and fruit, so William dined well. Continuing to be flattered by the attention he was accorded by the chiefs, he appeared unconcerned about the condition of the ship.

The crew now lived for the day, and the day was pretty good. But while *Bounty* rode gently at anchor at Toaroa, the season's constant dampness leached its way through her seams, below decks and into the holds. Content to ignore this, the crew carried out minimal duties then returned to their taios.

Their lassitude was interrupted by a couple of floggings. Muspratt was lashed for neglect of duties and Lamb received a dozen strokes for allowing a meat cleaver to be stolen by a native. But these punishments were out of the ordinary: in general an atmosphere of indolence reigned.

Fletcher, Peter and Ned now lived ashore with their lovers. Others, including Peckover, Stewart and Martin, spent most of their time on land. All spoke Tahitian well now.

Fletcher and Peter lay with their backs against palm trunks, drinking nuts beside them. Both wore breeches and the pandanus hats which Mauatua and Maire had woven for them. Fletcher's skin was like mahogany ('Brown as me, and I'm half-native,' as Ned put it), but Peter's skin was pink. Unlike Fletcher, he had stopped shaving, and his face was covered with auburn whiskers.

Peter picked up his coconut and swigged from it. Putting it down, wiping the juice from his mouth, he said, 'I've been writing about the arioi people. In my journal. Maire has been telling me about them.'

Eyes half-closed, Fletcher said, 'They're a class of priests, is that right?'

'Yes, but they're entertainers as well. They have great mana and are very privileged. They never marry. And if the females become pregnant, they bear the child then kill it at birth.'

'Why?'

'So they can continue their real role. Children would interfere with that.'

'That is so callous. Killing one's own children!'

'Indeed. But some arioi, Maire told me, commit infanticide over and over again.' He lay back on the sand. 'But apart from that barbarity, this is a wonderful island. I'm happy here, Fletcher. Happier than I thought possible. Aren't you?'

'Yes. I don't want to leave.' Lately the black fog had begun to hover on his horizon.

'But we must. It's our duty.' When Fletcher made no reply Peter asked, 'Isn't it?'

'Yes.' He paused. 'But what happens when duty and personal happiness conflict? Which wins?'

'If one is a naval man, duty does.'

'Yes.' A longer pause. 'But the thought of going back to sea for months … with that man …'

'I thought you and he were friends.'

'We were. But he has changed, and I don't like what he's become. He loves the adulation he gets from the Tahitian leaders. But it's my belief that they only fete him because he gives them the things they cherish, the nails, the iron tools, the trinkets, the English clothing. And because of the lie that he's Cook's son.'

Peter wiped beads of sweat from his brow. 'You may well be right. I have the feeling that many of the Tahitians don't really like him. Tu and Itia certainly do, though.'

'And they are well rewarded for it.'

'Indeed.' He frowned. 'But why have you changed your mind about the captain?'

'Never mind. It's not your problem.' Fletcher picked up a handful of sand and let it run through his fingers. 'But I have to say, Peter, I'm torn. Between Tahiti and the deep blue sea.'

Peter nodded. 'That I do understand. I've told Maire that I'll come back here. And I will, somehow.' He sat up. 'I'm going to be tattooed tomorrow.'

'Really? Where?'

'Here.' He touched his left breast. 'With a star of St George. Like the Order of the Garter. Maire's organising the tattooist. I've drawn a St George star for him, as a pattern.'

'Well, if you get one, then I shall too. To prove how Tahitian I've become.' Fletcher smiled. 'We shall be the Knights of Tahiti.'

From the direction of the lagoon came a shout. 'Christian! Heywood!'

They both stood up. Fletcher called out. 'Who's that? What is it?'

'It's Cole! You're both to report to the ship, immediately. There's an emergency.'

The crew assembled on deck, barefooted and dishevelled. Their women had been sent back to the shore. Fletcher stood alongside William on the quarterdeck, Fryer on his other side. William's face was puce.

'This morning the watch relief, Martin, found the duty officer, Hayward, asleep at his post. For that he will be punished severely.' He glowered at the crew. 'And I have reason to believe there have been desertions.' There was a collective intake of breath from the men. They looked at each other. Who was missing? 'Cole will now take a roll call. Cole!'

The boatswain read the list of names. As each was called, a hand went up, accompanied by an 'Aye.' Fryer ticked them all. Except for three: able seamen Millward and Muspratt, and master-at-arms Churchill.

William's eyes narrowed. 'So, Millward, Muspratt and Churchill. All guilty of desertion. And *Bounty*'s cutter has gone with them.' A tremor went through the assembly. 'And eight muskets and ammunition.' There was another shocked reaction. These were all hanging offences. A few, who had known of the deserters' plan, stared down at the deck.

William's expression darkened. 'All will pay heavily after they are captured. And they will be.' He called down to Cole. 'Take Hayward below and put him in irons. I'll go ashore and speak with chief Tu. He'll have informants who will seek rewards. They will know where the treacherous swine have gone!'

Next day the cutter was found abandoned in Matavai Bay. After it was returned to the ship by some local men they reported that the deserters had gone in a canoe to the atoll of Tetiaroa, twenty miles north-east of Tahiti.

Two of Tu's most trusted men, Ariipaea and Moana, agreed to sail to the island and return with the deserters. This was a risky proposition, given that Churchill, Millward and Muspratt were known to be armed.

Then the weather turned foul, with rain and gales, and it wasn't until nine days later that Tu's pair of vigilantes sailed off for Tetiaroa. But they did so determinedly, confident that Captain Parai would reward them for their work.

Shortly after the Tahitians left in their canoe, Fletcher was summoned to meet William in his cabin. He knocked, then entered.

'Ah, Mr Christian.'

Fletcher blinked. Mr Christian? William was holding a sheet of paper. He waved it. 'This was found after I searched Churchill's chest this morning.'

'What is it?'

'It's a list. Of the men who have been ashore.'

'Oh. What of it?'

'What of it? Your name is on it.' He looked down. 'Along with Heywood, Young, Peckover, Stewart and Martin.' He paused. 'And the deserters, Churchill, Millward and Muspratt.'

Fletcher nodded. 'Yes, we've all been staying ashore.'

'Then why are the deserters' names on this list?'

'Because they've been onshore as well. As I'm sure you know.'

Fletcher felt sweat starting to pour from his face and hands. The implications were obvious. As well as the names of those who had deserted, the others on Churchill's list could be construed as potential deserters. The other thing the men had in common was that they had all received a tattoo on the island, the St George star on the left breast. So Churchill's list comprised a kind of brotherhood. But Fletcher had no idea why he had written the names down.

William waved the list, looking at Fletcher sceptically, an expression which suggested that Fletcher and the others on it had collaborated in the trio's desertion.

Fletcher decided not to mention the tattooed brotherhood. It would only heighten the captain's suspicions. He simply said, 'I've had nothing to do with the list. I didn't know it existed.'

William kept staring at him. 'And you have no idea why those names are on it?'

'No. It is meaningless to me.'

William maintained his stare. Then he said, 'Well, I shall keep Churchill's list. And memorise the names that are on it.'

'That is your prerogative.'

'Yes.' William turned away. 'I need detain you no longer. Go.' Then he turned back. 'Oh yes, one other thing. That money I advanced you in Cape Town. You will be charged interest on the repayment.'

They all watched in silence as the deserters were brought aboard in irons. Their story had already been circulated: after Tetiaroa the trio had tried to sail to Moorea in their canoe, to seek sanctuary there with Tu's foe. But they had missed the island and had instead landed back on Tahiti, at Fa'a, a few miles west of Pare. Their ammunition was useless, as it had become saturated, Tu's informants reported. The captain and four armed sailors had gone in the launch to arrest the deserters and return them to the ship.

'From the Articles of War. "Every person in or belonging to the fleet, who shall desert or entice others to do so, shall suffer death, or such other punishment as the circumstances of the offence shall deserve, and a court martial shall judge fit.'"

Standing before the assembled company, Bligh set his commander's handbook aside. Churchill, Millward and Muspratt, shackled at the wrists and ankles, stood below him on the mid-deck, guarded by Cole and Morrison. An abject Hayward, hands together in front of him, stood to one side.

Bligh thrust back his shoulders, as if trying to make himself taller. 'The men you see before you have brought shame on His Majesty's Navy. Thomas Hayward slept on watch and so allowed these three scum to steal a boat, muskets and ammunition, and desert our ship. Were their labour not essential to our return voyage, they would already be hanging from the yardarm.' He stared up at the spar in question, then back at the company. 'Instead, until we return to England and they appear before a court martial, they will each be given two dozen lashes. They will be kept in irons for a fortnight, then given another two dozen.' He raised his chin. 'As for Hayward, he will be taken below and shackled again. Then sent before the mast.'

Those watching looked down, some with closed eyes. The guilty trio stared ahead impassively. Hayward looked close to tears.

Fletcher stood in silence, his eyes drifting in the direction of the shore, where he knew Mauatua would be waiting. He yearned to be off the ship again. He well understood why the trio had run. In his heart he was sorry they had been recaptured. He too longed to be free from this wooden prison, this place of brutality and incarceration. During these last weeks he had been living a completely different way of life, a freer, gentler, more loving one. The knowledge that he would soon have to leave it all behind was unbearable. He belonged on Tahiti now, not on a vermin-infested ship commanded by a vain, foul-mouthed, perverted dwarf.

On the horizon in his mind, the black fog was looming. He shut his eyes tightly, desperate to rid himself of it. And as soon as he could, he returned to shore.

Mauatua's family had a fare in the hills above Point Venus where they went to stay when the weather on the coast was oppressively humid. As it was now. When she suggested they spend a night there, Fletcher was only too pleased to agree. The further away from *Bounty* the better, he told her.

They walked up through the forest, along the same trail that led to the waterfall pool. There they stopped and swam in its cool water and Mauatua washed her hair under the cascade. Aroused by her nakedness, Fletcher led her to the side of the pool, where they made love.

Afterwards they lay there, bound by an afterglow. She took a tiare bloom from her garland and slipped it behind his left ear. 'Titereano, mauruuru roa. You are a nice man.'

'And you are so lovely. Ua here vau ia oe.'

'Ua here vau ia oe. I love you, too.' She touched his left breast, where the tattooed star was starting to heal. 'Does it still hurt?'

'Not as much.' He sat up. 'Shall we go on now?'

The trail led up a valley, then rose to a ridge. Mist clung about the mountain peaks and parakeets, doves and petrels flittered about the forest. Fletcher carried a pack containing some cooked pork and tuna, bananas and drinking nuts.

As the afternoon sun grew stronger the mist melted away. The fare was in a clearing atop the ridge. The foliage had been cleared on the side that faced the sea, giving views across the coast below. Forest giants grew over the rest of the clearing: puarata, tamanu and uru. The globular breadfruit were beginning to mature now.

They sat on the lip of the clearing, staring down at the coast below. Mauatua pointed and recited the names of the districts she knew, from east to west. 'Papenoo, Mahina, Pare, Atehuru ...' Point Venus protruded into the lagoon like a sprocket. Inland from it the knoll that Captain Wallis had named 'One Tree Hill' also stood out. They could see *Bounty* at her mooring, resembling a child's model boat afloat on a village pond.

Mauatua pointed to the north-east. 'There, Tetiaroa.' The atoll was just visible on the horizon, a bracelet of green, palm-covered islets, enclosing their cerulean lagoon.

To the north-west was Moorea, its jagged profile now backlit by the sinking sun. The shadowed side of the island was purple; a few gauzy clouds clung to its peaks. Between the two islands the sea had a pearly sheen. Fletcher wondered, could there be a lovelier sight in all the world?

His arm around Mauatua, he asked, 'Have you been there? To Moorea.'

'No. Enemies of my people live on the other side of that island.'

'But from here it is very beautiful.'

'Ae. Very beautiful. To see, but not to go.'

They stayed watching until the sun slipped below the horizon. Then the sky began to flare, suffused with different colours: red, pink, orange, vermilion. The display of brilliant light lasted only a few minutes, then the colours faded. Minutes later darkness fell, and from the forest came the din of shrieking insects. Away to the east, a rising crescent moon glowed through the velvet blackness and a few pinpricks of starlight began to appear. But to them it seemed that the world beyond the fare had ceased to exist.

Using his flint, Fletcher lit the candlenuts Mauatua had collected on the way up. Then, lying on the fare mats, they ate by their light.

Mauatua said, 'It is good to eat with a man. Before you, I never ate with a man.'

'Because it is ra'a?'

'Ae.' She took another mouthful of pork. 'It is good to share food with you, Titereano.'

Fletcher smiled. 'And I prefer to eat with you, rather than the crew. They are pigs. Pigs who eat pigs.'

They talked well into the night. He asked why the Tahitians had such a love for nails. 'Because iron is special. So strong,' she said. 'And we never had it.' She told him about the people from Hitia, on Tahiti's east coast. After Bougainville's men traded nails for their cunnies, the women planted the nails in the ground, thinking a tree would grow from them, bearing nails. She looked scornful. 'Hitia people are very stupid.'

She was still curious about him, his family, and Peretane. 'Where does King George live?'

'In London. In a very, very big fare.'

'How many wives does he have?'

'Only one. Queen Charlotte.'

'Do they have children?'

'Yes. Twelve, at the last count.'

'What is London like?'

'Very big. Many houses, many people. Beside a wide river.'

'Captain Tute brought horses with him to Tahiti. We had never seen such a creature. It was huge. We called it pua'a horo henua. Did you have a horse?'

'Yes, on the Isle of Man I rode a horse. To the top of the island.'

'Does Captain Parai live with his father, Tute, in Peretane?'

'No. Parai is not Tute's son, Mauatua. And Tute is dead. He was killed on Owhyhee.'

This shocked her. 'Aayaa. Not Tute's son? And Tute is killed? So Parai has told lies?'

'Yes. Parai is a liar.'

'Oh. That is not good.'

'No, it isn't.' But he was pleased that now one Tahitian knew the truth.

After they had again made love, as she lay in his arms he said: 'You call me by a Tahitian name, now I shall give you an English name.'

'Which name?'

'Isabella.'

'Izz-a-pella.' She laid her head on his chest. 'Why that name?'

'Because it's lovely. Like you.'

He did not add, because it was also the name of my first love.

* * *

On 6 March Fletcher and the others living ashore were summoned back to *Bounty*. Fryer and Cole were present, along with the midshipmen. Assembled on the quarterdeck, they were addressed by an irate William Bligh.

'This morning I ordered the men bring up and lay out the spare sails. After they did, I found them to be mildewed. Some were even rotten.' He stared at Fryer. 'Why did you not air the sails properly?'

'I was not instructed to.' Fryer's voice was icy.

'Huh? Must I instruct you to do everything? Do you have no awareness of your responsibilities as master of this ship?' His blazing eyes alighted on Cole. 'Furthermore, I also inspected the cutter. There is rot in its keel. There is also rot in the stock of the bower anchor. Why did you not note that, Mr Cole? And take steps to remedy these faults?'

'I was unaware of the rot, Captain.'

'Holy fucking shit, man, there's far too much unawareness on this ship! I doubt if any commander in naval history has had to put up with so much damnable unawareness.' He glared at them. 'The slackness you've all shown on this ship is shameful. You are all — and I include you midshipmen — guilty of dereliction of duty.' He paused to regain his breath. 'I have recorded every instance of it, and it will be reported fully, upon our return to England.

'Contrasting with your negligence, the work of Nelson and Brown has been splendid. We have more than a thousand breadfruit plants, as well as other living botanical specimens which will shortly be taken aboard. So our work here is almost done. From the first day of April we will prepare the ship for sailing, and be at sea as soon after that as possible.

'Fryer, instruct Lebogue to dry and repair the rotting sails. Cole, get Purcell to attend to defects in the cutter and the bower anchor. Fryer, oversee that work.' He flicked his hand dismissively. 'Now, all of you, leave, and attend to your duties. Properly.'

As they went below, Peter muttered to Fletcher, 'What about his own negligence? All he's done these last weeks is toady to Tu and his fat missus, and visit the other chiefs like a potentate. The biggest

182

slacker on *Bounty* is its commander. Bugger the duties, I'm going back ashore. Coming?'

'I am,' said Fletcher.

The first day of April. Fool's day. The thought of departure sickened him. The dark fog was rolling in.

Bounty's decks were scrubbed; more repairs were made to the sails and awnings. Provisions were bartered for by Peckover and taken aboard: green plantains, breadfruit and many coconuts. These were stowed below or piled about the decks. Pigs were butchered and the pork salted down. Two dozen live pigs and seventeen goats were brought aboard and penned mid-deck. Water casks were repaired and filled.

One thousand and fifteen flourishing breadfruit plants were stowed in the Great Cabin, in pots on the racks and in tubs and boxes on the quarterdeck. *Bounty* took on the appearance of a floating Kew Gardens. Nelson continued to fuss over the plants like a new parent with his babies: watering them, nurturing them and putting them to bed. But Brown, who had made a special taio on the island, had lost his enthusiasm for gardening.

As the word spread that Tute's son and the *Bounty* would soon be leaving, hundreds of Tahitians descended on Pare. Many came aboard, where they sang, chanted, danced, drummed and feasted on the produce they had brought with them. But there was also an overlying air of sadness as the departure impended.

For the last time, William hosted Tu and Itia on board. He inscribed his name and the dates of his stay on the back of the Webber portrait of Cook, thereby adding to its potency. There were rounds of gift-giving. From Tu to William: arioi costumes of bark cloth embellished with tropic bird tail feathers, and pigs, breadfruit, plantains and many coconuts. From William to Tu: shirts, mirrors, fish hooks, knives, gimlets, saws, dolls, a musket, a pair of pistols and hundreds of rounds of ammunition. This was the greatest gift of all, ensuring that Tu would from now on be Tahiti's most formidable ari'i.

Fletcher delayed boarding for as long as he possibly could. So too did Peter, George and Ned. They and several others were leaving special taios.

On the path below the fare, he held Isabella and buried his face in her hair. Feeling her trembling, for some time he couldn't speak. Then at last he drew back, parted her hair and told her, 'I will come back. I promise I will. And I will take you with me to Peretane. We will be man and wife. In London.' He stared into her lovely face for the last time. It was wet with tears, her eyes were tightly closed and she was shaking her head. It was as if she knew that it could never happen, knew that this was their final parting. There could be only heartache from now on, for both of them.

'Christian! The cutter's leaving! Now!' Cole's voice, coming up from the shore.

He released her, turned and walked away. Moments later he heard a cry, 'Aue!' Then her parting words. 'E eritape ta iti e, eiaha roa oe e faaru'e ia'u nei!' 'Do not leave me!'

He stumbled down to the shore as if mortally wounded.

All the Tahitians who had been on board were taken off the ship. Tu and Itia were the last to leave. When they left both wept inconsolably.

Bounty's anchors were weighed, buoys were placed in the channel and the boats prepared to tow her back to Matavai Bay, the point of final departure. When this was seen to be happening, the chanting, singing and drumming died. An eerie silence, a kind of mourning, descended on Pare. People of all ages lined the shore, staring at the *Bounty*. No Popa'a ship had ever stayed so long on the island. The Tahitian men were either silent or weeping; the women tore at their scalps with sharks' teeth, so that blood ran down their faces, reddening their tears.

Bounty, sails still furled, was hauled down the channel. William, in full uniform, stood on her quarterdeck, arms at his side. His jubilation was obvious. Mission accomplished, his stance declared. The red ensign was raised. Tu had requested that the ship fire a cannon salute, but William demurred, saying the noise might disturb the breadfruit plants. Instead he ordered the crew to line the starboard rail, and when he called for three cheers their cries rang out across the lagoon: 'Huzzah! Huzzah! Huzzah!'

Fletcher stood alone in the stern, staring back at the island that had changed his life. He felt hollowed out, as if a vital part of him had been removed and left there, a part he could never retrieve. He gripped the taffrail with damp hands. Isabella, Isabella. All he could see before him was her face. He closed his eyes tightly and her face vanished. Moments later, in its place was the black fog.

At Matavai Bay the boats were taken aboard and made fast. The capstan was turned, the anchors raised and catted. Men edged along the yards and let go the sails. They caught the afternoon breeze and began to billow. *Bounty* glided through the passage in the reef and into open sea. The helmsmen turned the wheel three points to larboard and she turned towards the sinking sun, settling into the west-north-west course that William had set for her.

Part Three

TO THE FRIENDLY ISLES

4–28 APRIL 1789

Aware that discipline had to be re-imposed after the inertia that Tahiti had produced, and knowing that testing conditions lay ahead, Bligh set the crew to work in a way they had not done for months. Sail and line-handling were practised daily, and the below-decks hygiene regime was once again strictly enforced.

Although the crew obeyed his commands, most performed the tasks perfunctorily. The contrast between the now and then could not have been starker. The minds of the men were mostly still ashore.

But they were not yet done with the Society Islands. *Bounty* called briefly at Huahine. There William was given the news of the death of Omai, the Society Islands native whom Cook had taken to England in 1773 aboard HMS *Adventure* and returned to Huahine during Cook's final voyage. The Raiatean's two New Zealand Maori servants had also died, William was told, and the house Cook had had built for Omai had been destroyed. But not before he had used the English guns he had been given, to defeat his enemies from Bora Bora.

Fletcher resumed his journal-writing.

10 April 1789

Time to write is precious. Bligh has once more instituted a regime of cleaning and washing, as well as regular small arms practice, so I have very little time to myself. The cleaning below decks is now done daily, Bligh insists, whereas before it was done only twice a week. Washing the hammocks is now also to be done every day. The men may be grubby, but they are not so unwashed that their hammocks need cleaning as frequently as that. They complain and curse as they scrub, and for that I don't blame them.

Furthermore, Bligh demands that these chores must always be carried out in the morning, during the period when I am the watch officer. I cannot help concluding that this is not a coincidence. He knows that heaping these extra duties upon me makes my life more difficult. This is nothing but spite on his part. For what reason does he single me out for this punishment? My conclusion, which I can confide to no one, is that it is because of my rejection of his unnatural overture while we were at Tahiti. That advance was deeply offensive to me, as he must have later realised.

Other factors, I also conclude, compound his antipathy towards me: the fact that I incurred a debt to him in Cape Town, and that on Tahiti I found a woman with whom I fell deeply in love. The first — the borrowing — was my error, done purely for the sake of lust. I regret that. The second — my love for Isabella — was something so wonderful that the memory of it will remain with me forever. How well do I now know the difference, the gulf, between lust and love!

Yet to Bligh these matters are evidently so disagreeable that he has determined that I will be punished for them. Although he heaps abuse on all his officers, accusing them of incompetence, it is me he singles out for particular criticism. Could he have discovered the improper use to which I put his loan money? Impossible. Only Peter would have suspected what happened, and he would never have informed on me to Bligh. He is a young man of honour, and a loyal shipmate. No, Bligh's vindictiveness is motivated by jealousy, I'm sure. And knowing that his is the ultimate authority aboard Bounty, he wields it on every occasion. He makes more reference to our backgrounds, contrasting mine with his. I am, it seems, a person of privilege. This to me is unjust. I did not choose my family or its status. It was thrust upon me, a fact so obvious that it should not need stating.

Bligh's bullying is becoming habitual. It puts me in mind of an incident when I was a lad, when one day I came upon a small boy being bullied by an older and stronger boy. This I thought so unfair that I attacked the bully and defeated him. Although I cannot now recall the names of either boy, what I do remember is how the bully retreated once I confronted him. He was, I then realised, a poltroon. If all bullies are so, as Charles pointed out to me, then Bligh must be one. But such are the circumstances on this ship

*that I cannot take action against him, as I did with the boy in Cockermouth.
So what am I to do?*

*I am powerless to take any action to alleviate these circumstances. I am
like the principal character in Shakespeare's Hamlet, a play which Edward
and I saw in the Haymarket in London two years ago. It was about a man
who was doomed to inaction. Although I am determined not to succumb to
Hamlet-like self-pity, the thought of enduring Bligh's malice for many more
months does induce in me a Hamlet-like melancholia.*

*Bligh makes threats to all his officers. He says that our incompetence will
lead us to destruction in the Endeavour Straits. If so, that day cannot come
quickly enough.*

I must end this entry now. My watch begins on the hour.

They resumed a westerly course, aware that the Friendly Isles, which
Bligh knew well from his time there with Cook in 1777, would be
raised before the end of April. There they would obtain more fresh
food and water in readiness for the haul north to the Endeavour
Straits, then through that perilous passage.

Fletcher carried out his duties in silence, still consumed by what
he had lost. Whenever possible he gave his captain a wide berth,
aware that since the bizarre incident on Tahiti their relationship had
fundamentally changed. They came together only over the dining
table, and then the conversation was stilted. Bligh would glance at
Fletcher from time to time, as if poised to say something significant,
then remain silent, as if he thought it better left unsaid. In this way
the resentments simmered. The only person Fletcher could confide
in was Peter, who was experiencing his own sense of loss, but he told
him nothing of what he suspected about their captain.

While on watch, staring out at *Bounty*'s wake, Fletcher could feel
the barometer within him plummeting. What he was feeling now was
beyond melancholia. He was not alone. With each day that passed the
atmosphere throughout the ship grew more depressed. Most of the
crew were too well aware of what they had lost, and what they were
now faced with: months of gruelling sailing, unyielding authority and

carnal deprivation. There was no sense of expectation, as there had been on the outward voyage, and the shipboard rigour was now unwelcome. Although well fed for the time being, the men went about their duties sullenly. They bridled at being ordered about, especially by Fryer, whose testiness increased by the day. Only Nelson, fussing constantly over his beloved breadfruit babies, showed any enthusiasm for his work. His colleague Brown was now as glum as the rest of the crew.

On Tahiti time had become meaningless. There was sunrise and sunset, light and darkness, with little but pleasure in between: bathing, feasting, fucking, laughing. Now on *Bounty* there was again the tyranny of the timepiece, the hourglass, the chronometer, the knot-line, the eight-hour watch. Nothing demonstrated the difference between the Tahitian day and the shipboard day more cruelly than these unyielding measurements of time.

Bligh was fractious. It seemed that after being treated royally for so long on the island, he resented the fact that he had been reduced to the status of a mere mortal again. Determined to reassert his authority, after young able seaman Sumner swore at Fryer, he ordered him to be given twelve lashes. All witnessed the flogging. As the lash rose and fell, it was another reminder that the good times had gone. From now on the cat would be let out of the bag for any infraction, Bligh warned his crew.

Fletcher thought constantly of Isabella, imagining every detail of her face and body. What was she doing today? Where was she going? To their pool? To the garden? To the fare in the mountains?

A small consolation was the journal he had begun on Tahiti. Writing of the present helped take his mind off the lost past. He now wrote in it whenever he could, retreating to his cabin to do so when not on watch or attending to other duties.

15 April 1789
Today, at 19° South latitude, 160° West longitude, we sighted an uncharted island, and stood off it. I saw through my spyglass that although the island is enclosed by a reef, it is not high like Tahiti. Neither does there appear to

be any pass through the reef. The island has a lagoon, white sand beaches and a humped mountain in its centre. I could see that the mountain — really just a hill approximately three hundred feet high — was covered in scrubby vegetation, and that around it is a fringing plain covered in coconut palms. Inhabited the island must be, for I saw smoke rising from the plain. In confirmation of this, four men came out to the ship in a canoe and came aboard. They were perfectly affable. Very like the Tahitians in their physiognomy, their language was also similar, so that those of us who spoke Tahitian were able to converse with them. They told us that their island was called Ay-too-tuck-ee and that its highest point is called Ma-un-ga Pu. After they showed amazement at our animals, never having seen such creatures, Bligh presented the men with a sow and a boar, in the hope that they might breed on the island. He also gave them some nails, beads and mirrors. In return, one of the men gave Bligh his handsome pearl shell breastplate, which had a cord of plaited human hair.

The captain was jubilant at coming across and recording the island, exclaiming to us, 'I have made a discovery! A new island! One that even Cook did not find!' Bligh's vanity is such that it was as if he had discovered the Great Southern Continent.

Resuming our westward course, on 17 April we sighted the place Cook named Savage Island in 1774. It has the appearance of having been raised a few hundred feet from the sea, and is composed of coral rock riddled with caves and coves. It has a level crown, covered with forest.

Curious about the people who inhabited the island, I suggested to Bligh . . .

'Should we not go ashore here? If only briefly?'

'Why?'

'To make contact with the natives. To show them we mean no harm.'

'Ah. You do like to make contact with the natives, don't you?'

'You misconstrue me, sir. I merely intended for us to establish with the people on the island that we are not hostile towards them.'

'I see. And do you not think that Captain Cook had the same intention?'

'I'm sure he did.'

'Yes. And the great man was attacked by the people here. On two occasions. Repelled by them, violently. So your suggestion is a foolish one. We will not make a landing on this island.'

He walked away, calling down to the helmsmen, 'Hold your course. West-north-west.'

The man has become a swine. A sarcastic swine. He seeks now to humiliate me, the way he humiliates all who disagree with him.

Two days later *Bounty* was struck by squally weather from the south-east. In the midst of the gale Fletcher was in the bow, helping Quintal and McCoy bring in the spritsail, which had been ripped by the wind. As they wrestled with the canvas, a caped figure appeared through the rain. It was Bligh. He shouted above the wind: 'What in hell's name are you doing?'

Fletcher turned. 'Bringing in the spritsail. It's torn.'

'Torn? Where?'

Fletcher pointed to the tear. 'There.'

'I see. And I know the cause.'

'So do I. The squall.'

'No, not the squall. You are the cause. You have not cared for the sails. You failed to air them properly while we were at Pare. Consequently, they have rotted.'

Fletcher felt his jaw drop. Quintal and McCoy, both drenched, looked at Bligh incredulously. This was unjust. Maintenance of the sails was the responsibility of Fryer and Lebogue, master and sailmaker, not a midshipman-promoted-acting-lieutenant.

Fletcher's voice rose above the wind. 'That allegation is unfair. You know that maintenance of the sails is not part of my duties. Why are you making this accusation?'

Bligh erupted. 'God damn your eyes, Christian, I'm making it because it needs to be made. You're the slackest officer a commander ever had to contend with!' He kicked at the heap of split canvas. 'Now get the sail below and tell Lebogue to mend it!'

As he stalked off through the rain towards the quarterdeck, McCoy shook his head in disbelief. 'The man's a nackle-arse.'

Quintal nodded. 'You shouldn't have to put up with that shit, Christian.' He stared balefully at Bligh's retreating figure. 'None of us should.'

Later that day, when Fletcher returned to his cabin to change out of his saturated clothing, he found a note under his cabin door. It read, 'Mr Christian, Mr Hayward is to be my guest at supper this evening. I hope you will be able to join us. Yours, William.'

Fletcher stared at the missive in disbelief. How could the man make such an offer, so soon after his tirade of abuse? What sort of a man was he dealing with now? Either Bligh was going out of his mind, or he was.

He screwed up the invitation.

22 April 1789

Yesterday we sighted some of the westernmost islands of the Friendly Isles. The most prominent is Kao, which rises like a pyramid from the sea. Its summit gives off smoke. Not far south of it is Tofua, which is steep-sided but lacks peaks. Bligh has decided we will not make a landing on either of these, but instead on Nomuka (20° South, 174° West), which he knows. This is a low island, as flat as a flounder, triangular shaped, with an unusual feature for a South Sea island — a large freshwater lake, a little way inland. This will enable us to replenish our water casks. We will also take aboard wood, as this will likely be the last opportunity to do so before we reach New Holland.

The first European to chart Nomuka was Abel Tasman, in 1643. He called it Rotterdam. We anchored on the north side of the island, in approximately the same place as Cook moored Resolution twelve years ago. After we anchored some canoes came out, bearing coconuts and yams, but it was not until the next day that a native came aboard. This was an old chief named Tapa, who walked with a limp and had a scar on one cheek. He offered us the use of a canoe house on the island.

Bligh went ashore with him, but was in a foul mood again after master's mate Elphinstone lost the bower anchor buoy. Bligh also told us that we

should not anticipate a warm welcome on Nomuka, since Cook had had
Tapa's son lashed after he killed a ship's cat. The Nomukans had not forgotten
this insult, we were warned. So Bligh urged us to be cautious at all times. He
also reported that the people here are in a poor state of health. Many have
fingers missing and there are sores on their bodies. How did they become so
diseased? Is it the venereals? Or leprosy?

Bligh has put me in charge of a watering party of eleven men. It will be
good to be ashore again, although I am still tormented by thoughts of Isabella
and Tahiti. No other island can compare.

'In view of the natives' likely restlessness, you are to take muskets and ammunition,' Bligh ordered Fletcher. 'But you are forbidden to fire them.'

'Will the fact that we are carrying firearms not be provocative?'

'You will not carry the muskets. You will leave them in the launch.'

'Then why bother to take them?'

'As a deterrent.'

Fletcher walked away. Ridiculous.

While Elphinstone went off with four men armed with axes for the wood cutting, Fletcher and eleven others walked to the lake. Some of his men carried the muskets, as he had considered it too great a risk to leave the weapons in the launch. Others rolled the water casks. The sky was graphite-grey, the humidity high.

As the party followed the track, several local men slipped in alongside them, carrying spears and clubs. They were different from the mostly slim Tahitians, Fletcher realised. They were bigger-boned, heavier, stronger. And threatening. Soon they began making darting attacks, jostling the sailors, snatching at their muskets and kicking the water casks. A tall youth leapt at Fletcher, trying to grab his tricorn, and he knocked him aside angrily. Minutes later there was a scuffle at the rear of the party and McCoy cried out, 'He's grabbed my axe!' A man ran towards the bush, wielding it. Fletcher brought his musket up to his shoulder and aimed it at him. The others did the same. But as they had been expressly forbidden to fire, aiming it was all he could do.

When the natives realised the muskets would not be fired they began to jeer. They taunted the sailors with their spears and clubs, waving them in their faces. Some began to throw stones.

Confused, the men looked at Fletcher. 'What do we do, sir?' McCoy asked.

'First, get the casks filled. Under guard.'

While three men stood guard at the lake's edge, the others filled the barrels and hammered in the bungs. Then, with the natives still hurling what were obviously insults or looking on menacingly, the barrels were rolled back to the shore and loaded into the launch.

Bligh was amidships, entertaining Tapa and three other chiefs, seated and wrapped in the mats the natives called ta'ovala. Fletcher and McCoy climbed up onto the deck.

'Are the casks filled?' Bligh demanded of Fletcher.

'They are. But we had great difficulty carrying out the duties.'

'How so?'

'The islanders threatened us.'

'Did you not have the muskets?'

'We did, but the natives were unafraid of them.'

'Why?'

Fletcher spoke through gritted teeth. 'Because your order prohibited us from using them.' He turned to McCoy. 'Was that not the order?'

McCoy nodded. Several of the others did too. They had all heard Bligh say it. Tapa and the other chiefs looked on, frowning, unable to comprehend this exchange.

Bligh took a step forward. His next words struck Fletcher like hurled gravel.

'You, Christian, are a coward. You are afraid of a few naked savages, even when you are bearing arms.'

Fletcher braced himself. Staring down at his commander, he asked, 'What use are arms, when your orders were expressly for us not to use them?'

Bligh's eyes narrowed. 'You are a disgrace to His Majesty's Navy. Of all my officers, you are the worst. You are a cowardly scoundrel.'

In the background, the men looked at one another, aghast. This was a very public shaming of a respected officer, and the very worst kind of insult for a commander to hurl at a lieutenant in front of his men. The Nomukan chiefs looked at one another, perplexed. What were these Papalagi doing to one another?

Fletcher could endure no more. Sweating profusely, he glared at Bligh but said nothing. His hands began to shake. Turning on his heels, he went down the aft stairway to his cabin. There he threw himself down on his bunk. What to do? What to do?

Next morning Fryer went ashore with several of the men to repair some barrels. While they were resting a man darted from the bush, snatched up the cooper's adze and ran off with it. It could not be recovered. Then at the beach, while Fryer's party was getting into the cutter, a crowd gathered around the boat, threatening to upset it. After Martin threw out a grapnel to stabilise the cutter, a boy dived down, cut the rope, grabbed the grapnel and ran inland with it. Fryer, close to panicking, ordered the men to row back to the ship.

'You lost an adze and a grapnel?' Bligh was apoplectic.

Fryer nodded. 'Yes. Both were stolen.'

Sensing another confrontation, Fletcher came down from the quarterdeck and joined them.

Bligh stamped his foot, Rumpelstiltskin-like. 'God damn your eyes, man, that brings our equipment losses to three.' He pointed at Fletcher. 'First, this one loses an axe, then you, Fryer, lose two more tools. Holy fucking shit, this is insupportable. It's negligence of the worst kind. You should both be court-martialled!'

Staring straight ahead, Fryer replied, 'I do not consider the losses very great, sir. We have more axes, and more grapnels, in the hold.'

'Get to hell and stay there, Fryer! The loss may not be very great to you, but it is to me!' Bligh bunched his right hand into a fist and shook it at the sky. 'Was ever a commander cursed with such a useless bunch of officers as I am? That grapnel is precious and I intend to get it back!'

Fletcher and Fryer exchanged glances but said nothing. Both walked away. The commander was out of control.

* * *

On Tahiti, Peckover had been in sole charge of trading. This system worked well, preventing the men from accumulating and hoarding native artefacts, which they knew could be sold for profit back in England. But since accumulating heaps of mementos would put pressure on the ship's stowage space, Bligh had forbidden the practice.

But on their fourth day at anchor off Nomuka, Bligh announced unexpectedly, 'The men may trade with the natives for what they wish.'

The word spread rapidly. Soon the ship was surrounded by canoes whose occupants brought out clubs, spears, carvings and tapa cloth. Food, too. There was an outbreak of trading, the crew offering their personal trinkets in exchange for what the natives offered them. The four Nomuka chiefs remained on board, mingling with the traders of both parties, offering comments and suggesting terms. There had been nothing like it during the voyage.

The decks became cluttered with artefacts. The carvings included turtles, whales, flying fish and kava bowls. The lengths of tapa, unlike the Tahitian cloth, were decorated with attractive brown patterns.

Fletcher and Peckover looked at the scene in bewilderment. Why had a sensible policy been abandoned in favour of this disorder?

In the midst of the bartering, Bligh climbed onto the quarterdeck and shouted down to Fryer, 'Order the anchors raised! We're leaving!' He waved at the natives. 'You lot, off! Off!' Clutching their trinkets, they returned to their canoes. But when the chiefs made to do so, Bligh raised his hand. 'No! No! You are to stay aboard! Cole and Morrison, stand by the gate and ensure those ones don't leave!'

Tapa and the other three chiefs were halted at the mid-deck gate. They looked up at Bligh furiously. Tapa shook his fist. Why were they not allowed to leave with the others?

Men raced to the capstan and the yards. The anchors were raised and catted, some sail made, and *Bounty* moved off to the west, propelled by a sou'easterly breeze.

Fletcher stood on the masthead platform, observing the confusion below. The small canoes had been paddled off, but one double-hulled canoe trailed in *Bounty*'s wake. It was clear to him why this was so: the men in the big canoe would not abandon their chiefs.

Bligh was shouting now, calling for the officers and crew to assemble on the mid-deck. The four chiefs sat by the rail, frowning, muttering among themselves, irate at being detained.

Fletcher joined the men on the mid-deck, not wanting to go near Bligh. Now he stood alone on the quarterdeck, his pistol tucked into his belt. He began to rant again.

'The slackness among this ship's company is deplorable! You are all, officers and crew, a disgrace to the King's navy! Yesterday a valuable grapnel was stolen by a native, under the very eyes of the officers and crew of this ship. But I intend to get the grapnel back! And I will get it back!'

He drew the pistol from his belt and began waving it about. 'Peckover, tell that lot in the big canoe the grapnel must be returned. Cole and Morrison, take the natives below. They are to be kept there until the grapnel is returned. And give the buggers some coconuts to husk.' He leaned over the rail. 'Do it now!'

The boatswain and his mate obeyed, although they looked far from happy at this order. The chiefs were outraged. This was the very worst kind of insult. Only kakai — commoners — husked coconuts. By being forced to do this work, the chiefs' mana was being publicly stripped away.

As the men were taken below, Fletcher realised what Bligh's tactic was. It had been Cook's strategy, if items of equipment were stolen, to take chiefs hostage and hold them until the objects were returned. Now Bligh was attempting to do the same as Cook had done, notably on the island of Raiatea, when he sought to force the return of some deserters by holding a chief and his family hostage. Yet this furore was over such a minor item. And it was obvious that the chiefs themselves were in no position to force the grapnel to be retrieved. Neither were those in the big canoe.

Fletcher shook his head in frustration. All this strife for one frigging grapnel?

Hours passed. Bligh had gone below. Norton and Linkletter were at the helm, Fryer beside them. Fletcher climbed up to the mainmast platform. The big canoe was still following them. Nomuka was now just a low line away to the south-east.

Without warning Bligh came back up the stairs to the deck. He yelled up at Fryer, 'Put her about!'

The sheets were loosed, *Bounty* went about, the sheets were pulled in and made fast. She began to sail on her reversed course. The canoe switched its lateen sail so that its course too was altered. Bligh yelled again, 'Cole, Morrison! Bring the buggers up from below!'

On the mid-deck, Bligh shook Tapa and the other three by the hand and presented each of them with an axe and a chisel. Although they accepted the tools, they continued to glower at Bligh.

The canoe drew up alongside and the chiefs got down into it. It was filled with furious-looking men.

The canoe's line was cast off and it quickly slipped away, a tall man controlling its steering paddle. Fletcher and *Bounty*'s crew watched its departure in silence. This visit had been a disaster. The Friendly Isles? More like the fiendly ones. And their commander was the fiendliest of all.

Bligh returned to the quarterdeck. He declared, 'You see how I treated those chiefs? That's the way to do it, show them who's in charge. The natives always respect a strong attitude.'

Fletcher thought, nothing could be further from the truth. The chiefs had realised they could not for the moment avenge the insult to their mana, so had made a pretence of acquiescing. But they were undoubtedly smouldering inside, like Kao, the nearby volcanic island. He would not like to be aboard the next British ship that called at Nomuka. Retribution would surely erupt towards the ship's company. And the grapnel has not been returned.

Fletcher kept staring southward towards the declining profile of Nomuka. But his mind lay far beyond it, in Tahiti. The island he had lost. He had many more months to endure on this floating prison, with its malicious gaoler. *Bounty* had become as much a penal vessel as those Thames prison hulks.

He looked north. Off the starboard bow he could see two spectral shapes, appearing to overlap, one conical and smoking, the other forested with a blunted summit. Kao and Tofua. Above them were dark clouds, bunched and crowded, like a herd of charging elephants. Storm clouds.

'Mr Christian, have you overseen the cleaning of the crew's quarters?'

'I have, sir.'

'And were they cleaned to your satisfaction?'

'They were.'

'Not to mine. I have just inspected them myself. I found filth in the crew's mess. Unwashed benches and cockroaches. It is not good enough.'

'I saw no evidence of filth when I left the mess an hour ago.'

'God damn you, man! I saw it with my own eyes. Filth! I won't stand for it on this ship!'

'As I said, the cleaning and washing was done to my satisfaction.'

'Oh, it was, was it? Well, it was not done to mine. We obviously have different standards, Christian. You may be from a superior class to mine, but always remember, on this ship that counts for nothing. Your Cumbrian pedigree is meaningless now.'

'I have never claimed otherwise.'

'But you think it, don't you? Yes, I know, you think you and your class are superior. But I am in charge here, I control this ship. Never forget that fact. Here your background counts for nothing. Furthermore, you owe me money. Never forget that.'

Fletcher walked away, sickened. To think he once respected the man.

Bligh next appeared on deck at noon the following day. Fletcher was on the quarterdeck with Peter Heywood and Ned Young; Norton and Simpson were on the wheel, Fryer beside them. The captain stalked along the larboard side of the ship. When he reached a pile of coconuts, he stopped. This was his personal supply, supplied by chief Tapa. Bligh turned and called up to *Bounty*'s master, 'Mr Fryer, this pile of coconuts appears somewhat reduced. Get down here.'

Fryer studied the pile. 'It does seem smaller. Perhaps the men walking over it has reduced its size. The deck is so crowded, what with all the livestock and the produce. It obliges the men to walk over the coconuts.'

Bligh shook his head. 'No, Fryer. I believe a theft has been committed.' His voice rose as he directed it at Cole. 'Call the ship's company together! And tell them to bring up every coconut stowed below!'

The crew stood beside their personal piles of nuts. Some grinned, conscious of the farcical nature of this exercise. The nuts had been traded on Nomuka at the rate of one nail for twenty nuts. Standing beside Fryer, Fletcher shook his head in exasperation.

Noticing the gesture, Bligh swung about. 'Was it you who stole my coconuts, Christian?'

'I took one, yes. It was hot last night, I was thirsty, and I thought the loss of one nut of no consequence.'

'One? One? You lying hound. I believe you have stolen half the pile.'

'I have not, sir. I took only one.'

Bligh strode over and thrust his face up at Fletcher's. 'You lie. You have stolen half of them!'

'That is not so, sir. Why do think I would be so mean as to steal half your nuts?'

'Because you are a thief. A thief and a liar.' He spun about. 'I'll get to the bottom of this!'

Later those who were present reported that this seemed like the first act in a charade which was to reach its climax a day later. Bligh interrogated each crew member in turn as he stood beside his personal pile of coconuts. Surrounded by the pig and goat pens, chicken coops and piles of fruit and vegetables, the scene resembled a disorderly country market overseen by an escaped lunatic. And as before, it was his officers at whom Bligh directed most of his vitriol.

'Young! How many nuts did you buy?'

'Twenty.'

'And how many have you eaten?'

Young shrugged. 'Dunno. I wasn't counting.'

'God damn you, man! You're a rogue as well! Like all my officers! All thieves and scoundrels. Next you'll be stealing my yams!' He turned to Samuel, his clerk. 'The men may take their nuts back below. The officers' nuts are to be stowed aft and they are not to have the use of them.' He faced the crew again. 'You lot, your grog is stopped, and your yam ration halved.' His voice rose further. 'I'll make half of you jump overboard before you get through the Endeavour Straits!'

Fletcher and the other officers stood in silence, astounded at this raving. In one fell swoop their commander had attacked their integrity, curtailed their private and public food supply, and stopped their liquor entitlements. Morrison muttered to Fletcher, 'He's not touching my nuts. I'll hide them under my cot.'

Bligh's eyes swept the assembly again. 'Attend to your duties!' He went below.

That afternoon, as Fletcher sat brooding on the after deck, Bligh appeared at the top of the stairway. 'Mr Christian!'

Fletcher looked up. 'What is it?'

'Have your nuts been taken below and stowed?'

'I did not trade for any nuts on Nomuka, so I have none to stow.'

'Ha! And I know why. Because you steal them from the others. The way you stole mine. You are a thieving swine, Christian. You are unfit to be an officer!'

Fletcher got up and walked away, his cheeks burning. Tears streamed from his eyes. He went along to the larboard side to the foredeck, trying to put as much distance between himself and the captain as was possible. He felt drained, emptied of hope. Beneath him, *Bounty* rose and fell with the swells. Now there was only one thing he could do.

Purcell was on the foredeck, working on a repair to the cutter's keel. The carpenter looked up, and frowned. 'What is it, Christian?'

'I can't take any more.'

'Of his rages?' Purcell snorted. 'You think you're alone in that?' He brought his hammer down on a spike nail. 'You've seen the way he treats me.' He attempted a smile. 'But bear an even strain, Christian. We have a following wind, and we're on our way home.'

'But think what we must endure before then.' Ashamed of his unmanly tears, Fletcher blinked them away. 'The Barrier Reef, the Endeavour Straits. He threatens us all with what he will do to us in those waters.' He shook his head. 'I tell you, Will, I can take no more of it. I'm leaving.'

'What do you mean, leaving? The ship?' Purcell looked around, to determine if anyone else could hear.

'Yes. I'll make a raft, and take it to that island.' He pointed towards distant Tofua. 'With your help.'

'That's a crazy notion.'

'It isn't. It would be crazy for me to stay. Bligh is driving me out of my mind. I have to go.'

'Christian, abandon that plan.' He waved at the sea. 'I've seen sharks out there. Big ones. And the natives of these islands are not well disposed towards us. If you made it ashore they would likely kill you. It would be madness to take that course.'

'I must. It's the only honourable course to take.'

'Honourable? A strange word to describe what you intend. Going to your certain death.'

'It is the right word, because for me to stay would be dishonourable.'

Purcell gave him a pitying look. 'So what do you need?'

'Planks, spars, ropes. If you get them for me tonight, I'll put a raft together and go over the side.'

There was a long pause, then Purcell nodded. 'I'll get the materials. Be back here at ten bells.'

'Thanks, Will.' Fletcher gripped the carpenter's arm. 'It has to be done. I can stand him no more. At ten bells, then.'

That evening a new moon rose in the east, a cuticle in the blackness. This presaged a full moon by the time they reached the reef-ridden New Holland coast. Helpful. To the north Kao's summit glowed like a firework; to starboard Tofua was an inky mass. The afternoon breeze had died away, the night was warm, the ocean lapped at *Bounty*'s hull. An unusual silence had befallen the ship, disturbed only by the creak of her timbers.

In his berth, Fletcher was beginning to get together his possessions. Bligh's servant, John Smith, appeared in the cabin doorway. Touching his forehead, he said, 'Scusing me Mr Christian, but Captain Bligh would be pleased if you could join him for supper this evening.'

Fletcher's jaw dropped. 'He wishes me to—'

Obviously appreciating the irony of the invitation — he had overheard Bligh's latest tirade — Smith nodded. 'Join him for supper, yes.'

Fletcher exhaled. 'Tell the captain that I will not be able to attend his supper as I am feeling unwell. But do give him my compliments.'

Getting the ironical message, Smith flicked up his eyebrows. As the man who had had to do Bligh's bidding day and night for a year and a half, he too had been on the receiving end of his verbal attacks.

Fletcher mulled over the supper invitation. It mystified him. Did the man have no idea how deeply his razor tongue cut? How wounding his words were? Had he no conception of how the victims of his abuse felt? Could he not imagine the feelings of others? The answers to all those questions was an emphatic 'no', Fletcher concluded.

Almost everyone had given up dining with Bligh. Only the toady Hayward, whom no one liked, still accepted the captain's invitation to dine with him. And below decks the men hissed Hayward for doing so.

Purcell kept his word: he had produced the materials Fletcher needed. Under cover of darkness on the foredeck, he lashed six planks to two spars. He had a pack full of provisions and a water flask. As he worked he felt fatalistic. If he drowned on the way to Tofua he didn't care, at least he would die a free man.

But now nature conspired against him. The night was stifling, *Bounty* was almost becalmed, and below decks the air was so muggy that nearly all the crew were lying topside, spread about the decks.

Fletcher had no hope of getting his raft over the side without the alarm being raised by one of them. Then he might be rescued, and incarcerated by Bligh for desertion.

His next watch would begin at four in the morning. He would wait till then, he decided, when it was cooler and the crew had gone below to their berths. Then he would go over the side. He returned to his cabin and his hammock.

Among Fletcher's closest shipmates — Peter, Ned and George — the word had been passed that their friend was planning to abandon the *Bounty*.

George was determined to dissuade his friend from deserting. Just before four he went below. Fletcher's berth was a few feet forward of the foot of the companionway ladder. A seal-oil lantern hung near the foot of the ladder, giving off a pallid light. Fletcher's berth was screened by a sheet of canvas.

Lifting the canvas, George growled in his Orkney accent, 'Fla-tcher!'

'What is it?'

Fletcher sat up. He had hardly slept, plagued by thoughts of his impending action and probable death. Crouching beside him, George spoke urgently. 'Don't take to the raft, it's a daft idea. Don't do it.'

'I must. It's the only way.'

'No, it is not the only way.'

'For my own sanity, George, I must leave.'

'You don't have to leave.' George paused, and Fletcher could hear his deep breathing. 'The men are ripe for anything, Fletcher.'

The canvas fell and George was gone. Fletcher lay for a few minutes, his mind churning. Ripe for anything. What did that mean? Did the men want Bligh taken down? He got up, pulled on his shirt and trousers and climbed the stairs. Topside, he replaced Peckover as watchman. Ellison was at the helm, with Mills. Fletcher greeted them with feigned casualness.

He settled in to his watch, standing at the base of the mainmast, one arm around it. His mind continued to seethe. *Bounty*'s timbers creaked as she rolled in the swells; above him the sails drooped and flapped.

Out of the darkness another figure appeared. Ned. 'Fletcher!' he whispered.

'What is it?'

'The raft notion. Drop it.'

'What else can I do? I've been in hell these past weeks.'

Ned glanced around, then murmured, 'We can seize the bastard and take the ship. Now's the time. All we need to do is get some of the men on our side and take control of the arms chests. With the arms we take the ship. We'll cast Bligh adrift in the cutter. There's no need for bloodshed. The people are ready, Fletcher.'

He slipped away.

Take the ship. Now's the time. Fletcher's mind was on another course now. If there was to be an insurrection, he was the one to lead it. The fact that Bligh had been his friend was irrelevant now. His mentor had become his tormentor. His brother Charles's advice beamed at him through the darkness: Despots must be stood up to, Fletcher.

Control of the ship meant deposing Bligh and establishing a new authority. He, Fletcher, would be free. Now's the time. Yes, those in authority — Bligh, Fryer, Elphinstone and Cole — were all below and still sleeping.

But who could he count on to support him? In his mind he drew up a list.

He thought of the ones whom Bligh had had lashed: Quintal, more than once, McCoy, Alex Smith, Thompson, Williams, Sumner. They had committed reckless acts and had been flogged for it. The would-be deserters, Millward and Muspratt, had been punished by Bligh. Martin? Yes, he too had been lashed and abused, and had been heard to curse the commander. Ned would join in. So, eleven men with motivation. Yes, that would probably be enough for them to take the ship. Provided they had the arms.

But at what price? If he failed, a fatal one. Confinement, a court martial, loss of honour and death by strangulation from a navy yardarm. A high price indeed. Yet what he was now experiencing —

false accusation, verbal abuse and humiliation — amounted to a kind of living death. He could, and would, endure it no longer. His mind had become filled with the blackest of thoughts, ones there was no hope of ridding himself of while he shared the ship with Bligh. The man's conduct, for whatever reason — envy, mania, or the worst to consider, his unnatural desire — had become insufferable. He was treating all his officers with disdain, but he, Fletcher, was being singled out for special contempt.

Again he brought to mind his brother Charles's case. He and his other insurgents had deposed their commander but had not been held culpable. The commander had been in effect found to be at fault. Was the case of Bligh not similar? Mutiny could in some circumstances be justified, surely. And Bligh's conduct may well not survive scrutiny by the authorities, should sworn eyewitness evidence of his misconduct be heard. As Charles's captain's had been.

Fletcher hugged the mainmast more tightly. Yes, rebellion was the only way. But first, a precaution. If he failed, he must die, and do so on his own terms.

He went aft to the mizzen mast, from which the sounding lines dangled. With his knife he cut one of the lines, with a heavy lead weight attached, and tied it round his neck, slipping the weight under his shirt. Should he fail, he would leap overboard and let the lead take him down with it. The sharks would do the rest.

Quintal and McCoy were among those still sleeping on the foredeck. Fletcher went to them. 'Matt! Will!' Both came to and looked at him groggily. 'What is it?' McCoy mumbled.

'I'm taking the ship. Are you both with me?'

They sat up. Quintal's expression became animated. 'Aye,' he said. 'I'm with you.' He turned to McCoy. 'Will?'

'Aye, me too.' Both scrambled to their feet.

Fletcher put his face close to theirs. 'Go below and rouse those who should be with us. Lamb, Martin, Churchill, Millward, Muspratt, Alex Smith. I'll let the others on watch know. But there is to be no bloodshed.'

Coleman was dozing by the starboard rail. Fletcher shook him awake. 'Joseph!' He stirred. Fletcher whispered, 'I'm taking the ship. Are you with me?'

The armourer's eyes gleamed. 'Sure I am.'

'We need the keys to the arms chests. Fryer will have them. Can you get them from his berth?'

Coleman grinned. He reached into his jacket pocket and withdrew two sets of keys. 'No need, Fletcher. Here they are.'

'How did you—'

'Fryer passed them to me. He was tired of being wakened by that dimwit Norman, wanting access to the chests at night so he could shoot at sharks.'

'Right. Unlock the chests. We'll all need pistols and cutlasses, as well as muskets. Ammunition, too, and bayonets.'

Below on the orlop deck, Quintal obeyed Fletcher's instructions. He knew who detested Bligh, knew who could be relied on to join the mutiny. One after another, roused figures came up on deck through the for'ard hatchway: Burkett, Lamb, Muspratt, Williams, Alex Smith. Now, the arms chests. One was below by the main hatchway, the other on the upper deck.

Two of the midshipmen, Hallett and Hayward, were asleep on the chests, Hayward on the one below, Hallett on the upper deck chest. Fletcher shook Hayward's shoulder. 'Wake up! Wake up!'

When he sat up, Fletcher admonished him. 'Get up on deck and attend to your duties, man!'

Hayward stumbled to the ladder and went topside.

The chest was now unguarded. Fletcher unlocked it, then eyed the contents. Muskets, pistols, cutlasses, cartons of ammunition. His heart began to race. Armed, they couldn't fail. Mustn't fail.

He helped himself to a musket with a fixed bayonet and a carton of cartridges. Pocketing the ammunition, he slipped a cutlass through his belt, then went back topside. The insurgents were clustered on the foredeck, speaking in low tones. When Fletcher appeared on deck, armed like a buccaneer, the men murmured approval. Quintal gripped his arm. 'You're in charge, now, Christian. Go for the bastard.'

'Not yet,' he replied. 'Thompson and Burkett, get to the chest below and collect the arms. And cartridges, enough for all of us. And make no noise. We mustn't wake Bligh, Fryer and the others before we're ready to.'

The pair nodded and crept off.

It was now after five. The eastern sky was becoming paler, although there was still no wind. Swells slopped and slurped against *Bounty*'s bow. Her timbers were moaning softly, like a cello ensemble. The figures on the foredeck were becoming more distinct, but they still could not be seen by the helmsmen at the other end of the ship. Looking at the lightening sky, Fletcher knew the point of no return had been reached. An impetus had built: now the moment had come for him to confront the man who had become his nemesis.

The door of Bligh's cabin was ajar. Cutlass in his right hand, Fletcher yanked it open. Behind him were Churchill, Burkett and Mills, all holding muskets with bayonets fixed. Bligh woke up. He was wearing a nightshirt and cap. Fletcher took a step forward and put the cutlass to his throat. Bligh struggled into an upright position, eyes bulging with disbelief. This is a nightmare, the popping eyes implied.

Fletcher gripped the cutlass. Now he had him. 'Get up!' he shouted. He grabbed the nightshirt with his left hand and hauled him from his cot.

Bligh began to yell. 'What is the meaning of this violence, Christian?'

'I'm taking the ship. Hold your tongue and you won't be hurt.'

'What's the matter? What's the matter?'

'The matter is that you have put me in hell these past weeks.'

Tearing off his cap, Bligh screamed. 'Murder! Murder! Murder!'

His howls were so loud they could be heard throughout the lower deck.

Churchill shoved his way forward, a length of cord in his hands. 'Sod you, Bligh,' he snarled. 'I'm trussing you.' Towering over the captain, he grabbed Bligh by the arm and spun him about. With Fletcher standing back, Churchill and Burkett tied Bligh's wrists and his arms behind his back, grunting with satisfaction as they tightened the rope. The tail of his nightshirt had become caught up in the rope, leaving his white bum exposed. He looked like a deranged patient who had wandered out of an infirmary.

Fryer's cabin was on the other side of the aft stairway. Having heard the yelling, he pushed his door open, but it was now guarded by Quintal and Sumner. They shoved him back inside.

'You're our prisoner, Fryer,' Quintal told him.

The master looked about wildly, as if expecting assistance from some of the others. Quintal grabbed his shirt front and shook him hard.

'Unhand me, Quintal, you swine!'

'Hold your tongue or you're a dead man! Mr Christian is the captain of the *Bounty* now.'

'What are you doing with the captain?'

Sumner pushed forward, grinning. 'We're putting him in the cutter and setting him adrift. Then we'll see if the bugger can survive on three quarters of a pound of yams a day!'

'Into the cutter? For what reason?'

'Oh, for Christ's sake, can't you understand? We're getting rid of the pig.'

Fryer cried out, 'But the cutter's not seaworthy! It's been eaten by worms.'

Fletcher came over to them, still brandishing the cutlass. Full of assurance now, he ordered Sumner and Quintal, 'Confine Fryer to his cabin.'

He turned back to Bligh, whose expression was dazed, his mouth hanging open. 'On deck with you,' Fletcher ordered, pointing to the stairs with the cutlass. Realising he had no option, Bligh shuffled to the stairs, one buttock still exposed. Fletcher was brimming with the power of authority and the satisfaction of redress. Now it is me who humiliates you, he thought, and it is a satisfying feeling.

He led Bligh up on deck. It was daylight now and the armed men were visible.

'What's the meaning of this?' Bligh demanded again, blinking at the insurgents.

Fletcher put his face close to his. 'How can you ask that, when you have treated me so abominably?'

'I, abominable? I taught you all you know! I advanced you money!'

Fletcher's reply was in a bitter tone. 'Yes, you were my benefactor for a time. Then, after I spurned your advances, you turned treacherous.' He drew back. 'You have treated me and the other officers like flunkies. You have abused and insulted us. You have proven unfit for command. Now, get aft!'

With the cutlass, Fletcher prodded Bligh to the mizzen mast, near *Bounty*'s stern. There, hands still tied behind his back, he was guarded by Churchill, Burkett and Alex Smith, all with bayonets pointed at him. 'Hold him there,' Fletcher ordered. Smith tugged Bligh's nightshirt tail out from under the rope in which it had become snagged.

Fletcher began to go for'ard, Bligh's cries following him. 'Infamy! Outrage! You'll fucking hang for this, Christian! You and all the other shits!'

Turning back, Fletcher stared at the abject figure. Lapsing into Tahitian, he shouted 'Mamoo! Hold your tongue and I'll not hurt you.'

To think he had once been friends with this stunted, foul-mouthed bully. How could he have so misjudged the man?

Ignoring Bligh's continuing cries, Fletcher went to the front of the ship. He tore the lead line from around his neck and flung it overboard. No need for that, now. He was in charge, and he had much to live for.

On the foredeck he carried out a head count. He reckoned there were now fifteen hard men on his side. And because they were all armed, they had control. Among those who had been doubtful, Millward had been ordered by his friend Churchill to join the mutineers. He concurred; nobody argued with Churchill. Young Ellison too had joined the revolt.

Fletcher now considered the Bligh loyalists. Of these, Fryer was still confined to his cabin. Cole, Lebogue and Coleman had not gone over to the side of the mutineers. Neither had Morrison, McIntosh,

Norman, Simpson and John Smith. Samuel, Hayward and Hallett would not join, and neither would purblind Byrne. Surprisingly, Will Purcell had declined to support the mutiny, despite loathing Bligh.

Gardener Nelson's allegiance lay with his breadfruit plants; he had been sleeping with them in the greenhouse since Tahiti. He remained loyal to Bligh. His colleague, Brown, did not. Loving Tahiti and despising Bligh, he willingly joined Fletcher's team.

Bligh's clerk, Samuel, showed courage by going below and asking Mills for entry to the captain's cabin. When consent was grudgingly given Samuel gathered up Bligh's compass, his purser's records and his commission authority. But Mills refused to let him take any charts, journals or navigational devices.

Fryer was still in his cabin, but his shouting could be heard topside. Quintal's head appeared at the top of the stairway. 'He's beggin' to talk to you,' he told Fletcher. 'Shall we let him?'

'Yes, bring him up. But keep him well guarded.'

Fryer strode up to Fletcher, his face distraught, his eyes wild. 'For God's sake, Christian, release the captain.'

'It's too late for that, Fryer. Bligh has brought this upon himself. He's to be set adrift. As are you and his other followers.'

'But why—'

'He's leaving the ship. And so are you!' He ordered Quintal and Sumner, 'Take Fryer back to his cabin!'

It was now seven-thirty. As Fletcher issued orders to his supporters, Bligh's loyalists stood about dumbly. A few, notably Hayward and Hallett, were tearful. Fryer, now allowed on deck, looked like a dead man standing. Some of Fletcher's supporters had not been issued with weapons, so were hard to define as his followers. Others had snatched up weapons in the excitement of the hour, without committing to the mutiny. Peter Heywood was one of these. He raced about the decks, waving a cutlass like a boy playing pirates.

Temporarily released from his bonds, Bligh pulled on his shirt, trousers and jacket, which had been brought up by his servant. Then, roped once again to the mast, he continued to stare about him in disbelief at what was happening.

Now that the boil had been lanced, the pus flowed. Relishing their newly won freedom of speech, the mutineers began taunting their deposed commander. 'Shoot the bugger!' Young shouted. 'Blow his brains out!' cried Churchill. 'Now you try and live on our rations!' Burkett yelled. 'No more fiddling our rations!' McCoy shouted. 'Scrub the deck yerself now, you short-arsed bastard!' Quintal bellowed.

Cole approached Fletcher on the mid-deck. He pleaded, 'I beg you to stop this scheme, Christian. Before it's too late.'

'It's already too late, Cole. You well know how the man has mistreated me.'

'We all know it. But you must drop your plan.'

'No. Bligh's tyranny is finished.'

The boatswain put his face in his hands.

On the foredeck, preparations were being made to launch the smaller cutter. Purcell confirmed that it was indeed rotting at the keel. But so was the larger boat, he reported. 'It will leak grievously,' he said. He begged Fletcher, 'We must use the launch instead.'

Fletcher gave this consideration. If the cutters weren't seaworthy, it was the ship's launch or nothing. He had no intention of committing murder, directly or indirectly. 'Very well,' he said. 'Prepare to lower the launch.'

Eighteen men volunteered to go with Bligh in the launch, which was tied alongside the ship, starboard side. After Fryer and the other loyalists got down into it, it became low in the water. There were barely seven inches of freeboard. Yet armourer Coleman and carpenter's mates Norman and McIntosh still pleaded with Fletcher to be allowed to go with their captain. He refused. 'You're staying with the ship,' he told them. 'Your skills are needed.'

Some supplies had to be taken aboard the launch. Cole and a few of the others had collected up bags of ship's biscuit, a cask of water and some coconuts. Reluctantly Fletcher also allowed four cutlasses and some of Purcell's woodworking tools to be taken into the launch. More food and some clothing was thrown down into the launch by the loyalists still on the *Bounty*.

Now came the turn of the man who just hours ago had been the commander. Fletcher led Bligh to the rail, prodding his side with his bayonet, resisting an urge to slide the steel between his ribs, having to again remind himself again that he must not commit murder.

At the rail, Fletcher untied Bligh's wrists. 'I must have a sextant,' Bligh said. 'And writing materials. My notebooks and journal. Is that too much to ask?'

Stripped of his authority and dignity, mocked and derided by many of his men, Bligh presented an ignominious figure. Fletcher felt a flash of compassion for the man. 'Very well,' he said, and told Martin to fetch what Bligh wanted.

When Martin returned with the sextant, books and writing materials, Bligh hugged them to his chest. Then he gave one last look at his captor, his mouth twisting into a sneer. Fletcher's hatred for the man came rushing back, but he said nothing more.

Not so Bligh. He raised a fist defiantly. 'You cannot hide, Christian,' he said, his chest rising and falling. 'We will find you. And after we do, you will hang like the common criminal you are.'

Fryer held out his hand to Bligh and he took a seat in the stern of the launch. Standing at the rail of *Bounty*, verging on tears, were loyalists Coleman, McIntosh and Norman. Fiddler Byrne was weeping, aware that there was no place for an almost blind man in a boat cast adrift. Coleman shouted down to Bligh, 'Remember, sir, I had no part in this hideous business!'

Looking up at them, Bligh yelled back, 'Never fear, my lads, I know you can't all come with me. I know which of you have not followed the mutineer Christian. And I'll do you justice if ever I reach England!'

There were now nineteen men in the launch and twenty-five aboard the ship. Fletcher cast its line off and the launch slipped sternward. On *Bounty*'s after deck, Young broke into a Tahitian dance, waving his arms, gyrating his hips and whooping with joy. Churchill, McCoy and Alex Smith were grinning like mad men as they swigged the grog ration that Fletcher had rewarded them with. They began to shout, 'Huzzah! Huzzah! Huzzah for Tahiti!'

The Bligh loyalists on board stood about in mute uncertainty, staring at the departing launch, not knowing where they would now be taken or what their fate would be.

In the launch, six men picked up the oars and began to row the overladen vessel. From *Bounty*'s decks they watched its solitary sail being raised. It caught the breeze. Then, with Bligh gripping the tiller, it turned and headed in the direction of Tofua, fifteen miles to the east.

Fletcher stood on the quarterdeck, watching the launch grow smaller. He had given Ellison the helm and told him to take a south-easterly course. The sun was high now, the wind a steady five knots. To larboard the islands of Kao and Tofua were fading into the mist and the launch was disappearing then appearing among the swells.

The breadfruit plants were tossed out *Bounty*'s stern windows, accompanied by shouts of glee from the throwers, among them gardener Brown. From the taffrail Fletcher watched the pots floating briefly in the wake, their foliage waving in the wind before they sank into the sea. The great breadfruit transplantation scheme was over.

We will now be able to claim the Great Cabin's space, Fletcher realised. And he wondered, what else can we claim?

Gilbert
Islands

Christmas Island

Phoenix
Islands

Tuvalu

Tokelau
Islands

Samoan
Islands

Fijian
Islands

Lau Group

Mutiny site

Niue

Aitutaki

Tofua

Nomuka

Tongatapu

Rarotonga

Manga

Friendly
Isles (Tonga)

Tropic of Capricorn

South

Pacific

Ocean

Marquesas
Islands

Voyage of HMAV *Bounty*
Tahiti to Pitcairn Island
4 Apr, 1789—15 Jan, 1790

——————— Route of the *Bounty* before the mutiny
●●●●●●●●●●● Route of the *Bounty* after the mutiny
☐　　　Places visited by the *Bounty*

ahine ☐ **Society Islands**
poorea ○☐ **Tahiti**

Gambier
Islands

☐ **Tupuai**

**Austral
Islands**

Henderson
Island ○

Ducie
Island ○

Pitcairn Island ☐

**Pitcairn
Group**

Part Four

THE RETURN

30 April 1789

After a break of several days, I am able to resume my journal writing.

I now command the Bounty, with a crew of twenty-four men under my authority. Although the sense of freedom I feel is uppermost in my mind, I am also aware that not all the crew are my followers. So my first task is to make it clear that I bear no grudge against those who did not join my rebellion. Men such as Coleman, McIntosh, Norman, Heywood, Morrison, Stewart and Byrne did not take action against Bligh, and that was their right. But neither did they suffer at his hands to the extent that I did.

Nevertheless my first duty as new commander is to instil unity into my crew, however disunited they may be. Since the ship is short-handed we must all work together to sail her. Accordingly, I have appointed Stewart as my second in command. Although a Bligh loyalist and hence not popular among my followers, the Orkney Islander is a consummate seaman. There was agitation to appoint Heywood to the role of second-in-command, but at seventeen I judged him to be far too young. Peter is but a boy, albeit a very bright one.

Order and discipline will be paramount from now on. I am conscious of the fact that our circumstances are unique. Although we are free of naval authority, from now on we must institute and maintain our own regime. We cannot hope to survive without being cohesive in our intent. This I stressed to the crew when they assembled yesterday. I told them firmly, 'It will be futile if, having overthrown one tyrannical regime, we find ourselves oppressed by another.' We also need to impress the natives we encounter, to show them we are not a rabble. To this end I have instructed that we will wear a uniform of sorts, cut and stitched from Bounty's old studding sails. I will donate my officer's uniform so that it can be cut up for edging this garb in blue. Muspratt has skills as a tailor, so he will be busy from now on with the sailmaker's shears, needle and thread. Also, Bounty's two cutters are being repaired, as we will have great need of them.

Although the mood aboard is buoyant and I am exhilarated from my newly won freedom, I am aware that factions still exist onboard and may emerge, to our detriment. Hence it is imperative that we find a safe haven as soon as possible, so that we can establish a shore-based settlement somewhere in this South Sea, one with activities of such benefits that they will forestall another insurrection.

I have moved myself into Bligh's cabin and given my own to Stewart. The Great Cabin is now given over to the stowage of the many artefacts the crew traded for at Nomuka, so that rather than resembling a greenhouse, it is now more like a London museum. My new berth contains many charts and journals of previous voyages, a resource which will be invaluable to us. Among these was the account of Captain Cook's third voyage, edited by Lieutenant James King. When perusing this I came upon this 1777 entry, while Cook was en route for Tahiti:

'... in the morning of 8th of August land was seen bearing NNE½E 9 or 10 leagues distant. At first it appeared in detached hills like so many islands but as we drew nearer we found they were all on one and the same island. I steered directly for it with a fine gale ... at day break the next Morning I steered for the NW, or lee side of the island, which we soon perceived to be guarded on every side by a reef of Coral rock which in some places extended a full mile from the land.'

Although Cook made no landing on this island, he established that its coordinates are 23° South and 210° East. As such it lies just north of the Tropic of Capricorn. From some natives who came out to his ship in canoes, Cook learned that its name is Tupuai. Although his ships Resolution and Discovery did not enter the lagoon, he left a useful description of the island. The men in the canoes

'... kept pointing to the shore and told us to go there. This we could very well have done as there was good anchorage without the reef and a break or opening in it, in which if there was not water for the Ships, there was more than sufficient for the boats, but I did not think proper to risk losing the advantage of a fair wind for the sake of examining an island that appeared of little consequence.'

So Cook's two ships sailed away.

Three hundred and fifty miles south of Tahiti, Tupuai resembles, from Cook's account, a smaller version of it, being encircled by a coral reef and well wooded, though less elevated. Since it was found by Cook to be inhabited it is probable that it also has sources of fresh water. Coconuts, breadfruit and fish too, most likely. I determined that this Tupuai may well be an island that has much to offer us as a place of refuge. Almost certainly it will be safer than Tahiti. As such, it will not be 'of little consequence' to us.

Although my thoughts are mainly with the day-to-day sailing of Bounty, I cannot help dwelling on Bligh and his followers in the launch. Will they survive? Will they find us? I very much doubt either eventuality. It is my belief that Bligh will take the launch first back to Tofua for provisioning, and thence south to the island of Tongatapu, where he spent time with Cook in '77. He became well acquainted with the chiefs there, he often boasted to me. Thus he will doubtless attempt to gain favour from them. But it is also my belief that he will not be able to leave that island, since there is no European outpost within reach of the launch. Instead he will have to wait for the arrival of the next European ship to visit Tongatapu, and that may not happen for years. Consequently no account of my insurrection can reach the Admiralty authorities for years. Thus we of the Bounty are free to choose whichever island we seek for a sanctuary, commencing with the island of Tupuai, towards which we are now headed. Once established there, we will return briefly to Tahiti to collect our lovers, then return to Tupuai to live. We cannot tarry on Tahiti. Other European vessels are bound to visit the island from now on, and these would alert the naval authorities to our presence should we stay. However we must return, albeit briefly. Young, McCoy, Quintal, Brown and Heywood have all told me how important it is to them to be reunited with their women, an emotion which I well understand. I too cannot wait to be with Isabella again, and to let her know that it is now possible for us to live together as man and wife.

While having supper with Stewart last evening, he asked me, 'Do you have any regrets about what has happened, Christian?'

I replied without hesitation, 'I do not. My life had become intolerable under Bligh. I could not endure many more months of his maltreatment. The course of action I took, I had to take.'

Although Stewart nodded, I could tell that he could not truly comprehend the depths of the despair I had felt these past weeks. What other course could I have taken, except self-murder? And at twenty-four years of age, and knowing that there is a wonderful woman who loves me, I have much to live for. Hence the new course I have taken.

Having declared that, I also admit that I carry Bligh's pistol, primed, under my belt at all times.

FC

28 May 1789

'Land! Land to starboard!'

The call came from Heywood, at the mainmast head. Half an hour later the island of Tupuai became visible from the decks. The crew stared at the new island. Under a cloudless sky they could see in its interior two forested hills, three or four miles apart, streaked with lesions of bare earth. A few miles ahead waves were breaking on the reef, and along the shoreline were white sand beaches, overlooked by coconut palms. The crew speculated about the island. Could they get through the reef? Would there be threatening natives? Would they have seen Europeans before? What would their women be like?

Spyglass to his eye, Fletcher ordered the helmsmen to steer for the north-west coast, where Cook had noted there was a passage. A mile or so off the island, Fletcher told Stewart, 'Go in the cutter and sound the pass. See if it's suitable for us to enter.'

Bounty hove to while Stewart, rowed by four men, entered the pass. In his belt he carried a pair of loaded pistols. As he put down a lead-line, those on the ship saw a canoe put off from the shore. To his alarm Fletcher saw that it contained several men armed with spears, and that it was being paddled at speed towards the cutter.

When they reached it a native leapt into the boat and tried to grab one of the sailor's jackets. Stewart stood up, waved his pistol, then fired it into the air. There was a puff of smoke and at the percussion the man took fright and jumped back into the canoe, which was paddled back to the shore.

Stewart returned to the ship. 'They are not well disposed towards us,' he told Fletcher. 'But they were fearful of my pistols.'

'And the pass?'

'Twelve fathoms, with a sandy bottom. It will admit *Bounty* to the lagoon. But we must be armed when we enter.'

Cautiously they worked the ship through the pass and into the lagoon. Several of the crew stood in the bow, primed muskets at the ready. *Bounty*'s anchor was lowered off a small bay. Standing on the beach watching the ship were warriors in bark cloth skirts, armed with spears and clubs.

Canoes put out and surrounded *Bounty*, the men in them waving the spears and clubs. Fletcher called down in Tahitian from the mid-deck rail. 'Ia ora na! Ia ora na! Maeva! Maeva!' He made beckoning gestures to the men.

Although they seemed to understand, they refused his invitation to come aboard. Some brandished their spears.

Young said to Fletcher, 'Why are they so hostile, do you suppose?'

'They are mistrustful of our weapons. They probably have memories of when some of Cook's men came here from Raiatea.'

'Why?'

'They were seeking two deserters from *Discovery*. I read of it last evening in Cook's journal. His sailors were armed, and although the deserters were recaptured, in the process some warriors from this island were killed by musket fire.'

'Ah. Then what shall we do?'

'Wait for their leaders to arrive, then shower them with gifts. Show them that we mean no harm.' He paused. 'We need this island, Ned.'

The next morning another canoe came out, bearing an elderly man. He climbed aboard. Grey hair tied in a topknot, he had tattooed upper arms. Fletcher greeted him on the main deck. The man touched his chest. 'Mahana,' he said. 'Ra'atira. To'erauetoru.'

Relieved that contact had been established, Fletcher presented him with a hatchet and a spike nail. The man nodded, pleased, but at the same time stared in astonishment at the penned pigs and goats on the deck. Obviously his island did not have these animals. He pointed back at the shore, then at himself, indicating that he would soon return with others. But his eyes also followed the men on deck. As he got back into his canoe, Churchill said to Fletcher, 'Did you notice the old bugger checking the crew? I reckon he was counting heads.'

'I did. Put the men on full alert when he comes back. He won't be alone.'

He wasn't. But rather than returning with male warriors, Mahana's double-hulled canoe was occupied by eighteen women and six men. They climbed aboard. The women were all young, with glossy hair which reached their waists and did not cover their breasts. They wore skirts of white cloth and coloured flowers woven into their hair.

The crew stared, mouths agape, at the women, who beamed at the sailors and chanted melodiously. As the men made to move towards them, Fletcher called out. 'No! Stay there! Look!'

He pointed towards the lagoon, where dozens of canoes were streaming out to *Bounty*, filled with men. It was obvious that the beauties were a diversion. He called down to Churchill:

'Arm the crew!'

As the men took up arms, the young women looked as disappointed as the sailors. Minutes later the native men climbed aboard, then immediately began helping themselves to anything not bolted to the decks: boat hooks, lead-lines, grapnels, belaying pins, fishing lines.

Fletcher waded into the mob, shouting 'Aita! Aita! No! No!' He began to snatch back what they were attempting to seize. Other crew members did the same. A boy ran up onto the quarterdeck and snatched the compass from beside the ship's wheel.

Fletcher picked up a nettle, a length of knotted rope, and began to strike the youth hard about his bare back and shoulders. He dropped the compass and fled back to his canoe, crying out. The others followed, including the young women. Then, from his canoe, one of the men hacked through the rope attached to the anchor buoy. Furious, from the foredeck Fletcher fired his musket at the man. It missed. He shouted to Churchill, who held a scatter gun, 'Fire into the canoe!' The shot struck the occupants, who howled with pain. Minutes later all the canoes began to paddle hurriedly back to the shore.

Determined to press home this advantage, Fletcher ordered the boats to follow. Both cutters were rowed in to the beach, all aboard armed with muskets and pistols. The canoes had been dragged up onto the sand. When the warriors began to hurl stones at the sailors, striking some of them, Fletcher told the men. 'Fire at them!'

Those holding muskets leapt from the boats, aimed and fired. Four warriors fell, dead or wounded. The rest turned and fled into the bush above the foreshore.

The sailors peered into the canoes. There they saw several lengths of plaited rope. Stewart picked one up. 'What are these for, do you suppose?'

'Trussing their prisoners, I'd say,' Fletcher replied. 'But for the muskets, we could have been tied up with them.' He called out to the others, 'We'll tow the canoes back to the ship, for added security.'

That evening they held a meeting by candlelight in the officers' mess, around a flask of Canary Island red wine. Present with Fletcher were the men he considered most reliable: Stewart, Mills, Churchill and Morrison. He told them: 'This island, I believe, should be the one we settle on.'

Stewart looked dismayed. 'Surely not, in view of today's fracas.'

'That was but a minor confrontation. And one that demonstrated our greatly superior force.'

Churchill leaned forward. 'But we don't know how many warriors the island holds. Its population may be considerable.'

Fletcher shook his head. 'I doubt it. A few hundred, perhaps. And we have the cannons, muskets and pistols. Suitably fortified, we could defend ourselves from any native attack.'

Silence descended on the cabin. Responding to it, Fletcher pressed his case. 'Because the lagoon is not easily accessible, and the island is

229

small, it's unlikely that any other European ships will call here. They would have no reason to do so. I believe Tupuai will offer us sanctuary.'

'And do you still intend that we first return to Tahiti?' asked Morrison.

'Yes. To obtain supplies, and our women.' Fletcher stood up. 'Tomorrow we will go ashore and leave gifts for the people here, then leave for Tahiti.'

The boats landed near the easternmost point of the island. After following a trail inland they came to a cluster of thatched fares. All had been abandoned. After witnessing the power of the muskets their inhabitants had evidently fled and were in hiding. Fletcher left half a dozen hatchets and some nails on the mat in one house, then they returned to the ship.

Later that day *Bounty* was towed through the pass. Her sails set, with Fletcher at the helm, she sailed on a northward course for Tahiti.

Matavai Bay, 6 June 1789

Canoes by the dozen came out to greet them, their occupants waving, chanting and beating drums. They surrounded *Bounty* even before her anchors were lowered. Delighted to be back, the crew rushed to the rails, seeking their special taios and waving to them.

The bushy-haired figure of Tu was first to come aboard, followed by his wife Itia and their retinue. He carried garlands of tiare flowers.

Fletcher bowed to the chiefly couple and Tu beamed. 'Ia ora na, Titereano.' He placed a garland around Fletcher's neck and they pressed noses. Then he looked around the deck. 'Where is Parai?'

Fletcher had prepared a story. He replied in Tahitian, 'Captain Parai is on an island we discovered after we left here.' He pointed west. 'It is called Ay-too-tuk-ee.' Tu nodded. His people knew of this island. Tupaia, who had been there, had told them about it. The Tahitians knew it as 'Tootate'.

Fletcher continued. 'And Captain Tute was living there, we also found.'

Tu's jaw dropped. 'Tute was on Tootate?'

'Ae. And his ship, *Resolution*, was there too. Tute is very well. He took Captain Parai, the breadfruit plants and some of *Bounty*'s men on board his ship.' As this lie was told, Fletcher noticed Itia's face fall. He had been aware that for some reason Itia fancied Bligh. Takes one short fatty to fancy another, he concluded.

Tu was frowning now. 'Why did not Parai or Tute return with you to Tahiti?' he demanded.

'They were needed on Ay-too-tuk-ee. To collect more breadfruit plants to take back to Peretane.'

Although Tu nodded, he seemed doubtful. Fletcher's hands had turned sweaty. I'm not a natural liar. Unlike Bligh.

He continued his fiction: 'Tute and his son Parai have sent me here to collect many goats, pigs and chickens, to take to them on Ay-too-tuk-ee. We will pay you for these goods in iron, of course.' He gestured towards the companionway. 'Now, please come below and share some wine with me.'

'You have come back, Titereano.'

'I promised I would, didn't I?'

'Ae. Maeva, maeva.'

He held her tightly, felt her heart beating against him. He put his face in her hair, drew in its fragrance of tiare and monoi. 'Ua here vauia oe, Isabella.'

She held him tightly, her tears wetting his neck. 'Titereano, ua here vauia oe.' Then she drew back, and led him into the fare, to the sleeping mats.

He cried out with relief. There had been so much hatred these past weeks, and so much despair. But now there was this love and comfort, and he felt reborn by it. He was at peace again.

Kneeling alongside him, Isabella dabbed his forehead and cheeks with a piece of 'ahu cloth. 'Rest now, Titereano, rest now.'

Gradually his breathing slowed. His heartbeat too.

Rain poured down. Sheets of water cascaded from the eaves, forming a watery curtain between them and the rest of the world. Isabella opened a drinking nut and they took turns swigging from it, letting the juice flow down their chins. Then, lying side by side, he told her what had happened. She sat up, shocked.

'You put Parai in a vaka? And he sailed away?'

'Yes. With eighteen others.'

She frowned. 'But why did you not kill Parai? For what he did to you.'

Avoiding her gaze he said, 'I could not kill him. But in that small vaka, with so many men …' He closed his eyes. 'It might as well have been murder.'

As the hideous events came rushing back he turned away, trying to block out what had happened. Then he said, 'Before the mutiny I thought I would kill myself. In every direction I looked, I saw only darkness. Killing myself seemed the only answer.'

'Don't ever speak of such an evil!'

'But when I thought of you, and our times together, I could not do it. My love for you was stronger than my hatred for Parai.' He forced a smile. 'So I overcame that terrible thought.'

Isabella nodded. 'Ae, that is good. For us.'

The rain had eased but the eaves were dripping. From the forest surrounding the fare, an insect chorus began. Again Isabella dabbed his face and chest with the cloth, murmuring affection as she did so. He loved the afterwards of their love-making; the grateful touching and embracing, their halting, hybrid conversation.

There was much to talk about.

'I must leave Tahiti again soon, Isabella.'

'Uh? But you have only just come back.'

'I know. But it would be death for me to stay. King George will send ships from Peretane to look for me, and to capture me and the others.'

He didn't add, *And I will be hanged aboard one of the king's ships. And in the naval tradition, not by a quick drop through a trapdoor, but by*

232

being trussed and noosed and hauled aloft to a yardarm. A death by slow strangulation, my choking and shitting and pissing watched by a drooling crowd.

'But where will you go?'

'To Tupuai.'

'No! Stay here, on Tahiti. I will hide you, in the mountains. We will live there.'

'Mauruuru, Isabella. But no, people would tell, and we would be found and I would be arrested.' He slipped his hand under her hair. 'I will take *Bounty* back to Tupuai. And you and the others must come too.'

17 June 1789

At last I can attend to my journal again.

The ten days we spent on Tahiti were frantic, as we took aboard supplies for our new settlement on Tupuai. We have aboard a menagerie, so that Bounty could be renamed Fletcher's Ark, as Morrison quipped to me yesterday. Hundreds of hogs, fifty goats, dozens of chickens and some cats and dogs. We even have a cow and a bull, left on Tahiti by Cook. For some reason these did not breed. I very much hope they will get over their reluctance to do so after we set them ashore on Tupuai. So the decks are crammed with the livestock and poultry and resound with the creatures' snuffling, braying and clucking. The ship stinks like a barnyard. Never mind, the animals will be indispensable to our future.

Our human cargo is no less interesting. Having necessarily left some Bligh loyalists such as Norman and Byrne on Tahiti, and sworn them to secrecy as to our destination should English ships later arrive, I have my own men and their women with us. Foremost among these is Isabella who, though she did not want me to leave Tahiti, elected to go with me when she realised I had no choice in the matter. If we had tried to hide, people on the island would be sure to give our location away to the English authorities, for reward. Bounty hunters, so to speak.

I could not wish for a more loyal or loving woman than Isabella. My men have nick-named her 'Mainmast', because of her tallness and upright bearing, but I prefer my English name for her. Her favourite place on *Bounty* is in the bow. She stands there whenever conditions permit, wearing an *ahufara* — a bark cloth shawl — around her shoulders, one hand on the spritsail halyard, staring ahead, the wind blowing her hair. She makes a living figurehead, a great deal lovelier than the real one fixed to the prow beneath her.

Other of the men who are with their Tahitian lovers are Stewart, who has his Teria, whom he calls Peggy after his mother. Alex Smith has Te'ehuteatuanonoa, whom he (understandably) prefers to call Jenny. Will McCoy has his Te'o, known as Mary and Tom McIntosh also has a Mary. They are all loyal women.

This is the very first time most of us have been on a Royal Navy vessel which carries women. I relish the difference it makes. The men take more care over their conduct and suppress their brutishness. For their part, the women assist in the galley, wash the men's clothes and feed the livestock. They are resented only by the men who do not have women of their own. These have declared that they will take women of Tupuai as their lovers, and in view of the beauties who came aboard when we were there previously, this ambition is understandable.

On our second day at sea several stowaways emerged from hiding below decks. These are mainly the friends of some of my men, such as Coleman's *taio*, Tupairu. More surprising was the emergence of Hitihiti, the Bora Boran who sailed with Cook on a segment of his voyage in 1773. He is such an eager participant in our venture that I feel he will be an asset. He is also high-born, which may give him *mana* with the Tupuaians. Less welcome, because of their vulnerability, are the seven local boys and one girl who secreted themselves aboard during our disorderly departure. But now, as before, there can be no turning back. We are obliged to keep them.

So our complement of supernumeraries consists of eight Tahitian men, nine Tahitian women, the boys and the girl. These, plus my sailors, will be the foundation settlers of our new community, which I am determined will be one of peace and productivity.

I recall once finding in my cousin's library on the Isle of Man a book entitled 'Utopia', by Sir Thomas More. It depicted a society on an island in *the Atlantic Ocean, one which possessed a perfect harmony of living. More's idea of such a society appeals to me greatly. Thus, in my mind's eye I envisage on Tupuai a community which has such qualities. It will be based on human cooperation, pastoralism, crop-growing and grazing, as on More's Utopia. There are sufficient seeds of English crops remaining in Bounty's hold, along with our many livestock, for this vision to be realised.*

We possess, in short, every ingredient for our own South Sea Utopia.

TUPUAI, 13 SEPTEMBER 1789

The spear flew from the bush, hurled by an unseen hand. It struck Burkett, standing alongside Fletcher, in his left side. Screaming, he fell to his knees. Fletcher called to Timoa, one of the Tahitians, 'Look to him!'

Timoa put his arm around Burkett and dragged him back. Another of the Tahitians, Niau, pulled out the spear.

A group of Tupuaian warriors burst from the trees, waving spears and clubs. They wore pandanus skirts and caps embellished with black feathers. Around their waists were belts and pouches which held stones. From yards away they took the stones from their pouches and hurled them at Fletcher's men with deadly accuracy. One struck Morrison on his forehead. He dropped, stunned. Then they ran straight at Fletcher's party, screaming and waving their spears. Niau hurled the spear he had removed from Burkett's side like a javelin, and it went deep into the chest of one of the warriors.

To Hitihiti, Fletcher shouted, 'Fire at them!' He did so, and the face of one of the warriors exploded. Fletcher raised his own musket and aimed at a thickset man. He fired and the warrior dropped, clutching his belly. Morrison, now recovered, fired at a warrior who crashed to the ground. Hitihiti had reloaded, and he aimed and fired again. He was a crack shot; another warrior fell. But more were rushing up from the rear. Realising they were outnumbered, Fletcher shouted to his group, 'Back to the taro garden! Take cover behind the embankment!'

They retreated to a clearing in which there were taro beds behind walls of earth. Lying under cover of one of the walls, musket barrels resting on them, they resumed firing upon the war party, who had pursued them to this open ground. Fletcher chose a target, aimed and fired. Another man dropped, struck in the belly. Quickly Fletcher reloaded.

The firing continued for another twenty minutes. Fletcher and his men, sheltered by the earth wall, were able to fire from their position unassailably. But the attackers kept coming, screaming and hurling their spears, most of which flew over the heads of the defenders.

Hitihiti lay next to Fletcher. 'That man their leader,' he said, pointing at an older warrior with a headdress. He was exhorting the warriors by brandishing his club. 'I get him,' Hitihiti said. He aimed, fired, and the leader spun about and fell to the ground, his chest torn open. The rest of the war party stopped in their tracks. Then two of them bent down, picked up the dead man and dragged him away into the bush.

Fletcher stood up. Placing the butt of his musket on the ground, he used it to support himself. He felt shattered, and his body streamed with sweat.

What had happened today was a terrible business, the culmination of weeks of misunderstandings and conflict.

Further along the embankment, Burkett's wound was being staunched with cloth by Timoa. Morrison lay on his back, swigging from a water flask.

Hitihiti grinned at Fletcher. 'We beat them, Titereano. Many killed.'

Fletcher nodded. But he thought, what has become of my Utopia?

Later that day he called the men to assemble on *Bounty*'s mid-deck. The ship was anchored in the lagoon off the north-east coast of the island, opposite the garrison they were constructing, which Fletcher had named Fort George.

Aware that he needed more than ever to demonstrate leadership, as Fletcher addressed the assembly he tried to suppress his disillusionment over what had happened.

'Today's battle resulted in many native deaths. And some of our people were wounded.' Burkett grunted, and pointed to his bandaged side. 'Tinarou and his warriors will doubtless seek vengeance. In the face of this continuing hostility, we must consider whether or not to continue to stay on Tupuai.' His eyes swept the group. 'If we stay we can finish building Fort George and thereby establish a secure base for our community. To this end, chief Ta'aroa, who rules over the Natieva district, is our ally.'

A hand went up. It was Churchill's. 'How much longer will it take to finish the fort?' he asked.

'I estimate, to complete the walls and moat, will take another three months' work,' Fletcher replied.

There were mutterings from the company. Digging the moat, shifting the sticky earth in the heat with hoes, spades and mattocks — hammered out on a makeshift anvil by armourer Coleman — was exhausting work, as Fletcher well knew. He had been the leader of the digging parties. And lately, work on the fort's construction had stalled.

'If we vote to leave Tupuai and return to Tahiti, those of you who did not mutiny will be able to remain there with your taios and be uplifted by the next English ship to call.'

'And the ones who got rid of Bligh?' This demand came from Alex Smith, who had begun a relationship with a Tupuaian woman.

'We cannot stay on Tahiti,' Fletcher replied. 'We will sail on, in search of another sanctuary.'

Silence descended on the meeting. All were aware that cracks had appeared in their community during these past weeks. The causes were differences over how they should proceed from now on. Several people wanted to leave this island. Tupuai's people had proved to be fractious, and resentful of the Popa'a presence. Some of the mutineers wanted the *Bounty* dismantled, so that it would not attract the attention of any passing ship; others wanted the vessel kept so that it would allow them to leave the island if it was necessary to do so. Most worrying, *Bounty*'s women had heard a rumour that the ship's Tahitian men and the Tupuaians were plotting an alliance in order to overthrow all the Popa'a men.

There was also a problem with Tupuai's women. While agreeing to have sex with *Bounty*'s men ashore, in exchange for red feathers from the Friendly Isles, they refused to stay aboard the ship or sleep with them at the fort. The fact that the Tupuaian women were so alluring did nothing to resolve this dilemma.

Now, following today's bloody battle — Morrison had estimated that altogether sixty of chief Tinarou's warriors had been killed — the community's future had to be decided.

Fletcher put the matter to a vote. 'Those in favour of abandoning this island and returning to Tahiti?'

Nine hands were raised.

'Those in favour of remaining on Tupuai?'

Sixteen hands went up.

'Very well, we will stay.' He placed his tricorn back on his head. 'And in recognition of the vote, I order a double ration of grog for this evening.'

There were cries of delight at this announcement. But as the meeting disbanded, Fletcher was aware of disquiet rippling through the company, like tremors before an earthquake. He sensed that the matter was far from settled. That night, in bed with Isabella, warmed by her and the grog, he asked, 'What is your wish that we should do?' The women had not attended the meeting, or been asked their opinion.

She stroked his face. 'I think … the people need to think more. I think you should ask them to say again what they want.'

Fletcher agreed. He should have given them more time to consider the matter.

The following morning he called the men together again. The lagoon was mirror-like. *Bounty*'s sails remained furled, as they had been for weeks. Fletcher addressed them from beside the ship's wheel. 'It has been suggested that we vote again on the proposal, to return to Tahiti or remain here at Tupuai.' The assembly looked at him in silence. Most had gone to their berths last night still pondering the question.

'Are you all in favour of taking another vote?'

They were.

'Those who favour a return to Tahiti?'

Fifteen hands went up.

'Those in favour of remaining here?'

Ten hands went up.

Fletcher nodded. 'A clear majority. Very well.' He stared up at the sails and the limp ensign at the top of the mainmast. 'We will begin preparations to return to Tahiti.'

There was a collective sigh of relief. After overnight reflection, and discussions below deck, the majority had decided they had had enough of Tupuai's spear-throwing men, its petulant women, its scheming priests, its clannish chiefs and the tormenting swampland mosquitoes.

Time to move on, again.

19 September 1789
We are at sea again, bound for Tahiti.

I am aggrieved at the failure of the community on Tupuai. I held high hopes for its success. But during the ten weeks we were on the island, little went as I planned. My ambitions were thwarted at every turn, and for that I must accept some of the blame.

Unwittingly I became embroiled in Tupuai's enmities and did not make myself sufficiently aware of them. Although Tupuai is only five miles across and three miles from north to south, it is separated into three rival districts. The one in the west is large, the other two much smaller. Each district is led by a chief who is jealous of the other two. Each chief wished to gain the favour of Bounty's people, mainly, I now realise, in order to acquire our weapons, in order to subjugate the people of their rival districts.

Chief Tamatoa, who controls the western side of Tupuai, made me his taio not long after we arrived. He was delighted to become my friend and we exchanged names according to the native custom. However

I subsequently chose the site for Fort George in Chief Ta'aroa's north-eastern bailiwick, Natieva, as it was physically much more suitable for the garrison. This incurred the wrath of Tamatoa, who saw it as a betrayal of our friendship. Knowing the sensitivity of native alliances, I should have foreseen this antipathy. It was naive of me not to do so. Thereafter Tamatoa formed an alliance with the third district chief, Tinarau, to forbid any intercourse of their people with those of the Bounty. From then on our settlement of Fort George was doomed and hostilities inevitable. Following a battle with Tinarou's warriors, with many native deaths, we elected to leave Tupuai.

We quit the island with some difficulty. Our pigs and goats, which had been running free on the island (and causing damage to the natives' crops and gardens, another source of friction with them) had to be rounded up and taken back aboard. Also, Bounty had been anchored in a shoal-strewn part of the lagoon, and had to be hauled back to the passage near what we named Bloody Bay, on the north-west coast of the island, the scene of our first fatal altercation.

There we made preparations for our departure. Three Tupuai men who had become my friends implored me to take them with us to Tahiti, since because of their known loyalty to me they would be killed if they stayed. I agreed to this request, as they will be helpful in working the ship. One of these men, Tetahiti, is a particularly fine fellow, and a leader.

We weighed on 17 September.

I anticipate raising Tahiti in two more days. From there I have decided we will separate, leaving on the island those who wish to remain there and those who were loyal to Bligh. These are Coleman, Heywood, McIntosh, Norman, Burkett, Morrison, Norman, Byrne, Sumner, Thompson, Millward, Muspratt, Heildbrandt and Stewart. Several of these have taios on Tahiti, so they will be well looked after there.

Those loyal to me, along with our women and six native men, will leave Tahiti in search of a more suitable haven. My men are Young, Williams, Quintal, Smith (who yesterday confessed to me that he had signed on under a false name and that his real name is John Adams!), McCoy, Martin, Mills and Brown.

After the experience of Tupuai, I now know that the island we seek is one which must not only supply all our physical needs, it must also be completely uninhabited by natives.

There must surely be such an island somewhere in the South Sea.

I remain deeply regretful that the community I envisaged on Tupuai, one which could have embodied the ideals of Thomas More's Utopia, had to be abandoned.

Even more troubling, I remembered also reading that More himself was later accused of treason by the English king, and was convicted and beheaded.

MATAVAI BAY, 22 SEPTEMBER 1789

Hitihiti and the others Tahitians left the ship first, delighted to be home again. Then the belongings of those sailors who were staying on Tahiti were taken ashore, along with goods considered essential to their well-being: carpenter's tools, cooking utensils, clothing and wine. Some of the clothing formerly belonged to those who had gone with Bligh. Each man except blind Byrne was also given a musket and cutlass, and three extra firearms were allocated to Heywood, Norman and Burkett in recognition of their rank.

To prevent any kind of insurrection against his followers, only when everything else had been landed did Fletcher allow any ammunition to be taken ashore. He remained on board during the transfers, although Isabella and the other women went ashore to visit and farewell their families.

When Heywood came back from one of the cutter's transfers across to Point Venus he brought unwelcome news. 'An English vessel has been here, Fletcher.'

The sweat on Fletcher's body turned cold. 'When?'

'She arrived on the fifteenth of August, and left here three weeks ago. *Mercury*, she was called.'

'Not a naval ship, then?'

'No. A privateer. A brig, sailing under the Swedish flag.' Fletcher's sweat became less cold. 'But captained by an Englishman, by the name of Cox.'

The coldness returned. Fletcher leaned on the quarterdeck rail. 'So our dissembling will have been exposed,' he said.

'About Cook being alive and with Bligh on Ay-too-tuk-ee?'

'Yes.'

The two were silent for a time. For Fletcher the implications were ominous. Tu, Itia and the other leaders would know of the lies they had been fed, and he could imagine their fury at the way they had been deceived. They would be vengeful, understandably so.

'Tu has not appeared. Do you know where he is?' he asked Peter.

'He is visiting relatives in the south of the island. But before he left Cox told him of Cook's death in Hawaii. And Tu told Cox of *Bounty*'s return.' Peter's expression was grim. He too was aware that these developments were grave for the mutineers.

Staring back at the island, Fletcher cursed. This changed matters greatly. The lies had been exposed and the news of the mutiny would go abroad. This would bring retribution sooner. *Bounty*'s departure was now a matter of urgency.

Although there was no one within earshot, Fletcher spoke in a low voice. 'Peter, my party must leave Tahiti as soon as possible. When you return ashore inform my men of that, and tell them to send word to their women that all who wish to leave with me must be aboard *Bounty* tonight.' He put his hand on Peter's shoulder. 'I will write a note for you, testifying to the fact that you took no part in the mutiny. You will return to England a free man. But I would rather die than be taken back there, shackled and shamed, to face the naval authorities.'

He looked into the midshipman's boyish face. How much the pair of them had been through, this past year and a half. 'Will you continue to work on your dictionary?'

'I'm keen to do so, yes.'

'Good. It will prove valuable.' His voice catching with emotion, Fletcher said, 'And when you return to England, I would like you to take a letter from me to my family. Will you promise to do that?'

'Certainly I will.'

Tahiti, 22 September 1789

My Beloved Family,

This is the hardest letter I have ever had to write. It seeks to explain, but not diminish, the actions I have been forced to take during these past months.

You often heard me speak of William Bligh, and the voyages I took to the West Indies under his command. These were successful, and resulted in friendship between us. As you know, this also led to my joining the expedition of HMAV Bounty to Tahiti. During this voyage I was promoted by Bligh to acting lieutenant, a role I relished.

Subsequently, and especially after we left Tahiti, Bligh's behaviour towards me changed greatly. His criticism of me became constant, and ultimately, intolerable. Like Bunyan's Pilgrim, I fell into a 'slough of despond'. My consequent melancholia reached a stage in which I considered taking my own life rather than endure more of it. Instead, with the support of others who shared my loathing of Bligh, in the waters of the Friendly Isles I deposed him. I took command of the Bounty, and set Bligh and eighteen of his followers adrift in the ship's launch. Their fate is not known to me.

I am still in command of Bounty, and will leave Tahiti shortly in her, to seek a sanctuary elsewhere in the South Sea. As yet, that place is unknown, but when I find it, that is where I must stay. I cannot return to England. It was never my expectation to become a fugitive, that role was thrust upon me. But now that I have become one, I will apply all my willpower to discovering, establishing and maintaining a new community of British men and Tahitian women.

My heart breaks to think that I shall never again see you or England, but it cannot be otherwise. The navy will be merciless in its response to my actions, as they will be judged in violation of the Articles of War. But I wish you to know that those actions were necessary, and inevitable. Bligh's behaviour towards me had become unbearable. Thus, far from acting dishonourably, the action I took was the only option available to me. To not depose Bligh would have been a craven reaction to his conduct towards myself and others of Bounty's crew.

Should a naval enquiry eventuate regarding Bligh's loss of the Bounty, there will be many witnesses among the crew who will swear to the veracity of my statements. Several of these men are on Tahiti, awaiting their repatriation.

I am now in the company of eight of the men who supported my overthrowing of Bligh. Our women companions accompany us. Mine is as loyal and loving a woman as a man could wish for. Her Tahitian name is Mauatua, but I call her Isabella. Her family is of Tahiti's nobility.

It is our hope that some day Isabella and I will have children. Should that eventuate it may be of some comfort for you to know that although I can never return to England, there will be a branch of the Christian family tree, planted and flourishing on an island in the South Sea, and that that branch will continue to flourish for ensuing generations.

In this way the honourable family name, 'Christian', will endure.

My deepest love to you, always,

Fletcher

He blotted the sheet of notepaper, folded it, and placed it in an envelope. His eyes had become filmy. He closed them, seeing in his mind's eye his mother, his brothers, and a portrait of his father.

Fletcher handed Tetahiti the axe. 'Take this and cut the anchor cable.'

The Tupuaian frowned. 'Cut it?'

'Yes. Now.'

'Why?'

'We are leaving Tahiti. Go for'ard and cut the cable.'

A full moon cast beams of light across the lagoon and streaks of moonlight illuminated the pass through the reef. There was a faint breeze, insufficient to fill *Bounty*'s sails, but enough to move the ship. White water rose and fell at the margins of the pass, marking the place where the reef began.

From below decks came the sounds of laughter and song. Weeping, too. The taios had come aboard — men and women — to farewell their friends, the vahines and their companions.

Young and Brown were on watch on the quarterdeck with Fletcher. He told them: 'We're leaving, immediately.'

Ned looked askance. 'Why?'

'The others will try to prevent us. And they have arms now.'

Ned nodded, understanding. They felt *Bounty*'s position beginning to shift. Her bow swung slowly to larboard. As it did so Tetahiti returned, the axe in his hand.

'You have done it?'

'Yes.' He mimed a chopping motion and grinned.

'Good.' Fletcher said to Will and Ned, 'I'll take the helm. You two lower the foresail, and the fore topsail.'

The pair of them scuttled away and began to climb the rigging. Ten minutes later the two sails were dropped and *Bounty* swung to starboard. Fletcher turned the wheel three points and she began to move steadily towards the pass. The water was as smooth as satin, the only sound the rippling of the water under *Bounty*'s bow.

'Aue! Aue! Aue!'

The cries came from the women who had come up on deck to see what was happening. All middle-aged and wearing bark cloth skirts and cloaks, hair tied atop their heads, they had been guests aboard the ship. They ran to the stern, their cries becoming louder as they realised what their position was. *Bounty* was now beyond the reef, Fletcher holding her on a north-west course. Abaft, the profile of Tahiti was becoming fainter. Realising they were being taken away without their consent, the women continued to weep. The mutineers' women surrounded them, attempting to console the older ones.

Martin's woman, Jenny, rushed up to Fletcher on the quarterdeck, her expression desperate.

'These ones do not want to come with us, Titereano. We must take them back.'

'We cannot.'

Jenny wrung her hands. 'But they are frightened. And upset.'

He held his course. It would be fatal to return to Tahiti. Looking down at the weeping women on the mid-deck, he thought, but what use would these ones be? They were past the age of child-bearing, so could never contribute to a growing community. But neither could he abandon them. They would have to be taken off the ship. He looked to starboard, towards Tahiti's sister island. He said to Jenny, 'We will take them to Moorea at first light. The people on that side of the island are not hostile, like the ones on the other side. And Otuana — our oldest one — came from the village on the nearest side.'

A large canoe put out from the island's shore, paddled by young men. After it drew alongside *Bounty*, the women climbed down into it, still crying, but now with relief. As they were paddled away to the island, they stared back at the ship, throwing up their hands and tearing at their scalps with pearl shell, in sorrow at their parting from the young ones remaining on board.

The sun was still rising when Fletcher ordered all *Bounty*'s sails unfurled. After they caught the south-east breeze, he turned the wheel to larboard and she settled onto a WWN course.

15 November 1789

We have now been at sea for five weeks, and have little to show for it. The haven we seek proves elusive. We first sailed due west, bound for the Friendly Isles, but before we reached them we came upon an uncharted island which the natives told us was called Purutea. It appeared to be a raised atoll, not unlike Cook's Savage Island, with a forested crown and a reef close in to the shore. After we hove to, an outrigger canoe came out to greet us. Its occupants were males, and shy but friendly. They came aboard. Their leader, a sturdy fellow wearing a wreath of leaves around his head came up to me and ran his hands admiringly over my officer's jacket. He was especially taken with its pearl shell buttons. I removed the jacket, passed it to him and indicated that he could try it on. Delighted to do so, he stood at the rail gate and shouted in triumph. As he did so ...

The shot came from the foredeck, where McCoy was standing, musket at his shoulder. The man with the jacket screamed, clutched his chest and toppled backwards into the sea. His compatriots, terrified, ran to the gate. Howling with shock, they dropped down into the canoe and dragged the dead man aboard. *Bounty's* company, men and women, stood about the main deck, speechless at this act.

Fletcher ran forward and yelled at McCoy, 'Why did you shoot?'

McCoy shrugged. 'He were stealing your jacket.'

'Good God, man, I gave it to him. Didn't you see that?'

'Yes, but you loaned it to him, and he was going to keep it.'

'You had no need to shoot,' Fletcher hissed. 'That was a murderous, unprovoked act.'

McCoy's cheeks had turned red, but his expression remained defiant. Fletcher eyeballed the Scotsman. 'This island may well have provided us with what we seek. But now, through your wanton killing, we will not be welcome there.'

McCoy turned away. 'There'll be other islands,' he muttered.

Fletcher swore. How to account for such stupidity? And how to cope with it? Irate, he walked back to the quarterdeck, where John Williams was at the helm. He shouted at him, 'We'll not tarry here. Put the helm over and bring her before the wind.'

He went below to his cabin, struck by a fresh bout of gloom. McCoy's brutish tendencies, never far from the surface, had broken through it again, causing a gratuitous death. And the worst part of it was, Fletcher was powerless to prevent such incidents occurring. Yes, he was in authority, but he did not have the means to enforce it, as a bone fide commander would.

He picked up his journal and quill.

I admonished McCoy verbally but could do no more, a lack that he is well aware of. What such incidents demonstrate is that we are an exceedingly motley crew, perhaps the motliest that ever sailed a naval ship. My mutineers are ill-disciplined and at times rancorous, especially when in liquor. They feel it is their right to order the native men to do their bidding. As for those, the Tahitians mistrust the Tupuaians and vice versa, while our Raiatean is a loner who does not get on well with the other native men. I do my best to instruct them in the skills of seamanship, but this is by no means straightforward.

Only our Tahitian women show common sense and decency towards each other and the rest, especially my Isabella and Alex Smith's woman, Jenny. They remain calm at all times, and are a fine example to the others. All the women also take care of Sully, Te'o's little daughter. The women are the hoops of iron which hold the disparate staves of Bounty's company together. And their bodies provide carnal relief for the men, at the same time reducing their aggressive instincts.

I worry about the condition of Bounty. That she is the victim of neglect is clearly evident now. The sails are in a poor state and we have lost spare spars and anchors. The decks need re-caulking but we are without the materials to carry this out. Our vessel has become like an ageing dowager who has fallen on hard times. (Like my mother. An unkind comparison, but an irresistible one to draw.)

We are also lacking in provisions, so I intend making landfall on Tongatapu, an island which Cook and Bligh were familiar with.

They entered the lagoon to the north of the island, then anchored near where Cook had moored *Resolution*, close to a village called Mu'a. There they were able to trade for hogs, coconuts and plantains and take aboard water. Unlike Nomuka, the natives on Tongatapu were not hostile, although they were puzzled by the presence of women on a Papalagi ship. After Fletcher asked the chiefs whether Bligh's launch had landed here, they replied in the negative. One chief, Paulaho, remembered Bligh, but assured Fletcher he had not been on Tongatapu since he came with Tute.

After Fletcher called a meeting of his men, they decided that however friendly the people here were, they could not stay on Tongatapu. It was too well charted and documented. More European ships would be bound to call at the island and report their presence. They had to keep searching.

They now took a north-westward course, giving Nomuka and Tofua a wide berth.

After four days they came upon a cluster of low islands which appeared on none of the charts they had. Standing off the atolls, Fletcher observed through his spyglass that they were inhabited by black, frizzy-haired natives. He and Ned had lately read the account of Cook's third voyage, and tried to work out which islands these were.

'They must be part of the Feejee islands,' Ned surmised. 'A place Cook was warned not to go to.'

'With good reason. They are inhabited by man-eaters.'

He and Ned exchanged glances. There could be no haven here. All around the decks, the ship's company was looking in their direction, awaiting a decision. Brown was at the wheel, keeping *Bounty* turned into the wind.

Placing his spyglass to his eye, Fletcher saw about a mile away an islet covered in palm trees but without houses. He called down to the others, 'The natives on these islands are cannibals, so we cannot linger here. But some of us will go ashore on the nearest one with an armed party and collect coconuts.' He sought out his men. 'Smith, Mills, Martin, prepare to hoist the larger cutter.'

With *Bounty* hove to and rolling gently, and after the cutter was lowered, Fletcher returned to his cabin. He was becoming more and more downcast. The further west they sailed among these islands, the more likely it was that they would encounter European outposts, thereby placing themselves in jeopardy. So their future could not lie in that direction.

Fletcher knew that this was the time, when their future was so much in doubt, to show more leadership and determination. That was the responsibility he had taken upon himself. They had come too far to compromise by landing on a populated island. Surely there was a suitable refuge for them, an uninhabited place, somewhere in this ocean.

Glancing up at Bligh's book collection in the cabin's corner cabinet, he noticed again the copy of *Voyages*, by John Hawkesworth. It had been published in 1773. While skimming the book recently he had read something which chimed in his mind. Flicking through the book's pages, he came to the section which included the log of Philip Carteret's South Sea voyage of 1767. The Englishman's sloop *Swallow* had become separated in a gale from its consort, *Dolphin*. While searching for her:

We continued our course westward till the evening of Thursday the 2nd of July when we discovered land to the northward of us. Upon approaching it the next day, it appeared like a great rock rising out of the sea. It was not more than five miles in circumference, and seemed to be uninhabited ... I would have landed upon it, but the surf, which at this season broke upon it with great violence, rendered it impossible ... It is so high that we saw it at a distance of more than fifteen leagues, and it having been discovered by a young gentleman, son to Major Pitcairn of the marines, who was unfortunately lost in the Aurora, we called it Pitcairn's Island.

Carteret had calculated and noted the island's coordinates: latitude 25° 02' south; longitude 133° 30' west.

Fletcher reread the entry: 'a great rock ... uninhabited'.

Freshly hopeful now, he went topside, calling, 'Ned!'

Together they pored over a chart of the South Sea. Fletcher ran his finger along the Tropic of Capricorn. 'An uninhabited island, just south of the Tropic. It's what we need.'

Ned looked doubtful. 'Longitude 133° west.' He looked again at the chart. 'That would mean sailing east for nearly three thousand miles. Against the trade winds.'

Fletcher persisted, 'But if we first sail southward, into the higher latitudes, we can then go east, pick up the westerly winds and currents to take us to the island.'

Ned grimaced. 'The higher latitudes? Think of the cold, Fletcher.'

'Think of the island, Ned. Pitcairn's Island.' He stood up. 'Call the company together.'

14 December 1789

We have not seen land for weeks, only ocean and more ocean. I feel like Odysseus. The women and men are depressed in spirit, and remain below decks for the most part. When they come topside they stare forlornly at the grey sea. The natives suffer from the cold. Fortunately we have the extra clothing that belonged formerly to Bligh's loyalists: trousers, shirts, jackets. The women have their bark cloth capes, but these do not keep out the cold to great effect. Their noses stream and their joints ache. Isabella is silent for long periods, trying to conceal her anxiety, but I know how worried she is. The Tahitians implore me to return to Tahiti; the Tupuaians wish to return to their island. My men become more morose. These various entreaties raise great doubts in my mind. Is it right to put my people through this ordeal? Was I right in pursuing this course? Is this voyage east a terrible mistake?

Squalls bring us fresh water, but leach into the lower deck, causing further discomfort. However as I informed the company yesterday, I will soon put Bounty on a northern course. That will take us again into the warmer latitudes. The people showed great relief at this prospect.

Ned made his noon calculations. Then, lowering the sextant, he came onto the quarterdeck. His expression disconsolate, he announced to Fletcher, 'We have arrived at Carteret's 1767 position.'

'Are you certain?'

'Yes. I checked. Twice.'

They stared into the distance. The sky was clear, visibility unimpeded. So clear, so unimpeded, that they could see that towards every point of the compass there was no land. No Pitcairn's Island.

Ned looked scathing.

'Carteret's island is a fiction, Fletcher. A fantasy, a chimera.'

'It is not. He didn't invent such an island. He was not a writer of novels, he was a chronicler. If he logged that he discovered an island, then he did.'

'Then where is it?'

'Think. This was over two decades ago. Carteret could establish latitude accurately, but longitude was then much more problematic.

He lacked our timekeepers.' Fletcher looked eastward. 'Therefore, if we continue to sail east, holding this approximate line of latitude, we must eventually reach Pitcairn's Island.'

Ned grunted. 'I really hope so. The crew are restive, Fletcher, they are verging on the rebellious. Quintal said to me last night while on watch, "Christian's sodding island doesn't exist. And even if it does, he'll never find it." That's a warning.'

'When we find the island, it will be greatly to our advantage.'

'*If* we find it. I'm now of the belief that young Pitcairn and Carteret were dreaming.'

Fletcher turned away. If Ned was right, there may not be only one mutiny on the *Bounty*. More troubled than ever, he went below to his cabin, where Isabella was waiting. Now, more than ever, he needed her closeness. In the bunk they held each other tightly, but for Fletcher sleep proved elusive.

'Fenua! Fenua! Fenua!'

At the masthead, Tetahiti pointed to starboard. 'Look! Look!'

Everyone ran to the side. And there it was. Rising — protruding — from the dark ocean. A perpendicular rock, hundreds of feet high, its crown 'thickly wooded', in Carteret's words. Cliffs, streaked with ginger earth. And swells, dashing themselves onto the rocks at their base.

All aboard were transfixed.

In Hawkesworth's book there was an engraving of the island Carteret had come across. Fletcher held it open at the illustration. Although it was early evening, the sun was still strong enough to illuminate the island's profile. He showed it to Ned, standing alongside him. The features were unmistakable. This was Pitcairn's Island.

Ned laughed. 'Carteret's longitude was wrong. By nearly two hundred miles.'

Fletcher nodded. 'And what a wonderful mistake to make.' He trained his spyglass on the island. 'Charted wrongly. The navy will never find us.'

Next morning he brought the ship closer to the island, but not too close, as the swells were surging against the boulders below the cliffs. He and Isabella stood in the stern, she holding his arm. It was a fine morning with just a light southerly breeze. Staring at the island, she murmured, 'No smoke, Titereano. No fires.'

'No. So perhaps no people.'

She gripped his arm. 'No people is good, yes?'

He nodded. No smoke meant that the island could be uninhabited. He was also thinking, those cliffs are so steep it would be impregnable. Nine months after the mutiny, they had perhaps found their refuge.

Not yet, however. For two days the swells were so strong that they made a landing impossible. And while *Bounty* sailed around the island, they all stared at its tantalising closeness, all wondering the same things. Where could they land? Was there fresh water? Which plants grew there? Was it really uninhabited?

On the third day, standing off the island's west coast, Tetahiti urged Fletcher to let him lead a landing party. Pointing to a shelf of land below the cliffs, he said, 'There, Titereano, we can go in there.'

Fletcher trained his spyglass on the coast. Yes, the wind was from the east, so the swells were less strong there. But the shore was strewn with boulders and the swells were still breaking heavily. As a landing site it would still be hazardous. But they were now desperate to go ashore.

'All right,' Fletcher told Tetahiti, 'we'll take the cutter in there.'

He chose six men to make the landing with him. Tetahiti, Niau and Timoa were selected for their experience at landing canoes in surf; Brown, Williams and McCoy he added for their brute strength. 'You're in charge of the ship, Ned,' he told Young.

With the women watching anxiously from *Bounty*'s stern, they took the cutter in. The European men all had muskets across their backs.

The swells were even bigger than they appeared from the ship. When one of them passed under the cutter it rose steeply and they saw ahead of them promontories, boulders and a cauldron of white water. Knowing that there was no going back, Fletcher chose his moment.

'Go, now!' he shouted, and the boat surged towards the rocks. Gripping his oar over the stern as a steering aid, he managed to guide the cutter between two boulders. Behind them another swell rose, then crashed, hurling the cutter forward. It veered to the left and they heard the rasp of wood against rock. 'Get out!' he shouted to Tetahiti, 'and drag her in!'

The Tupuaian leapt into the surf, carrying the painter with him. Fletcher slipped over the side and into the surf, gripping the stern. The other five stayed aboard, their oars shipped. Another wave rose and crashed over Fletcher, flinging him forward. His knee struck a rock. Yelping with pain, he maintained his grip on the boat, feeling it sliding towards the shore, seeing Tetahiti hauling the cutter between the boulders.

They dragged the boat up onto the rocks, and made it secure with a grapnel and line. Some of them were soaked; Fletcher's knee was gashed and bleeding. He ignored it. Surrounding them were rocks, black and twisted into strange shapes, resembling burnt toffee. There was a patch of sand among the rocks which they sank down onto then stared up at the land.

Above them was a slope, about three hundred feet high, covered with vegetation: palms, pandanus, plantains and a species of pale green tree. In places patches of ochre-coloured earth showed through the vegetation.

Fletcher bound his knee with his kerchief then stood up. 'Right, let's get to the top,' he said, and led the way towards the slope.

It took two hours to reach the top of the island. They fought their way up through the bush, grabbing tree roots and branches, skidding and struggling to get a foothold in the glutinous mud. All were wondering, what would they find at the top? Villages? Hostile natives? They had primed their muskets in case of attack.

At last they emerged, filthy and exhausted, onto the crown of the island. There they stopped and stared.

The day was cloudless and very hot, and from this height they could see so far that the horizon was curved. The sea was darkest blue, scuffed with white tops. Below them, a mile out from the rocky shore and the only man-made object in sight, *Bounty* was being rocked by the swells.

His gaze sweeping the scene, Fletcher said, 'This place isn't just an island, it's a fortress.'

Williams nodded. 'Yes. The height, the cliffs …'

They wandered across the top of the island, pushing through scrub, pandanus and grass. Occasionally the vegetation was broken by a banyan, its roots trailing the ground like a brown curtain. Fairy terns fluttered around the banyans, making chirruping sounds like chattering girls.

After half an hour they reached the other side of the island. Here the land descended to the ocean in a series of terraces. They stopped again to rest and take in the view. Frigate birds rode the air waves above the terraces, rising and falling gracefully. To the north-west the land rose to a rock escarpment whose face was pocked with caves and a huge hollow. To the north the terraced slope was more gradual, culminating in a drop to a relatively sheltered bay. Overlooked by a sheer cliff, this place was the nearest thing to a secure anchorage they had seen.

They made their way down to one of the terraces. It was covered in forest: coconut palms, banana palms, breadfruit heavy with fruit and other large trees.

'What are those other trees?' Fletcher asked Timoa.

'Miro, rata. And tamanu,' he replied. 'Tamanu is very strong.'

'*Calophyllum inophyllum*,' prompted Brown. 'There's one in Kew Gardens.' He bent down, picked up some soil and rolled it in his palm. 'Friable, probably volcanic in origin.' He nodded. 'Fertile. Anything will grow here.'

Tetahiti looked around, nodding. 'Fenua maitai,' he said. 'Good land.'

Fletcher pointed down at the little bay. 'We could put *Bounty* in there, I think.'

The more they explored, the more resources they discovered. Halfway along another of the terraces they came upon a spring bursting from the ground. Parched by now, they drank from it, finding its water cold, clear and sweet. Brown identified the plants they came across which would be of benefit to them: pandanus palms for weaving material, breadfruit and plantains for fresh food, mulberry trees for bark cloth, candlenut trees for lighting, coconut palms whose nuts could be drunk and whose fronds could be used for thatching. Brown also found a patch of sweet potatoes, long gone to seed. The surrounding sea, they surmised, would be rich with fish.

The only thing they hadn't found was people.

Not like Tupuai, Fletcher thought with relief.

Returning to the crown of the island, they came upon a platform of stones, half covered by creepers and ferns. 'Ah, marae,' Tetahiti declared. They pulled away some of the creeper. There were sun-bleached jaw bones amid the stones, and a coarse figure carved from scoria. 'Tiki,' said Tetahiti. 'Like on our island.' Timoa picked up a basalt adze and mimed cutting movements with it. Further away were the stone foundations of buildings, and charcoal from fires.

'So, native people have lived here,' Fletcher mused.

Williams nodded. 'But not for some time, judging by the whiteness of those bones.' He stared at the marae. 'Where did they come from, and where did they go?'

Fletcher laughed. 'It matters not, Jack. The thing is, they've gone. So Pitcairn's Island is ours.' He hadn't felt as hopeful as this for weeks. Brushing the mud from his trousers, he told the others, 'Now, let's get back to the ship. And let them know of our discoveries.'

20 JANUARY 1790

Fletcher and Isabella sat on the lip of rock they had already named 'The Edge', which overlooked the bay on the north-east coast of the island. *Bounty* had been brought close in two days ago. All sails furled, she rode at anchor below them. Some of her fittings were being carried up the steep track from the bay by the Tahitian men and women. Adams had christened the track the Hill of Difficulty. To Fletcher he explained, 'The name comes from another Christian, and another pilgrim's progress.' Ned had been reading Bligh's copy of John Bunyan's allegory to Adams.

His arm around Isabella, Fletcher said, 'I will build a house for us here.'

'On this rock?'

He laughed. 'No. On this side of the island. In a sheltered place.'

'That will be so good.' She put her head on his shoulder. 'Titereano …'

'What is it?'

She placed a hand on her belly. 'I have no toto now. No bleeding.'

'For how long?'

'One and a half moons.'

He stared at her, absorbing the implications of this. Did it mean what he thought it did?

'I talked about the no bleeding with Jenny last night. She knows about such things.' Isabella gave a sigh. 'I am hapu, Titereano.'

'Pregnant.'

'Preg-nant.' She kept her hand on her belly. 'Tamari'i is in here. Our tamari'i.'

With a surge of joy, Fletcher drew her closer to him. A child. Their child. To be born on this island they had discovered. He pressed his lips to her forehead. 'Isabella, ua here vauia oe. I love you.'

'Ae, ae.'

Then he thought, our tribulations are over. They had found their sanctuary. Here they would live in freedom, in a real Utopia. He would be a father, and a landowner. Here they would raise their children on their own land. His sons would inherit their property. Their sons, too.

He looked down at the bay, where *Bounty* was rolling in the swells. From now on, everything was going to be the way he had hoped it would. They had a secure future now, all of them.

23 January 1790

Most of us are now living in shelters made from Bounty's sails, pulled over a frame of tree boughs. The encampment is a little way back from the cliff edge, in a grove above the place we have named 'Bounty Bay'. The ship itself has been brought in closer and made fast to the land with cables and grapnels. For some reason a few prefer to live aboard the ship with their women, among them Quintal and his Sarah and McCoy and his Mary. This puzzles me, as the shore camp is much more spacious. Could Q. and Mc. be draining the last of the ship's liquor?

Onshore, we white men and our women are in one area, while the six native men and their three women — Nancy, Mareva and Tinafanaea — have occupied an area further away. This was their choice, as they seem to want to be separate from us. Our accommodation is adequate for the time being, until we build proper houses.

Everything which will be of use to us has been taken off the ship: pigs, goats and chickens, plants and seeds, carpenter's tools and nails, armourer's forge, iron ballast, weapons and ammunition, sails, buckets, cooking equipment, cutlery and crockery, spare spars, cordage, seine nets, fishing lines, cabin fittings, hammocks, ladders, companionways and rails, the livestock pens. I ensured that Bligh's books, charts, writing paper, ink and quills were among the first items to be transferred. They are safe in my shelter.

Everything will be useful to us!

Not wanting to risk losing the cutter, I devised a system whereby two rafts were improvised from the ship's hatches. The goods were lashed to them, then hauled ashore with ropes by our women. All the materials are now stowed, out of reach of the tide, at the foot of the cliff at Bounty Bay. It will take many more days of hard labour before everything is lugged up the Hill of Difficulty to the Edge.

I have made it very clear to everyone that by dint of my naval rank and the fact that I succeeded in bringing them to this haven, that I am to be in charge of the community. Ned is my appointed deputy. Our settlement must have regulations and it must be disciplined. Nearly all appear to accept this.

In my capacity as leader I have already declared certain edicts.

Firstly, no fires are to be lit during the daylight hours, since smoke could attract the attention of a passing vessel. Secondly, a lookout watch must be kept during the day. This is to be held at the top of the headland in the north of the island, which we have named Lookout Point. Ned has set a roster for this watch. Thirdly, I insisted that the materials unladen from the ship are to be available for everyone's use. They are a communal resource, kept under canvas above the Edge. After any of the tools are used, they are to be returned there. There is not to be any personal usurpation of the implements or materials.

As I issued these regulations, a certain resentment emanated from some of the men, in particular the habitually intractable Quintal, McCoy and Williams. 'We've had a gutsful of rules,' McCoy declared. 'We're free men now.' Fixing him with my harshest look, I told him, 'Without rules we will not survive. Light a fire by day and it will be seen from the ocean. And that will mean the end of our refuge. And if we do not share the resources, a few will thrive but the majority will not. Do you not understand that?'

Avoiding my gaze, McCoy looked down and mumbled, 'Aye.' Troublemakers, like bullies, must be stood up to.

Isabella continues to be a tower of support for me, fully deserving of the men's name for her, 'Mainmast'. We are both delighted in the knowledge that our child will be born before the year is out.

After reconnoitring the island thoroughly, I have selected a plot of land in the north-west for Isabella and myself. There I will build our house.

Being high-born, Isabella is the natural leader of the Tahitian women. All of them appreciate their new freedoms. They prepare the food, but no longer are they obliged to eat it separately from the men. We all eat together, under a canopy. The native men show some antipathy towards me for permitting this, particularly Tetahiti and Niau, who were chiefs on their home islands. But as I emphasise to them, ours is a different community, with rules unique to our circumstances.

We all relish our new diet. What a difference from what we endured during those long weeks at sea! We have fresh fish daily, caught with ease with a line from the rocks in the bay. The women gather seabirds' eggs from cliff ledges. We have breadfruit, sweet potatoes, sugar cane, taro, plantains —

all of which grow wild. Plentiful coconuts too. Here we gather and share the nuts, and I have no fear of being accused of stealing anyone else's! Our pigs, chickens and goats run free. They too will breed, giving us a source of fresh meat and …'

'Titereano!'

Isabella's cry came from the direction of the Edge, a hundred yards from their shelter. Fletcher closed his journal and sprinted down the hill. Before he got there he smelt, then saw, what was alarming her.

Smoke and flames, rising from the bay.

Bounty was ablaze. Flames engulfed her and smoke spiralled upwards. As Fletcher, Isabella and the others stared at the inferno, shocked at the sight, there was an explosion in the ship's stern. A shower of sparks like a fireworks display, then another, burst from her superstructure. Where the flames met the water, steam fizzed and billowed. As they watched, too stunned to speak, the mainmast toppled like a felled oak. Freed of its rigging, the mast crashed for'ard onto the foredeck, sending up another shower of sparks.

Fletcher felt part of his world collapsing. His home for more than three years, the ship in which he had crossed the world, and the South Sea, being destroyed before his eyes. This must have been deliberate.

'Who did this?' he asked bitterly.

Isabella pointed. 'There. By the rocks.'

Quintal and McCoy were sitting on the sand above the bay. Quintal held a rum bottle. He swigged from it, then passed it to McCoy. Fletcher began to run, and slide, down the hill.

'Did you do this?' he demanded of Quintal.

The Cornishman grinned. 'We both did. Me and Will. Set fire to a cask of pitch from the carpenter's store.'

McCoy guffawed. 'And up the old girl went. Whoom!' He took another swig of rum.

'Why?' Fletcher demanded, bunching his fists, wanting to hit both of them. He could feel the heat from the burning ship on his back, hear the crackle of blazing timbers, smell the tarry stench of *Bounty*'s cremation. She was by now burnt almost to the waterline.

'Why?' Quintal echoed, then belched. Dribble ran down his chin. 'Cos the niggers could of used it to sail away, with our women, and leave us civilised men behind.'

For a few moments Fletcher was speechless with fury. At the lack of consultation, and the thoughtlessness and destructiveness of the act. He advanced on the pair, fists still clenched. 'And now we have no means of leaving this island, should we wish to.'

McCoy sniggered. 'Why should we leave? We've only just arrived.'

Quintal laughed mockingly. 'Christian, Christian, don't be upset.' He waved a hand at the burning hulk. 'Before, *Bounty*'s mainmast were sticking up as tall and stiff as a nigger's cock. It were bound to draw attention. But now, no ship will ever see her, and find us.'

Fletcher turned away. Although sickened by the arson, he knew Quintal was right. This would help them evade attention and likely capture. But he also knew that now their only connection to the outside world had been destroyed. And as a consequence, all twenty-eight souls had been sentenced to life on this lonely crag in the middle of the South Sea.

1 OCTOBER 1790

It took eight months for Fletcher to build a one-room house for him and Isabella. Located on a large plot of land he had allocated them, the house was in a hollow. Sheltered from all but winds directly from the north, the site was surrounded by forest trees, banana and coconut palms. Made from posts of tamanu and planking from the *Bounty*, the house was roofed with several layers of coconut palm fronds. The lockable door Fletcher had also purloined from the *Bounty*. It was the door of Bligh's cabin, with its nameplate removed. There was a spring two minutes' walk from the house, bubbling from a cavity in the forest. Its water was cool and pure.

Building the house had been a labour of love, taking him from dawn to dusk every day for the thirty weeks. The others were building houses too, so the *Bounty*'s saws, hammers and axes had to be shared, the nails distributed among the builders. He and Isabella's house was some distance from the rest, something which pleased him. Already the others had given the property a name: Down Fletcher.

When the house was finished, he began to clear a plot of land and dig a garden. This was on the upland near the centre of the island, a twenty-minute hike up from the house, on the area they had named 'Flatland', since it was the largest area of level terrain on the island. A giant banyan tree grew beside the garden, sheltering it from the south-west wind.

He took pleasure in the physical effort of building the house and starting the garden. The work was hard but fulfilling and he had never felt so fit and strong. Now tanned as dark as the native men, he also wore his hair tied in a topknot, island-style.

'You are like Tahitian man now,' Isabella told him one morning, as she plucked hairs from his chest. 'Not English man any more.'

When they were able to sleep in their house, he and Isabella felt contented. At last, a place of their own, where they were free to be themselves. How different from the poky, airless conditions aboard *Bounty*, and how good it was to be away from the prying eyes of shipmates and neighbours!

After negotiations, Fletcher and Ned had divided the island into nine sections for themselves and the other seven white men. The six native men and their three women were allocated no land as such: they were told to settle wherever they wanted to, so long as it was outside the boundaries of the white men's properties.

The land the natives chose was a little way back from the cliff above Bounty Bay. Here, on level land, they built six rudimentary houses from salvaged materials, old sails and palm fronds.

Quintal, McCoy and Williams made something clear from the beginning — the native men were to make themselves available for physical labour, such as cutting firewood and carrying water for them.

Fletcher took issue with them over this, and admonished the trio. 'They're not your servants. They have rights too.'

The others scoffed at this. 'We're landed fuckin' aristocracy now, Christian,' McCoy told him. 'And as aristos, we have to have servants. That's what the niggers are for.'

But when Quintal, McCoy and Williams tried to order the native men about, their leaders resisted. Tetahiti spat at the white men's feet. 'You are not ari'i. On my island, I am ari'i. Ohoo is my servant.'

'But you ain't on your island now, sunshine,' Quintal sneered. 'You're on our island.'

Tetahiti strode away, muttering imprecations beyond their understanding.

Resentment began to seethe, attitudes began to harden.

Unable to settle these tensions, Fletcher divided his time between the house and his garden. His vegetable plot was about thirty yards square. It had first to be cleared of the rampant weed which covered the ground, but once he stripped it away with a mattock, then dug the earth over, it was suitable for planting.

When the spring rains came the soil was well watered, and nourished the seeds he planted. Following Brown's suggestions he sowed beans, pumpkin, melons, carrots, cabbages and corn. He also planted tubers from the yams and sweet potatoes that grew wild on the island, and sugar cane.

The crops thrived. Six months after the seeds were planted he and Isabella were eating their own beans and cabbages. She cooked fish, shellfish and pork in the umu next to the house. The fish and meat scraps Fletcher buried in his garden, to increase the soil's fertility. And with the warmer weather of September, the vegetables grew faster than ever.

In Isabella's womb, the baby grew too.

Fletcher was hoeing a row of beans when a call came wafting up from the bush below Flatland.

'Tit-er-re- ano! Te fanau ra oia i tana ai'u!'

The baby is coming! It was the voice of Jenny, Martin's woman and Isabella's friend. Fletcher dropped his mattock and ran down through the trees. Jenny had raced back ahead of him and the house door was closed. From inside he could hear loud cries. Heart racing, he banged on the door. 'Isabella!'

'Mamoo! Do not come in! Wait there!' This was Jenny's voice.

He sank down against the wall. Jenny had reckoned the baby's arrival would be about now. Inside the house, the cries turned to screams, punctuated by sobbing. Fletcher crouched, sweating and anxious, feeling useless.

The cries continued. Then, after another hour, he heard a different cry, long and low, of prolonged relief. Then yet another, reedy and uncertain at first, then stronger. This was followed by high-pitched laughter, and cries of 'Ae, ae, manuia, Mauatua! E tama!'

The door swung open. Jenny, her face flushed, her hands bloody, beckoned him in.

Isabella was lying on the pandanus sleeping mat, naked and bleeding. While Jenny wiped her face and neck with a pad of bark cloth, her eyes were fixed on the small creature who lay beside her. Its round face was scrunched into a red knot and its body was streaked with blood. The genitals were disproportionately large for the small body and the umbilical cord, still attached, and the placenta, lay in a heap beside the baby. Over the mother and baby hung the smell of blood, sweat, coconut and gardenia oil.

Isabella looked up at Fletcher. Although her eyes were bloodshot, her expression was radiant. 'Tama. A son for us,' she murmured.

Fletcher stared in wonder at the newborn. As he did so the baby gasped, drew in a breath, then let out a bellow so loud Fletcher thought it would bring the palm-frond ceiling down upon them. It bellowed over and over again, as if testing and approving of its own strength.

There was a canvas bucket of water beside Isabella. In it was a pair of sailmaker's shears from the ship. Handing them to Fletcher, Jenny said 'You cut.'

Not understanding at first, she pointed to the cord that joined the baby to the afterbirth. Hands trembling, Fletcher opened the shears and sliced through the cord. The baby yelled again. Jenny passed it to Isabella. Clutching the baby, she offered it her breast. It took the nipple, then sucked greedily. Isabella stared down dreamily at the child.

Too moved to speak, Fletcher stared in wonder at their feeding son. New life, created by Isabella and himself. Until this moment he had thought that the carnal act was merely for gratification. He now appreciated that it also prefigured the creation of life. And this child, their newborn son, was the result of a special kind of union, one between England and Tahiti, between the old world and the new. It was a miracle.

When the baby had finished feeding, Jenny took it, rubbed its back until it brought up wind, then wrapped it in a length of bark cloth. Then, rocking him gently, she closed her eyes and intoned a blessing:

'Ia haamaitaihia oe no tea ho ora ta oe i ho ma i te hotu o te here o na metua nei! Mauruuru no to oe here ia raua, e no tei o faahia hia ta oe e pupu nei a raua.'

Although Fletcher couldn't understand it all, he caught the gist of Jenny's benediction to the Tahitian gods. 'Thank you for this new life that you have given to these loving parents. Thank you for your love for them and this marvellous gift you offer them.'

'Mauruuru, Jenny,' he said, then kissed Isabella softly on her cheek. 'And mauruuru to you, Isabella, for our son.'

In hours the whole community knew of the birth at Down Fletcher, a first for the island's community. His parents named him Thursday October, after his birth day and date.

The women brought pulau blooms and the sweet-scented flowers they called aalihau. They also brought baked breadfruit and bananas boiled in coconut milk. The men brought cooked groper, mullet, tuna and butterfish. Martin brought a bottle of Canary Islands wine he had been hoarding; Adams brought a little turtle he had carved from tamanu wood. But there were no gifts or visits from Quintal, McCoy or Williams.

Gardener Brown brought something else. He opened his hand to Fletcher. In it were four acorns. 'I took these onto the *Bounty*. They're from Richmond Park in London. Thought I might plant them in Tahiti.' He gave a little laugh. 'But I forgot about them. Now they should be planted here. My woman Teatuahitea tells me that a tree should grow where a baby's afterbirth's been buried. It's a Tahitian tradition. The mother and child then know that part of them nourishes the tree.'

Nodding, Fletcher took the handful of acorns. He would plant them, and bury the afterbirth beside their house, so that a very English tree — an oak — would be joined with this very Tahitian belief.

7 November 1792
I write mainly to record the birth of another Christian.

We have a second son, a brother for Thursday October! He was born this morning, with Isabella again assisted by the ever-dependable Jenny. He is a fine, healthy baby, like his brother. Isabella and I agreed that he should be named after my brother, Charles. I can never forget Charles's advice to me regarding a despotic sea captain. Without Charles's counsel, our second son may never have been born. If we are blessed with another, he will be named after brother Edward.

Isabella is a wonderful mother, devoted to her baby sons. I sometimes hear her murmuring to them the endearments she once said to me! Never mind, her love and caring will ensure that they grow up strong, healthy and respectful to their parents. Not really remembering my own father, I am determined that my sons will know and love theirs.

Our community continues to be fully occupied. There is always much to do: gardening, weeding, fishing, building. The free-foraging pigs are a pest, necessitating the building of walls around the gardens. The stones of the old maraes prove excellent for this purpose, so we have dismantled all of them. The Tahitian men reproached us for this, especially after some human remains were found beneath the marae stones.

'Ra'a,' Tetahiti said severely, when he saw me carrying some of the stones away for my garden wall. 'Taboo.'

'I need them,' I rejoined, 'for my garden wall. And the maraes were old and abandoned.'

Tetahiti fell silent, but his expression remained disapproving. I was unapologetic, however; we cannot allow ancient superstitions to override our present endeavours.

Having seen pictures of English women in a book from Bounty's library, the women have made gowns for themselves, from Bounty's sails. Cut out with shears and stitched together, the canvas makes hard-wearing garments. The women are delighted with them. Making clothing this way is far less tedious and time-consuming than beating cloth from the bark of the pulau shrubs!

More children have been born this year. Quintal and McCoy's women, Sarah and Mary, have both been delivered of sons, and Mills' woman, Vahineatua, has presented him with a daughter. In this way our community grows.

But it is not a contented one. Isabella tells me that Quintal and McCoy beat their women, something I find reprehensible. She also tells me that Mary has to protect Sully, her little daughter, whom she brought with her from Tahiti. The behaviour of McCoy, Quintal and Williams becomes more thuggish by the day. Last week, after Ohoo was slow at bringing them a meal, they tied him to a tree and McCoy flogged him with Bounty's cat-o'-nine-tails. Quintal then rubbed salt into his gashes. A despicable act that appalled me. But how can I stop such acts? We have no authority over the trio any more. They are a law unto themselves.

There is also unhappiness in the native camp. The three Tahitian women, Nancy, Tinafanaea and Mareva, must endure much carnal attention from the six native men. This makes them dejected, particularly poor Mareva, who must suffer the untrammelled lust of the three Tahitian commoners. No wonder she displays an unhappy expression.

The watch from Lookout Point is still maintained during the daylight hours, but we continue to see nothing but empty ocean. A nearby natural feature, a hollow in the cliff face below the lookout, has become a favourite place of mine. Already the others refer to it as 'Christian's Cave'. It is a hard climb to get there, but worth it, since there I can be alone with my thoughts.

At least once a week I climb to the hollow and sit for hours, reflecting on what happened since I left England.

I wonder, often, what happened to Bligh and his eighteen loyalists. Are they dead or alive? Will I ever know? And my family, what of them?

These unanswerable questions bring me a melancholic disposition, relieved only by thoughts of Isabella and our children.

There has been a death. Williams' woman, Fa'ahotu, fell and was killed while collecting seabirds' eggs at the place we call St Paul's Point. She slipped on gravel and plunged to the rocks below. This was bad enough, but to make matters worse, Williams has demanded a replacement woman. This is Nancy, the consort of the young chief from Raiatea, Tararo. Hearing of this demand, I urged Williams to desist. I told him, 'You can have Sully, when she's old enough.' He looked at me as if I was insane. 'She's four now. You expect me to not fuck anyone for ten years?'

I walked away, fearing that no good can come of this situation.

McCoy, Quintal and Williams forced the native men to draw lots. The result was that Nancy received the short straw. The unruly trio then took her from Tararo, against her will, and handed her over to Williams.

All this was reported to Ned and me by Martin, who witnessed the shameful proceedings but was powerless to stop it.

Isabella, holding little Charles, looked afraid. 'It's Tararo, Titereano.'

'What about him?'

'Vahineatua told me that he, and Tetahiti and Ohoo, are planning to kill the *Bounty* men. She saw them sharpening axes.'

'That's probably just boastful talk.'

Clutching the baby, the creases in her brow deepened. 'I worry. At the spring today, I heard Vahineatua singing a Tahitian song. It is an old song, but she was giving it new words. She is singing, "Why does black man sharpen axe? To kill white man".' She shivered. 'I am frightened, Titereano.'

Fletcher considered this. Was Vahineatua right? Could the warning be genuine? Perhaps. The Tahitians were certainly aggrieved. In any event, it was time he reasserted his authority, or what little of it was left. He told Isabella, 'I'll go up and speak to Tararo and the others.'

He loaded his musket with small shot and slipped his unloaded pistol into his belt. Then he walked up to the native encampment. Tararo, Tetahiti and Ohoo were seated under a tree, whittling driftwood. There was no sign of the women. A long-handled axe was leaning against the tree trunk. As he approached, musket at his hip, the men got to their feet. Tararo spoke first.

'What you want, Titereano?' he demanded.

'I want no trouble. I want peace between us.'

'Peace?' Tararo gave a bitter laugh. 'White men only want peace so they can attack black men.' He made a slashing gesture with his hand. '*Bounty* men are bad. They whip Ohoo, they steal my wife.'

'That won't happen again. I will talk again to Williams. Tell him to give Nancy back to you.'

Tararo sneered. 'Hah! Williams take no notice of you. White men only take notice of this.' He turned and picked up the axe. The other two crouched, seeming ready to attack.

Fletcher squeezed the musket trigger. It fired, showering the three men with small shot. They yelled and put their arms over their faces. Bluffing, Fletcher pulled the unprimed pistol from his belt and aimed it. When he did the three men turned and ran, up the rise that led to the bush on the other side of the island.

He made his way back to the house, close to despair. Things were falling apart. The island was becoming corrupted from within. It was like some exotic fruit, ripe and lovely on the outside, but with a core that was decaying. The island was rotting with carnal envy and racial hatred. It was a long way from More's Utopia. Was there a word for the opposite of Utopia? He didn't know, but if there was one, Pitcairn was turning into it.

How could he stop the rot? Incarcerate McCoy, Quintal and Williams? Impossible, without provoking retaliation. Arrest the native men? That too would invite violence. Could the wounds in the community ever be healed?

He could see no way that they could.

His despondency deepened. He needed to return to his cave.

20 SEPTEMBER 1793

He slid down the slope below the escarpment. Since the single musket shot there had been no more. But the shot had come from Down Fletcher. Had there been a killing there? If so, who was it? Heart pumping, he reached the trail at the foot of the slope and broke into a run. Past the boulders and the taypau trees, then up through the forest to the house. In front of it he stopped. A musket — his musket — was leaning against the front wall of the house. From inside came the sounds of crying. Female crying. Confused, he pushed the door open a little.

Jenny's face appeared. There was a wet cloth in her hands.

'What's happening?' Fletcher demanded. 'Who fired the musket?'

'I did. To tell you that you needed to come. And to know.'

'Know what?'

'That the next baby is coming.'

Fletcher exhaled with relief. 'How much longer will it be?'

'I think, toru.'

Three hours. He nodded, then was struck by another thought. 'Where are Thursday and Charles?'

'At Brown's. With Teatuahitea.'

Fletcher heaved another sigh. They would be safe there. From inside came another cry. Jenny turned. 'Mauatua. I must be with her.'

'Yes, yes.' The door closed.

Three hours. He was useless here. He would go up to the garden and work for a couple of hours, then return in time for the baby's arrival.

He went to the spring, drank from it and filled his water flask. Three years, three babies. That compensated for all the rest of it. Then, mattock over his shoulder, he climbed up through the bush to Flatland.

270

The garden was flush with spring growth. The beans were entwining themselves around their poles, the sweet corn was three feet high already, the pumpkin plants were sending out tendrils. But the weeds too were prolific, shooting up between the rows, threatening to choke the yams. He took a swig from the water bottle, set it aside, picked up the mattock and began to hoe between the rows of yams.

'Titereano.'

Tararo, coming around the banyan. Barefoot, hair tied up, wearing grubby sailor's trousers. Musket in hand, hatchet at his belt. The whites of his eyes stood out in his dark, fuming face.

Fletcher stood up. He gripped the mattock with one hand, let the other fall. 'What do you want?' he said, calmly.

Tararo's eyes bulged. 'I want this!'

He brought the musket up to his shoulder, and fired.

Fletcher flew back, his chest struck. Gasping, he clutched at his heart. Through the fiery shock came a parade of faces. MotherEdwardCharlesJohnIsabellaIsabella. Blood spurted from his chest and gushed over his hands. The faces vanished, blackness rushed in. He fell.

Tararo laid the musket on the ground and took the hatchet from his belt. With hard, deft movements he chopped through the neck. When it was severed he picked up the head up by its hair. He grunted with satisfaction at the staring eyes, the gaped mouth, the bleeding neck and ragged sinews, the severed spinal column. Done.

He lobbed the head into the garden, then dragged the corpse in among the vegetables. The neck was still pumping and gushing blood.

Then he walked down the hill to join his friends. And plan the next killing.

An hour later, Isabella was delivered of a daughter.

She named her Mary Ann.

Part Five

DISCOVERY

28 SEPTEMBER 1808

It was seventeen-year-old Thursday October Christian who first saw the ship, from Lookout Point. Although official watches had ended years ago, people still climbed up here to enjoy the view.

Thursday stared at the three-masted ship. He had never seen such a sight, only illustrations in a book of his father's of such vessels. Coming from the north-east, it was in full sail, and heading towards the island.

Thrilled by the sight, Thursday got to his feet. With his brother Charles and James Young, he launched their outrigger canoe at Bounty Bay and paddled out through the swells to the ship, which had anchored a few hundred yards offshore. Awed by its size, the boys drew up alongside. A line was thrown down and they climbed aboard.

The boys gazed around at the decks and up at the rigging in astonishment. They had never seen anything like this. For their part, the ship's crew had gathered mid-deck and stared in fascination at the strange boys. They had European features, but were as dark as natives. All wore only loincloths. The boy who looked the oldest was tall and slim, with curly black hair that came down to his shoulders.

The ship was the sealer *Topaz*. The *Bounty* mutiny had occurred nineteen years ago; the island had been occupied for eighteen years.

Among the watching crew was Nathaniel Wescott, twenty-eight, who had signed on to *Topaz* in Boston in 1807. Although he was working aboard as a sealer, Wescott was an avid reader of sea stories and harboured an ambition to have his own adventures and write about them. Accordingly, he had persuaded Zachariah Poulson, the editor of a Philadelphia newspaper, *Poulson's American Daily Advertiser*, to commission him to write a series of stories about the South Sea sealing trade. Poulson had agreed to this proposal.

But after sailing around Patagonia and doubling Cape Horn, seals had proved elusive. To his great disappointment Wescott had found little to write about, except how wretched the onboard conditions were. But now, with *Topaz* low on fresh food, wood and water, they had come across this uncharted island in the middle of nowhere. And now these three strange boys had come aboard. Intensely curious, Wescott pushed through to the front of the crew, the better to study them.

The ship's captain was Mayhew Folger. Aged thirty-four, he had brown hair and a hawkish countenance. He addressed the three boys: 'Captain Folger. Do you speak English?'

The tallest boy grinned. 'We are English, sir.' He had an open, intelligent face.

'Who are your parents?'

'Our fathers be all dead, sir, but our mothers are not. My family are Christians.'

Confused, Folger asked, 'You are all Christians?'

'Me and brother Charles are, sir.' He pointed at James. 'And his family is Youngs.'

Wescott leaned forward, listening avidly.

'Were you all born on the island?' Folger asked.

'Yerr, we was all born on Pitkern Ilan.'

'And how long have your families been there?'

'Eighteen years. Our mothers and fathers came to Pitkern in 1790. In a ship called the *Bounty*.'

There was a stunned silence among the captain and crew. News of the mutiny on the *Bounty* had reached England early in 1790, and over subsequent years the notorious event and its aftermath had fascinated the public on both sides of the Atlantic. Wescott had followed the trial of the mutineers closely. Like all followers of the story, he had wondered what had happened to Fletcher Christian and the other mutineers. They had seemingly vanished from the face of the Earth. So this island represented the missing piece of what had been a worldwide puzzle.

Seeking verification, Folger asked the eldest boy, 'What was the name of your father?'

'He were Fletcher Christian, sir. He were killed by a native.'

'And the ship? The *Bounty*? Where is she?'

Thursday pointed shoreward, at the bay. 'She were burned. And sunk. There.'

'Are all the crew of the *Bounty* dead?'

'Not all, sir. Mr Adams is still alive. He is our leader.'

Nathaniel Wescott was transfixed. Now, from out of the blue, here was the solution to the mystery, embodied in these boys. And he would be the first to write the story.

The two-level thatched house was in a clearing surrounded by lush vegetation: miro trees, coconut palms, plantains and pandanus shrubs. There was a water barrel by the front door, along with some gardening tools.

Writing materials in his pack, Wescott had been led up to the house by Thursday October. He knew he had only a few more hours on the island before *Topaz* sailed on after her provisioning.

Notified yesterday of the forthcoming visit, John Adams was waiting to meet him.

Aged about forty, Adams was balding, but with long sideburns. His lank remaining hair came down to his shoulders. He wore a loose-fitting shirt and well-weathered calico trousers. There was a knotted kerchief around his neck and his feet were bare.

Wescott held out his hand. 'Nathaniel Wescott, from the *Topaz*.'

Although he shook his hand, Adams gave him a mistrustful look. His hazel eyes were deep-set, his face lined and pitted with smallpox scars. His nose was prominent, the eyebrows tangled.

'Are you English?' he asked Wescott.

'No, I'm American.'

Adams' expression softened a little. He said, 'A drink? I've only water to offer you, but it's from the spring.' He told Thursday, 'Fetch us water, boy.'

277

Wescott took the mug. He noticed how big Adams' hands were. They were covered in tattoos and the two middle fingers on his right hand were crumpled.

'Thank you, sir. Now, do you mind if I ask you some questions?'

Although he looked far from enthusiastic, Adams gave a nod.

They sat in the upstairs room of the house, which was connected to the ground floor by a ladder. The lower level was a junk room: it held lengths of planking, coils of cordage, a heap of unhusked coconuts, bits of canvas and a fishing net. Upstairs was obviously his living room. Woven mats covered the floor and the furniture was made from rough-sawn planking. A hammock was slung in one corner and on a table under an unglazed window was a big Bible.

Wescott opened his notebook and dipped his quill in the ink pot. 'Where were you born, Mr Adams?'

'In 'ackney, London. Our parents couldn't care for us, so me and me bruvvers were sent to the poorhouse. Soon as I could, I went to sea.'

'How did you get to be aboard the *Bounty*?'

'I heard around the docks that she were bound for Tahiti, and I had an urge to go there. I had deserted from my first ship, the merchantman Delia, 'cause the captain were a swine. So I signed onto *Bounty* as an AB under a false name, Alexander Smith.' He gave a little laugh. 'Little did I expect, Bligh turned out to be worse.'

'You blame him for the mutiny?'

'Oh yes. 'E were a bully. He 'ated me as much as he came to 'ate poor Mr Christian. He 'ad me flogged, in Tahiti. But it weren't just the floggings — some said Cook flogged men more — but 'is tongue were vicious. He enjoyed lashing men with it.' He shook his head at the memory. 'I'm a Christian man now, but I tell you, I were pleased that we sent Bligh to 'is death.'

'William Bligh is still alive, Mr Adams.'

Adams' face turned to stone. 'You're codding me, mister.'

'I'm not. One man was killed by the natives on Tofua Island. Bligh then sailed from Tofua to Timor, without the loss of a single other man. Three thousand, six hundred miles, in forty-one days.'

Adams looked as he had been poleaxed. He tried to speak, but couldn't. At last he blurted out, 'Is Bligh in England, then?'

'In 1807, when we sailed *Topaz* from Boston, Bligh was the governor of New South Wales.'

Adams brought his hands up to his face. 'Still alive. That means I can be taken back to England and hanged.' He looked at Wescott. 'If you or your captain let the navy know I'm 'ere, that is.'

Wescott didn't reply. He was on the horns of a dilemma. He thought, I must write this story, but I don't want to condemn this man to the noose. What to do?

Biding for time, he asked, 'What happened to the other mutineers?'

'All dead. Every one, 'cepting me.'

'How?'

Staring at his hands, Adams began. 'It started when McCoy, Quintal and Williams mistreated the black men. And they brewed liquor, from ti plant roots. They became drunken sots, on top of all else.' Adams shook his head. 'A kind of madness set in after that. One of the black men, Ohoo from Tupuai, who we also called Timiti, beat up his woman, Mareva. Knocked 'er front teeth out. She complained to Fletcher, an' 'e called Ohoo to account in a sort of court 'e set up. But Ohoo excaped from the court and ran down to Tautama to hide.

'The mutineers ordered Menalee, the Tahitian, to kill Ohoo. If he didn't they would kill him, they said. So Menalee caught Ohoo and killed him with an axe. Chucked his body into a split in the rock at Tautama. A place wot we now calls Timiti's Crack.'

Adams heaved a sigh. 'That were just the first killin'. After that the natives went crazy. They murdered Mr Christian, and Mills, Martin and Brown. They were after me an' all. Shot me in the shoulder and smashed two of me fingers. The women sheltered me from them. Those white men wot was left — Quintal and McCoy — then killed some of the blacks. One of the women shot another native, and so did Ned Young. That meant all the blacks were gone. Then McCoy, mad with the liquor, threw hisself off the cliff at St Pauls.' Adams scowled.

'Then Quintal threatened to kill Mr Christian's three children if he couldn't 'ave his widow, Isabella, for his wife.'

'And did he?'

'No. Ned shot Quintal for that. Then he took Isabella for his wife.'

The effort of recalling all this made Adams groan. He took a mouthful of water. 'From the mutineers, that left juss me and Ned. For an 'alf darkie, Ned were a good man. 'E taught me to read and write, proper like. Then, five year ago, poor Ned died. One day 'e couldn't breathe, and choked to death. I couldn't save 'im.' Adams studied his hands again. 'So then there were just me an' the women an' the little 'uns. The women was our salvation, especially Isabella and Jenny.'

Rocked by this account of hatred and mayhem, Wescott said quietly, 'So many violent deaths, in this beautiful place.'

'Aye. The massacre were a terrible time.' He wiped his eyes with his hand. 'But the babies had come afore that. And now we 'ave twenty-three young 'uns, and the eleven women.'

Adams went silent for a few moments, looking up at the ceiling. 'I too were drunk with the ti liquor for a time. Then I read the scriptures and the Lord's teachings. And the Archangel Gabriel appeared before me, and told me to bring Christ into my life, and the life of every other person on Pitkern. So I did. I 'ad been a sinner, but the Lord saved me. And now every woman and child on this island is a God-fearing Christian too.' He pointed towards the Bible on the table. 'I read the good book every day.' He gave a dry laugh. 'The Bible were Bligh's, don't you know? So, odd to say, the Bible wot 'ad belonged to a human devil saved me from Satan and eternal damnation.' He sighed. 'I know the Lord will forgive me my sins, 'cause I made this whole island true believers.

'Every Sabbath, twice a day, I take Christian services in front of this house. We sing hymns, and praise the good Lord who looks down on us all.' He placed his hands on his knees. 'And I've built a schoolhouse, where I teach the young 'uns to read and write.' He exhaled with satisfaction. 'Christ's presence is everywhere on this island now, Mr Wescott.'

It needs to be, Nathaniel thought, to atone for all the killings. He asked Adams, 'What did you think of Fletcher Christian, and what he did?'

There was a long pause. 'Mr Christian were a good man. He did what he had to do. To Bligh, I mean. He were driven to it.' He waved a hand. 'And he brought us here, to this island. He was our leader. He did his best. It were not his fault that things fell apart.'

Wescott noted this, then set his quill down. 'Mr Adams, there are other things I must tell you about the *Bounty* men. After Bligh made it back to England he was given a court martial and found not guilty of losing the *Bounty*. He became a hero in the eyes of the English public, by all accounts. The navy then dispatched a ship to Tahiti to take the mutineers into custody and bring them back to England for court martial. The ship was a frigate called the *Pandora*, commanded by Captain Edward Edwards.

'When *Pandora* got to Tahiti Edwards arrested the fourteen *Bounty* men who were on the island. He treated them dreadfully. They were kept them in chains, in a cage on the deck. Then on the way home *Pandora* went aground on the Great Barrier Reef. Thirty-five of her crew died, including four of the prisoners.'

Aghast, Adams said, 'But most of them what stayed on Tahiti were loyal to Bligh. Heywood, Morrison, Norman, McIntosh and the rest of 'em — they weren't in the mutiny. They only didn't go with Bligh in the launch because there weren't no room.'

Wescott nodded. 'Yes, that became evident during their trial in 1792. We followed it all in the news sheets in Pennsylvania. It was a huge story, just as Bligh's return had been two years earlier.'

Adams said sourly, 'I expect Bligh testified at the men's court martial.'

'No. He was on his way to Tahiti again, in HMS *Providence*, on a second voyage to get breadfruit plants for the West Indies.'

'Good Lord. The bugger's a trier, I'll give 'im that.'

'Yes. And this time he succeeded. He got the breadfruit plants to the West Indies. But the slaves refused to eat the breadfruit. So the whole scheme had proved futile.'

Adams ignored this. 'What was the result of the court martial?'

'Some were found not guilty, some were sentenced to death.'

'Do you remember the names of those judged guilty?'

Wescott thought for a few moments. The names had been in the news sheets for weeks during the court martial. He recalled them: 'Heywood, Morrison, Burkett, Ellison, Millward and Muspratt. All were found guilty and sentenced to hang.'

Adams glowered. 'Heywood and Morrison were never mutineers.' He conceded, 'But the others were.'

Wescott nodded. 'Eventually, the court agreed too. After public agitation, the case against Heywood and Morrison was dismissed. Muspratt was discharged on a legal technicality — I can't recall what — but the other three were hanged, on the deck of HMS *Brunswick*, in front of a big crowd. In October 1792.'

Adams closed his eyes. 'The other three. Tom Ellison, Johnny Millward, Tom Burkett. All mates of mine. Good men, driven to mutiny by William Bligh. May the Lord 'ave mercy on their poor souls.'

Covering his face with his big hands, he began to sob.

Nathaniel now needed to talk to Fletcher Christian's widow. The boys, Thursday and Charles, led him to the house. With them was their sister, Mary Ann, a pretty, long-haired girl of about fifteen. It was a fine spring afternoon as they made their way along a forest trail to the family home at Down Fletcher.

The children's mother was sitting cross-legged on the ground in front of the house, weaving a basket from strips of pandanus. Thursday announced, 'Mama, here come Mr Wescott, from the big ship. He want to talk with you.'

Nathaniel saw a fine-looking woman. Although seamed, her face was delicately sculpted, the cheekbones prominent. Her coal-black hair was parted in the centre and tied back in a bun. She wore a long-sleeved gown, done up to the neck, and a pearl-shell pendant. Her feet were bare, the toes splayed. Nathaniel estimated her to be in her late thirties.

Setting aside her weaving, she stood up. 'Ia ora na. Please, come inside.' The children left them and Isabella led the way into the house, tall and straight-backed. Nathaniel was reminded of her nickname, Mainmast.

In the living area were sleeping mats and a table and chairs made from planking. On the table were cooking pots, a basket of bananas and a plate of coconut pieces. Bouquets of brightly coloured flowers — ginger, tiare, oleander, hibiscus — were tied around the matting walls, scenting the big room.

Isabella offered Nathaniel a piece of coconut, then gestured towards one of the chairs. Her manner was dignified and considerate. He noticed her long fingers, which were laced with tattoos. They sat facing each other, Nathaniel with his notebook open.

Aware of the need for tact, he first asked her, 'Did Fletcher talk to you much about the mutiny?'

'At first, yes. But it upset him to talk of it, so after a time we did not. We was more concerned about today than what happened before.'

Nathaniel was struck by her accent, which seemed a mixture of old-fashioned English and a native tongue.

Isabella looked at him intently. 'Mr Adams has told you about the killings?'

'Yes.'

'Very bad time. But now, good time. We look after the children, and the Lord Jesus Christ look after us.'

'Yes. It seems to be a very peaceful island.'

'Ae, peaceful now.' She smiled.

'How do you remember your husband?'

'Titereano was a good man, a good husband. A good father to our children.' She looked away, her expression misted in memory. 'We had aroha nui, great love, for one another. And our children.'

'How sad that he did not see them grow.'

'Ae, so sad.' Then she brightened. 'But we had good times with our babies.' She was struck by another thought: 'And much good upa upa.'

Nathaniel stayed his quill. 'Upa upa?'

283

'What Titereano call "fucking".'

'Oh.' Disconcerted for a moment by her frankness, he wrote the new word down.

Isabella added, 'We have much 'ata, too. Laughter.'

They continued to chat. She recalled how entranced she had been with Titereano from the moment she first saw him at her family's fare in Tahiti. 'He were diff'ren to Tahitian men. He talk to me about many diff'ren things. About Peretane, his mama, his brothers, his school, his Ilen of Man.' Although she spoke matter-of-factly, her love for her dead husband was obvious.

When Isabella told him that Titereano had kept a book in his last years, on the *Bounty* and on the island, Nathaniel's writerly instincts were instantly aroused. He asked, 'Can I read his book?'

Isabella thought for a moment, then shook her head. 'No. My husband book is only for the feti'i.' She waved a hand around the room. 'This family.'

Though disappointed, Nathaniel understood. It would be too personal, too private, to show a stranger. But what a record it must contain!

To change the subject, he asked Isabella, 'Would you like to go back to Tahiti?'

'Oh, ae, I very much like to go back. But no ship to take me.' Then she was struck by another thought. 'But maybe, now your ship come and tell of Pitkern, other ship will come, and maybe take me back to Tahiti.'

Nathaniel nodded. After his story was published, other ships would surely visit. He closed his notebook. 'Isabella, thank you very much for talking to me.' He paused. 'Just one more thing. Where is your husband's grave? I would like to see it before I leave.'

She shook her head. 'No grave for Titereano. After he was kill, I leave him in his garden.'

Nathaniel started. 'You left his body there?'

'Ae. Then, came all covered in weeds. An' hogs an' birds an' worms an' maggots ate all his body. Later, I bury skellington in his garden.'

284

She related this dispassionately, as if talking about fly-blown meat. Then she smiled benignly. 'But his head, I doan bury.'

Nathaniel inhaled sharply. 'You kept your husband's head?'

'Ae. Me and Vahineatua — Mills's vahine wot was — we take our men's skulls an' clean 'em. So just bone left, no eyes, no rotten meat. All clean.'

Nathaniel tried not to betray his shock. 'Why do you keep the skulls of your loved ones?'

'Because that is our Maohi custom. Before in Tahiti, I go to see the skull of my grandmother, in a cave in the mountains. Loved ones' skulls, they bring messages from our ancestors to us. We talk to them. And listen to them.' Again she smiled. 'They talk to us, like Jesus talk to us through Mr Adams's Bible.'

Wondering what sort of ancestral messages Fletcher's skull would bring, and knowing that this macabre custom must comprise part of his story, Nathaniel pressed her. 'So do you keep Fletcher's skull in a cave?'

She shook her head. Turning, she pointed upwards, to a far corner of the room. There, on a triangular wooden shelf close to the ceiling, its long dark hair intact, its teeth and bones bright white, rested the skull of Fletcher Christian.

Afterword

John Adams (176?–1829). In 1814, six years after Mayhew Folger's rediscovery of Pitcairn, two Royal Navy ships called at the island. Adams, its patriarch, went aboard the ships and related the events of the mutiny and its aftermath to the naval captains. He described these in a manner that placed his own actions in as innocent a light as possible. But since he was the sole survivor of the mutiny, there was no one else left to gainsay his version of the events. Although technically still guilty of mutiny, in view of his ostensible piety and leadership of the island community, Adams was not arrested. In 1825 he married Mary, formerly Will McCoy's woman. They had one son, named George. Adams' marked grave lies alongside that of Mary, behind where his house was. Pitcairn's one tiny township, Adamstown, commemorates him.

William Bligh (1754–1817). When Bligh returned to England in 1790, after his epic open-boat voyage, he was hailed as a hero. His version of the mutiny, *A Narrative of the Mutiny on the Bounty*, published in 1790, heightened his celebrity status, as did his second breadfruit voyage. However when the other men of the *Bounty* were returned to England in 1792, alternative accounts of the mutiny were made public. The influential Heywood and Christian families disputed Bligh's version, and public opinion became much less favourable to him. Nevertheless, always fearless, he resumed his naval career and commanded Royal Navy ships with distinction in battles against the Dutch in 1797 and the Danish-Norwegian fleet in 1801. He was elected a fellow of the Royal Society in 1801, for services to navigation and exploration. In 1805 Bligh was appointed governor of the penal colony of New South Wales. Three years later he became embroiled in a mutiny in Sydney while attempting to break up the monopoly of the army, known as the Rum Corps. After being imprisoned for two years, he returned to England, where he was exonerated. He was promoted again, first to Rear Admiral of the Blue, then in 1814 to Vice Admiral of the Blue. He died aged sixty-three and is buried in Lambeth churchyard.

Ann Christian (1730–1820). Fletcher's mother discovered what had happened to her youngest son after the story of the mutiny and Bligh's voyage was made public, early in 1790. The anguish she must have felt when her son's notoriety was publicised can be imagined. By the time the discovery of the Pitcairn community by Captain Folger was brought to the world's attention in 1808, Fletcher had been dead for fourteen years and Ann was elderly. So she learned of but could never meet her Tahitian daughter-in-law and Fletcher and Mauatua's three children. Ann had no other grandchildren. She was living with her son Charles in Douglas, on the Isle of Man, when she died in 1820, aged ninety.

Charles Christian (1762–1822). After studying medicine in Edinburgh, Charles joined the West Yorkshire Regiment as an assistant surgeon, and three years later studied again at Edinburgh and qualified as a surgeon. He then served in that capacity on the merchantman *Middlesex*. Horrified when he received news of the mutiny and his brother's part in it, Charles attributed Fletcher's actions to the extreme mental stress which can develop below decks on a sailing ship. In 1808 he joined his mother Ann on the Isle of Man, where he spent the rest of his life.

Edward Christian (1758–1823). After graduating from Cambridge University Edward was admitted to Gray's Inn in 1782. In 1788 he was appointed Downing Professor of the Laws of England and was Chief Justice of the Isle of Ely. He also 'published some of the most respected papers and legal opinions of his time' (*Fragile Paradise*, p435). At Edward's urging, in 1794 Stephen Barney, counsel to *Bounty* mutineer William Muspratt, published the *Minutes of the Bounty Court Martial*. This included an Appendix, written by Edward. In it he did not excuse Fletcher's conduct but recounted some of the excesses of Bligh, using as his source interviews with prominent people who had spoken to some of those who had witnessed the mutiny, such as Peter Heywood. The publication of Edward's Appendix led to the tide of public opinion turning against Bligh and in Fletcher Christian's favour. Bligh then published a rejoinder, which prompted Edward to publish *A Short Reply to Capt. William Bligh's Answer*. Edward held the Downing College professorship until his death.

Thursday October Christian (1790–1831). The first child born on Pitcairn after the arrival of the mutineers and their Tahitian women, Thursday was only three when his father was killed. At the age of sixteen he married Teraura, also known as Susannah, formerly Ned Young's consort, who was then about thirty. Tall young Thursday impressed the visitors on the ships that called at Pitcairn in 1808 and 1814. They admired his open countenance and respectful manner. During his brief visit to HMS *Tagus* in 1814, Thursday had his portrait drawn. In it he wears a straw hat decorated with rooster's feathers. *Tagus*'s Captain Pipon described him as 'a tall fine young Man about 6 feet high … with a great share of good humour & a disposition & willingness to oblige, we were very glad to trace in his benevolent countenance, all the features of an honest English face'. Thursday also spoke good English. Later informed that his father had not taken the loss of a day into account while sailing east on the *Bounty*, Thursday changed his Christian name to Friday. In 1831 a group of Pitcairners, including Thursday-Friday, sailed to Tahiti, where he died of an infectious disease. He and Susannah had six children. She died in 1850.

Isabella-Mauatua-Maumiti-Mainmast Christian (176?–1841). It is said that she remembered Cook's last visit to Tahiti in 1777, which means that she was probably older than Fletcher. After his death she became the partner of Ned Young. She had two sons and a daughter by Fletcher and one son and two daughters by Young. She returned to Tahiti in 1831 with a party of Pitcairners, but found her homeland defiled by contacts with dissolute Europeans and went back to Pitcairn. White-haired in her old age, she was well-known for the stories she related to other members of her family.

Peter Heywood (1772–1831). Although he played no active role in the 1789 mutiny, Bligh cited Heywood as one of the mutineers. Now eighteen, he was arrested and taken back to England aboard *Pandora* to be court-martialled. Along with five others he was sentenced to death by hanging. However, after his influential family lobbied on his behalf, mercy was recommended and he was pardoned by King George III. Resuming his naval career, Heywood was given his first command at twenty-seven and made a post-captain at thirty-one. He remained in the navy until 1816, earning a reputation as a fine hydrographer. He married Frances Joliffe but they had no children. In his retirement Heywood published his dictionary of the Tahitian language.

Pitcairn Island: The Aftermath

During the first decades of the nineteenth century the population of Pitcairn Island increased rapidly. The descendants of the *Bounty* mutineers and their Polynesian women lived peacefully and communally, gardening, fishing and raising goats, pigs and chickens, much as Fletcher Christian envisaged that they might before the conflicts and killings erupted. Law-abiding and God-fearing, physically strong and healthy, the next generation of Pitcairners knew little of the outside world, had no need of money, and displayed an innocence and devoutness which impressed those who visited the island. They were, in a manner of speaking, true Christians.

By 1831 the population of the island had reached eighty-seven, and it was feared by the outside authorities that the small island could not sustain any further increase. At the instigation of an English missionary, all the Pitcairners were uplifted from the island and transported on the *Lucy Ann* to Tahiti, the land of so many of their forebears.

Tahiti had now been exposed to the wider world for over half a century, and many European ships had called at the island. The Pitcairn people were horrified at what they found there. They considered the Tahitians and the Europeans who lived there to be dissolute and promiscuous. They could not accept their lax morality. Furthermore, the Pitcairners contracted diseases such as tuberculosis and venereal disease from the much more worldly Tahitians. Eleven Pitcairn adults and children died over the next two months, including Thursday October Christian, Fletcher and Mauatua's first-born. The transfer had been a tragic mistake. Consequently a ship was chartered and the Pitcairners were returned to their home island.

Pitcairn became a British colony officially in 1838. That year, led by the strong Tahitian women, the island was among the first territories in the world to extend voting rights to females.

The population continued to increase rapidly. By the mid-1850s there were nearly two hundred Pitcairners living on an island only one and three-quarter square miles (4.5 square kilometres) in size, less than ten percent of which was arable land. The population again needed to be evacuated, but where could they move to this time?

Three thousand seven hundred miles (5955 kilometres) west of Pitcairn is another much larger Pacific island, named Norfolk in 1774 by James Cook, its first European discoverer. For most of the first half of the nineteenth century Norfolk was an English penal colony, a place so harsh in its treatment of transported convicts that its very name struck horror in the hearts of even hardened felons. Two mutinies occurred on the island, in 1834 and 1846. Both failed, and wholesale executions followed.

Word of the cruelty and depravity of the Norfolk Island penal regime eventually moved the authorities in England. After agitation from prominent members of the English clergy, in 1854 the Norfolk Island gulag was abandoned and its convicts shipped to Port Arthur, in Van Diemen's Land (now Tasmania).

The leaders of Pitcairn Island had written to Queen Victoria requesting her help to find another home. In a compassionate gesture she offered them recently evacuated Norfolk Island. At first there was some resistance to the move, but on 3 May 1856 the entire population of 193 people was uplifted from Pitcairn and transferred to the ship *Morayshire*.

The voyage west to Norfolk Island took five weeks and conditions aboard were miserable, but on 8 June 1856 *Morayshire* stood off the island — which like Pitcairn has no sheltered harbour — and the immigrants were lightered ashore.

For the Pitcairners, this must have been like arriving on another planet. The new island seemed massive, although it was only five miles by three miles (eight kilometres by five kilometres). There were things the Pitcairners had never set eyes on before, such as stone houses and civic buildings, horses and cows, roads and wagons. But the settlers brought with them their unique shared history, the laws and customs as they had evolved on Pitcairn, their language and their Christian faith.

Later some of the migrants returned to Pitcairn: seventeen members of the Young family in 1858, then some of the Christian clan in 1864. The rest remained on Norfolk Island, where many of their descendants still live.

Today, one third of Norfolk Island's population is directly descended from the Pitcairners. Every 8 June the anniversary of the arrival of the *Morayshire* is celebrated with Bounty Day, when a re-enactment of the landing is held at Emily Bay and period costumes are worn.

Like today's Pitcairn islanders, the people of Norfolk have their own language, a blend of eighteenth-century English and Tahitian. On a wall in many houses is the triskelion, the flag of Fletcher Christian's first island, the Isle of Man, along with those of Tahiti and Norfolk. In other homes there are scale models of the *Bounty*, copies of the Robert Dodd painting of Bligh's launch being set adrift, pictures of Pitcairn and photographs of their forebears. Norfolk Island place names also commemorate the *Bounty* mutiny participants: Captain [sic] Quintal Drive, Edward Young Road, Fletcher Christian Road. There are so many Christians living on Norfolk that there is a special section in the phone book where one can more usefully 'fast find' ('faasfain' in the Pitcairn patois) particular Christians just by their nicknames. Trent Christian, country and western singer, greets visitors to Norfolk with songs he performs in the centre of the island's principal town, Burnt Pine. Just outside the town is a fine Cyclorama depicting the events of the mutiny, the settlement of Pitcairn Island and the move to Norfolk Island.

Other *Bounty* mutineer surnames in the Norfolk Island phone book are: Adams, McCoy and Quintal. But there is no feature on either Norfolk or Pitcairn Island named after William Bligh. He is commemorated geographically only by Bligh Water, the stretch of sea in Fiji that lies between Viti Levu and the Yasawa Islands. Bligh and the men loyal to him sailed through this sea in *Bounty*'s launch, during their epic voyage to Timor. Truly it can be said of William Bligh, 'Here lies one whose name was writ in water.'

Pitcairn Island in the 21st Century

Pitcairn Island today is a British Overseas Territory, with the same status as other vestiges of Britain's empire, such as Ascension Island, Bermuda and Gibraltar.

Although Pitcairn is now connected to the internet and has efficient telecommunications with the rest of the world, it remains one of the most isolated islands on earth. Ships can stand off the island and transfer passengers only when sea conditions are favourable. This does not occur often. A supply ship brings cargo and some passengers to the island three times a year, with goods and people being transferred to the island by longboats skilfully deployed by the Pitcairn men.

Most of the island's population follow the teachings of the Seventh Day Adventist Church, which was introduced to Pitcairn by a missionary in 1890.

Isolation, a lack of employment and educational opportunities mean that Pitcairn has suffered a steady loss of population since the beginning of this century. Email has decimated the once-profitable philatelic industry. In 2011 the island's population was sixty-eight; in 2016 it had declined to forty-nine. Young Pitcairners are sent to New Zealand for their secondary schooling, and seldom return.

Pitcairn's reputation was severely damaged by a series of sexual assault trials in 2004. Charges were laid against seven men living on the island and six living overseas. After lengthy trials which divided the island's tiny community, in October 2004 nearly all those charged were convicted. After their final appeals were lost, the British government set up a prison on the island, a prefabricated building made in New Zealand, and in 2006 the convicted men began serving their sentences. By 2010 they had either completed their sentences or been granted home detention. In 2016 a former mayor of the island, Michael Warren, was convicted of possessing multiple images and videos of child pornography on his computer. This dealt another blow to Pitcairn's reputation.

Today's Pitcairners, although numerically in decline, have a sincere wish to move on from these traumatic events and build a positive future for their island. Tourism is the best prospect. Aware of Pitcairn's unique history, the islanders know that many people would like to visit their island and see for themselves the place where the *Bounty* mutineers found sanctuary. It is possible to dive at the site where the *Bounty* was scuttled, in Bounty Bay, and see remnants of the ship. The graves of John Adams and his wife, and the main graveyard below Adamstown, tell the story of the island's history.

A plaque on the Edge, above Bounty Bay, lists the names of all the Tahitian women who accompanied the mutineers and contributed so much to the eventual survival of the Pitcairn community.

Everywhere on Pitcairn there are reminders of the *Bounty* mutineers and the settlement they established on the island 226 years ago: the Hill of Difficulty, now a sealed road; Christian's Cave below Lookout Point; a cannon from the *Bounty* in Adamstown's square; evocative place names — McCoy's Valley Road, Point Christian, Brown's Water, John Mills' Road.

Isolation remains an impediment, as neither Pitcairn nor her three sister islands — Henderson, Ducie and Oeno — have any air connections. The nearest inhabited island is Mangareva in French Polynesia, hundreds of miles to the north-west.

One significant recent development is the construction of a second jetty, at Tedside on the north coast of the island. Funded by the European Union, this major addition to Pitcairn's infrastructure will allow ships to moor here when weather conditions are unfavourable on the island's east coast.

Like their forebears, the people of the island are hard-working and resourceful — and they still speak the distinctive Pitkern dialect.

Acknowledgements

Much has been written about William Bligh and the mutiny on the *Bounty*, and there have been several movies based on the story, the last released in 1984. Not so much has been written about the early life of Fletcher Christian, or how he and Bligh came to be together on the *Bounty*.

Fletcher of the Bounty is a work of fiction, but it is based on real events. It might thus be classed as 'imagined fact'. Some episodes – such as Fletcher's defence of the boy Wordsworth, and the attack on Fletcher at Madras – are products of the novelist's imagination. Several characters too are invented, such as Meike the Dutch woman in Cape Town, and the American journalist Nathaniel Wescott, on Pitcairn.

The sources of those facts are many and varied. There has been a multitude of publications documenting the *Bounty* mutiny story. Of these, five books in particular were of help in acquainting me with the facts of Fletcher Christian's life.

It was my good fortune when I visited Pitcairn Island in 2011 to have in my suitcase a manuscript copy of a work by Glynn Christian, the great-great-great-great-grandson of Fletcher Christian: *Mrs Christian, Bounty Mutineer* (Ashton Books, 2011). Having learnt that I was going to Pitcairn, Glynn sent me the manuscript and asked that I present it to Betty Christian, a relative of Glynn's by marriage and an island resident. I was happy to do so, because I had earlier read and much admired Glynn's book *Fragile Paradise* (Doubleday, 1999). This account of the mutiny and subsequent events was extremely helpful in understanding Fletcher Christian's part in it. The book also disproves some of the mutiny myths which have sprung up over the years. *Fragile Paradise* was more than a reference, it was a guiding light.

A more traditional source was *The Bounty* by Richard Hough (Corgi Books, 1984). An experienced naval man himself, and someone who had been to Pitcairn Island, Hough brings a seaman's viewpoint to the saga. More pro-Bligh than some accounts, *The Bounty* nevertheless sheets home a key catalyst for the mutiny, Bligh's inability to see events through anyone else's eyes except his own. I, too, felt that this failure of the imagination by Bligh was a key reason for Christian's actions aboard the *Bounty* after the ship left Tahiti in April, 1789.

There is no more comprehensive biography of *Bounty*'s commander than *Bligh: William Bligh in the South Seas* by Anne Salmond (Viking, 2011). This must be the definitive account of Bligh's remarkable life and career. It is particularly illuminating with regard to Bligh's time with James Cook during his third and fatal world voyage aboard HMS *Resolution*.

For background reading, the novel *Transit of Venus* by Rowan Metcalfe (Huia, 2004) is unique. Also a descendant of Fletcher Christian and Mauatua-Isabella, and a prize-winning short story writer, Rowan tells the *Bounty* story from the perspective of the Tahitian women. Although fiction, it provides many insights into traditional Tahitian cultural practices. *Transit of Venus* is rendered more moving by the fact that Rowan died tragically in 2003, shortly before the novel was published.

Fish and Ships! Food on the Voyages of Captain Cook (Captain Cook Memorial Museum, 2012) provided me with specialist information regarding the preparation and serving of food on Royal Navy vessels in the eighteenth century.

While on Pitcairn Island I spent a good deal of time in the company of Dave Evans, a geophysicist from Alaska. Dave had earlier worked on Pitcairn and knew the island intimately. As well as showing me its every crevice and gully via quad-bike, he presented me with a copy of his booklet, *Pitkern Ilan* (2007). This proved to be a little gem, filled with relevant information about Pitcairn, past and present. I referred constantly to Dave's map of the island in the booklet.

I am also grateful to my Tahitian-Kiwi friend, Lola Carter, for providing me with the Tahitian phrases which are included at times in the text. Lola and I have made several visits to the islands of French Polynesia in the course of our work, and no one is more familiar with the culture of Tahiti and her sister islands than she is. Mauruuru Lola, for all your help.

Thanks, too, to Robert Thompson and Tahiti Tourisme for assisting me with travel to Mangareva in French Polynesia, the stepping stone to Pitcairn Island.

On Pitcairn I stayed with Charlene and Vaine Warren-Peu. They and their extended family could not have been kinder to me while I was on the island, and I have the most affectionate memories of my time with them.

I wish to thank the New Zealand company Stoney Creek Shipping, which sponsored my visit to Pitcairn Island aboard their vessel *Claymore II*. It was this visit which was the catalyst for my interest in the mutiny on the HMAV *Bounty* and the life of Fletcher Christian.

Thanks also to Betty Christian, who is now living in Auckland, for providing me with additional information about Fletcher Christian.

I am greatly indebted to maritime historian and renowned author Joan Druett for her expert advice regarding the nautical world.

My gratitude also to my editor, Stephen Stratford, for his unerring judgments and eagle eye for anachronisms, and to my tireless agent Linda Cassells, who takes my books into the wider world. I wish to thank HarperCollins' senior editor in Sydney, Nicola Robinson, for her thorough professionalism, and my publishers at HarperCollins, Shona Martyn and Alex Hedley, for their advice, support and good humour.

Graeme Lay

Graeme Lay was born in 1944 in Foxton. He grew up in two small coastal towns in Taranaki, first in Oakura, where he began school, then Opunake. Growing up on the coast instilled in him a great love of the sea.

Graeme Lay began writing short stories in the late 1970s. After several of his stories were published in magazines, he began his first novel, *The Mentor*, which was published in 1978. His first collection of short stories, *Dear Mr Cairney*, was published in 1985. Since then he has published or edited forty works of fiction and non-fiction, including novels for adults and young adults, two more collections of short stories and three books of travel writing. In the late 1990s and early 2000s he also devised and edited five collections of New Zealand short short stories, three of which became bestsellers.

From the 1990s onwards, after travelling to New Caledonia and Rarotonga, Graeme Lay developed a deep interest in the islands of the

South Pacific and the history and culture of the region's indigenous peoples. Many of his books, both fiction and non-fiction, are set in the South Pacific. For example his trilogy for young adults, *Leaving One Foot Island* (1998), *Return to One Foot Island* (2001) and *The Pearl of One Foot Island* (2004) are set mainly on Aitutaki, in the Cook Islands, and his adult thriller, *Temptation Island* (2000) is set on a fictional South Pacific island, Savaiki.

Graeme Lay's other works include the travel collection *The Miss Tutti Frutti Contest* (2004); an historical novel, *Alice & Luigi* (2006); a travel memoir, *Inside the Cannibal Pot* (2007); *The New Zealand Book of the Beach* (2007) and *The New Zealand Book of the Beach 2* (2008); *In Search of Paradise: Artists and Writers in the Colonial South Pacific* (2008) and *Whangapoua: Harbour of the Shellfish* (2009). He also compiled and edited the anthology *Way Back Then, Before We Were Ten: New Zealand Writers and Childhood* (2009) and *Home and Away* (2012), a collection of New Zealand travel writing. His *Globetrotter Guide to New Zealand* is now in its seventh edition.

The first novel in his bestselling trilogy based on Captain Cook's career, *The Secret Life of James Cook*, was published in 2013. The second novel, *James Cook's New World*, was published in 2014 and the final novel, *James Cook's Lost World*, in 2015. All three are published by HarperCollins under the Fourth Estate imprint.

An updated version of Graeme Lay's entry in
The Oxford Companion to New Zealand Literature is at:
www.bookcouncil.org.nz/writer/lay-graeme/.

From Graeme Lay,
a masterful trilogy on the life and voyages of
James Cook.

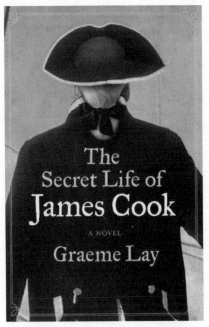

'A compelling account of this towering but enigmatic figure … both insightful and a great read.'
– *New Zealand Herald*

'Graeme Lay knows his Pacific … and is well placed to attempt what no one has ever managed to achieve, by telling us not just what Cook did, but what he was like.'
– *North & South Magazine*

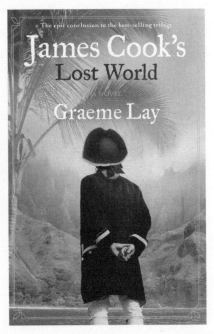